THE MAFIA AND HIS OBSESSION

PART 1

Tainted Hearts Series

By Lylah James

THE MAFIA AND HIS OBSESSION PART 1

Copyright © 2018 by Lylah James.
All rights reserved.
Second Print Edition: August 2018

Limitless Publishing, LLC
Kailua, HI 96734
www.limitlesspublishing.com

Formatting: Limitless Publishing

ISBN-13: 978-1-64034-999-5

No part of this book may be reproduced, scanned, or distributed in any printed or electronic form without permission. Please do not participate in or encourage piracy of copyrighted materials in violation of the author's rights. Thank you for respecting the hard work of this author.

This is a work of fiction. Names, characters, places, and incidents either are the product of the author's imagination or are used fictitiously, and any resemblance to locales, events, business establishments, or actual persons—living or dead—is entirely coincidental.

Dedication

For everyone who chooses to pick flowers in their darkest times.

CONTENT WARNING

This book contains dark—and sometimes violent—depictions of the world of organized crime and sexual assault. Some events might be triggers for some readers.

Author's Note:

The Mafia and His Obsession: Part 1 should be read after *Blood and Roses*. This is the fifth book in the Tainted Hearts Series.

The characters make their appearances throughout the series. To better understand their story, it is recommended to read the series in order.

Tainted Heart Series Reading Order:

The Mafia and His Angel: Part 1 (Now Available)
The Mafia and His Angel: Part 2 (Now Available)
The Mafia and His Angel: Part 3 (Now Available)
Blood and Roses (Now Available)
The Mafia and His Obsession: Part 1
The Mafia and His Obsession: Part 2 (Coming soon)

Prologue

Him

The smell of blood touched my nostrils, and I almost fucking laughed. Perfect. Just perfect.

I dug the knife deeper and watched the man scream. He writhed on the cold, hard, bloodied ground.

"Man, can you stop playing Joker?" Phoenix said behind my back.

"If I dye my hair green and wear red lipstick, will I look like Joker?" I replied, twisting the knife in the captive's flesh before pulling it away.

He laughed mockingly. "No. You will look like a clown."

He was mocking me. *Maybe I'll shave his head off in his sleep.* That would teach him.

Slowly twirling the knife between my fingers, I stared at the man. He seemed captivated with each twirl and twist. I cocked my head to the side, regarding him.

And then, I threw the knife behind me.

"Goddamn it!"

My lips curved upward at the outburst. It looked like the knife had hit its target.

"Are you fucking serious? It almost took a chunk of my flesh!" Phoenix bellowed.

"So dramatic," Alessio muttered from his position against the wall. "And hurry up! Ayla is waiting for me."

From the corner of my eyes, I saw him pushing away from the wall. Taking two steps forward, he stopped behind me. "Finish him."

Two words in the deadly silence of the dark alley. Two words spoken by my Boss. My King.

And his words were my command.

It had been for years.

Taking out an army knife from my breast pocket, I showed my captive the blade. He trembled in absolute fear. The shock and agony in his eyes were not mistaken. It could never be.

That was exactly what we fed on.

Fear. Our enemies' fear. The look in their eyes when they were about die, it was what we lived for.

Some say we were cruel. Disgusting human beings. Heartless. Ruthless.

I would agree.

But I liked the word barbaric better. Unsympathetic. Sadistic. Vicious.

After all, we were killers.

We were born into this life. Since the very beginning, we breathed it.

From first breath…till our last.

His whimpers snapped me out of my thoughts. Was that piss I smelled?

THE MAFIA AND HIS OBSESSION PART 1

Most probably. They always turned into disgusting carcasses when their death flashed in front of their eyes. Too bad for them it was always too late.

He opened his mouth to speak, but I never gave him a chance. My fingers tightened around the knife before I drove it down, right in the middle of his throat.

The man gurgled his last breath as his blood poured around him...and on me. Shaking my head in disgust, I spat on him.

"Foolish. They know the consequences, but they still try and play us," I sneered at him.

His chest expanded as he took his last breath...and then silence. Nobody spoke a word as we stared at the dead man, his eyes still open. Still staring into mine.

The only difference was that his were empty, while mine were still very much alive, glowing with power.

I heard Phoenix talking over the phone while I stood up. My handkerchief was already out of my pocket, and I cleaned my hands, trying to remove the blood. My face was next. It felt sticky where the blood had splattered.

Appalling filth. I need a fucking shower now.

Why didn't Alessio do it himself?

Oh, wait...because he didn't want to get his hands dirty this time. His Angel was waiting for him at home.

Like that made him the lesser evil.

He was just as fucked up.

We were all fucked.

But we had *her* to bring us some light. A little bit of happiness. Some smiles…some occasional laughter. Some scraps of love.

She gave it all to us, without expecting anything in return. She loved so much and so hard that sometimes our hearts were not big enough to take it all.

Someone swore behind me. My eyebrows furrowed in confusion as I was brought back to the present.

Annoyingly, I had been lost in my thoughts too much lately. Very bad.

I was going to get killed if I don't get my shit together.

"Boss," I heard Phoenix warn.

What the fuck is he warning Alessio about? I turned around, facing the others.

Only to come face to face with Alessio pointing his gun at me.

"Seriously? We don't have time for this," I said, my eyes on the gun. He cocked his head to the side, his eyebrows lifted in amusement.

"Can we do this later? After we have disposed of the body? C'mon, man."

I rolled my eyes, knowing Alessio wasn't going to do something stupid. He wouldn't. Not after everything.

Turning my back to him again, I put my life…everything in his hands. I gave him my full trust.

That was my first mistake.

I heard the gunshot first. It rang so loud in the silent alley. My heart thumped in response.

THE MAFIA AND HIS OBSESSION PART 1

Then I felt it. The indescribable pain and burn that came after the bullet pierced my body.

He shot me.

He actually shot me.

In the ass.

What the ever-loving fuck?

He did not just fucking shoot me.

I swiveled around to face him, ignoring the pain. Trying so hard to ignore the fact that I had just been shot in the ass. I had a hole in my ass cheek!

This wasn't some *Deadpool* bullshit. And I sure as hell wasn't some super mutant who could pop bullets out of their asses.

Yeah…he was a dead man.

"Ayla's going to be pissed when we get back home and she finds both of us shot," I drawled, reaching behind me.

I never got a chance to get my gun. He was now aiming at my chest, right over my heart.

I froze. My muscles locked as I stared at Alessio in surprise. He wouldn't…

Raising my hands in surrender, I took a step back. "Alessio, we can talk about this."

At least not my heart. He could shoot anywhere but the heart. Or my dick.

"No. We can't," he simply replied. His eyes appeared darker than usual, anger glistening in them. Alessio was a madman when he was angry.

He would blur the lines between right or wrong. Nothing mattered to him except his revenge. He would do anything and…everything.

In that moment, I was on the other side. Not beside him. But against him. For the first time since

I had known him.

Instead of our guns pointing at some other bastards, his gun was pointed at me. And only one reason made sense.

"Did you think I wouldn't find out?" he hissed. I saw his fingers tightening around the gun. His index finger laid on the trigger, waiting for the right moment, dragging out the suspense.

He loved the chase, the adrenaline in making others shake and whimper in fear. Except I wasn't shaking or whimpering.

That probably pissed him off more.

"I was going to tell you," I answered.

Lies. I wasn't.

Because there was nothing to tell. Nothing was what it seemed to be. Every action, every word had a meaning behind it.

Nothing in our world was the perfect image. Everything was in pieces, and we had to put all of them together to find the truth. A piece in the puzzle to get the whole vision.

Everything was a lie.

Everyone was a lie.

Every fucking day was a game to play. A game we had mastered.

Believe nothing. Whatever you see or hear is a lie.

That was one of the lessons learned and a lesson to remember.

"Let me explain," I tried to convince him. Anything but another bullet in my body.

"You know damn well that I never give anyone a chance to explain," he snapped. Thrusting his gun

THE MAFIA AND HIS OBSESSION PART 1

toward my chest, his lips curled in disgust. "And you aren't any different."

"Boss," I heard someone say. There was a warning in his tone. Maybe he was trying to save me? We were a brotherhood after all.

Alessio smirked, just the corner of his lips turning up, and I just knew. My death had just been signed, and I had no choice over it.

The veins in my neck throbbed. Blood rushed to my ears until the only thing I could hear was the pounding of my heart.

Their voices sounded like they were underwater as my dreadful life flashed in front of my eyes. This was it.

The end.

BANG!

I closed my eyes as the gun went off, sounding so loud, so evil to my ears. The connection of the metal and my skin was quick. So quick that I could have missed it.

But when the pain came later…there was no escaping it.

Sweat dripped down my forehead as my blood dripped down my body. The cold bullet penetrated my chest, and I prayed it didn't hit my heart.

A laughable thought that was.

Alessio had the perfect aim. If he wanted me dead, shot in the heart, there was no escaping death.

He was death.

My eyes fluttered open as I regarded my *brother* for one final time. His hand dropped to his side, still holding the gun.

The anger in his eyes was gone, replaced with

hurt and pain. His expression changed to one of regret. "I didn't want to do this, but you gave me no choice. You fucked up. And you fucked up bad."

I know that!

I wanted to scream, but my lips felt numb. My throat grew tighter as the pain spread across my body. It felt like I was burning from the inside as the ground turned darker with the red shade of blood.

Through blurry vision, I saw Alessio pointing the gun at me again. I closed my eyes, waiting for him to end this. Waiting for this indescribable pain to finally end.

The fired round seemed to float through fragile air, my ears barely registering the gunshot. It pierced my chest without consideration, without real meaning or relevance.

A sacrifice made from my part. A sacrifice I was willing to make. For my family. For her.

The small wounds leaked blood similar to how crying eyes leaked tears.

I sank to my knees, my body too weak to hold myself any longer. I gasped for breath, pleading for air.

Maybe I heard him whisper *sorry*. Maybe it was my mind playing tricks on me, but there was no mistaking the anguish in his voice.

I wanted to open my eyes, to give them a final look. A final goodbye. But my weakness won over.

"The only reason why I can regret this is because Ayla will be hurt. She is going to cry, and I won't be able to do anything," Alessio said. His voice sounded nearer but still so far away.

THE MAFIA AND HIS OBSESSION PART 1

I was drifting. Falling deeper and deeper into the dark abyss.

Suddenly everything went completely silent. All movement around me slowed down to an excruciating pace. I could feel my pulse pounding through me as visions flashed behind my closed eyes.

The images swirled before me right until the end, leaving that last scene of her imprinted upon my mind without the oxygen to sustain it.

Her smile. Her laughter. The look of love as she gazed up at him. Never me. Always him.

I bled out, losing consciousness faster…falling faster…until I hit hard ground.

I was jostled, and pain racked through me. It felt like my unbeating heart just started again, pumping blood through my body.

I died. I knew I died…then the voices…

What's happening?

I opened my mouth to speak, but no words found their way out. The burning sensation in my chest never ended. It hurt more and more every second.

"He's flat lining!"

The noises grew louder over the pounding of my heart.

"Don't let him die!"

New voices. They didn't belong to Alessio or any of our men.

"Fuck! I need him alive, damn it!"

No. I was dead.

"He needs to live," the voice hissed.

"You need to live. Do you hear me, son?" It sounded nearer now.

Is he talking to me?

My body was moved, pushed, pulled, and I bore down on the agony.

Leave me alone, I wanted to scream. I was with her…at least in my death moment, she loved me.

But now some stupid bastards were taking me away. I could see her fading, turning away from me.

I reached for her, but it was too late. She was gone, fading into the darkness. She left me alone again.

"This is what happens when you choose the wrong side."

Huh?

"Fucking Ivanshov. They would pay for this. All of them."

No.

"I told you to join us, but you didn't listen. Now bear the pain of being betrayed by your *brother*. Over whom? Some fucked up Italian *blyad*."

Don't fucking call her a whore.

Anger swirled inside of me before realization finally dawned.

They were speaking Russian.

Ah, fuck my life.

"Don't worry. You will get your revenge. They all betrayed you. You will live and get your revenge."

His words penetrated through my mind, and I held them close, wrapping myself around the words.

They all betrayed you.

Other words were mumbled, but I ignored them.

You will live and get your revenge.

In my head, I smiled. *Oh, yes I will.*

THE MAFIA AND HIS OBSESSION PART 1

I was going to live…fuck death. It was not my time yet.

"Get him to the estate. When he wakes up, we will put our plans into action. The time has come for my heir to join me."

The smile turned into a smirk. It was time.

Blood would be spilled, and only the strong would live. There can only be one conqueror. Everyone else was going to be ten feet under the cold, hard ground.

Deceit. Betrayal. Lies. Traitors. Hate. Revenge. Fraud.

We lived with them every day. We breathed them. We played them. And we welcomed them.

The game has begun.

Chapter 1

Konstantin

One year later

"Are you fucking serious? We have been planning this for a year and *now* you want to change the plans?" He bellowed so loud that the walls shook. Probably. Because my ears were now definitely ringing.

"It's the only way and you know it," I returned calmly.

His fist slammed on the table, and I internally rolled my eyes. *Here we go again.* One of his tantrums that made me want to wring his neck and drop him in a ditch somewhere.

"Or is it that you don't trust me?" I raised an eyebrow in question.

A small change in his expression. The tiniest flinch. A little furrow in his eyebrows. But I caught it all.

Bullseye.

THE MAFIA AND HIS OBSESSION PART 1

Crossing my arms, I leaned back against the couch, getting comfortable. "I just hit the eye, didn't I?"

"No," he growled low.

I was itching to take out my knife and cut his tongue out for lying to me. But I had mastered the art of controlling myself over the years.

Right now, he was the Boss, and I was the underdog.

Not for long, though, the devil on my shoulder whispered. He liked challenging me, laughing in my ears, reminding me of the games that were being played.

But oh, how he tested my limits every single time. Him and the fuck face sitting behind that table.

"You are scared this little plan of yours will fail. You are scared I will betray you and go back to *them*," I hissed, just to make him angrier.

I liked him angry. The way his face would turn red like he was tempted to shoot me. But unfortunately for him, he couldn't.

It was all part of the game. A little ruse we had built around us.

"They think I am dead. They even had a little funeral for me. We have kept the charade on for a year. They have no idea what's waiting for them," I continued before he could say anything.

I hated it when they would interrupt while I spoke. He knew that and stayed silent. Not surprising. He was a little coward in disguise. Without me, he was nothing.

Sitting back in his chair, he regarded me silently,

waiting, calculating. "And what will you do when you go back there?"

"Gain their trust again."

He laughed, a full belly laugh that I was highly hoping he would choke on.

Unfortunately for me, he didn't. Sad life.

"You think you can gain their trust? After everything? After disappearing for a year and making them believe you are dead," he grumbled, his thick Russian accent very obvious.

Whenever he was angry or frustrated, his fake English accent would vanish into thin air and reality would take its place.

"I believe you are questioning my abilities now," I returned rather very calmly.

"I am not, but your plan does not seem easy, Konstantin."

Konstantin. I fucking hated this name. Every time it was uttered, I wanted to smash someone's head into the wall.

But *he* would purposely say it every time. A way to remind me of who I actually was. Whose family I belonged to.

Not the Ivanshov.

I was no longer an Ivanshov.

I cleared my throat, trying to calm the anger rising inside of me. "What makes you say that? Artur did it for years. Why can't I? If they were able to fall into his trap, imagine how easy it would be for them to fall into mine?"

Artur had played the Russian King, infiltrated their home, and stayed there as family. Except he was just a pawn, a player of the game. He was a cunning liar and betrayed the family. He had sided with the enemy and chosen the wrong side. In the end, it had led to his death.

But before his blood was spilled, he had played his game well, for many *years*.

If he could do it, I easily could too.

"They won't believe it," Valentin said through gritted teeth, now losing his thin patience. "*Alessio ne poverit.*"

The veins in his neck bulged in fury, and I fought the urge to laugh. So much anger yet he couldn't do a single thing about it.

Alessio wouldn't believe it, he said. Of course not. But someone else would...

"Ayla will."

My voice was loud and clear. I spoke the two words that silenced everyone. He took a deep breath through his nose, holding it in.

His eyes flared in surprise as I smirked for him to see. He started to shake his head, but I raised a hand, stopping his tirade.

Standing up, I walked over to his desk. Both my palms made contact on the surface as I leaned forward, caging him in. "She will believe me. One word and she will believe me. Ayla is too fucking naïve for this game. The moment I have her wrapped around my fingers, Alessio will have no choice but to follow. He is like a little dog after her. If Alessio falls in my trap, the whole *family* will."

My face was mere inches apart from his when I spat the words. "Guess what? The little Queen is going to be their...unfortunate downfall."

His lips curled up in distaste at the mention of

Ayla. "You think you can win her?"

"Absolutely. You know, I am deeply hurt by your lack of faith in me," I added before leaning back.

I tugged at my tie, suddenly feeling like I was going to suffocate. "For a year, I have been trying to get you to trust me, yet you still don't."

He quickly stood up, shaking his head in disbelief. "Of course, I do. You are my heir. My reign is coming to an end. I am doing this for you. If we win this little game, one day, the four families will belong to you," he sputtered.

Moving forward in a flash, I grabbed his collar and pulled him closer, his feet almost leaving the ground. "Then start treating me like your heir instead of your fucking slave. You don't want to test me, because the moment I am in control, your ass will be in a gutter somewhere, understood?"

He choked, his face turning bright red. "I know," he breathed.

"Good," I said as I released him.

"If you're scared that I will choose them again, then your fear is misplaced. Remember, they left me for dead," I grumbled, facing the wide windows.

The darkness of the night shadowed everything. Every evil in this world.

I was killed in the darkness too.

And then I was resurrected in the darkness.

This time…I was the Master of the game. Everyone else would just be dancing to my tune.

Without turning my back, I spoke. "Don't forget. This is my game. My war. You are just a part of it."

He didn't answer, but I felt his fear vibrating,

feeding my dark soul. Such a sad sight, to see him cowering to me. And it was just the beginning.

"Konstantin, I wouldn't have saved you if I didn't trust you," he said slowly. He meant his words to be believed.

Funnily, I believed them. Because they really were the truth.

Unfortunately for him, his first mistake was saving my life.

From the corner of my eyes, I saw him rubbing his neck. It was already bruising. He stared at me with wide eyes, waiting for my next response.

"Then show it. From now on, I will be living in your main estate. Since you saved me, I had to stay here. I wonder what you are hiding in your estate?" I replied slowly, watching his every reaction through the dark-tinted glass.

He fidgeted with his tie before answering. "Nothing. I made you stay here in order to protect you. We had to hide your identity. But if this is what you want, then I will have your stuff moved to the main estate. You can stay there for however long you want. It's yours, after all."

I hummed in response. My eyes tracked every single fidget. He was nervous, and I was more curious.

This was another move on the chess board. Every move was part of the perfect ruse.

Perfect betrayal. Perfect lie. Perfect revenge.

I loved the chase. The prey falling willingly into the jaw of the predator. Too bad, so sad.

Without making eye contact with him, I swiveled around. He stayed beside his desk, watching me walk away with hawk eyes that I felt burning into my back.

My men followed behind me, and I reveled in the power of having everyone underneath me, on their knees. The corner of my lips turned up as I thought of how this was going to end.

My feet stopped just in front of the door. The room was silent, waiting for my next words, my next move.

With my hand on the door knob, I spoke loud for everyone to hear. Dominance and power swirled with my words, masking the real threat underneath.

"If you want to win this game, then it's about time you trust me, Valentin Solonik."

I didn't wait for his answer before walking out. I didn't need his reply. He knew exactly what he had to do.

And that was to surrender.

I was in control now.

Chapter 2

Konstantin

I walked down the dark lengthy hallway. It was silent, everyone in their beds, all doors closed.

As I neared my room, something or someone caught my eyes. Smiling, I moved forward fluidly. Perfect. Just what I needed.

A good fuck before a good night's sleep.

When I finally spoke, my voice was low, only for her to hear. "Get in the bedroom. I want you on the bed, naked, your legs spread, and your wet pussy bare for me to see."

The fact that we were living in Russia and dealing with Russians every single day, I had to master its language. But sometimes, English still spilled out. Thank fuck a lot of them understood English.

She nodded without a word and went inside the room. The door closed behind her with a soft click. My steps slowed until I came to a stop in front of the heavy, dark wooden door.

The seconds ticked by as I waited, letting the anticipation seep into us. After what felt like the longest time, I opened the door and walked inside.

Just like instructed, I found her on the bed, readily waiting for me.

She pushed herself on her elbows, peeking up at me with a tiny seductive smile. Her tongue slipped past her lips, licking the seams slowly.

"Did I say you could move?" I questioned in a thick Russian accent.

She giggled, and I internally rolled my eyes. I hated it when they giggled for no fucking reason. Like some desperate whores looking for attention.

On second thought…she was a whore. Well, she had an excuse.

"Lay down." My voice came out as a bark. Her eyes widened, but the excitement there was undeniable.

"Spread your legs wider," I muttered while unzipping my pants. They dropped to my feet with my underwear, and I stepped out of them. Her legs opened wider at my command, and I palmed my hard shaft.

"Ya hotela tebya ves' den," she whispered softly. My eyes narrowed on her hand as it went between her legs.

"You have been waiting for me?" I asked while she stroked herself, her two fingers working in and out.

"*Da*," she replied, a little breathless. I hummed in response, watching her bring herself to an orgasm.

I rubbed my length faster and harder. It was hard,

THE MAFIA AND HIS OBSESSION PART 1

already dripping from the tip. Her eyes flitted below my stomach, and she licked her lips hungrily.

"You want it?" I asked, moving closer to the bed.

She nodded silently, her fingers pumping faster with her thumb now circling her little nub. Her back bowed off the bed, her orgasm closer than before.

Her eyes were hooded as she waited for me. "You can't come."

"*Konstantin*," she breathed, her legs spreading wider, a very tempting and welcoming sight.

My legs started to cramp, and I knew I was close. Releasing my throbbing hardness, I joined her on the bed. She smiled, a happy look on her face.

Slapping her hand away, she laughed and removed her fingers from her wet heat. I crawled forward before flipping her on her front.

"You always…" she started to complain, but a hard slap on her round ass shut her up.

"You have no place to complain. We do this my way or not all," I hissed in her ear before biting the sensitive skin just below.

I never looked into their faces while fucking them. To me, they were faceless. Nameless. Nothing but whores to satisfy my dick and my needs.

And they knew the rules. Understood them, yet still chose to submit.

My knees widened her legs apart, my hardness pushing between her folds. She was dripping, already so wet, and I had barely touched her. "Such a dirty girl."

"Yes. *Pozhaluysta*," she begged, pushing her ass

back toward me.

"You like begging?" I tsked in her ear before pressing further into her wet heat. She moaned out loud, her head falling backward.

I nipped on her shoulder, but my teeth didn't leave their marks. She wasn't mine to claim.

My thoughts went back to the woman I wished I could claim as *mine*.

I wanted her lips swollen from my kisses. Her skin flushed, my fingers leaving their marks from my tight hold as I thrust into her pussy. Her moans belonging to me. Her kisses mine to take. Her body mine to love and cherish. Her heart entwined with mine.

"Konstantin."

My name snapped me back to the present, the image of *her* disappearing from my foggy mind.

My hips drove forward, my cock filling the woman underneath me in one long, hard stroke.

She screamed, her hips bucking forward under my relentless thrusts. Her head was buried in the pillows as she took everything I was giving her, taking from her.

She submitted, and I took.

I continued thrusting into her willing body, using her for my pleasure. Closing my eyes, I let myself imagine the impossible.

My mind replaced the whore underneath me with someone else.

Behind my closed eyes, I envisioned *her*.

A black-haired beauty with green eyes that looked like the rainforest.

Green eyes so vibrant that they took my breath

away the first time I ever gazed in them.

It was *her* moans I heard. *Her* laughter. *Her* smile. I was making love to *her*. Only her.

And she loved me in return.

The thought of her had me coming hard into the whore's warm heat instead of the woman I wanted as my own. Her orgasm hit her at the same time, her screams snapping me out of my perfect dream.

My eyes opened as the woman collapsed underneath me. I rolled over, breaking the contact we had.

My breathing was harsher, the blood roaring in my ears. My pulse was thumbing harder as I tried catching my breath.

It was always like this. Fucking other women, but always thinking of *her*. Always wishing it was her.

Just the mere thought of her would make me come harder and faster. The wet pussies I had and were laid on a silver platter for me never did the work.

Dragging the black comforter over my body, I closed my eyes. "You can leave now," I ordered, my voice still husky from the recent activity.

"Konstantin." Only my name made it past her lips before I interrupted.

"We are not to the point where you can say my name when we aren't fucking. It's Mr. Solonik, Sir, or Boss to you."

"Sorry," she muttered before falling silent.

"I will see you tomorrow?" she asked softly after a few seconds.

I peeked at her with one eye as she got out of

bed. Her eyes were on me, looking strangely innocent. She smiled while dressing, having a content look on her face.

My answer took that smile away. "No, you won't."

She froze, her arms hanging to the sides. "What do you mean?"

"It's my last day here. I am moving to the main estate tomorrow," I replied, relaxing into the soft mattress.

I didn't owe her any explanation, but for weird, fucked-up reasons, I still gave her one. Maybe it was the sad look on her face. Maybe it was the way she was looking at me—as if I were her savior.

I almost laughed at that thought.

"I need a new pussy, anyway," I muttered low. It was partly for her to hear, letting her know whatever we had was just fun.

And she did hear. Her gasp told me she did.

I scoffed, waiting for the outburst. When I didn't get one, I opened my eyes.

She quickly dressed up, staying strangely silent. Once her body was covered, she tied her hair in a tight bun.

After, she stood still. Her throat worked up and down as she swallowed. "I thought I was your favorite."

I released a long, frustrated breath. *Here we go again.*

"Look, In—" *What the fuck is her name?*

Inessa? Inna? Anna? Wait no, those were the other three.

"Irina. My name is Irina," she replied quietly.

THE MAFIA AND HIS OBSESSION PART 1

The sadness in her voice was not mistaken.

"Right, *Irina*. Look, I don't have any favorites. I'm a simple guy who wants a simple thing. And I thought you were aware of that when you got involved with me," I started, now sitting against the headboard.

She opened her mouth to say something, but I stopped her with a hard look.

"To put it simply, I needed a good fuck. A warm pussy to dip myself in. What guy doesn't need one? And you, Irina, your pussy was wet, warm, and tight enough to keep me entertained for a longer time. That's it."

Yeah, I heard her heart break. Too bad, so sad. She knew the rules. They were pretty fucking simple.

"I thought—"

"Well, you thought wrong," I quickly interrupted. "Now, it's time for you to move on. Forget about me and my lovely ten-inch anaconda, which I know you love so much. And I will forget about your tight pussy. Got it, baby?"

I raised an eyebrow, waiting for her reply. She swallowed again, blinking away unshed tears. Finally, she nodded. A small heartbreaking nod before turning on her heel and walking away.

The slump of her shoulders and quiet sniffles almost made me feel bad.

Okay, fine. I *did* feel bad, like a heartless asshole.

But the words were needed. I couldn't have an ex-fling coming at me and thinking we would get married or some shit.

Not gonna happen. Never ever. Like nope. Zero possibilities.

Did I mention *never*?

Before she could walk out of my room, I stopped her, feeling bad for being a *little* too harsh.

"Irina, I am not saying this to hurt you. Or to be an asshole. I am just stating the truth. It's not your fault. And it's most definitely not you. Just find a good guy who actually deserves you," I said quietly. "You are a good girl."

I heard her taking a deep breath and then exhaled. "Thank you for the sentiment, Mr. Solonik. I appreciate it. And thank you for your time. I also appreciate that. I will now bid you goodbye."

She didn't turn around as she spoke. Her words held no anger. They sounded empty.

The door opened, and she walked out. I closed my eyes with a tired sigh.

"I also hope you find a good woman. One who will not make you so heartless anymore. A woman who will actually teach you to be good and how to show compassion."

My eyes snapped open, but I didn't catch a final glimpse of her before she closed the door with a soft click.

Her words left a gaping hole in my chest, and they rung loudly in my ears.

I pinched my eyes closed, fighting against the pain in my heart. I never realized that words could actually hurt this much.

Shoot me in the ass and I could bear it.

Shoot me in the heart and I would smile.

But those words…they haunted me.

It hurt so much, knowing that I did find that woman.

Only difference…she wasn't mine.

"Fuck this shit! Fuck my life! Fuck my whole fucking existence!" I hissed, dropping more f-bombs than I could count.

Punching the mattress, I pulled the comforter over my head, still swearing loudly.

It appeared that sleep wasn't going to come easily.

Chapter 3

Her

My fingers froze when I saw the doorknob turning. The sunlight was bright in my eyes as I looked outside, not blinking, completely frozen.

It was still too early.

The sun was still high up in the sky. Darkness hadn't covered the city yet, so why was *he* coming for me?

I was supposed to still have some time. I was supposed to have time to prepare myself for tonight.

But the plans had changed. He didn't care.

And now I had to bear it.

The pain. The endless tears. The unspoken words. The unleashed screams.

The newly given scars.

I had thought my body would grow numb over time, but it hurt to realize that you could never go numb.

Every pain was made to be felt.

Over the years, I had learned my lesson. I found

THE MAFIA AND HIS OBSESSION PART 1

a way to fight him. Not physically. Just mentally.

The door opened, and I sucked in a deep breath, waiting for the unexpected. Because with him, it was always unexpected. It was always something new that I had to grow accustomed to.

He always found new ways to defile me. New ways to hurt me.

Sometimes my body. Sometimes my heart. And other times, my mind.

He played me masterfully. He knew every button to push that would lead me over the edge, hanging over the cliff, falling yet not reaching the bottom.

Hurting but not dying.

Tears but no sound.

Everything was silent in my world. Silent and dark.

Sometimes, I wished he would kill me. Death would be easier, but funnily, I was scared of death.

So I fought for each breath I took. It was a battle I won every day he would come into our bedroom.

My body might not have been numb to his games, but my heart was.

It was unfeeling.

My heart would beat to a rhythm. *Thump thump. Thump thump.*

I was alive. But that was all.

Just breathing. My heart just beating.

He molded me, creating a shell out of a living person. One who once knew how to laugh, smile, and talk. But now...while looking inside, you would find it empty. A dark pit of emptiness that would lead you to a road map of nowhere.

From the corner of my eyes, I saw his feet

coming closer. One step at a time. One step closer with each passing second.

Thump thump. Thump thump.

My heart continued beating. I inhaled. I exhaled.

Breathe in. Breathe out.

Another step forward. Another step closer to me.

Another step that reminded me of my lack of freedom.

Freedom.

A foreign word to someone who had none. It held such little power to those who had it. But to the ones who didn't, it was something we could only dream of. A wish made to a flying star in the darkness of the night.

To us, it was only a fading hope.

He paused at my chair, waiting, soundless. Always silent.

In some ways, that was my power. My hidden strength. One he couldn't take away from me.

The silence was my gift.

Once upon a time, I hated it. And now, I reveled in it.

I stayed still, my fingers still wrapped around the knitting cloth and needle. My eyes stayed fixated on the window, watching the blue sky, a beautiful sight that reminded me of what I had lost.

The clouds moved just as the seconds ticked by. The sun shined, casting the breathtaking glow around the lands.

In some parts of the world, some people were enjoying the sun. Loving it. Praising it.

Other parts, we were trapped inside with just a glimpse of it. It was not ours to feel and breathe in.

THE MAFIA AND HIS OBSESSION PART 1

His movement caught my eyes again. He moved away from my chair, walking toward the bed. Closing my eyes, I continued to breathe.

Thump thump. Thump thump.

I counted the seconds in my head.

One. Two. Three. Four. Five.

Five seconds was all he gave me. Five seconds to prepare myself. Five seconds to wish for my death. Only in those five seconds I always wished for my end.

But as soon as those five seconds were over, the steel cage around my heart came back up, folding and molding. Protecting me in the only way it knew how.

My five seconds were over.

It was time for his entertainment and my ruination.

Standing up, firm, stiff, and poised, just like I had been taught, I placed my knitting materials on the chair.

Shoulders back, head up but eyes cast down, I walked toward him.

My thoughts flew elsewhere. Like always. Like right now. My gaze tracked the floor, and I was thinking how ugly the carpet was. It was brown, and the woven wool was almost coming apart. I dug my toes into it, feeling its softness on my bare skin.

It was a lesson learned.

Sometimes, the ugliness in the world could bring softness and gentleness.

Other times, the most beautiful and captivating thing could bring pain and tears.

Something we all needed to remember but

always forgot. A long time ago, I forgot too. I fell into a dark trap by a beautiful, captivating thing.

When my feet finally came a stop, I closed my eyes for a brief second. A sharp pain in my ankle brought me to my knees.

A reminder to kneel down. So I knelt down with my thighs slightly spread apart.

My eyes opened at the feel of his feet pushing my legs wider. I did as I was silently commanded.

Always listen, even when the words are not uttered. Always listen, so it will hurt less.

My mother had whispered into my ear before. The last time I had seen her.

At first, the words were forgotten. And now, those words were my mantra to staying alive.

A small tap on my head brought my eyes up to meet his aging ones. Dark brown eyes with deep wrinkles around them, a sign that he was getting older. *Already old.*

My gaze traveled south, wanting to escape the sight but couldn't. When my eyes landed on his lips, I waited.

He waited too, dragging out the suspense. Forcing me to feel it. Little did he know that I had mastered this game.

It was a weak ploy to weaken me. But I had learned how to use his game on himself.

He thought he was dragging out the suspense. For me, I was just using each passing second to strengthen myself against the pain I knew was coming.

"Come here," he finally said. Snapping his fingers with the words, he only stared at me.

Emotionless. Just like the heartless man he was.

I moved forward, crawling closer between his legs. My body tightened in disgust, hating every moment of this. My skin itched with the urge to hide and run away. To fade away into nothingness.

He grasped my chin, pulling me closer. "I said come here."

Pushing myself up, I crawled on his lap. With my thighs on either side of his hips, I straddled him, waiting for his next command.

"You have been spacing out a lot lately," he continued, his eyes roaming my face diligently.

Only so I could escape you.

But even in my dreams, he was there. Always haunting me. Always making me cry soundless tears.

I shook my head mutely, and his eyes narrowed. His fingers dug into my thighs, slowly pushing my long dress up.

The hem grew closer and closer to my crotch, bunching tightly around my middle. Every time he touched me, I wanted to return the touch.

But in a different way. I wanted to claw his eyes out and watch his blood drip around us. I wanted to slice his throat open.

I wanted to stare into his soulless eyes.

His touch made me violent. Only problem was...the violence only existed in my head, buried deep inside. If only I could unleash it, then maybe I would get the taste of freedom.

But my freedom was a craving that would never be fulfilled.

His fingers inched closer, following an upward

path. I trembled slightly but such a small shiver that even he missed it.

I am strong.

A soft whisper in my head resonated through my ears. *I am strong.*

Taking a deep breath, I released it quietly. Just as he touched me *there*. His thumb pressed harder, a slightly painful pressure. But not one I couldn't bear.

I had been through worse than that.

Suddenly, he moved. And then I was under his body. Underneath him. Like always.

His body pressed against mine, trapping me into the soft mattress. His lips moved over my neck, placing kisses as he went. Biting softly and then harder.

Hard enough to break skin. He left his mark there as my blood slid down my neck in a single trail. Like a tear falling down your cheek.

Disgust filled me to full capacity, but still, I was frozen.

His wet kisses continued down to the valley of my breasts. He paused before slowly pulling away. My dress was ripped apart in mere seconds.

I blinked, waiting for this to be over.

Thump thump. Thump thump.

More kisses…more claiming. More marks on my body. His marks.

I had to bear them with pride, for they were my crown. My title. They showed who I belonged to.

I laid naked under him, my body bare to his pleasure. So he played me however he wanted. Pulling whatever strings he desired. Pressing

THE MAFIA AND HIS OBSESSION PART 1

whatever notes he wished.

My eyes widened at the prickling feeling in my arm. It was sudden, harsh, and then gone just as quickly as it came.

A few seconds passed before he propped himself on his elbows, hovering above me. His hardened bulge pressed against my core as he circled his hips, a tiny smirk on his face.

My eyes fluttered closed as I realized his game.

Forced pleasure.

He was going to make me crack under his hands. And like the whore I was...I was going to crack. Like every time he had played this game.

My jaw clenched as his hand traveled south between my legs. I refused. My body refused. My mind roared. My heart cracked a little.

But no matter how much I hated it, refused to want it, he made me want it.

My body might give in, but my soul was intact. He would not feast on my soul and heart. They were mine to keep.

His fingers invaded me, and my teeth snapped together, pressing hard, fighting against the invasion.

He pressed deeper. Another finger, opening me wider.

My eyes snapped opened as his other hand gripped my breast hard, pinching the nipple. "You are responding to me, just like the little whore you are."

I hate you.

His thumb pressed over the tiny nub, circling over and over again, dragging a pleasure from deep within me. My thighs trembled in the effort of keeping my dignity.

My chest heaved with each breath, my vision clouding with unshed tears. The pressure of his fingers intensified, forcing me to feel it.

I hate you.

The tears trickled down my temple, soundlessly.

I hate you.

His fingers moved roughly inside of me, stretching me, hitting spots that jolted my insides. I clenched around him, my body wanting what he was giving but hating it at the same time.

I felt betrayed, like always. I loathed myself.

I hate you.

He pressed his body over mine, his hips thrusting against me with the movement of his fingers.

"I want to hear you scream."

I won't.

The torture continued, and I knew he wouldn't stop until I let go. So I did.

I let go, letting my mind open to feel whatever he was giving me. Bile made its way up my throat and I fought against the urge to vomit.

Don't.

My lips trembled as more tears fell, the pillow now wet with my pain.

Finally, my body spasmed, my legs shaking and my mind shutting.

I gave him what he wanted.

I hate you.

He smirked, licking his fingers. "Perfect." His eyes went between my legs, watching.

I let out a small breath, feeling my shame

dripping down the inside of my thighs.

It was all that was left of me.

Shame.

I hate you. But I hate myself too.

I laid there, letting my mind swirl with dizziness. Black spots appeared in front of my eyes, and I tried to shake it away.

His body covered mine again as I stared up at the ceiling. He entered my body with a single hard thrust. Hard enough to hurt, my body jolting with agony.

He thrust in and out, not for my pleasure. But his.

And I let him.

I surrendered underneath my *husband*.

Time passed, the seconds flew by, the minutes crawled, and finally, he fell beside me. My eyes closed, knowing this was the end.

I hate you.

Relief filled me when I felt him getting up. The bed shifted and then nothing.

I waited as my body ached. So much pain. My thighs hurt, and my core felt like glass was cutting through me. The marks over my body left a dull pain, one that was still vibrating through my mind.

When my eyes opened, he had already left the room.

Relief. Tears of relief and happiness.

Even with my body violated and my soul tortured, I cried silent tears of happiness.

He took something, but in the end, I had won.

I didn't scream. He didn't hear my screams.

He lost yet again.

I hate you.

Finally pulling the courage deep within me, I got off the bed. My legs shook, my body almost falling to the floor.

Holding on to the bed, I steadied myself, but it hurt too much. My knees met the ground as my body weakened.

I crawled to the bathroom, each movement causing jolts of agony through my body. My muscles protested, but I still crawled. In the bathroom, with the help of the counter, I stood in front of the mirror. I wasn't surprised with what I saw.

It was a sight I saw every day.

Teeth marks. Hand marks. Marks that looked like he had clawed at my skin. Some were deep red. Others already turning purple.

Blood dripping from open wounds that he left with his teeth. Blood coating the scratches left on my body.

My eyes drifted lower, following every piece he left me. My gaze stopped between my thighs.

Blood.

My panties were in shreds, bloodied. He made me bleed. He left me bleeding. It wasn't new. Just another day living my nightmare.

The red represented my humiliation. A fitting color.

I hate you.

Refusing to look into the mirror anymore, refusing to face my shame any longer, I walked into the shower.

Sitting against the wall, I curled into myself,

letting the raining water wash away my shame. After a long time, I walked out.

My body was sensitive to the towel, and I winced as my long dress covered my body. My skin felt scratched raw, my body aching with every step as I walked out of the bathroom.

My feet took me slowly toward the chair, the one facing the window. The sun was going to sleep, the sky now a mixture of orange, yellow, and pink.

Another beauty…in the darkness of my world.

The tears were long gone as I sat down, holding my knitting cloth and needle in my hand. Watching the sunset, I resumed my knitting.

As if nothing happened.

As if everything was perfect.

I was the perfect wife.

He was the perfect husband.

We were a perfect lie.

Chapter 4

Konstantin

My men followed me out, their steps close to mine but still behind. Just the way it should be. The harsh winter air hit me hard in the face, and I winced.

Fucking Russia and its winter.

"Are you ready?" Valentin asked, his voice ruining my mood further. Always yapping. Maybe I should shut his mouth for him. Shove a block of snow in his face or something.

Keep dreaming, the devil currently perched on my shoulder laughed. My lips curled up in distaste, and I almost shooed him away, but that would look weird.

Shooing away something that wasn't even there. My men would think me crazy.

Maybe I was. Living with Valentin Solonik for a year had driven me crazier than when I was living with Alessio.

Crazy to say, but I almost missed the poor

bastard.

You can't miss your enemy, the devil laughed in my ears.

Another reminder of what I had to do. What I was actually born to do. My legacy. Those years spent with the Ivanshovs, I was on borrowed time, living a life that wasn't mine.

A character who was made up. A killer who was dancing to someone else's tunes.

Little did I know, I was born to lead a family. I was born to have everyone else bowing to me.

I was born to succeed Valentin Solonik.

"Konstantin, are you listening to me?"

His voice broke into my thoughts, and my head snapped up, regarding him with a glare. He swallowed and smiled, almost nervously.

"What?" I asked, my legs moving again. He matched my steps, following next to me.

"The estate is ready for your arrival. One of my men will lead you through and show you around, just to get yourself familiar. I have to stay behind and take care of some club business," he answered, almost robotic, like he practiced it.

"I don't need anyone to lead me around." With a raised eyebrow, I waited for his answer.

His silence was his answer as he opened the car door for me. Ha. In your face, Valentin Solonik. The Boss opening the door for his heir. *That's new.*

He would be bowing to me soon too. I had been waiting for this day for a very long time. Only a few months now and everything would be just the way it was supposed to be.

I used to hate games; now I was just loving it.

You can only love a game when you are the Master. The leader. When the reins are in your hands, you can move the chest piece anywhere you want, the others will just have to follow, silently and obediently.

After I was seated in the car, Valentin closed the door and gave me another tight smile.

Rolling the windows down, I motioned him over. He came closer and I whispered so only he could hear. "Do you need the bathroom?"

"What?" he stuttered.

"The bathroom. You look like you are constipating. I don't think your men would enjoy the foul smell, no matter how much they love you," I continued.

He could only stare, his mouth opened, speechless. Tipping my black hat toward him, I winked. "Boss," I mumbled, just to rustle his feathers a little.

One point for me.

Before he could move, I rolled up the windows. My body settled back against the seat, relaxing as the car started moving.

With my eyes on the front, I took a deep breath. Another step on the chess board. Another piece played.

In the rearview mirror, Valentin's figure grew smaller and smaller, until it completely disappeared.

It was his turn now. How fucking exciting.

Closing my eyes, I let myself think of every moment leading to this one. Every step I took was for one purpose. In the end, was I going to get what I wanted most?

THE MAFIA AND HIS OBSESSION PART 1

A game was being played...it might have appeared that I was the winner for now, but for how long?

How long before I fall, because we always fall? From the top, everything crumbles under your feet and you hit rock bottom again.

It must have been a long thinking process, because the next time I was brought back to the present, the car had stopped and my driver was speaking to me.

"Sir, we are here."

I opened my eyes to see it was dark outside, the sun already down, casting the perfect darkness for people like me.

Perfect start for a new beginning.

The driver opened the door for me, and I stepped out, staring at the estate in front of me. It was dark, except for the lamps around it.

In the night, it looked like those ghost houses in Halloween movies. A castle that was hiding the Devil.

I fucking loved it.

But I knew in the morning, it would be the perfect beautiful estate for the filthiest and richest man in Russia. Also known as Valentin Solonik.

But soon, it would be me. *Konstantin Solonik.*

Have I mentioned how much I hated that name? I wondered how much my mother hated me to name me after a fucking theatre actor. More like an opera actor. I shuddered at the thought.

"This way," Yegor said, nodding his way toward the entrance.

"Do I have to do this?" I questioned, taking a

step forward.

"You have no choice, Konstantin," he replied quietly, only for my ears.

He was right. Only because a year ago, I made a choice to lie and play a part in the game of *power*. And now, here I was.

Yegor slapped my back in encouragement. "Think of relief after all this shit is done."

I laughed before slapping his back too, maybe a little too hard. He stumbled forward before quickly catching himself. He grumbled something under his breath, his glare not one to miss.

He was lucky I considered him a friend or he would have been dead, his eyes gouged out for even *thinking* of glaring my way. Nodding toward my men, I made my way inside. The cold was left outside, thank fucking God for that.

The door closed behind us, and I stared. It wasn't much different than the Ivanshov estate. Almost the same, just more sterile.

No warmth. No feelings. No laughter or sweet smiles.

Sometimes, I missed it. Other times, I was thankful.

At least now I didn't have to look at someone who was forbidden to me. I didn't have look at her and crave her touch, knowing well I couldn't have her.

I made a mistake once. I touched her before, almost kissed her…our little secret.

"The kitchen is to your left, but it doesn't matter. You have the maids to bring your food, whatever you need," Yegor continued his useless introduction. His voice broke through my depressing thoughts.

"My room?" I asked, already moving toward the imperial staircase.

"You're so fucking impatient," he muttered under his breath.

"I need my beauty sleep, asshole. I'm taking an early flight tomorrow morning," I growled, stomping upstairs.

"Back to the States?"

I huffed in response. Back into the enemy's cave. *Time to play with the little Queen,* Valentin's voice resonated through my ears.

He was absent yet his words wouldn't leave me. Fucking bastard. Just ruined my night.

Through the silence, I walked down the hall, trying to find a suitable room. Maybe the last room in the corner? More privacy while fucking someone.

"Are the walls soundproof?" I asked, going door by door.

"No—" he started, but I quickly shut him up with a raise of my hand.

"Just fucking great. I love this shit...*not*," I hissed. "It's not my fault when you won't be able to sleep at night. Just saying. The women always turn into screamers, even when they aren't."

He rolled his eyes. "Whatever, man."

"Jealous?" He didn't answer. No problem, I already got my answer.

I was still walking, still looking, when my eyes fell onto something—or someone.

My feet stop, my body frozen at the sight that beheld me.

The door was partially open, but it was the sight from behind the door that got me intrigued.

Against my better judgment, I moved closer, just a step, toward the door. I leaned forward, peering inside, wanting a better view.

The light was on, the chandelier casting a beautiful glow around the room. But that wasn't what caught my attention.

It was the woman sitting underneath the chandelier.

The world stilled for one fucking moment. Maybe I was robbed of my breath. Whatever it was, I could only stare at her.

She was a sight to see.

My eyebrows fused together in confusion. "What is she wearing?"

My gaze followed the length of her body. The plain navy gown shielded everything. It was loose around her body. The white collar was high, covering her neck. Her arms were hidden with long sleeves, except her hands.

She was dressed specifically not to tempt any man. Yet…

"She looks like a fucking nun."

A beautiful nun.

After my shock at her clothes, my eyes moved upward to her face. Her head was down, looking at her lap. She was knitting in the silence, while the chandelier glowed around her.

She was glowing under the light.

Her long blonde hair fell behind her back. Some wavy strands were hanging loose around her face, shielding her from my eyes. And I wanted to see more.

A nun with a tempting figure, one that made any man want to sin.

Her fingers continued to work the needles, threading whatever was in her hand. Slowly she brought her head up, like she knew she was being watched.

Our eyes met for the briefest second. She cocked her head to the side, staring at me fully, almost like she was memorizing my face before she looked down again.

One look, so quick, and then it was gone. Like I wasn't even there.

One look was enough to make me want more.

My thoughts came to a screeching halt when a hand pulled me away from the door. "You shouldn't be here, Konstantin," Yegor whispered.

"Who is she?" I asked, my eyes still on her.

"Solonik's wife."

I froze, my eyes widening. It felt like cold water had just been dumped over my head, shaking me awake. Bringing me back to the present.

Forget about having cold water dumped over my head. It felt more like I was drowning in the cold ocean with no escape. Just dark and a seeping coldness that could make anyone go numb.

"Valentin's wife," I whispered. My gaze was fixated on her, finding it hard to move away.

Yegor came to stand in front of me, shaking his head slowly. "You aren't allowed here. This is where his wife stays. She is always in there. Nobody is allowed to come in here except for her bodyguard. He is in there with her right now, always watching her."

"She is so young," I muttered.

"Are you listening to me?"

I nodded, my gaze still on the door. "Yeah, I am."

"She won't speak to you. Don't worry about that. She stays by herself so you won't have any problem avoiding her. Just choose a room on the other side," he said, releasing a long breath.

"She is so young," I repeated, and Yegor closed his eyes.

"Konstantin—" he hissed, but I shook my head. "Look, I don't know the story. Nobody does. One day Valentin was single with a limp dick, and the next day they were married."

My eyes met his with a fierce glare. "She doesn't belong here."

"You are right. She doesn't. But that's not our problem," he practically bellowed the last word.

"What the fuck! She can hear you," I said. My fists raised to punch his ugly face, but he quickly ducked away.

"Even if she does, she can't speak," he muttered. His eyes went to the door, and I almost saw a hint of emotion there before he quickly went back to being a cold bastard.

That stopped me. "She can't speak or won't speak?"

"Can't speak. She is mute."

A mute nun who married Solonik. Well, shit just got more interesting.

Yegor pushed my shoulders in frustration. "Konstantin, listen to me. You need to listen or you

THE MAFIA AND HIS OBSESSION PART 1

will be fucked. Valentin is crazy about his wife. If he finds you anywhere near her, your dead body will be found the next morning. Trust me, you won't be the first."

I was half listening to him and half thinking how the fuck did Solonik get a wife like her. She was probably younger than me, and Valentin was old enough to be my father.

She was too young to be here. To be in this life.

"This is my warning. More like my helpful warning. Stay away from her and focus on why you are here. We have come this far, and we can't lose now," he continued in panic.

That captured my attention. Fuck, I couldn't lose focus now. He was right.

Who cared about Valentin's wife? She wasn't part of the plan. And I had to stay far, far away from her.

Taking a deep breath, I released it slowly. "You are right."

I couldn't fuck this up. Now was not the time to get distracted by a woman with pretty blonde hair and dressed like a fucking nun in a convent or something.

"Punch me," I whispered.

"What?"

"Just do it."

He punched him. Right in the face. Fuck, I didn't think he would actually do it. So I kicked him in his knee instead. "I didn't fucking mean it."

Although the punch did bring me back to my senses.

No blondes for you, Konstantin. Keep your dick

in your pants. For tonight, at least.

"I'm going to bed," I called out, walking away from Yegor. Away from *her*.

After a few minutes of getting lost, I finally found a bedroom that suited me. Without wasting any time, I got into bed and closed my eyes.

Another game to be played tomorrow.

Unfortunately, sleep didn't come to me. It stayed away like a fucking stubborn child. I rolled around in bed the whole night, actually begging to the moon for sleep.

But nope. Nada. Zilch.

When the sun started to make its appearance, I was pissed as fuck.

Pissed to the point that I wanted to yell, *Off with their heads*, to everyone I saw. Just great. A perfect morning to see.

I avoided everyone, even my pilot and hostess. The plane ride was enough for me to gather all my information. Everything was locked and ready to fire.

When the plane touched ground, I was fucking ready to start the day.

All thoughts about a pretty blonde girl were gone from my head. Only my destination mattered.

With the help from Valentin, he had a car waiting for me. Giving the address to the driver, he drove me to where I wanted…needed to be.

I closed my eyes when the car made its final stop.

One year.

One fucking year.

I was back, motherfucker.

THE MAFIA AND HIS OBSESSION PART 1

Are you ready for me? I didn't think so. Nobody was ready.

I inhaled and then exhaled. On my next breath, I opened my eyes and stepped out of the car. My legs didn't stop until I was standing in front of the door that I walked out of one year ago.

A year ago, *she* hugged me goodbye. Right there. In front of that door.

Little did she know, I wouldn't be back. Not until now.

The door opened. I heard gasps. I saw shocked faces. Familiar faces.

And then I saw her.

Standing on the top of the stairs, her hand covering her mouth in shock.

One second. Two. Three.

Her next step was slow and then she was running down the stairs at full force. Pregnant belly and all, almost giving me a heart attack.

I stepped forward, trying to stop her from her thoughtless action. Protectiveness made its way into my heart at the sight of her running toward me.

My arms opened wide, and she jumped into my embrace, holding me close. Her tears soaked my shirt as she sobbed brokenly.

I held her tighter, as close as I could with her rounded stomach. Burying my face into her neck, I breathed in her sweet smell.

Home. This was what home felt like.

My lips touched her skin in the slightest touch, my whisper only for her ears to hear.

"*Baby girl.*"

Chapter 5

Ayla

It was a moment when everything stilled. My feet froze on the landing above the staircase, and it felt like I had been robbed of my breath. My heart flipped, and then the tears came.

My throat closed, trying so hard not to cry as I ran down the stairs toward him. In the back of my mind, I knew Alessio was going to be mad at me for running in my current state. I could already see his face turning red with frustration but trying his best not to yell at me.

But in that moment, nothing mattered.

One year.

One whole year since I had seen him.

One year since Alessio came back home and gave me news that broke my heart.

"Ayla! Alessio is home!" Maddie screamed at the top of her lungs.

My heart jumped and then accelerated, my face

THE MAFIA AND HIS OBSESSION PART 1

breaking into a wide smile that I couldn't hold in anymore.

I really hated it when he had to go away for more than just a day or two. It had been almost a week—five days to be exact—since I last saw him. But Alessio always made sure we spoke on the phone every day. Even through his busy schedules, he always found time for me and Princess.

I felt a kick on my thigh and laughed quietly. Speaking of Princess.

Looking down at my bundle of joy, she cooed at me, her lips pursing cutely. "Papa is home, pretty Princess."

Her tiny legs kicked at me again excitedly, as if she understood what I was saying. "Let's get you dressed and we can welcome him home. What do you say?" I murmured, tickling her sides.

She laughed, her cute little dimple showing. Maila had her papa's dimple, even on the same cheek. Poking the dent softly, I placed a kiss on her nose.

Princess kicked again, her giggles never ending, as she tried to roll on her back. Her tiny body moved around, trying to escape my hands. At four months old, she was already rolling around, almost giving Alessio a heart attack the first time she did it.

"Well, aren't you excited today?" I continued talking, making sure to dress her up quickly.

After making sure she was presentable, her pretty blue dress adorning her tiny body and her headband in place, we both made our way downstairs.

Just in time to see Alessio walking through the

doors with his men following closely behind him. I smiled at the sight.

The entry was filled with so much power and dominance. Each step they took spoke of authority. The suits made them look like gentlemen, rich billionaires. But the looks on their faces, the harsh and unveiled look that didn't hide anything, showed the true monsters underneath.

No smiles from them. No laughter. Emotionless stares. Stiff bodies.

As I stepped off the last landing, I practically ran to Alessio. He opened his arms for me, and I sunk into his embrace. He held us close, Princess against his chest, cushioned between him and me.

His warm embrace felt like sunlight, erasing the harsh coldness I felt during his absence. "Princess missed you," *I muttered.*

"*I think you mean you missed me,*" *he replied with a dry chuckle.*

"*You know I did,*" *I retorted as he pulled away slightly.*

To my surprise, he wasn't smiling. The soft gentle look he always wore around Princess and me was gone. In its place was a man I had met the first time, when our story started. The very first time I had seen him.

"*What's wrong?*" *I asked, placing my palm over his cheek. He didn't reply; instead, he brought his attention to Princess.*

His thumb brushed over her nose softly, and her smile widened. She was definitely her papa's girl. "*How is my little Princess doing?*"

His mood seemed off. Not the Alessio I had

THE MAFIA AND HIS OBSESSION PART 1

grown accustomed to. My gaze went behind me, looking at the other men.

Every time they would leave the house, it felt like something big had settled over my heart. And when they would come back home, I always found myself giving them a once-over, making sure they were all okay. They were older than me, meaner, harder...killers.

Yet I found myself watching over them like they were my babies.

They stood silently, their shoulders rigid, their bodies locked and ready for battle. Nikolay wore a frown, while Phoenix appeared like he was mourning.

Everyone seemed fine...except nothing was fine.

They were all here, except one.

"Where is Viktor?"

My question was met with silence. It lasted for a few seconds until I couldn't handle the suffocating silence anymore.

"I asked, where is Viktor?" The panic in my voice couldn't be mistaken.

One of my boys was missing. One of Alessio's men, his brother, was missing.

I looked at everyone, but their faces told me nothing. My heart dropped to the pit of my stomach. This couldn't be happening.

Not Viktor.

It was a joke, like always. They loved to worry me and pull my leg during unexpected times. It must have been Viktor's plan. He was the player, the one who could make me laugh even when I wanted to cry.

But this time, I wasn't in the mood to joke.

Turning to Alessio, I grabbed his arm. "Are you going to answer me, Alessio? Or just stand there? I asked a question. Where is Viktor?"

His furious blue eyes met mine, and he pulled his arm back, almost causing me to stumble back. "He will not be coming back."

"What do you mean by that? Where is he?"

I suddenly felt sick. This couldn't be happening.

Viktor was more than Alessio's second in command. He was his best friend. His brother. They were bonded not by blood but by choice. By hearts.

This moment was one that left me speechless. And then angry. Tears clouded my vision as realization sunk in.

"What have you done, Alessio?" I asked quietly but already knowing the answer. When he didn't answer, his gaze moving away from mine, he confirmed what I already knew.

"I asked a question, and I want an answer."

His glare could cut through glass. He stared at me, unflinching, like my anger and sadness meant nothing to him. "And I already answered, Angel."

His voice was surprisingly soft even when his gaze held red hot fury.

"Don't call me that," I hissed, finally breaking into cold sweats. Each word had become harder to speak.

It made me realize that I had been blinded for so long. Nothing was perfect...I just thought it was. I wanted to believe that it was.

A perfect family.

Without another glance, Alessio started to walk

away. My back straightened as he bluntly ignored me.

"Don't walk away from me. I am speaking to you," I said, louder.

Maila flinched in my arms, and I heard a small whimper as she started to struggle. Her chin wobbled as if she was about to cry.

I rocked her back and forth, soothingly. All the while my gaze stayed on her father's back, glaring at the sight.

"Maddie, can you take Maila?" I asked, already handing her over. Maddie shook her head, trying to clear her shock from Alessio's announcement.

"I got her."

I went upstairs, following behind my husband. I found him in our bedroom. His back was to me as he stared off into the distance, his gaze on the wall.

"He is dead, Ayla. I left him bleeding in a dark alley. You won't be seeing him again," he murmured. The anger in his voice wasn't mistaken.

"Why would you do that? How could you?" I asked rather softly. It was the moment when I didn't know if I should be crying or yelling. Maybe both. Yet I couldn't bring myself to do either.

"You know why."

"Is it because of what happened? Alessio, I thought we talked about that. I explained what happened!"

I walked closer. Alessio stepped away, his back rigid. Almost like he couldn't bear for me to be close to him.

"He touched you!" he growled low in this chest.

Once upon a time, I would have loved those

words, that tone. Today, I just hated it.

"He was drunk!" I hissed back, suddenly wanting to shake some sense into Alessio. "He didn't realize what he was doing, and I stopped him before he could do anything else."

It had happened weeks ago. In the middle of the night, I had caught Viktor stumbling in the corridor, looking for his room. But he was drunk...he didn't know what he was doing. He tried to kiss me, but it never happened.

I thought Alessio understood that.

He swiveled around, a dangerous glint in those blue eyes I loved so much. "He touched what is mine. And he had no right to touch you."

I swallowed, already knowing I was losing this battle. It was never mine to win.

Desperately, I tried to reason with Alessio. But knowing him, it would make no difference. "I told you. He didn't touch me because he wanted to. It was a mistake. I stopped him before anything happened. Why are you acting like this?"

He stalked forward, forcing me to take several steps back. When I hit the wall behind me, Alessio crowded my space. With his hands leaning on the wall on either side of my head, he caged me in.

"He touched my wife," he repeated, his voice dangerously low.

His head bent forward slightly until his lips were so close to mine. With his gaze on mine, holding me in place, he continued. "His lips were this close. His fucking lips almost touched yours, Ayla. And you know damn well I don't play nice to anyone who touches you."

THE MAFIA AND HIS OBSESSION PART 1

I breathed in, trying to stop my wildly racing heart. Remembering the scene clearly, I knew it looked bad. Alessio would never forgive Viktor. Not when it came to me.

"I stopped him," I replied softly.

"It doesn't matter."

"He didn't mean it."

His lips turned up into a smirk. Not a nice beautiful one. More like an evil smirk, one that said Alessio Ivanshov was about to kill you and you had no choice but to accept your fate.

"Do you really think that, Ayla?"

Shaking my head, I tried to push him away. "What you did was wrong. Worse than what Viktor did. Only because he didn't do anything wrong. He didn't kiss me. He was drunk and not in his right mind. He didn't mean to hurt you."

When he finally moved, I walked away from the wall and his furious gaze. "But you? You hurt him knowingly."

His hands fisted at his sides, and I knew I had hit him straight in the heart. "You killed him," I whispered. The tears finally escaped, falling down my cheeks.

I saw his eyes tracking my tears, following the drops. His jaw tightened as he gritted his teeth. Was it in anger, or was he hiding his pain...I didn't know.

I made no move to swipe the tears away, letting him feel my pain. "He trusted you, Alessio."

"And I trusted him. But he broke that trust. The moment he thought of you as someone to be desired and fucked, he broke that trust."

My eyes widened, and I took a step back. "You are disgusting."

"Truth hurts, doesn't it, Angel?"

When I didn't answer, he let out a dry laugh. With a broken heart, I couldn't even say anything. There was nothing to say.

Alessio had already made up his mind. He did the one thing I thought he would never do.

The world tilted, and it felt like everything was crashing around me, falling underneath my feet. Alessio started to walk away, and I could only stare at his retreating back.

Before he could step out of the room, my voice stopped him.

"He was your brother."

My final words. I had hoped they would make a difference. But what a laughable thought. Those words wouldn't bring Viktor back.

He was...really gone.

Alessio paused at the doorway. His voice was low and rough as he spoke.

"You are right. He...was."

The door closed behind him, leaving me in the silence of the storm he left behind.

Decades of friendship. Decades of brotherhood. All gone within days.

Viktor was gone.

The man who could make me laugh. The man who sometimes had wiped my tears away. He loved Maila unconditionally. He loved Alessio.

He was a man who would do anything for his family. Lay his life down for those he loved. In his eyes, we always came first.

THE MAFIA AND HIS OBSESSION PART 1

For Alessio to kill a man like that, it was despairing.

"How could you, Alessio?" I whispered brokenly.

The world slowed to a stop as the past faded into the present. My mind swirled with each image, and then I saw him…

His arms opened wide, and I jumped into his embrace, holding him tight. My tears soaked his shirt, but he didn't seem to care. He held me just as tightly.

"You came back," I choked through my cries.

"Yeah. I'm home, baby girl." His reply was soft as he moved slightly. With my body no longer hugging his, we faced each other.

He gave me a small smile and then winked. "Miss me?"

I shook my head. "Not really. Phoenix and Nikolay kept me entertained enough."

"Ha. Those fuckers are boring without me," he replied, looking behind my shoulders.

"I can't believe you're finally home," I whispered, my eyes taking all of him in.

He winked mischievously. "It took me long enough, but I am here now."

His teasing laughter brought a smile to my face. Everything felt surreal. Viktor was home. After one year, he was back where he belonged.

"Viktor!" I heard a squeal, and then Maddie flew into his arms.

"Are you trying to kill me?" he asked, hugging her just as tightly.

"How? I don't understand…" she cried in her chest.

"Don't worry about it. I'm home now. We will discuss everything later."

Maddie pulled away, questions burning in her eyes. "But…"

His stern voice stopped her flow of words. "Let's forget about this for now. I don't want to talk about it, Maddie."

Viktor turned to me. "Where is my potato?"

Just then, I heard babbling coming from my right. Turning to my side, I saw Princess and Lena standing near the kitchen. Lena appeared like she had seen death, while Maila was oblivious.

"There is your potato," I announced, pointing at my little firecracker.

"She's walking," he said in astonishment, his eyes practically bulging out.

"Of course, she is. She doesn't sit for more than five minutes now."

"Mama," she said in her cute baby voice, walking toward me.

Bending down as far as my pregnant belly would let me, I smiled at my baby. "Come here, Princess."

Her smile widened, and I smiled at the sight of drool covering her chin. As I opened my arms for her, she started running as fast as her little chubby legs would let her.

But before she could make it into my arms, Viktor swooped forward. Maila quieted down, her eyes widening in shock and fear.

She looked back at me and then at Viktor again. Back at me again and then at the rather strange man holding her in his arms.

Her chin wobbled as she started to struggle out of his arms. "Mama," she whimpered, reaching for me. "No. Mama."

Viktor panicked at the sight of Maila crying. "Why is she crying?"

Maila practically slapped him in the face as she tried to reach for me again, sobbing her heart out. Quickly, I took her in my arms, soothing my frightened baby.

"I'm sorry. She was just shocked, that's all," I apologized as Maila finally settled, giving Viktor a weird look.

She wrinkled her nose at him before burying her face in my neck.

"She doesn't remember me," Viktor said quietly.

Biting on my lips, I looked down at her. "She was so little when you…"

My words died in my throat, and silence fell around us. Viktor nodded, without any words.

All too quickly, it felt like a cold air had hit me. Viktor's soft eyes turned into a glare as he stared behind me. It was deadly. If his glare could burn someone on the spot, the person would only be ashes right now.

Without turning around, I knew who was standing behind me. My heart went to my throat, suddenly suffocating me.

"Excuse me. I have to deal with something," Viktor said, walking past me. Not something. *Someone.*

I grabbed onto his arm. "Please, Viktor."

If I had to beg, I would.

From the corner of my eye, I saw Alessio already making his way upstairs. Viktor tracked his movement, his hands fisting at his sides.

My voice brought his attention back on me. "Please don't fight."

"Ayla…"

"I know what he did was wrong, but maybe just talk without fighting," I quickly spoke.

"I would really appreciate if you stay out of this. It doesn't concern you," he replied stiffly. I flinched at his tone. "Whatever happened is between Alessio and me."

He pulled his arm back, walking away.

"Don't hurt him," I murmured.

He continued walking without turning around. But I heard his voice. "Did you beg for my life too? Or is this a special treatment only for Alessio?"

"You know that's not true. I just don't want you fighting with each other. Your loyalty was one that I used to admire," I returned, desperately trying to calm him.

He paused at the staircase, slightly turning toward me. "Like Alessio's loyalty? Fantastic brother he was, wasn't he?"

He dug deeper into my heart with his words, taunting me, forcing me to face the truth.

It's a lie, I reminded myself. *He is just angry. He will get over it.*

When no reply came from me, he continued his way upstairs. My shoulders slumped down in defeat, and I could only hope.

I just prayed that this encounter didn't end with either being shot.

Chapter 6

Konstantin aka Viktor

It was hard turning away from Ayla when all I wanted to do was hold her in my arms and never let go. I wanted to soothe her worry and fear.

I wanted to hold her and tell her how much I missed her. Her voice. Her laughter. Her smile. Everything about her.

But I had something to deal with first. Someone to deal with…a past to put at rest. Another step in the game.

Another step toward the throne that only one person could hold.

There can only be one King.

And in the end, there *would* only be *one* King standing.

A promise made before, a promise to hold. A promise that would be fulfilled.

The door to his office was open, an invitation to enter. I found Alessio sitting behind his desk, looking just as dangerous as he always did.

His elbows were on the table, his chin resting against his steepled fingers. He stared at me with emotionless eyes, but I could tell they held plenty of promises. The anger was hidden but always there.

Alessio was silent, just calmly staring me. It was his way of making his enemies nervous and cower underneath him. I grew numb to those stares many years ago. They didn't faze me any longer.

"I am thinking if it would be polite to offer you a drink."

He finally broke the silence, his words loud and clear. Walking forward, I stopped beside the couch.

"That would be appropriate, but I am not here for a drink," I drawled, crossing my arms.

He shrugged. "What are you here for then?"

I raised an eyebrow, chuckling lightly. "I am surprised you're even asking."

"Just trying to build up a conversation. I haven't seen you in a year," he replied, standing up to his full height, looking bigger and meaner.

"Right. I remember. The last time we saw each other, you left me for dead. After shooting me in the heart and my ass."

He cocked his head to the side. "So you are here to return the favor?"

"That's the plan."

Alessio looked unfazed as he poured himself a drink, his glass full of brandy. He filled another glass before pointing it toward me.

I accepted the glass. "I think a drink is in favour. To warm ourselves up. The night is still young." He spoke slowly, sipping as he stared at me.

THE MAFIA AND HIS OBSESSION PART 1

With a raised eyebrow, he watched my reaction. Alessio was an asshole. Plain and simple. An arrogant asshole that I was tempted many times to shoot in the face.

Holding the glass to my lips, I poured the entire contents in my mouth, drinking the whole thing in one large gulp. It burned my throat, but only slightly.

Slapping the glass on the table, I rolled my shoulders. The tensed muscles started to relax, and I breathed out.

The corner of Alessio's lips turned up slightly in a small smirk.

"You know, I should win a fucking Oscar for this shit. Hollywood would be stupid not to bag me as a lead role," I started, feeling my own lips turning up. "I'm thinking of changing careers."

He placed his glass down, next to mine. The smirk still was present on his face.

Alessio took a step toward me before wrapping an arm around my neck. His other hand went to my back, slapping me hard. And then hugging me.

I heard his voice over the roaring of my blood.

"Welcome home, brother."

I wasn't crying. I swear I wasn't crying.

Chapter 7

Viktor

Brothers till death.

It was what our fathers taught us. Something we had lived by for the last thirty years of our lives. Words to remember and never forget.

I was born to stand beside Alessio, on his left. While his wife would stand on his right.

Our fates were decided long before we even took our first breath. *Brothers till death.*

How Valentin Solonik thought he could break this was still a fucking shock to me. Was he that stupid?

Well, that was a dumb question. He was *that* stupid. Stupid fucker who kept me away from my family for a year. A whole fucking year. For what?

Revenge. A dangerous game he wanted to play.

He didn't care what he destroyed in his path. He wanted to be the King, the *Pakhan*. The God-fucking-father.

What he didn't realize was that as long as I was

breathing, that would never happen. I had always lived with only one purpose. To protect my family. Fight for them. Kill for them. Hell, I would even lay my body down, waiting for death if that meant protecting them.

Just like in a game of chess, the knight protects the King. And the Queen.

If Solonik wanted to play a game, I would give him one. My gaze met Alessio's again, his darker than usual. Giving me a nod, like he could read my mind and agreed to my every single thought.

My lips turned up, matching Alessio's smirk. Hell yeah, we were about to give Solonik one hell of a game. He forgot who the Ring Master was. I almost...*almost* felt bad for the poor bastard.

He was about to learn what it meant to test the Ivanshovs' fury. He did a big mistake by threatening my brother. And my Queen.

And that would be his last mistake. Because the ball was in our court now.

"I should be asking how you are doing. But I have a feeling that I already know the answer," Alessio spoke, breaking the tensed silence.

Shaking my head, I took the half empty bottle and quickly guzzled it down. My throat burned, but it was a good burn. It woke me up and reminded me what I was here for. What I had to do.

"I am feeling a little on edge. Solonik is not backing down. He thinks I'm on his side for now, but what happens when he has even a slight silver lining of doubt?"

Alessio stared at me with hard eyes, analyzing my words like he always did. "You just have to play the card right. You said so yourself. He trusts you. As long as you can keep his trust, you can pull the strings in whatever direction you want and he will follow."

"It's not that fucking easy, Alessio," I snapped, feeling frustrated with myself. "Do you realize how fucking hard it has been? A whole year acting like I hate my family? Deep loathing of them? I have to act disgusted every time your names are mention. Laughing with him while he calls Ayla a whore and a fucking bitch. Listening to him talk about how he's going fuck her and make you watch?"

Alessio's back straightened at my words, his fingers curling at his sides. He stared past me into the distance, his jaw gritted and his eyes so fucking angry that it would make anyone piss their pants.

"What did you say?" he asked, his voice pointed and coming out in a low growl.

"Exactly what I said, Alessio. You heard it. Don't make me repeat myself," I replied, looking at the floor, suddenly feeling ashamed. "It fucking hurts. And I'm ashamed of myself. Even though I know I'm doing it because I have to. I have to make it look believable, but it still fucking kills me when I have to laugh with him and accept his words without taking my gun out and shooting his limp dick."

"He called Ayla a whore?" he asked again. I knew what he was doing. Alessio was using the words to fuel his anger, and the look in his eyes at the moment...it was deranged. Almost a wild look filled with promises of making someone bleed red.

He was a mad man. And Solonik made the worst

mistake by going after Alessio's Queen.

Moral of the day?

Don't go after the Queen. The King will follow.

This was some Harley and Joker type of shit.

Taking a deep breath, I prepared myself to make it worse. "Worse than that."

"Tell me. I need to know every single fucking detail."

This was a bad idea. *You should have kept your mouth shut, asshole.*

"Alessio—"

"Tell me!" he bellowed, effectively cutting me off.

I did as I was commanded, spilling out every word. A year filled with hatred. I lived it. I breathed it. I became it so I could play with the Devil.

Alessio had no idea what type of shithole I was living in while he enjoyed the day with his Angel. Like a big fucked-up happily ever after.

He had no fucking idea. But he was about to know.

"He said all of that?" Alessio repeated when I fell silent. I nodded mutely, because for once I didn't know what to say.

His breathing was harsher as he tried to control himself, the anger evident in his posture. His rigid shoulders told me he was about to lose it.

But now was not the time. We still had a long way to go before we reached where we wanted to be. With Solonik ten feet underground while I pissed on his grave and screamed *fina-fucking-lly.*

Reaching to his side, he threw the glass across the room. It slammed against the wall, breaking into pieces. "I'm going to fucking kill him and make him wish he was never born," he snapped, punching the wall behind him.

Alessio's face contorted in an all-consuming fury, his eyes flashing with killing intent, his nostrils flaring as his fists clenched and then unclenched at his sides. He looked very much like the ruthless made man he was. The one everyone feared and cowered underneath.

"Alessio."

My eyes widened. I swiveled around to see Ayla peeking into the room from behind the door.

"Alessio," she said again, her voice so soft like velvet. It caressed me in a soothing manner.

From the corner of my eyes, I saw Alessio's angry demeanor was instantly gone, the monster inside of him shackled yet again. Only from the voice of Ayla.

"Can I come in?" she asked quietly, still hiding behind the door.

Alessio smiled sweetly, making my head spin at how he could change so fucking fast. Placing his palm out, he beckoned for her to come forward.

"You never have to ask, Angel. Come in," he replied, his voice soft yet still a little rough.

Ayla walked forward, practically skipping into Alessio's arms. They hugged, her tiny body burrowed into his as he held her tightly in his arms. He placed a kiss on top her head, his hard eyes meeting mine briefly.

It told me everything I needed to know. The anger was still there, just hidden.

Alessio was a dangerous man when he was

angry. A raging bull, a monster underneath ready to be unleashed. His judgments clouded by his fury. He was someone not to be crossed. Ever.

But there was only one person he would never take it out on.

If there was someone who has never felt the brutality of his anger, that would be his Angel. His woman. His wife.

Just like they say...a King only bows down to his Queen.

Witnessing such a moment, the sudden pang in my heart almost made me flinch. I fucking hated it. Watching them together. Watching them be so in love.

In their small world, nothing mattered. No one else could break what they had.

And I was just an outsider, taking a peek and wishing I had the same thing. Wishing I had *her*.

Ayla Ivanshov.

My brother's wife.

The thought almost made me retch. Feeling disgusted at myself yet again, I turned away from them, looking into the distance.

She whispered something to him, too soft for me to hear. I wished it was me she was whispering to.

I wished it was me she was holding and showering her love upon.

Shut up! My brain screamed at the same time my heart squeezed painfully at the sound of her quiet laughter. While the Devil on my shoulder hollered with laughter.

Why was I torturing myself? Why couldn't I just forget her? Every single time, just a glance in her direction, and my fucked-up heart would break again and again.

It knew I couldn't have her, yet the yearning was still there. I still wanted her. So fucking badly that sometimes I wished I could…steal her away.

"So did you guys kiss and make up?" she teased loudly. "Please tell me you did. I can't handle all the tension and brewing testosterone coming off you both."

This right there was proof that she hanging around Maddie too much.

I couldn't help but laugh. Even with my heart feeling heavy, I still laughed. Ayla had this charm around her. She made everyone feel welcome, comfortable. Her sweet smile would just draw you in, no matter how much you fought it.

Turning around, I faced them again. She was smiling cutely at me, her green eyes practically twinkling in the light with her excitement.

I shrugged before winking. "We made up. But we didn't kiss yet. We're going to need some privacy for that, baby girl. You do know that kissing leads to other things…like me being balls deep in—"

"If you finish that sentence, I am shooting you in the dick this time," Alessio warned, but I could tell he was trying to hold his laughter in.

I sauntered forward, wiggling my eyebrows at Alessio. "But I thought you loved it."

"Shut the fuck up, Viktor! Do you not have an off-switch button? You are in the presence of a lady. Act like a fucking gentleman."

This time, I laughed, almost wheezing before I

could speak again. "Ha. Like you act like a gentleman. We can hear all the *boom boom clack* every night from across the estate. Not very gentlemanly, I would say."

"You little fucker—"

"Okay stop! Both of you!"

And silence.

Alessio paused mid-sentence, and even I straightened up.

Ayla smiled sweetly at us. "Alessio, play nice. I am so happy to have you back home, Viktor. But I think I'm happier to see you both bicker back and forth. I missed it."

"I didn't miss him," Alessio muttered under his breath.

"Oh, please. You did. I think I heard you cry once." Ayla raised an eyebrow.

Oops, she just took his man card away. Savage little Angel.

She was probably joking, but this shit was funny. For a brief moment, I forgot about wanting my brother's wife. I just basked in the feeling of being home again.

I was finally able to laugh freely. And in return, I could see her smile. Right there, in front of me. That was enough.

"Breakfast. We need breakfast," Alessio sputtered, his eyes wide in horror at Ayla's words.

"And that was exactly why I came up. We went a little off track." She giggled.

I hated it when women giggled for no reason. But when Ayla did it, it was the cutest fucking thing ever.

"I'm hungry. This little one—" She caressed her swollen stomach. "—is hungry too."

Speaking of the little one.

"How far along are you?" I asked, walking forward. Without waiting for me to ask, she took my hand and placed it over her baby bump.

"Five months." She smiled when the baby moved. A small kick and I couldn't help but smile too.

"A boy or another girl?"

Ayla looked up at Alessio as his hands went around her hips, holding her more firmly. "No, we want it to be a surprise this time," Alessio said.

"But I think Baby is a boy," Ayla quickly said.

"Baby could be a girl," he retorted.

"What do you want?" I asked, sincerely curious, because Alessio was about to be fucked.

"It doesn't matter. As long Ayla and the baby are both healthy," he quickly replied, caressing her stomach. I took my hand away, giving the parents their moment.

"So, it doesn't matter if it's another girl—" I drawled, watching for his reaction.

Alessio paused, only now realizing what this meant. When my words registered through his brain, his eyes widened in horror.

"Shit. No. We can't have another girl. Ayla, I can't handle another girl. We need a boy. It has to be a boy," he panicked.

Bending forward so that my face was close to Ayla's stomach, I muttered. "Did you hear that? You have to come out as a boy. If not, you're going back in and changing your gender. Trust me, this family can't handle another girl."

If it's another girl, we might as well switch careers and work at Disneyland, dressing as Prince fucking Charming. How wonderful—not.

Ayla swatted my head playfully. "You and the others are the goofiest uncles ever."

"You mean we are the best uncles," I replied with a wink before standing up to my full height. "Let's eat. I'm starving."

Ayla nodded before quickly hugging me. "Welcome home, Viktor."

"Thanks." Holding her for just a moment longer, I reveled in the feel of having her in my arms before pulling away.

"I can eat three whole plates!" she exclaimed. "But I also can't. My stomach won't fit everything." Ayla pouted as we walked out of the office.

"If you eat anymore, you're going to burst," I joked, swatting her rear.

Alessio growled dangerously, his eyes flashing in warning. But Ayla…she paused.

She looked up at me with tears in her eyes.

What the fuck?

When Alessio noticed, he quickly started shaking his head, his gaze meeting mine in panic. "No. No. No. No. No. No. He didn't mean it, Angel."

He looked like he was about to murder me, and I was completely fucking lost.

Ayla sniffled before palming her pregnant belly.

"Did you just call me fat?"

Huh?

And then she busted into tears, loud sobbing, like

someone just died.

I backpedaled quickly, my arms thrown out in front of me in caution. "What?"

I am going to kill you, Alessio mouthed as he tried to soothe her.

"He called me fat, Alessio," Ayla wailed.

"No. No. No. He didn't. Viktor, say something!"

"I didn't call you fat. I just said you are going to burst—" I paused when she sobbed louder.

"You called me fat again!"

Alessio sighed, rubbing his forehead tiredly. "Here we go again," he muttered under his breath.

Wait…what? I didn't call her fat. Did I?

Chapter 8

Viktor

Alessio glared daggers at me across the table. He was probably thinking of multiple ways to mutilate my body.

And I was thinking of multiple ways to not only escape his wrath but also Ayla's cries.

She had long stopped crying, after several minutes of Alessio trying to calm her down. But her quiet sniffles were breaking my heart a little bit. There was lots of confusion clouding my fucked-up mind.

After taking our seats, I saw the other guys coming forward. Phoenix slapped me behind the head, almost causing me to hit the table.

"Welcome home, fucker."

"That's a nice *welcome*, asshole," I muttered, rubbing my head.

He shrugged before taking a seat beside me. "That's the only welcome you're getting. Don't expect me to kiss and make up. I don't swing that way."

I looked at Nikolay, watching him take his seat on the opposite side. "It's nice to have you home," he said in acknowledgment.

"Well, it's nice to be home."

Maddie and Lena came forward, joining us at the table. Poor Mama Lena. She looked pale and confused. It was time to give her break.

"Don't worry, Lena. I'm okay. We're okay. It was business," I explained quietly. Her eyes widened, and she nodded mutely.

That was all the information she needed. *It was business.*

In other ways, it was *our* business, and she didn't need to worry herself about it. Those words explained everything.

"You boys will give me a heart attack one day. Give this poor old lady a break, will you?" she replied gruffly, glaring at us.

"Sorry," Phoenix mumbled around his spoon before continuing to stuff food in his mouth.

My stomach rumbled at the thought of food. Staring at my plate, I sighed in relief. "I missed your cooking, Lena."

She nodded before sending me a small smile. Lena couldn't stay mad at us for long. It was impossible.

Damn, was I glad to be home.

At the thought, everything came crashing down and then stilled. How fucking stupid was I?

This wouldn't last long. I had to go back to Solonik. I had to leave my family again and crawl back into the hellhole I was trying desperately to

THE MAFIA AND HIS OBSESSION PART 1

escape from.

Well, this was the true definition of *fuck my life*.

Feeling frustrated, I concentrated on the plate until Maddie's voice broke through the silence. "Ayla, why aren't you eating?"

My head snapped up to see Ayla staring at her plate, but instead of eating, she was only pushing her food around. My heart tightened a little at the sorrowful look on her face.

"I don't feel very hungry," she answered softly before sending Maddie a tight smile. It didn't convince anyone. And sure as hell not Alessio.

Alessio was seated between Ayla and me, so I was forced to lean across him. "I didn't mean to say that, baby girl. You misunderstood my words. I didn't call you fat. You are the most beautiful girl," I whispered, hoping this time she wouldn't cry.

Ayla nodded but didn't meet my eyes. Alessio pushed me back into my chair with a low growl. His frown told me he was majorly pissed that I had hurt Ayla with my careless words.

Everyone continued eating, but from the corner of my eyes, I saw Alessio leaning forward and whispering something in Ayla's ears.

Then she blushed.

Even the tip of her nose turned red—whether in embarrassment or something else, I didn't know.

But when Alessio's hand disappeared underneath the table and Ayla's breathing changed, I got the idea.

My hands fisted on the table, the feeling of jealousy suffocating me again.

She bit on her lips, looking so sexy and innocent

at the same time. The way her cheeks colored beautifully, the slight shakiness of her hand as she brought her glass to her lips, I got the idea so fucking well.

Every time I gazed into her face, I tortured myself with the impossible. I let myself believe in a fantasy where it was *me*. Not Alessio. But me loving Ayla.

It was *me* touching her.

Not my brother.

Until even the fantasy felt like it was strangling the air out of me.

Fantasy would always be a fantasy. It could never be reality.

And that was my fucking problem.

I couldn't have the reality I wanted, so I tortured myself by dreaming about it. Every fucking day. Every moment I saw them together, happily married.

"Viktor…Viktor…"

My name brought me out of my reverie, and I turned toward the voice. Maddie smiled cheerfully before speaking again. "Evaline is coming back."

At my sister's name, the tightness in my chest disappeared a little. "Does she know?" I asked, looking at Alessio.

He shook his head. "Since the day I came home and announced your *death*, she left and never came back again. Nikolay has been keeping an eye on her, though. To make sure she's okay."

Nikolay nodded in quick acknowledgment before he focused on his plate again. I reminded myself to thank him later. If it was Nikolay keeping an eye on my sister, then I knew she was in the best hands.

"She has been mourning your death, Viktor," Ayla whispered. She reached out and placed a hand on mine, giving it a soothing squeeze before pulling away.

I missed her touch instantly.

"We couldn't tell her the truth. It would have been too dangerous," Phoenix explained.

Nodding, I faced Maddie. "You told her I'm back?" I questioned.

She confirmed with a nod. "Eva is already in the city. She's dealing with a business contract for the law firm she is working at. When I called her, she said she'll be here in thirty minutes. I explained as much as I could quickly so she doesn't, you know, try to stab you to death."

I took a deep breath before releasing it again. "That's very helpful."

She winked. "I might have given her some ideas, though."

Fuck my life again.

These two were psychopaths.

Ayla snickered, and I caught her wink too. Annnnd…they have corrupted Angel too.

Great. Just fucking great. What an amazing family.

With multiple killers, throw in some made men, then add some crazy women who are probably psychopaths, mix it well with a walking potato…and we had one big happy family.

I wouldn't change it for anything.

"She should be here any time now," Maddie continued, looking toward the entrance.

My eyes followed her gaze, and speaking of the cheeky devil, there she was.

"I'm giving you a head start, Viktor. Run while you can, because I'm about to chop you to pieces, you fucking bastard!" she bellowed by the entrance before throwing her handbag on the floor.

Why? Why is it always me? my mind screamed as I stood up. I faked a shudder at her glare as she stomped forward.

I was almost scared she was going to be true to her words. *Oh, the horror.*

Rolling my eyes, I opened my arms for my sister. She was too cute to chop me to pieces. That job should be left for Nina, our little assassin, with a mind just as fucked up as the rest of us. And damn, she was good at her job.

Evaline ran into my arms, and both of us stumbled back before I regained my footing again. "I missed you too, little hedgehog."

"You little shit…I am so mad right now," she snapped seconds before busting into tears. "I am…going…to squeeze the life out of your balls and…and…murder your small dick."

I winced at that image. Fuck, what ideas did Maddie give her?

She was a fucking savage in her attacks as she started punching my chest.

I couldn't help but laugh as I restrained her crazy-ass movements. "Please spare my dick and balls. I need it to reproduce some Viktors in the future. Without it, we're doomed!"

"I'm not joking!" she screamed, punching me right in the eye. Well, damn. Bullseye.

THE MAFIA AND HIS OBSESSION PART 1

Never underestimate the power of an angry woman.

I quickly stepped back when she went for my dick. "Okay, Evaline. I think that's enough. You don't want me to punch your boobs."

She gasped, her glare fiercer now. "You wouldn't dare."

"I would if you touch my preciousness."

Evaline was silent for a moment before her tearwork came yet again. "You…have…no…idea what I went through," she sobbed brokenly. "I thought…you died. I thought I lost you."

Walking forward, I pulled her into my arms. "It's okay. I'm fine and very much alive. I'm sorry, Eva. It was needed."

She looked up at me, her face red from crying. I swiped her tears away while whispering, "It was important for the *family*."

The seriousness in her eyes came back at my words. "And family always comes first," she whispered back with a nod.

I smiled, my chest puffing up proudly at the fact my sister had the same beliefs. Each word had been drilled into our heads since we were little kids.

Family comes first. Always. Protect the King. Protect the Queen.

"Correct, little hedgehog."

She nodded again as an understanding found its way into her eyes. A small smile appeared on her lips. "I am not sorry about the punch, though," she said with a shrug.

Laughing, I gave her another hug. "I know you aren't. Hell will freeze over before you ever apologize for this punch."

I felt a hand on my back, and already knowing who it was, I let out a small, breathy sigh. I turned around to see Ayla standing there. But her eyes were focused on Evaline.

"Come and join us for breakfast," she said, smiling. Evaline moved forward before wrapping Ayla in a hug.

"God, I missed you so much. Sorry for being a total bitch and leaving like that," my sister muttered before pulling away.

Ayla shook her head. "No. It's okay. It was understandable."

With the little fiasco now over, we moved to the table again. The rest of breakfast went like usual.

Just like before. Like nothing had happened.

As if that one year never happened.

We were a family again.

***

I followed Alessio silently into his office. Phoenix and Nikolay followed behind me, and they closed the door.

It was late at night, and everyone was asleep. It was the perfect time to discuss business. The rest of the day had been catching up with everyone else. We had no time to talk about why I was back and what the next move was. Or if there was even a next move.

Alessio seated himself behind his desk, and he released a long breath. Now that I studied him better, he looked tired and stressed out. Something was weighing heavily on his shoulders.

Before he met Ayla, nothing mattered except becoming a richer fucking man and playing games with the less fortunate souls who thought they could cross us.

But now...he had a wife. A daughter. And another baby on the way.

And his perfect little family had just been threatened.

No wonder they said *love* was a weakness. It really was. Love was a twisted son of a bitch who fucked us all up. We fell into its trap without even realizing it.

It was a simple rule. *Don't fall in love.*

Isaak and Lyov were right. This was the moment I wished we had listened to them.

I looked at Alessio again and noticed where his eyes were staring. A picture of Ayla on his desk. She was laughing while staring at the camera. In the background, I could see the creek.

She was happy.

And I knew, when Alessio took that picture, he was at his happiest.

The thing that Ayla taught all of us was that love could be a weakness and multiple shades of fucked up, but it was still someone's strength.

She taught Alessio that.

She taught *me* that.

"He's going to pay. For whatever he has done, he is going to pay ten times worse. He will pay for even thinking about hurting Ayla," Alessio muttered, breaking the silence.

His voice was rough and held the edge of anger.

When his eyes met mine, I saw the killer there. I knew his fingers were itching to end Solonik's life. But not now.

Not before we knew his real plan, or whatever Valentin was planning behind closed doors.

He might have thought of me as his *heir,* but he never trusted me fully. There were things I still didn't know. And to know them, I had to become the Devil. I had to become part of his little puppets and play along.

"What's the plan now?" I asked, moving forward.

Alessio looked away from the photo, his eyes meeting mine. He leaned back against the chair before crossing his right ankle over his knees.

"Go back there. And tell him I sent you to spy on him."

My eyebrows furrowed in confusion, and I heard Phoenix swear under his breath.

"Here's the thing. We need to play his game. He thinks you're coming here to gain our trust again. It's simple. I hate you and want you to show your loyalty. Tell Solonik that I have given you a way to gain my trust again. All you have to do is spy on him and give me information. Of course, he's going to think that you're still on his side. Two birds with one stone. This way you can stay with him and figure out what he's planning. In the meantime, he's going to think that you're playing me and giving me false information. He'll think I have grown weaker. Except it's just the opposite," Alessio explained masterfully.

"That makes sense. It could work if you play it

well and make it all believable," Nikolay pointed out.

"After all, he needs you on his side. He's desperate for it. Without you, Solonik can't move forward with any plans," Phoenix added.

I had done this shit for a year, and I knew I could do it again. I just had to fuck Solonik's head up a little and *kaboom.*

"For how long?" I simply asked.

"Just keep playing, Viktor. A game never stops until there's a winner," Alessio replied, leaning forward. His elbows rested on the table, his chin on his entwined fingers.

The furious look on his face could make anyone whimper. "And this game won't end until one of us is dead."

Alessio stared at me straight in the eyes before continuing, his voice low. "In the end, only one person will be standing and left breathing. And there are only two choices. Me or Solonik."

I heard the silent, unsaid words. The true meaning behind what he said.

In the end, only one person would be standing and left breathing. And there were only two choices. Alessio or Solonik. My King or my enemy.

And everything depended on how well I played this little fucked-up game.

Chapter 9

Her

I felt his groan against my skin as he pushed inside of me again. My body wasn't my own as he used me as his toy.

For a brief moment, I fantasized. I replaced the image of Valentin with someone else. Someone who actually cared about me.

Instead of taking me against my will, he was making love to me. I thought of a man who loved me.

Closing my eyes, I imagined someone younger than my husband. I imagined someone handsome. Strong. Beautiful. Someone worthy of my love.

Instead of leaving scars, the man was filling me with hope.

The fingers that were touching me caressed my skin softly.

The lips touching my neck were whispering sweet words.

Each thrust into my body, he was making sweet

love to me.

I imagined a future where instead of getting raped, I was being loved. Instead of living in fear, I was carefree and smiling. I imagined it all.

And in my dreams, the handsome man looked very much like the man behind the doors that separated us.

A small glimpse. One look. Our gazes connected and it felt like the world had stilled for a moment.

Then it was gone. The moment broken when I remembered the rules.

But those eyes stayed with me longer. The look he gave me, one which was very different from what I was used to, it stayed with me even after he was gone.

But just like the doors that separated us, we were two worlds apart. Just a far away look that haunted me since then, but a look I had to forget.

Fingers bit into my hips, causing me to hiss in pain. My eyes snapped open to see Valentin glaring down at me. His anger caused my insides to tremble, knowing whatever pain was coming next would be ten times worse.

"When I am fucking you, I want your eyes on me," he growled, thrusting harder. "Remember who owns you, little girl."

I will never forget. Not when you remind me every day.

No words. No sounds were made from me. He craved my pain, my tears, he wanted my voice—to hear me scream. But he took that away from me long ago.

He took everything...until I had nothing left. Yet

it was never enough for him.

I was owned. Never an equal.

A payment to a debt that couldn't be repaid.

A sacrifice from my part—I just didn't realize that this sacrifice would cost me everything. Until it was too late.

Now, I just had to stay alive and bear the pain. I just had to survive. Just breathe. As long as I was breathing, *they* were safe.

I was just unwilling collateral in this game of war and revenge. A battle I wanted no part of. Just like they said, everything is fair in love and war.

Only difference, this was just war. No love. No emotions. Just bloodshed and pain along the way, until one person was sitting on the mighty throne.

My head snapped to the side, my mind freezing and thoughts scattering as the slap brought me back to the present. I tasted blood on my tongue, and the corner of my lips stung, proof enough that he had hurt me, made me bleed.

His hand wrapped around my neck, his strength undeniable even in his old age. My eyes widened as his fingers tightened around my throat, blocking my air passage. I struggled for air, my vision blurred from the lack of oxygen.

I clawed at his hand, desperate to break free.

I can't breathe! I screamed in my head.

Seconds passed as he continued to thrust into my body, scarring me inside and out. The hold around my neck only became worse with each hard thrust as he picked up his pace. His release was close and he used me as his toy.

The last thing I saw was his face tightening, his

head thrown back in pleasure as he came inside my unwilling body. My vision faded into nothingness.

A black void pit as I fell deeper and deeper into the darkness before hitting the bottom, my body in shambles, broken and bleeding.

A sacrifice. Every day was a sacrifice. I accepted death so *they* could live.

The next time my eyes opened, my mind felt numb. My body was hurting, sore in all places, and I knew it was marked with my husband's sadistic pleasure. Just the way he loved it.

I blinked against the sun, showing me that it was morning already. Another daylight in the darkness of my world.

I tried to move, but my throat closed up as pain racked my body, and I trembled, feeling both cold and too hot. One second it felt like I was burning from the inside and then it felt like I had been dumped into freezing water.

I gritted my teeth against the pain and forced myself to move. My naked body pressed against the mattress, and I bit on my lips, holding back my cries.

The tears were silent on my bruised cheeks, and I swiped them away.

No tears, honey. They won't get you anywhere. They make you weak.

The voice rung through my ears like the words were being spoken to me right in this moment. Except they were the words by my mother—from the very last time I saw her.

She had held me in her arms and cried while telling me to never shed tears.

Don't cry. Be strong. Promise me you will be strong.

Stupid words that held no meaning. How could I be strong when I was not even my own anymore?

She had forced me to walk away with my head held high, like I was a Queen, not someone meant for sacrifice.

After struggling out of bed, I didn't bother to clothe my naked body. Instead, I limped into the bathroom, my body ravaged in the worst way possible. I knew when I looked into the mirror, I would see the damaged girl with no dreams or hopes left.

A pretty face with an empty soul. Eyes with no life, just staring, just observing, just living.

The door closed behind me, and I locked it, safe in my sanctuary. At least here, he wouldn't follow me. It was a place where I could hide and try to clean my body the only way I could. Wash away my shame as I cried silent tears. Bathe myself while hoping I could bathe away the pain.

My eyes met my reflection in the mirror, and I smiled.

Just like I predicted. My reflection told the real story. My reality.

I walked closer, my fingers softly touching my face where my husband had bruised me. The touch moved to my swollen lips where he had hit me. The blood had dried, but it was still aching.

My gaze followed down the length of my neck, the red marks now slowly turning a deep shade of green and red. I touched the skin but winced at how sore and sensitive it felt.

He tried to strangle me for disobeying him.

When I am fucking you, I want your eyes on me.

I wished I was blind; at least then I didn't have to look at his face and relive my nightmare every time. At least then, I could just stare into the darkness and act like this was just a bad dream.

I huffed a small laugh from my chest and then flinched. Giving myself a final look, I walked into the shower and turned on the water.

It cascaded around me, falling like beautiful waterfall. I reveled in the freshness and soothing rhythm, closing my eyes and just enjoying this slight touch of happiness.

I didn't care how long I stood there, but by the time I walked out, my skin was red from the hot water and I was no longer cold. Instead, I felt warm, like I was almost floating.

Breathe in. Breathe out.

Another smile touched my face. Valentin could try however much he wanted, but he would never own my soul.

I might have felt like an empty shell inside, but I was still living.

He could break me every day, but the fact that I was still breathing proved I was strong. He would break me and then I would stand up again.

He would rape me but I would clean my body of his filth.

At the end of the day, I was winning this game. His game was to break me. He did break me. Every day. But because my will power—my will to protect *them* was stronger than his will to break me. I was still alive because of it.

I will live. And I will protect. I was born to protect. I was born for this. And I will die only when I have fulfilled my duties.

After drying my body, I wore another black dress—clothes he had custom made for me. To hide my body for any other eyes. After all, I was only *his*.

I looked into the mirror and laughed silently. How stupid. How foolish. His own actions contradicted him.

He clothed me so that nobody could see me, yet he would take me in front of his *friends*. A prize he won so he would celebrate to show his victory.

I combed my hair, watching the silky strands flow behind my back after I was done. The marks he left me were now hidden.

We were back to being the perfect couple. Perfect wife. Perfect husband. Perfect life.

Only problem—the mirror showed our reality. I had the sudden urge to break it into pieces. An act of rebellion, just for a moment I wanted to show my anger. I wanted to take it out. I wanted to see the scattered pieces on the floor—just like the scattered pieces of my life.

Instead of doing just that, I took a step away. And another. I kept moving back until the door was against my back.

An act of rebellion meant more pain. Not just for me.

So I didn't let my anger out. I reined it in, deep inside of me, locking it there, hiding it. With another glance, I walked out of the bathroom and into my bedroom again.

THE MAFIA AND HIS OBSESSION PART 1

My eyes moved around the bedroom, everything polished and perfect. Except the bed.

Taking a deep breath, I fixed it and made it perfect—just like everything.

The sun shone into the room, bathing it with warmth. I craved to feel it on my skin yet here I was, trapped inside with just a glimpse.

I shook the thought from my head before taking my wool and knitting materials in my hand. Sitting on the chair that faced the window, I started knitting.

A shawl for my sister.

The closet to my left was filled with them. Shawls with different colors. Different patterns. All for my sister. And every night I dreamed of giving them to her—a token of my love. To show her my love without being able to say the words.

To silently tell her that she was my heart and how I wished I could have hugged her one last time.

Every day I missed her. But every day I was thankful that it was me, not her. Every day I sent a silent prayer and thanked God that Valentin chose me.

At least then my little sister could live a normal life. A happy life.

My gaze moved across the room, where the nightstand stood beside the bed. I smiled, knowing what was in the drawer.

A photo of her. Her beautiful smile. Her twinkling eyes. The sun shining on her face as she stared into the camera.

But then I lost that smile, when I remembered how I got the photo.

Another nightmare. Another day spent with the Devil.

Every year he would show me a picture of my family—for me to see that they were happy and healthy. To show my sacrifice was not for nothing.

And every year, I only had five minutes to stare at those pictures before they were ripped away from my hands, never to be seen again.

I only had five minutes to see my family. I only had five minutes to see their smiles.

But a few years ago, one look at my happy sister, I couldn't let her go. Five minutes wasn't enough.

So I begged. I begged so much. So hard. I cried, my cheeks pressed against his feet, begging. My heart cracked open as I hoped for his mercy.

But every gift meant that something was taken away from me. That night, I gave him my submission willingly so he could let me keep my sister. I submitted, gave him my body and soul.

He asked me to suck his cock; I did. He came into my mouth, his cum dripping down my body as he watched in depraved lust. He marked my body with his filth, branding me as his slave.

He asked me to open my legs wide so he could fuck me; I did. I spread them open and welcomed him into my body.

He asked me to parade around his friends with his cum dripping down between my legs; I did as I was commanded.

He asked me to be on my knees as he fucked my ass raw, and I went on my knees just like he wanted. While he fucked me again, causing me to cry out in pain, his friends shot their cum on my skin.

Their moans and groans could still be heard in my ears as if it was just minutes ago. Their laughter was haunting, just like my broken cries were melodious to them.

That night, I let my husband do every depraved thing he wanted to my body. I let him abuse me—I let him own me, willingly.

That night, I became what he wanted. A disgusting whore. A filthy slave. A pet who did as she was commanded.

But it was all worth it in the end. Because by early morning, when he had enough fun, he left the room.

Not before throwing my sister's picture next to my ravaged, broken body.

I remembered holding it in my hand so gently as I caressed her face. It was mine to keep. I had fought for it, and I won.

The drawer kept my sister safe, and I smiled yet again.

I miss you.

I continued knitting while dreaming that one day, one day I would be united with her. With my family.

One day, I would be able to give her these shawls.

One day, I would no longer hold a picture, but I would hold her in my arms.

Chapter 10

Viktor

Maila poked my cheek, her lips pursing out in concentration. "Hi."

"Hi," I replied, trying to hold back my laughter.

"Hi."

I nodded when she poked my cheek again. "Hi."

"Hi."

"Hiiii." She dragged it out, almost slapping me in the face with her excitement.

We had been at it for about thirty minutes, and she was still stuck on "*Hi.*" I wasn't complaining one fucking bit. At least she was talking to me and not crying her heart out.

After I spent almost two days trying to gain her trust, she finally felt comfortable enough to let me hold her while her mother wasn't in the same room.

Mission accomplished.

Her Royal Highness was now on Uncle Viktor's side. Fuck yeah!

Let's do some dirty dancing in our heads, shall

we?

"Is she still playing the Hi game with you?"

Ayla walked into the room. She smiled, her eyes going straight to her daughter. Maila bounced on my lap at the sight of her mother.

I grabbed hold of her when she tried to reach out to Ayla. "Careful there," I mumbled. Her tiny body was held close to my chest for a second, breathing in her sweet baby scent before handing her over to Ayla.

Not before I caught Ayla's scent on Maila. It was mixed with the baby smell, and I closed my eyes, holding this moment close to my chest.

"I have to put her to bed," Ayla muttered. "Is it okay if I take her away?"

I nodded with a tight smile. "Yeah. She seems a little worn out. Wouldn't want the *potato* to lose her beauty sleep."

Ayla laughed while rocking Maila in her arms. The little one was already yawning before cuddling closer to her mother's chest.

"Are you ever going to stop calling her that, Viktor? I can imagine her wanting to rip your hair off when she's fifteen and you're still calling her potato," she said quietly.

"Never. She is forever my potato Princess." I winked before standing up. I wrapped them both in my arms, holding them in my embrace before letting them go, far too quickly for my liking.

I tried to clear the stupid fucking thoughts from my head—the ones that whispered in my ears like the Devil they were. Always taunting me. Pulling and pushing me in the wrong fucking direction.

Every time, I had to fight the urge to succumb to the Devil's taunting. I could feel the tip of its tongue flicking against my ear, whispering, laughing.

I stared at Ayla and she gave me a sweet smile, oblivious to the effect she had on me. Clearing my throat, I glanced at the open doors. "I have to go. Alessio called for a meeting," I finally said.

She nodded mutely, her eyes now on Maila. A sign of dismissal. Taking a deep breath, and with a final look toward the woman who had been haunting me for months, I walked away.

It was the best I could do. Walk away. Walk in the opposite direction because she was already taken. A wife and a mother.

A heavy heart was hard to bear, but in my situation, it meant nothing, because I couldn't let my heart control my actions. My mind and my dick were in my favour right now.

And I needed to fuck someone—fuck Ayla out of my system.

Find a new tight pussy and a new obsession.

Maybe I'll fuck a redhead this time. Or a blondie. Whoever is willing.

The doors to Alessio's office were open, and I walked inside before closing them behind me.

Everyone was there, including the mafia daddies. Oh, how fucking sweet. I rolled my eyes at the look they gave me.

"Happy to see me, Father dearest?" I asked with raised eyebrows. "Surprised I'm still alive? I should be thanking for you for that, by the way."

He shook his head before leveling me with a

glare. I didn't give a fuck. I was in this stupid, fucked-up mess because of him.

Because he couldn't keep his dick away from a willing pussy.

I paused at the thought. *Oh well, like father, like son. Fuck my life.*

"Are you ever going to let this go?" he asked, crossing his arms and leaning against the wall.

I shrugged at the question. "Let it go? Ha. Maybe in a few hundred...years? Give or take."

"Viktor—" Lyov started, but Alessio cut him off.

"Don't start, old man. You're just as guilty."

"It seems you two have forgotten who Isaak and I are. You might be the Boss now, Alessio. But that doesn't mean I'm powerless. You make it so fucking difficult not to blow your brains out," Lyov hissed.

And the glaring contest has started. A—fucking—gain.

"And make Maila fatherless? Ayla a widow?" Alessio asked, just chilling in his chair like his father didn't just threaten him. Oh, you know. Just the daily life of the Ivanshov family.

Lyov's mouth snapped shut, and Alessio held back a smirk. "I didn't think so."

"Why do you two make everything so difficult? Why go against us on every step?" Isaak muttered. "We're trying to help!"

"You have helped enough, Isaak," I quickly cut in.

He growled, taking a step forward. "I am done with your disrespect, boy. This ends here or I will be forced to take you down, got it? Don't embarrass yourself in front of your brothers."

Game on, *Father*.

His eyes sparked in warning and anger. When I took a step forward, he snapped.

Moving forward in a flash, his fist made contact with my face before I could move. He grabbed me by the throat, slamming me into the wall. I winced at the impact but stayed stubbornly quiet.

Whatever he believed, and the disrespect I pushed his way, I wasn't going to raise my hands on my *father*. Call me a pussy and make me wear a fucking pink tutu, at least I knew when to draw a line.

His fingers tightened around my throat, but I didn't give him the satisfaction of wincing again. I bore the pain and stared straight into his eyes. "This isn't going to make me submit..." I strained to get the words out.

His hold loosened just a little, giving me enough space to talk without choking me. "You fucked up and now I'm paying for it. Before I was even born, you messed up my life."

At my words, he lost the angry demeanor. His expression turned almost sorrowful. "I didn't think it would come to this. If I knew what I was doing then, I would have stopped. I would never fuck up your life willingly, son. Believe me or not, if I had a choice, I would have protected you from this stupid game."

He let me go and took a step back. The regret in his voice couldn't be mistaken, and for a moment I forgot my anger too.

Isaak shook his head, his eyes staring down at

THE MAFIA AND HIS OBSESSION PART 1

his feet for a moment before his hard stare pinned me against the wall again. "But we are too deep into this shit—and we have no choice. To protect those we care about, we make sacrifices. And this is a sacrifice you have to make. I'm just sorry that my past brought you to this path."

When I remembered the shit hole I had to crawl back into, the anger came back. Ten times worse.

His past fucked up my future, and now I was an unwilling piece in this game. Some days I was the pawn and others, I was the knight. A slave and then a fighter.

"Because of you, now Solonik thinks he owns me. He thinks I am someone he can use. All because of you, Isaak. If you're looking for forgiveness, you aren't getting it," I mumbled.

I moved away from the wall and turned my attention to Alessio, who was watching the scene silently, his face void of any emotions.

"You are leaving tomorrow," he said when Isaak didn't reply.

I nodded, my back straightening at his order. "Get back to Solonik and do whatever you have to do. Make him believe you, play the cards carefully, and when the time is right, he will fall and we will rise yet again."

Alessio looked thoughtful for a moment, but he didn't say anything. I knew whatever he was thinking was another fucked up plan. He loved games, and he never did anything without a back-up plan.

"Back to the hell hole, huh?" Phoenix muttered from the other side of the room.

"Couldn't have said it better," I agreed.

Alessio's expression didn't change. No sympathy whatsoever. One minute he was a caring brother, but he could be a heartless son of a bitch when he wanted.

Speaking of being a heartless bastard...there was a big fucking loophole here.

"Why is Ayla not pissed off or surprised that I'm alive? Actually, Maddie doesn't seem that surprised either," I asked.

Alessio closed his eyes before resting his head back against his chair.

"Oh! That's a story you would want to know. Epic, man!" Phoenix laughed. Even Nikolay was smiling—or half smiling—well, smiling in *his* standards.

"Fuck you," Alessio snapped, his eyes still closed. If I knew better, he was probably hoping a hole would open and swallow him whole.

Well, that was new.

"Ayla heard us talking a few months ago. She was *spying* behind the door," Alessio started. "When I went back to our room, she confronted me. I couldn't lie anymore. It was no use. She already heard us talking."

"Tell him what happened afterwards," Phoenix pushed, still laughing like a fucking hyena.

"Shethrewavaseatme."

"Huh?" I asked, not understanding a word he said during his gibberish.

"She threw a fucking vase at my head!"

Cue. Laughing like a hyena.

"He has a scar to prove it," Lyov jumped in. His

THE MAFIA AND HIS OBSESSION PART 1

face was red as he tried to hold in his laughter too. "It's close to his hair line, so it's hidden."

"Ayla threw a vase at your head?" I asked again, not believing them.

He shook his head, finally opening his eyes. Alessio threw everyone a glare, effectively shutting them down. "Her…umm…hormones have been a little off since she became pregnant again. I don't know if today is the day she cries her eyes out every minute, or she wants to kill me or she suddenly decides that I am the perfect husband."

Ah. Now everything made sense.

"Like yesterday?"

"Exactly."

"She even kicked him out of their room," Phoenix mumbled in between.

"If you don't shut up, I will shoot your ass—then you and Viktor will have matching holes!"

Speaking of holes in our asses…

"Why the fuck did you shoot me in the ass, you fucking bastard?" I finally exploded. "That wasn't part of the plan."

Alessio cleared his throat and then shrugged. "I just wanted to know how it felt to shoot someone in the ass. Trust me, it felt so fucking good. You should try it sometimes. Stress reliever."

His words were met with silence.

"We should go to…sleep," Lyov intervened when nobody said anything.

Nikolay and Phoenix nodded, while I stood there—contemplating if I should take Alessio's advice. Maybe I should shoot him in the ass too. Great fucking stress reliever.

Isaak started to make his way out but not before he stopped by me. "It was a mistake, Viktor. I'm sorry you're in this mess now because of a mistake I made years ago," he whispered.

"A mistake? A fucking mistake?" I growled.

"It was an accident," he snapped back when I didn't accept his stupid apologies.

"Oh, like you accidentally slip out of one sister's pussy and end up accidentally dipping into the other's? Wow, very accidental, I would say."

He made a frustrated sound at the back of his throat, and I was tempted to ruffle his feathers more. So, I did.

Turning around, I faced him head on. "Next time, remember not to dip your dick into sisters' pussies. Or better yet, don't dip it into the enemy's sisters' pussies!"

He scratched the back of his head, his hands curling into fists. I bet he wanted to take a swing at me now. But I wasn't finished yet.

I took a menacing step forward, but I was still a foot away from Isaak. My voice came out harsher than I wanted, but I didn't give a fuck. "Now that you have fucked Solonik's sister and I am the outcome of that, he sees me as his *heir*. How fucking awesome is that, huh, Father dearest? I am next in line for the family who wants to destroy us."

"Okay, that's enough!" Alessio finally said.

"So yeah, next time, keep your tiny di—" I finished off.

That got his attention well. "Fuck you. It's a python."

"Ha. Mine is an anaconda."

THE MAFIA AND HIS OBSESSION PART 1

"Are you guys comparing your dicks?"

All of us swiveled around to see Evaline standing by the door. Great. Just what we needed. Another person added to the drama.

She walked forward nonchalantly. Evaline stopped beside Nikolay, throwing him a wink. And she smacked his ass.

Wait what?

"What's your size?" she asked, loud enough for the room to hear. Nikolay's eyes widened in horror, and I took a step forward.

Hell to the no.

Not happening. Never ever.

"What size?"

Another voice joined in, and I rolled my eyes. What the fuck was this? A circus?

Ayla walked in, her eyes instantly going to Alessio's.

"Oh, they're just comparing their dick sizes," my dear sister replied. *I am going to permanently shut you up if you don't stop talking!*

Ayla blushed, her cheeks reddening as she made her way to Alessio. "Oh."

"Ayla, what's Alessio's size, by the way?" Evaline asked. *What the fuckity fuck?*

Ayla's blushed deepened. "Huh?" she sputtered.

Alessio was already backpedaling. He wrapped an arm around Ayla's waist, pulling her away from the chaos. "That's it. I'm taking my wife out."

"More like taking her to bed," I muttered before I could stop myself.

There we go. My fucked-up feelings made their ugly appearance yet again.

"Jealous?" Alessio taunted, not realizing what effect his words had.

Shrugging off like his taunting meant nothing, I replied, "You're still a puppy."

"You're still single."

A shot straight to the heart. Bullseye. My heart squeezed almost painfully, and I looked away from the happy couple.

Fuck you, brother. Just fuck you.

"Ouch," Phoenix chuckled. "That's gotta hurt."

Leveling him with a glare, I let my anger out. "Look who is fucking talking. Has Maddie threatened to cut your dick off yet?"

Maddie and Phoenix have been doing the tango dance for years. I wondered when she would finally give in and give the poor bastard a break.

Phoenix glared back and mumbled under his breath. "Yeah, she did. Last night. When I tried to sneak into her room."

This family deserved an Oscar award. Right fucking now.

I saw Phoenix turning his head toward Nikolay, which brought everyone's attention to the brooding, silent man.

"What?" he asked, looking completely horrified. The image itself made me want to laugh.

Evaline clapped her hands. "Oh, I know!" She smiled sweetly at Nikolay, batting her eyelashes. "You're still a cuddly teddy bear."

Silence. Complete utter silence.

"What?" Nikolay finally sputtered.

My sister, oblivious to the mess she just created, winked. "The girls and I have decided that you're a cuddly teddy bear."

"That's worse than all of us combined," I whispered to Phoenix, who was already nodding his head.

"I'm almost embarrassed for him. Well fuck."

"I'm not a fucking teddy bear," he finally growled.

"Prove it," Evaline laughed before slapping his ass again.

Moving forward quickly, I grabbed hold of her arm and pulled her away. "Okay, that's it. Too much touching now."

Alessio cleared his throat. "We're out," he announced before dragging Ayla out of the office.

What a fiasco.

But I couldn't help but smile. This was what I missed.

Being a family.

Isaak and Lyov quietly left too. Everyone walked out, one by one, until only Nikolay and I were left behind.

"Are you going to be okay?" He finally broke the silence after minutes of us not speaking a single word.

"You mean, if I will come back alive again?" I questioned.

"Will you?"

"I'll try."

"Good. The family needs you. I hope all of this ends quickly and you can come back home—where everyone is waiting for you."

With those as his final whispered words, he walked out. I was left alone in the office, with only my thoughts.

Taking a deep breath, I closed my eyes. Time to play.

They might have had the King, but the Ace was in our hands now.

Chapter 11

Evaline

The lights were off, the estate now dark as everyone went to their rooms. I could hear a few doors closing and then silence. I laid in my bed, my heart thumping wildly for some reason.

Wait, actually, I knew the reason.

I was only two doors away from Nikolay.

My heart thumped harder at the thought, just like always whenever I thought of him. When my eyes would find his, it still felt like the first time I had gazed into his face. The same bolt of electricity, the same shiver…every time felt like the first.

Every look felt like the first look.

And every touch was just as good as the first, if not better.

The same emotion clawed at my throat, wanting to be let out. My heart wanted me to feel and let go. He was only two doors away. I could go to him. Maybe he was waiting for me.

Or maybe not.

Seven years ago, he would have been waiting for me. His doors unlocked, his naked body half covered by the bedsheet, as he waited for me to silently come into his room. And then we would make love in the darkness of the night until next morning.

Just wrapped in each other's arms, cocooned in each other's love. Just us.

And now, he avoided my eyes every time he could. He kept himself hidden in shadows, so that nobody could touch him, see him, hold him.

One moment we had everything and the next, we lost it all.

Thump thump.

My heart continued to beat for him.

Thump thump.

My breathing accelerated with the possibilities. Would he push me away again?

He used me whenever and however he wanted. Nikolay would always come to me during his darkest moments. He would take me, use me, and then disappear into the shadows again, leaving me empty in the midst of my broken love for him.

Until the next time he lost control.

Thump thump.

I needed him tonight. Maybe I could use him this time—an excuse to hold him while I could. I wanted to give him the love he needed but was trying so hard to fight.

Thump thump.

I pressed my hand over my chest before taking a deep breath. I closed my eyes, and when I opened them again, my decision was made.

THE MAFIA AND HIS OBSESSION PART 1

Without a second thought, I jumped out of bed. *Get your inner badass bitch out and go claim your man.*

My feet were light against the wooden floor as I walked out of my bedroom and made my way to his.

One step ahead. Another step forward. And repeat, until I was standing outside Nikolay's room.

Thump thump.

My palms felt sweaty, and I licked my lips nervously. Wait, why the fuck was I nervous?

Shaking my head, I scowled at his door. It wasn't like this was our first time. Hell no, we had been doing this for a long time now.

Maybe it was the fact that I hadn't see him for months—five months to be exact. The last time I had seen him, he had fucked me in my bed and left without a word. Just like always.

Our once beautiful love story was now tainted. No longer a love story. Just broken moments between us. Shattered hearts that left both of us drowning in the fucked-up mess of love.

But tonight...it was going to be different.

"Well, I fucking hope it is," I muttered to myself, still scowling at his door. "God, woman. Get yourself together and stop acting like a fifteen-year-old virgin."

I patted my hair down and bit on my lips, trying to give it a more reddish color and look plump. "Time for mission impossible, babe."

But my words were drowned by a sudden, muffled scream.

My eyes widened, and I took a step forward,

almost plastering my body against the door. There was another scream, it sounded almost tortured. And so broken.

My heart ached at the sound, and without thinking, I turned the doorknob. I knew the door would be open. He hated being confined in a room. It took him months to finally be able to close his door, but he never locked it.

The doors were always partially open, never fully closed.

It gave him a sense of freedom. He needed it. Nikolay craved it.

I walked inside and closed the door behind me. My eyes found Nikolay in the darkness. The small lamp on his nightstand barely cast any light.

Another scream made me flinch, and my eyes blurred with tears at the sight of my man fighting against invisible chains—monsters.

His body thrashed around on his bed, the bedsheet twisted around his ankles as he fought his torturers in his sleep.

"*No!*" His fingers clawed at his throat, his legs kicking out in desperation. He cried out again. My heart cracked at how raw and painful his cries sounded.

Without thinking, I lurched forward and ran to his side.

The warning bells rang loud in my ears, telling me what a big mistake this was. But I didn't care.

With a knee on the bed, I leaned over him. My fingers dug into his shoulders as I tried to shake him awake.

"Nik. Nikolay. Nikolay, baby, open your eyes," I

begged, my tears now falling in endless streams down my cheeks. "*Lyubov moya.*"

His screams turned into an angry growl, and before I could blink, his body moved swiftly and quickly.

I found myself underneath him, his legs straddling my hips with his fingers wrapped around my throat.

Nikolay didn't give me a chance to speak. His fingers tightened, blocking my air passage as I struggled against his hold. I choked and sputtered, trying to cry out. Desperate for him to hear me and snap out of whatever nightmare he was going through.

My vision blurred with my unshed tears, and finally, his eyes snapped open. He stared at me, looking confused at first.

"It's…okay. You…are okay. We are okay…it was just…a…nightmare," I tried to choke out. My hands released his and went around his shoulders. "You…are safe. You are okay."

My touch was featherlight, a soft touch, a gentle caress as I waited for him to come back fully to his senses.

His gaze moved from my red face to his hand around my neck, and his eyes widened in horror. "Fuck!" he swore, quickly pulling away from me. He rubbed a hand over his face in an agitated manner before leveling me with a glare.

I held my neck and gasped for air, my throat burning so bad I could barely swallow.

"How many times do I have to tell you not to touch me when I am like this?" he snapped, his black eyes looking even darker and more dangerous with his fury. "I could have hurt you! Damn it!"

I rubbed my throat and shook my head. My heart drummed harder like the wings of a caged bird. My voice was suddenly gone, my tears just rolling down my cheeks as I stared at Nikolay.

He looked so angry…and so tortured. His body was covered in sweat, his breathing harsher, and his chest heaved with each labored breath.

He looked like he just escaped hell. In some ways, he just did.

For most of us, when we sleep, we relax and just float away. For Nikolay, the demons hunted him down even in his sleep.

His torturers were long gone but still haunted him. As if they were right here, next to him—hurting him.

It hurt…not because my throat was sore, but I hurt for him. And I just wished he would let me hold him. Just for once. I wanted him to share his pain with me, to let me take some of the burden, but I saw how his expression shuttered when I didn't answer.

Nikolay retrieved back into himself, his expression turning cold and dark. Vicious. He looked almost frightening. His scars looked more pronounce and deeper, like they were fresh and not fully healed yet.

His eyes were darker, almost looking soulless.

Everyone else would have been scared. I wasn't.

I welcomed it because I knew, beneath all those scars and the raging façade was a gentle man who once called me *Beauty*.

"I was trying to wake you up. It was a really bad nightmare," I said finally. My voice came out croaky and too soft for my own ears. "I was worried you would hurt yourself."

He scoffed, his gaze quickly going to my neck before meeting mine again. "What are you doing here?" he finally asked, his glare almost causing me to shiver.

Taken aback by the question, I sat up against the headboard and tried to think of an appropriate answer. Whatever I had in mind had just disappeared into thin air. The situation was different now that he just woke up from a nightmare.

He rubbed his head before digging his fingers into his scalp in frustration. His once buzz cut hair has grown a little longer. Enough for him to pull on them.

His arms fell to his sides again as he knelt beside my body. His fingers clenched into fists and then unclenched again. His teeth grinded together, and I saw a muscle tick in his jaw as he clenched it too tight.

"Why are you here?" he asked again, his time his voice louder. I knew he was about to lose whatever control he had left. "Answer the fucking question, *Evaline*."

I could no longer hold his eyes, instead my gaze shifted to his chest. "You know why," I whispered.

"You came here to be fucked?" he sneered, his body inching closer to mine.

I flinched at his tone and the way his words were thrown at me. "Your pussy miss being used, Evaline?"

"Nikolay—" I started, but my sentence was cut short when he grabbed my ankle and pulled.

A shocked yelp escaped me when I found myself on my back, with his huge body looming over mine. My throat suddenly felt dry, and I could only stare into his mesmerizing eyes.

I always found myself lost in the depths of those beautiful dark irises.

Without much of an effort, he ripped my nightdress, peeling it away. Nikolay pushed himself up, until his lower body was cradled between my spread legs. "I'll give you exactly what you came here for. I'll fuck your pretty cunt until you can't walk for days."

I was powerless against his words, and my body wasn't my own anymore. His hands trailed down my torso, moving south toward my pussy.

Everything else that happened minutes ago was long forgotten.

We were both lost in a lustful euphoria.

I was already wet, weeping for him. I squirmed underneath his hard body, needing him to touch me everywhere. His fingers grazed my clit, and I threw my head back, my body jolting with a moan.

"I have barely touched you and you're already so fucking wet," he growled in approval, his thumb now working over my clit.

He dragged a finger over my slit before his palm cupped me roughly. "What do you want, Evaline? Tell me."

"I…I…want…no, I need…"

My words were lost when he took my tiny nub between his thumb and forefinger, giving me a soft pinch. "Fuck," I swore, my hips pushing against his fingers for more.

My hand went behind his neck, pulling his head toward me. My mouth slammed against his for a hard kiss. My lips parted, and his shoved his tongue into mouth, taking control of the kiss.

I needed his touch, his kisses—just like I knew he craved mine.

While his thumb played with my clit just the way I liked it, he pushed a finger inside me, stretching my walls. I moaned into his kiss, moving my hips with his fingers.

He inched another finger inside me, working both fingers in and out, pumping harder with each thrust.

When his fingers slipped out, he dragged a disappointed mewl from me. I felt empty, but not for long, when his length bumped against my throbbing opening.

I bit on his lips and then kissed him harder. His wet fingers circled my nipples, tweaking the hardened buds. I cried out at the sensation, my hips thrusting upward.

Nikolay dragged his cock against my folds, back and forth. Again and again, but never entering me. He continued to torture me, running his hard length up and down my wet folds. I could feel myself dripping, and yet he refused to give me what I needed.

I trembled underneath his body as my legs spread wider, his hips pressing into mine. "Please…"

Finally, he tore his lips away from mine, and our

eyes locked. The tip of him teased my opening, and I shuddered in pleasure.

His hand inched upward until his fingers were wrapped around my throat. My eyes widened, and I grabbed his wrist.

He didn't give me a chance to think. With a powerful, relentless thrust, he drove into my willing pussy.

I cried out, my hips bucking upward, trying to dislodge him as he stretched me almost painfully. My fingers desperately clawed at his shoulders.

He continued to thrust into me, pounding me hard. My ankles locked behind his back as I surrendered to him.

He quickly found his stride as he tilted my hips upward, my ass leaving the bed as he continued to slam into me.

With his cock buried to the hilt, he paused. I was stretched impossibly full. It almost hurt but I loved the burn.

"It doesn't matter how many times I have taken you. Countless times, over and over again. Your pussy is still as tight and grips my cock just as perfectly, as the first time I fucked you." His voice lowered to a possessive growl. "Remember when I popped your cherry?"

With my gaze on his, I felt myself smile. "How can I forget? It was the best night of my life, *lyubov moya.*"

My love.

His face softened for a second before he lost the loving look again. Nikolay pulled out of me, and I moaned in response, pulling him closer again. He drove into me again with a punishing thrust.

I winced, but I was so wet, practically gushing around him, that it wasn't as painful. Another trust and I screamed in pleasure, my body tightening as he continued to use me. With his hand around my throat, he pulled me up until I was straddling him.

His cock slipped out almost fully before slamming into me again. "Shhh, be quiet. You don't want your brother to hear me fucking this tight pussy, do you?"

I buried my face into his neck, my teeth marking his skin, trying so hard to muffle my cries. I closed my eyes and gave myself to him...letting him fuck me senseless in however way he wanted.

His fingers around my throat tightened as he fucked me like an animal. His grunts drove me over the edge, and when I felt his cock swell inside of me, I knew he was close.

His thrusting became faster and harder. With his other arm around my hips, he pulled me down on his hard length at the same time he would thrust upward.

"Fuck. Fuck. Fuck!" I screamed into his neck.

I realized...Nikolay wasn't just fucking me.

He was hate-fucking me. Taking all his anger out in the only way he knew how. He fucked me raw and deep...filled with passion but also with so much hate.

I was rendered powerless as he continued to ram himself into me. Again and again. I bucked into his arms. I wasn't sure if I wanted him to stop or if I was begging him for more.

"You will be the death of me," he whispered in

my ear, his voice hard and strained—filled with dark lust. His fingers released my hips and traveled south between our bodies.

I squeezed my eyes closed, the pleasure too much to bear. A strangled moan ripped from my throat when he pushed his thumb hard against my little bundle of nerves. It was my point of pleasure. I rolled my hips with each of his thrust, matching his movements. I was stretched tightly, almost forcefully around his hard length, and my clit throbbed.

I was close…so fucking close…

I just needed…

My body shook as he buried himself deep inside of me again with a brutal thrust. It felt like I was being split open as I cried out, my orgasm hitting me harder than I could imagine.

My vision blurred, and I continued to milk his cock as he found his release too. I felt his hard length throbbing inside me, stretching me as he pumped his release into me.

His groan made my head spin. The feel of him coating my inner walls, filling me with his own cum, drove me over the edge again. When his thumb pulled at my clit, demanding another orgasm from me, I gave it to him.

I never wanted it to end.

I clenched around his cock, wanting him to stay deep within me.

His fingers finally released their vise grip around my throat, and my head laid limply against his neck, completely spent.

I felt our mixed cum drip between us, coating my

inner thighs with our pleasure. Still shuddering from my orgasm, I clenched around him again.

I gasped when I felt him starting to pull out. My arms tightened around his back, and I placed a soft kiss on the side of his neck, right over his scar while my fingers gently traced the scars on his back.

"No," I whispered. My hips moved against his as I continued to work him in my pussy.

I was impossibly full and wanted more. Nikolay growled low in his chest, and he grabbed hold of my hips before pulling me off him.

I whimpered, my eyes going between us where we were still joined. I watched as he pulled me off, watching his cock leave my pussy and his release trickling down between my legs.

I gasped when he left my body, feeling strangely empty. Nikolay pushed me on the bed and stood up. My legs were still spread wide, my body limp and too tired to move a muscle.

His gaze went between my legs, and I saw the heated look he gave me, but then his lips curled up in anger. Confused, I could only stare up at him.

"You can leave now," he said, his voice rough, deep, and just so perfect from our recent fucking.

But I didn't have a chance to love his voice when his words registered through my foggy brain. "What?" I asked. *How fucking dumb of you, Evaline.*

I struggled into a sitting position, my body sore. He used me savagely, and I loved it. But now…

He shifted his focus from my body to my eyes. "I said you can leave. The door is right there." He nodded toward the door.

I stared dumbly at it before moving my gaze back to the man standing in front of me, in all his naked glory. My eyes went to his semi-hard cock, which was wet with signs of our pleasure. The tingling between my pussy didn't stop, and I shook my head.

My eyes blinked in confusion as I wrapped the bedsheet around my body and stood up. My legs wobbled, and I almost went down. Nikolay moved forward, grabbing me by the hips and helping me find my footing again.

When I went to lean into his body, he stepped away, leaving me cold and empty. Nikolay turned around, giving me his back. I saw my red harsh lines where I had savagely dragged my nails. His skin was scratched raw. I watched him quickly pull on his sweatpants, my mind still foggy.

"What do you mean?" I asked. Actually, I knew what he meant. It was always like this. He would find me, fuck me, and then leave.

Only difference was this time I came to him. But he still fucked me. And now he was making me leave.

The blissful moment that I was completely lost in seconds ago was now shattered.

He turned to face me, his expression so cold—almost deadly. I shivered and brought the sheet closer to my body, seeking comfort from it.

"You came here to be fucked, and I gave your greedy cunt what it needed. Now you can fucking leave, Evaline. We both got what we wanted," he hissed.

Forget about hurting for him…all of a sudden, I

was blinded by anger, and I lurched forward. His body was stiff as he stood still.

When my palm met his cheek, he didn't even flinch. The corner of his lips bled, and he touched the cut.

His expression thundered with fury, and he grabbed me by the neck before slamming me against the wall. "I would suggest you never hit me again, Evaline. You won't like the result. I'll let it go this time," he growled low.

"I am not a whore or someone you buy from a fucking prostitution ring, Nikolay. So don't treat me like one," I hissed back, fighting unshed tears.

How dared he? His words had cut deeper than he could imagine.

You came here to be fucked, and I gave your greedy cunt what it needed. Now you can fucking leave, Evaline. We both got what we wanted.

He spoke as if I was someone cheap...only be used for someone's pleasure.

"But isn't that exactly what we've been doing for the last couple of years, *Evaline*?" he sneered into my face, his lips curled up in anger.

Why are you angry? I wanted to scream. *What have I done?*

"*Beauty*," I whispered, a single tear falling down my cheek. It made a wet trail, and Nikolay's eyes tracked it.

His jaw clenched, and I could almost hear his teeth grinding together.

"*Evaline*. I used you and you let me...what exactly does that make you, huh? I won't be surprised if you're fucking around. In my book, that makes you a filthy whore. So don't be offended when I call you one," he whispered harshly into my ear.

My lungs squeezed as I fought for breath, his words cutting me deeper.

This was not the man who called me *Beauty*.

This was not the man who made sweet love to me.

"You are so fucking stubborn, Nikolay! Just stop it," I almost screamed. "Please," my words turned to begging.

His fingers released my neck, and I slumped against the wall, watching him take a step away.

"You know damn well that you're the only man I have ever been with. The only man who has ever touched me. You're the only man who has ever made love to me—or, in your case, fucked me," I whispered now. My words came out so soft, sounding so broken even to my own ears.

"Too bad, you aren't the only woman I have fucked."

My heart slammed to a stop, and I plastered myself against the wall, hoping it would shield me away from Nikolay's cruel words.

"What did you say?" I murmured, watching his face—watching for any lie.

"*Evaline,* your pussy isn't so special that I only want to fuck it alone. I have had plenty of women over the last few years who kept me company," he said with a dry laugh.

My fingers curled into fists at my sides, my nails biting hard into my palms.

"You're lying," I whispered. "I know you are

lying."

He shrugged. "It doesn't matter if you believe me or not."

I stayed silent, my eyes boring into his. Swiping away the tears, I opened my mouth to say something, but then snapped it shut again.

Me, who never ran out of words, was now speechless.

"Leave," he said, pointing at the door.

I stared at him before taking in a shaky breath. "I have known you for eleven years. I have loved you for eleven years, Nikolay. I know you better than anyone else. When you were brought back to us, I knew *we* would never be the same again. I knew that, and I accepted it. Seven years and I am still fighting for you," I whispered.

"Even when you push me away, I'm still here. I'm still waiting for you, just like I promised before." I paused and wiped away from tears. "I am still waiting. Why can't you see that?"

"I never asked you to wait," he replied quietly.

Closing my eyes, I brought a hand to my lips—trying hard to hold back my cries. I thought I was strong; I thought I could be strong for both of us.

But with each day, I became weaker, my heart becoming more fragile.

Until it was completely broken.

He turned away from me, facing the other wall. The muscles in his back were rigid. The scars looked hauntingly beautiful, and I choked back a sob.

I loved him…even when he was being a fucking beast, I loved him.

"Then tell me you don't love me," I murmured into the darkness of the room.

His hands curled into fists, his shoulders straightening like he had been hit.

"I don't love you."

I rubbed my chest, trying to get rid of the pain, but it wouldn't go away. It hurt. It hurt more than I could ever imagine.

It hurt more than when I saw him bloodied and broken.

"You're a shitty liar, *lyubov moya*. Look me in the fucking eyes and tell me you don't love me."

I waited for him to turn around and almost wished he wouldn't. Nikolay could never lie to me. He could never look into my eyes and lie. As long as his back was to me and he whispered those words, I knew he was lying.

But then he turned around.

His eyes met mine, our gazes locked. His were empty, dark…and soulless.

"I don't love you, Evaline."

I wished in that moment that I had been shot straight in the heart…I wished I had died. It would have hurt less than hearing him say those words while holding my gaze.

"You don't love me?" I whispered brokenly.

"No. I don't love you, Evaline," he said again.

My lungs squeezed, and I rubbed my chest harder as I fought for breath. My heart felt heavy, and my stomach rolled, like I was going to throw up.

"Is that your final decision?" I asked, my back straightening even when all I wanted to do was crumple to the floor and just disappear.

"Yes."

I wanted to kneel at his feet and beg him.

"When I walk out of this room, Nikolay, it's over. Everything is over, do you understand that? You can't come to me when you lose your mind again—when you fall back into the dark and you completely lose it, you can't come to me anymore. When your mind is fucked up again and even when your nightmares are fucking killing you, you can't come to me. I have been doing this for seven years. You'd come to me and I would open my arms and hold you when you needed me. And when you don't need me anymore, you walk away. You can't do that anymore," I said softly.

He didn't blink, like my words meant nothing. Nikolay just stared at me.

"I will give you nothing. Is that what you want?" I asked, hoping he would say no…hoping he would hold me and apologize. I just wanted his arms around me; I just wanted to melt into his embrace.

But he gave me nothing.

"Yes."

One word. Just one fucking word and he ended everything.

"I won't wait for you anymore. I won't fight for you anymore," I whispered, my tears blinding my vision.

He nodded without a word.

We stared at each other—and I hoped he could see what he had done. He broke us. He broke me. I stared into his eyes, hoping I could see even one bit of humanity in it.

Nikolay just looked…dead.

Finally, I shifted my gaze away, and I held the bedsheets tightly around my body as I took a step forward. He didn't move as I walked closer.

His eyes stayed on my face as I went on my tip-toes. My mouth touched his scarred cheek, and I laid gentle kisses the length of his scars.

He hissed quietly, a quick intake of breath that broke me further.

I stepped back, our eyes meeting again. Swiping my tears away and with a final glance, I walked away.

I closed the door behind me and leaned against it.

A minute later, something crashed against the wall. I heard him—his anger, his pain.

"You are such a shitty liar, Nikolay."

But it didn't matter anymore. His words had hit me right where he wanted them to. There was no taking them back—he couldn't unbreak us.

Touching the doors, I placed my lips softly against it.

"Good bye, *lyubov moya.*"

Chapter 12

Viktor

I tried to ignore Ayla's moan when I passed their room, but my feet stopped, and I leaned against the door, my chest aching.

The bed squeaked, and she moaned louder—Alessio's name on her lips.

Not being able to bear it any longer, I stalked away, and at the end of the hall where my room was, I slammed the door harder than needed, but the anger inside of me, the buried jealousy, was now burning.

I tugged my tie off roughly and practically ripped my shirt off as I got naked. I needed a cold fucking shower and to fuck Ayla out of my head.

But it was late, and I had an early flight tomorrow morning. No pussy for me tonight. Turning my neck left and right, I tried to release the tension there. My skin prickled with the need to hit something and fuck someone. Ride her hard and rough—fuck both of us into a coma so I could get the thought of my brother's wife out of my head.

I got into the water and turned the water to *cold*, letting it seep into my bones until I was shivering and almost blue. It felt like even my teeth were shivering. After my mind started to numb with my body, I turned the water to *hot*.

It was painful and practically suicide but exactly what I needed.

My body started to hurt. It felt like my skin was being scratched raw, but I bore with it. The pain helped me clear my fucked-up mind.

When my body was warm enough and no longer hurting, I sagged against the shower wall and just closed my eyes.

My head was hurting like a son of a bitch, and for the first time in my life, I wanted to escape here. I wanted to escape seeing Alessio and Ayla together.

They were happy, and I really was fucking happy for them. No one deserved happiness more than these two. And they belonged together. They were one. Fated and all that shit.

Yet the small part of me that was hurting every time, I couldn't stop it. The Devil flicking his tail and laughing on my shoulder wasn't any help, either.

I needed some kind of relief…and I knew full well how to find it.

No pretty pussy…then my hand gotta do. It wasn't the same, but the only substitute I got.

I needed to come, find some fucked-up kind of relief, and then sleep for a century. Yup, that plan sounded much better than me sulking after someone who was forbidden to me.

I quickly soaped up my body, and my hand drifted down my dick. I stroked myself once, twice, and my cock jerked as I put more pressure. It wasn't enough.

I fisted my cock tight, pumping my length hard. The water continued to cascade around me, giving me the right lubrication. My hand glided around my dick easily, and I almost hissed when the pressure became worse.

I leaned my forehead against the wall, my breathing getting heavier with each second. I closed my eyes and knew who would be appearing in my fantasy.

But instead of seeing black hair and green eyes, I was surprised to see someone else.

Eyes that looked beautifully haunted and blonde hair so smooth, almost silky.

What the fuck?

My eyes snapped opened, and my hardness jerked in my fist, pre-cum covering the tip, and my balls grew tight between my legs.

I pumped my throbbing dick harder, and the ache intensified with the desperate need to come. Closing my eyes again, the vision of the beautiful nun still didn't escape me.

I was assaulted with every image of her. It was a sudden change. From Ayla to an image of the exotic, mute nun.

Confused, I rubbed my cock harder and let my body mix with the pleasure of what my mind was conjuring.

I imagined her lying down on the bed. My hands

slowly removing the ugly long dress covering her body. I would be undressing her—prepare her for every one of my sinful thoughts.

She was a nun made for sinning, and I would gladly take it.

I imagined how she would be naked, pale, beautiful, rosy as she would blush—just beautiful. When I had seen her, her body had been fully covered. Only her head was visible.

But that was the thing about imagination. You could turn it into anything you wanted.

And that was exactly what I did. In my head, I undressed her so that instead of a fucking nun, she was laid bare—ready for my cock.

The idea of her being forbidden, covered and shielded away from my gaze, made me want her more. The idea of jerking my cock off for the mute forbidden girl did strange things to my head and apparently, my dick, because it obviously fucking liked that.

Behind my closed eyes, her naked body laid in front of me, and I pushed my knees between her legs, spreading her wide for my eyes. Her pretty cunt glistened with her need, her wetness coating every inch of her labia and her pussy lips.

I imagined thrusting two fingers into her needy pussy, and she would be weeping for me, dripping with wetness, and only I would be able to satisfy her. Her face would twist in pain because of how tight she would be and then her expression—it turned into pleasure.

I wouldn't be able to hear her moans, but the look on her face would be enough. I jerked my cock faster now. My legs shook, and I pressed against the wall.

I moved upward over her body, feasting on her pretty tits while the tip of my cock rested against her tight entrance. I drove into her pussy in one single, powerful thrust.

She screamed under me, clawing at my shoulder. After a few thrusts, her pussy milked my cock as she found her orgasm.

"Fuck. Fuck. Shit!" I swore, punching the wall. This was a bad fucking idea, but I couldn't stop myself.

I hated to admit that I fucking loved the idea of making the mute nun sin. The Devil whispered dark promises into my eyes.

Oh, you are going to take her. And you are going to make her sin...and she is going to sin so beautifully.

One last pump, my fist as tight as a pussy could get—although it was fucking nothing to the real thing. My balls tightened as I imagined her body writhing underneath mine as I filled her up nicely with my cum.

Her cunt would be full—and she would be begging me for more.

The pressure finally released, and I came with a hiss, my head banging against the wall. My legs trembled, and I fought to hold myself up. Thick ropes of cum shoot out, coating my hands and instantly being washed off by the raining water.

I kept fisting my cock until every last drop was spent...for the beautiful blonde girl. Squeezing my eyes shut, I tried to get my breathing under control.

What a fucking mess.

But a mess that I apparently just took a liking to. Or should I say, my cock took a sudden liking to *her*.

I quickly washed off and walked out, drying myself and wrapping a towel around my waist. My legs dragged behind me as I made my way to the bed. Dropping on it, I removed the towel and crawled under the covers.

My eyes started to droop without any problem, fatigue finally taking over. Jerking off always did the job.

But when I closed my eyes again, all I saw was *her*.

"She isn't part of the plan," I muttered to myself. *Get your head together. Don't think with your dick, asshole.*

But my thoughts did nothing to appease my sudden hunger. A hunger for a girl that wasn't meant for me.

"She isn't part of the game," I said again.

I was almost drifting off to sleep and felt my lips tilting up in a smile.

Maybe she could be...it would be our little secret.

That was my last thought before sleep took over and dragged me into the darkness.

Where *she* was waiting for me.

***

"Are you sure you don't want to meet Ayla one last time? She'll be disappointed," Alessio said

THE MAFIA AND HIS OBSESSION PART 1

when we reached the main doors.

"No. Don't wake her up. Let Maila sleep too. I will see them—and everyone else—when I get back home again," I muttered.

He stared at me silently and then nodded. I could almost hear his thoughts.

Will you be back home? What happens if you can't make it—what happens if you never make it back?

The thought left me reeling because it was true. *What if I never make it out alive?*

But I quickly shook my head. *Be optimistic, fucker. Like how you're optimistic about getting pussies. Just like that.*

Nikolay and Phoenix were standing behind Alessio, their faces impassive, hiding their true feelings. Being away from them for a year and now going back again, it was hard. I knew it would be hard, but I didn't expect it to hurt.

These guys were my family, my brothers, and I didn't even know if I was going to see them again.

"Ready?" Alessio said.

I took a deep breath and nodded. "As ready as I can be if I was getting fucked in the ass—without lube."

They cracked a smile and shook their heads. Yeah, that was what I wanted to see. Alessio walked me to the car. The driver opened the door for me, but I paused.

I turned around and looked at Alessio. His fists clenched at his sides, but he nodded, giving me his permission.

Before I could get into the car, he moved

forward and wrapped an arm around my neck, pulling me close.

I didn't think; I just laid my forehead on his shoulder.

It wasn't weakness. Fuck no. It was love for my *brother*.

"Promise me you will be back, Viktor," he said quietly, only for my ears. His voice was rough, maybe even a little hoarse.

I nodded. "I promise," I returned.

A promise made to my Boss. My king. My *brother*. A promise to hold and never break.

"Just come back to us safe. Everyone will be waiting for you. Believe it or not, we need you. *I* need you."

His hold tightened before he slapped me on the back and stepped away. His face was emotionless again, and I straightened to my full height.

We both nodded, and with a final glace at the estate and him, I got into the car.

The drive to the airport was a blur. Hell, the plane ride was a fucking blur too. I barely remembered anything. I drifted off to sleep and then woke up again as the plane touched down.

Well, I'm back, motherfuckers. Trust me, you aren't ready for this sexy ass.

I laughed at my own joke. We all needed a little comedy sometime, just to take the fucking stress away. *My stress?* It was to make sure I stayed alive long enough to protect my family.

A car was already waiting for me. I barely felt the Russian winter as I buckled up safely and warmly into the car.

THE MAFIA AND HIS OBSESSION PART 1

The drive back to the estate was silent. Valentin knew I was coming, yet he didn't come pick me up himself.

"Where is Valentin?" I asked Yegor.

He cleared his throat before replying. "He is out of the country. He left this morning, and I have no fucking idea why. Valentin just said it was business after he told me to welcome you back home."

Our eyes met in the rearview mirror, and he shrugged. The driver stayed silent, not saying a word.

I leaned against my seat and wondered what *business* he had to take care of.

But all of that was forgotten as we got nearer to the estate.

Valentin wasn't home.

That meant...*she* was alone.

My eyes widened when the blonde beauty made her way into my thoughts yet again. Well, fuck me, but did this *game* just become easy?

I pressed a finger to my lips, and I couldn't help but smile.

Just fucking perfect.

All worry seeped out. In its place, anticipation leaked in. My knees bounced, and I looked outside, feeling my heart pumping faster. My blood roared in my ears as we got closer to where the silent girl stayed in all her glorious, forbidden beauty.

A nun in a tower, waiting for her Prince to save her.

But I was no Prince Charming. I was the wolf, ready to pounce.

My cock twitched in my slacks at the thought,

and I mentally stroked it before patting it, like the good boy it was. *It's okay, boy. We are about to get lucky.*

When the car made its final stop, I didn't wait for the driver to open my door. I was already out and walking toward the entrance.

The door was opened, the men slightly bowing at my presence. I didn't spare them a glance, for they didn't deserve my attention.

My attention belonged up there—down the long hall, hidden in a room.

My steps were filled with purpose and determination as I made my way up.

Your loss, Valentin. My gain.

Since the very first time I had laid eyes on *her*, she had gotten me intrigued. She had made my heart still for one fucking moment, capturing all my attention.

And now that I had her all for myself, I was going to let out my wolf to play.

I was going to uncover all her secrets, the hidden ones she kept locked inside her heart. *Like it or not, baby…but you just became part of this game.*

Slowly, she was going to open for me, like the petals of a flower after showering it.

Just like her legs would spread open soon.

My heart continued to drum to a strange beat—faster and harder as I drew closer to her door. It was closed, shielding her away from me.

My palms were sweaty, and I glared at the shakiness of my hands. What the fuck? Was I nervous?

Hell to the No.

I stared at my hands before looking at the door again. My chest suddenly felt tight, and I scowled. Shaking my head, I tried to clear the clouds in my head.

And without a second thought, I placed my hand on the doorknob and twisted it open.

Chapter 13

Her

I placed my knitting material next to me and stared at the sunset. It was so beautiful that I wanted to reach out and grab it, hold it close to me.

The large windows were my escape from reality. Just a glimpse of the outside world. I liked it. It was enough for me.

I admired the view and wished I could be on the hillside, with my sister by my side. We would both look at the sunset, gazing into the beauty. Just the two of us. Happy and safe.

She loved the sunrise and the sunset. Before, I never appreciated them. But now, they reminded me of my sister, so I held them close. They were the only thing I had of my sister. The only way I could feel close to her.

I thought of the picture in my drawer—something else that was close to my heart. I had very few meaningful things in my life, but the few I had, I treasured them.

THE MAFIA AND HIS OBSESSION PART 1

I was lost in my thoughts and didn't feel anyone entering my room until it was too late.

Until I felt the presence right next to me, the heat of someone next to my body. Frozen in my chair, I stared straight ahead.

The cologne that touched my nose told me it wasn't my husband.

It was someone else.

Someone I didn't know.

The scent was soft. It didn't give a headache like Valentin's. It was manly enough but not too hard.

I felt the person moving closer, his heat wrapping around my body. Licking my lips, I tried not to move. But it was getting hard not to fidget when the silence started to become too much to bear.

He wasn't doing anything. His body was just close to mine yet not moving. I could only feel him.

We stayed like that for what felt like hours, even though it was only minutes. Until he moved. Slowly and swiftly. His steps were filled with determination. The way he moved around, it was as if he owned the room. The presence around him felt commanding.

He stopped in front of me, blocking my view of the sunset. Blocking my beautiful escape with his huge frame.

Curiosity got the best of me, and my eyes drifted upward, following the path up his strong legs. And then his chest. He was wearing black slacks and the grey dress shirt he wore was tight around his chest. He wasn't wearing a suit jacket, so I could see every muscle definition.

I knew instantly he was young, not old like Valentin.

He was tall, his shoulders wide, and his frame huge. This man definitely looked like he could snap someone in half without missing a beat or even be out of breath.

I cowered back into my chair, feeling intimidated, and a sense of fear filled me. Who was he? And why was he in my room?

No one was allowed in my room—not unless Valentin allowed them.

If it wasn't my husband in the room then it was Igor, my bodyguard. And this man, he was definitely *not* Igor.

From the corner of my eyes, I saw that my bodyguard was standing by the door, his arms crossed over his chest as he stared straight ahead, his face hard and monotone—emotionless. He was younger than Valentin but many years older than me.

I glanced back at the man standing in front of me, my eyes on his chest. The warning bells rang loud in my ears, but I didn't stop myself. My eyes continued upward.

His cheeks were rough with a few days of stubble, his lips full, and there was small smirk there.

And finally, our eyes met.

Chocolate brown eyes—the same ones I couldn't forget. No matter how much I had tried.

The same eyes that had haunted me since I caught a glimpse of them behind my partially closed doors.

My heart stalled, and I couldn't breathe for a moment. I could only stare at *him*.

When he noticed that my eyes had finally met his, his lips tilted up in the obvious smirk he was trying to hide before.

He looked…dangerous while smirking. But playful too. I couldn't wrap my head around it. He appeared to be closer to my age, maybe a few years older. He looked mature, a man set to conquer the world.

"Hello," he said in Russian.

My heart accelerated. He was talking to *me*. Nobody was allowed to talk to me.

He said something else, but I didn't hear it. His eyes narrowed on me as he cocked his head to the side, regarding me with a strange expression.

As if he were trying to figure me out.

I stayed still, trying to make myself as small as possible. His presence was overbearing—almost too much for me. There was something about him that I couldn't quite catch. His eyes were hard and dark, reminding me of Valentin.

I knew he wasn't a good man. If he was here, in this estate, he wasn't a good man. He was just as dangerous. Another made man. Another killer. Another monster.

But he felt different than Valentin.

Even with the fear inside of me, he wasn't doing anything to hurt me.

"So are you going to say something?" he asked, this time in English. When I stayed silent, he let out a breath and raised an eyebrow.

"You are not going to talk? Silence is very rude

when someone is speaking to you," he continued in English. Maybe he caught the understanding in my eyes when he spoke before.

I still didn't say anything, his stares warm on my face as I continued to gaze into his. My lips were tightly shut, waiting for him to continue his babbling.

He could speak, taunt me however he wanted—I would never find my voice. That gift was taken away from me before I could even appreciate it. Exactly like my life. It was just like the saying—*you don't know what you've got till it's gone.*

I wish my mother had said to me, let me know to appreciate every single moment in my life for it could be taken away from you in the blink of an eye.

The man snapped his fingers in front of my face, bringing me back to the present. Sometimes, I got lost in my head. It was a safer place to be instead of living with the pain every day.

He smirked again, his eyes still focused on mine. Almost like he couldn't take them away. His hand went to his pocket, and from the corner of my eyes, I saw him taking out a lighter.

My eyes drifted downward as I watched him click the lighter open, my gaze mesmerized and my mind fascinated by the swirl of his thumb around the little fire. He kept clicking it on and then off. He repeated the process again and again, and my gaze never wavered.

Until he shut it off completely and my eyes went up to his face again. He nodded, as if he approved of me looking up at him. My heart did a little crazy

THE MAFIA AND HIS OBSESSION PART 1

beat again, and I pressed my shaky hands against my thighs.

It was weird, but this close, he was making me nervous, and my stomach kept dipping dangerously.

"So?" he asked, still looking at me with a strange expression. I couldn't quite read this man. For years, I had learned how to read people's faces and their reactions—it taught me what to expect and how to prepare myself.

But this man, he was a big mystery, and I couldn't figure him out. It was a strange combination.

We stayed like this for a few seconds before he shook his head and then chuckled, his perfect white teeth showing.

"Oh right. You can't speak," he said, still shaking his head. "I forgot. My bad."

My eyes narrowed on him, feeling the lash of his words almost as bad as Valentin hitting me. He knew I couldn't speak yet he still asked. Why? To hurt me more? To make me feel the loss more than I already do?

It appeared like he was tsking at me. "How unfortunate. My sincere condolences."

There was nothing sincere about his words.

His lips tilted up in an amused smirk, his gaze moving to my lips then my eyes. In his eyes, there was no sympathy or any care. Instead, all I saw was amusement, almost like he was taunting me.

This beautiful man was mocking me.

He was mocking me for not being able to use my voice—for losing a beautiful piece of myself.

His callous smile made my heart ache, because

for a brief moment I thought he was different. When I had seen him behind that door, he seemed…different. The look in his eyes, it appeared almost like he wanted to run in and steal me away from this dark chaos.

But now that he was standing in front of me, his body so close to mine, it seemed like he was just the same as my husband.

Or maybe I was just trying to convince myself? Maybe I was just trying to instill fear in me, believing something that wasn't there.

He leaned forward, and my breath caught in my throat. When he touched me, it felt like my skin was on my fire—like I had been touched by a bolt of electricity. So hard and vibrant. One touch and he had my stomach in knots. My body trembled, but I stayed still, my eyes wide as I stared into his face.

His index finger trailed up my neck, leaving goosebumps behind and causing me to shiver again. He touched my hair before twirling a blonde lock around his first knuckle. When I felt a tug, my body moved against my will.

We were so close, our faces almost touching. I could feel him breathing, and his eyes bored into mine, holding me captive.

Strangely, I didn't want to escape. He wasn't hurting me—something I wasn't accustomed to. For the first time in many years, a man was touching me, speaking to me without hurting me.

So our gaze stayed locked while I stared into his chocolate brown eyes. I could see my reflection in them; I could see what he was seeing.

I wondered if he saw a weak, broken girl—

something dirty, a whore?

Or does he see me, the real me?

He tugged at my hair again, bringing me closer until our noses were touching. "What happened to you, silent *myshka*?"

I almost missed his words. My body felt overheated being in his presence. His warmth seeped into my pores, feeding my insides until I was no longer cold.

He spoke again, but I didn't get it. It felt like I was submerged underwater. I couldn't breathe. I couldn't think.

I could only stare into his eyes that had captivated me and weren't ready to let me go.

I wanted more of his warmth. After feeling cold for so long, I craved this feeling, whatever it was. My heart did another dance again, beating a little faster.

Thump. Beat.

It wasn't the same beat when I was with Valentin.

It was different. A different melody.

I should have stopped it. I should have pulled away. I should have remembered the rules—the punishments.

Thump. Beat.

But I couldn't.

Who are you? I wanted to say. My lips begged to say those words, to whisper them to him. My throat closed and nothing came out. No voice. No sound.

Who are you? I screeched in my head as my heart continued to beat in an usual symphony.

He cocked his head to the side when my silence

was all he got. Letting my hair go, he stood up straight again and took a step back.

The moment was broken, and suddenly, he took all the warmth away.

I was left feeling cold again—empty. I was left craving more of the warmth he had given me.

Shaking my head, my eyes went to my lap, and I took a deep breath. This was wrong. It was so wrong, and Valentin would hurt me so bad if he ever found out.

And he would. He was going to find out. *No*, my battered mind screamed. *No*, my broken heart wept.

My thoughts reeled, and I shuddered even before the pain could happen.

My bodyguard, Igor—he was going to tell Valentin.

While I was lost in this man's eyes, lost in this moment that brought me warmth, I had forgotten that Igor was standing there by the door—watching everything, watching us.

And now I had to bear the pain of looking into another man's eyes other than my husband.

My fingers twisted in the fabric of my dress, my nails digging into my thighs as my stomach rolled, and I had to fight the urge of throwing up.

How could I forget? How could I have been so reckless and careless?

Confusion clouded my mind, and I glared at my lap. *Stupid girl. It's all your fault now when Valentin hurts you. You have no one to blame but yourself.*

From the corner of my eyes, I saw his feet moving away. I didn't dare to look up. Maybe he was leaving.

The sudden thought caused my heart to squeeze, and my chest ached—it hurt. I pressed my nails deeper into my skin, trying to stop my rains of thoughts.

I wanted to lurch forward and stop him from leaving.

Stop! I squeezed my eyes shut.

Seconds turned into minutes, and slowly my heart started to calm. The crazy, dangerous melody turned to a dull beat.

My breathing turned to normal, and my chest didn't feel so tight anymore. When he was close to me, it felt like he had brought havoc to my heart and mind.

But now…everything felt empty again.

My eyes burned because I wasn't sure what I wanted. The chaos he brought with him or the emptiness I felt in the darkness.

Suddenly, something dropped on my lap and I jumped, my thoughts screeching to a halt.

I froze with fear, and my eyes snapped open. I looked up, and my throat closed, my lips turning dry.

My heart did the same pitter patter dance again. The same melodious beat. The storm of emotions hit me hard, and I could only stare into his brown eyes, mesmerized yet again. Completely and utterly swept by his presence.

Just like before, he held me captive.

He hadn't left.

He nodded at me and then at my lap. Confused, I followed his gaze.

A notebook and a pen rested there.

I touched the beige papers with gentle fingers, holding it with my thumb and forefinger. After staring at the items for a good five seconds, I looked up again.

Our gazes met and locked.

And then he smiled—a true smile—and it met his eyes beautifully.

My eyes moved down to his smiling lips. He looked beautiful—even more handsome and so different when smiling.

"Talk."

One word and my eyebrows furrowed. The man nodded toward the notebook and pen again.

"Talk," he repeated, looking at me expectantly.

Breaking our eye contact, I looked down at my lap again. My heart danced again, my body no longer cold.

He wants me to speak?

He wanted me to speak—not by using my voice. But with pen and paper.

Even though I was someone filled with silence, he still wanted to hear my thoughts. He still wanted me to *talk*.

I didn't think my heart could get any crazier. But it did.

This man...he didn't realize what he had just given me.

He didn't want my silence—he wanted my words.

So I would give him my words.

Because he had earned them. With one simple action, he had earned them.

THE MAFIA AND HIS OBSESSION PART 1

Taking the pen in my hand, I held it to the paper.

Chapter 14

Viktor

My imagination was nothing now that I was this close to her. So close that I could see the green speckles in her doe hazel eyes. She looked up at me, her eyes wide with a hidden innocence, some naivety and a hint of fire. They were the most beautiful eyes I had ever seen.

I bent down a little, until our faces were mere inches away. Her breathing quickened, a sharp intake of breath that told me she was affected by my presence. Our first touch—my skin against hers, she gasped, her eyes fluttering.

My fingertips tingled at the sensation as I dragged my fingers down her cheek and the top of her neck, where the high neckline stopped. She licked her lips nervously before biting on them softly. Her eyes were still on mine, as if she couldn't take them away.

I found that I couldn't stop looking at her either.

Twirling my first knuckle around a lock of her

blonde hair, I tugged her closer. She came willingly, without any fight. Her body moved toward me effortlessly, like it was made to respond to my touch.

I gave her hair another gentle tug, our bodies so deliciously close. Her hair smelt of roses, the fragrance so sweet and soft. I inhaled, breathing her sweet smell in. With our noses almost touching, I said, "What happened to you, silent *myshka*?"

Because I knew something had happened to her. Nobody would willingly become Valentin's wife. Especially not a mute girl who was decades younger than him.

Whatever had happened to her—Valentin had a hand in it.

She was hiding in this tower, a forbidden secret, kept away from the world—it was all under her husband's command.

It was clear as day. But me being a reckless bastard, I wanted to play with fire. I wanted to uncover her secrets, because those that are forbidden are always more tempting, more intriguing.

The taste of something forbidden was always more delectable. *And I can't wait to taste her secrets on my lips.*

Her wide hazel eyes were unblinking. She looked lost in her thoughts, her chest moving up and down with each breath—the only indication that she was feeling something. Feeling my touch and I was going to make her want it—crave it, until it was the only thing she needed.

"Do you feel this?" I asked quietly, for her ears

only. Her bodyguard, Igor, was there. His stares were burning into my back. I ignored him, but that didn't mean he had to know what we were talking about.

Our words—mine and hers, they were only for each other.

The mute girl didn't answer my question, just like I knew she wouldn't. She didn't even move. Her body was a frozen statue, her mind under my spell.

The corner of my lips lifted up in a smirk. I couldn't even stop it. This was much easier than I had thought. I already had her in my trap—she fell almost so easily that I was left wondering if I had already won.

Or maybe I had won just this round. After all, we still had a long way to go.

"I want to know what you're thinking," I whispered, my nose brushing against her. She blinked this time, her lips parting, but no sound was made.

Her gaze drifted to my lips and then my eyes again. My finger unlocked around her hair, and I stood back up, pulling away.

The moment was shattered as she blinked again, her eyes widening in shock. It was the same moment that I saw fear in them before she bowed her head.

I saw true real fear, her body slightly trembling. She wasn't scared of me. If she was—she would have tried to escape before, not willingly succumb to my advances. Instead, she had let me touch her.

The terror I had seen in her gaze, it was fear of

THE MAFIA AND HIS OBSESSION PART 1

the unknown. And Valentin Solonik, the bastard, her *husband,* and my so-called *beloved* uncle, was the only explanation.

Stepping away from her trembling frame, I stared at her a second. Her hands twisted agitatedly on her lap, her fingers digging into her thighs as she tried to regain some of her control again.

Little did she know…whatever control she had before, it would all be gone now. Her thoughts belonged to me, whether she liked it or not.

She was an itch I had to get rid of. *I'll have my fun while I can. Valentin is gone…his wife is alone. And wolves like to come out and play, so I'll play a little bit.*

"You shouldn't be here, Konstantin."

Annnd…here we go again. Let me actually introduce myself.

Viktor Konstantin Ivanshov, also known as Konstantin Solonik.

And now, I was back to being only Konstantin. *Farewell, Viktor. Adieu. Until next time. I will fucking miss you.* Cue sad, dramatic music.

Taking a deep breath, I turned around and faced Igor, who had rudely interrupted my moment with my mute nun.

"That's Sir or Boss to you, Igor. You better remember that. I will not tolerate any disrespect. If you need a reminder of what your rank is and where you actually belong, let me know. I will gladly remind you," I said slowly, making sure he understood every single word. "And please know, my ways are *very* different than Valentin's."

His throat moved as he swallowed nervously

before bowing his head. "I am sorry, Sir. That won't happen again. It's just that Boss doesn't allow anyone in this room. And you are also talking to her. That's not allowed. It's the rule of the estate," he explained weakly.

I felt a sudden surge of anger at his words. They treated her like a fucking dog, someone not worthy. Like the lowest type of slaves. Hell, even the dogs at the Ivanshov estate were treated better than this.

My hands turned into fists at my sides, but I took a deep breath in. *Fucking control it, Viktor. You'll only get yourself killed. And everyone else.*

Instead of replying or showing my moment of weakness, I scoffed and turned my back to him again. He wasn't worthy of my attention.

My gaze drifted toward the blonde woman. The one with the most beautiful eyes, with hair so soft that I wanted them wrapped around my wrist as I fucked her pretty pussy.

This woman...she was worthy of my attention.

My dick twitched in my pants at the thought. I squeezed my eyes shut. *Not yet, boy. Settle down.*

I didn't give a fuck about the estate's rules. I was going to take what I wanted, satisfy my thirst for something I knew I shouldn't take. Yet I was going to take it—take her. And she would be willing.

The woman who had my attention closed her eyes, her chin wobbling as if she were about to cry. Taking my eyes away from her, I looked around the room. When I found what I was looking for, I stepped away from her and walked toward it.

She was mute—she didn't speak. Her voice was something I would never hear.

THE MAFIA AND HIS OBSESSION PART 1

I couldn't have her voice—but I would have her words.

The notebook and pen laid on the dresser, next to a small lamp, as if it was placed there just for this moment. Taking them in my hands, I glanced back at the mute girl. Her eyes were still closed, her body still trembling.

My heart clenched at the sight of her tortured expression. She reminded me so much of someone...

Ayla, the devil whispered in my ear. He sat perched on my shoulders, watching the show. Enjoying it. Laughing at me. *She reminds you of Ayla.*

Shaking my head, I tried to clear the thought of Ayla from my head. She was there...I was here, with my mute nun. I clenched my fists, my teeth grinding together in frustration.

You can't have Ayla. But you can have this one, the devil continued whispering. He tsked at me, and I glanced at the woman sitting across the room again.

She is all yours. No one is stopping you.

That was true. The devil and I for once were in agreement.

"You can't speak, but that doesn't mean you don't have thoughts," I said out loud. Walking closer to her, I continued softly. "I want to know what you are thinking."

My eyebrows furrowed in confusion when she didn't show any response. Her eyes stayed closed, her head and shoulders hanging low in despair.

It appeared as if she was hiding into herself,

hiding away from everything and everyone. Protecting herself against the unknown. And that included me.

Too bad for her, she didn't have a choice. She couldn't hide from me, no matter how much she would try.

And I sure as hell didn't like being ignored.

Maybe I'll teach her a lesson…on what happens when I am ignored.

Smirking at the thought, I stopped in front of her. "Are you seriously going to ignore me?" I asked, my voice low and a little rough. The thoughts of teaching her my ways got my dick excited.

She didn't lift her head up, but when I dropped the notebook and pen in her lap, her eyes snapped open. Her lips parted with a soft gasp as she stared up at me in shock.

Her hazel eyes were wide…looking so beautifully lost as she gazed into my eyes. For some strange, fucked-up reasons, my chest tightened as I held her gaze—completely and voluntarily lost in this moment.

My heart did a crazy beat as she continued to stare up at me, as if I was the only one she could see.

I liked that…I liked that very much.

My lips pulled up in a smile—my first true smile since I stepped foot into this estate. Hell, since I stepped foot in Russia a year ago.

This mute nun was a temptress I couldn't hide from. She got me feeling all kinds of fucked-up emotions.

Just like the devil said…she was mine to take.

THE MAFIA AND HIS OBSESSION PART 1

Someone forbidden but I could still have her.

"Talk," I said, my head nodding toward her lap.

We had been wasting away the minutes, but now, all I wanted were her words. I wanted to see what she was thinking.

Her eyes broke away from mine and went to her lap. She looked confused for a second, staring blankly at the notebook and pen.

She fingered the papers softly and then looked up at me again. I waited, but she didn't make any move.

"Talk," I repeated. I knew she understood my words—she wasn't dumb.

But as each minute ticked by, I grew both anxious and impatient. Our time together was being counted down, and she still hadn't said a word.

Her confused eyes met mine again, and she held my gaze. I didn't dare speak again. I just waited—letting her lead from here. The decision would be hers.

Finally, the confusion cleared from her eyes. Giving me a final glance, she then looked down.

My breath caught in my throat when I saw her holding the pen in her hand. The tip touched the paper, and I waited. My heart did that fucking beat again, clenching and then beating faster to a strange rhythm.

I hated it. I hated things that I didn't understand—and I sure as hell didn't understand what was wrong with me.

She looked up at me expectantly, her lips parting as if she wanted to say something, but then she closed her mouth, waiting.

When realization dawned to me, I cleared my throat and fought another smile. She was waiting for me.

"What's your name?" I asked, my voice strangely soft.

Don't frighten her. Be gentle and you will have her in the palm of your hand, the devil muttered. For a brief second, I imagined him crossing his legs and sipping tea in a cup, being all sassy and shit.

She looked down at her lap again, her hand moving. I peered into the notebook but saw it was blank.

I waited, but instead of writing, she handed the pen to me.

"What is it?" I questioned, taking the pen from her hand. "Is it not working?"

I expected no reaction. But she moved. Her head gave me a small single nod.

The little nun just kept surprising me. *Interesting.* I cleared my throat again and threw the pen across the room.

"Well, it's useless then," I muttered.

She nodded again, peeking up at me behind her eyelashes, almost shyly. I found it…endearing. Giving her my best smile, I fished out a pen that I always kept in my pocket.

I handed it to her without a second thought. "You can use my pen then."

Taking the pen from my hand, she stared down at the paper. I leaned closer, until her knees were touching my legs. The small shiver of her body gave her away.

I saw the pen moving as she wrote for me. The

pen stopped, and she glanced up at me before showing me the notebook. In beautiful penmanship, the letters were written in cursive.

Val

My forehead furrowed in confusion. "Val?" I questioned before hiding my laugh with a cough. "That's your name? What, did your parents hate you?"

She lifted her chin up in defiance at my insult, her eyes narrowing with a slight glare. Ah, there was the fire I was looking for. She had been hiding it before—but I wanted it.

Looking down at the paper again, she scribbled quickly and then showed me the notebook again.

No. Val is for short. My name is Valerie.

Valerie. My eyes traced each letter slowly, saying the name in my head.

"Valerie," I whispered, our eyes meeting. Her cheeks turned a soft pink as she blushed beautifully. "Valerie."

So fucking sweet and beautiful. Just like her.

Her lips parted as she breathed in, her tongue peeking out to run over her fuck-me lips. Heat rolled over me, bathing me with fire. She really was temptress. A beautiful nun—without her voice, but a temptress still.

"Don't you mean Valeria?" I asked, breaking the moment. That would have been the correct Russian pronunciation. Except…if she wasn't Russian. She appeared to understand English fluently. Maybe she was American.

I saw her scowl, and it snapped me out of my thoughts. She looked very unhappy at the name *Valeria*, almost as if she detested it. She wrinkled her nose at me, and I chuckled. Well, damn, the mute nun was a spitfire.

No. My name is Valerie. V.A.L.E.R.I.E.

Pressing my lips together, I tried to hold my laugh in. But it was almost impossible.

She stared at me for a second before blinking away. Valerie took the notebook back before writing again. Bending forward, I peered down on the paper.

What is your na—

She didn't even finish her question, I placed my hand over hers, and I was already speaking. She looked up in surprise.

"Viktor," I answered quickly, without thinking.

When I heard a harsh intake of breath behind me, I realized my mistake. Fuck! Double fuck.

But just as quickly as I realized my mistake, when the corner of her lips turned up in a small, barely there smile, I forgot about Igor yet again.

She mouthed my name, and my heart stuttered.

Viktor

Her eyes went from mine to our hands. I

followed her gaze, staring at my hand over hers. She didn't move or try to escape my touch. She sat still, waiting…

My thumb caressed the back of her hand, her skin so soft, almost silky. From the corner of my eyes, I watched her. Her reaction was another boost to my ego.

She appeared transfixed, watching every swipe of my thumb intensely. I leaned closer, my lips almost touching the corner of her ear. Her eyes fluttered closed, and her other hand went to her stomach, her fingers twisting around the fabric of her dress.

"You are so beautiful; do you know that?" I whispered for her ears only. "And I like you better when you are nervous, silent *myshka*."

My hand tightened around hers, and her eyes snapped open, watching our intertwined hands. She turned her head to the side, facing me.

When someone cleared their throat behind us, I slammed my teeth together in frustration.

I let Valerie go, and she inhaled, her brows furrowing as she stared down at her hands. I straightened before stepping back.

Valerie swallowed nervously before staring up at me again. "I think that's about it for today. Thank you for telling me your name," I said quietly.

She nodded, her hazel eyes losing the little spark I had seen there. Taking another step back, I turned to walk away.

But the sight of her scribbling quickly on her notebook stopped me. Valerie showed me her paper and I stared at the words.

Thank you for telling me your name too, Viktor.

I nodded without any words, because for the first fucking time—I didn't know what to say.

When I didn't reply, she started writing again.

Thank you for the pen too.

She showed me the notebook and then placed her hand out, the pen in her palm. I moved toward her again. I folded her fingers over the pen and placed her hand over her lap.

"It's yours now. Take it."

With that as my final words, I took a step back and walked away.

But not before I saw her staring at the pen as if it was her lifeline. A single tear trailed down her cheek.

That was the last thing I saw.

With my heart in my throat, I stared down at Igor, giving him a menacing look. He quickly looked down, his head bowing. He closed the door behind me when I walked out.

I left the beautiful mute nun there—in her tower.

Chapter 15

Alessio

She stood in the middle of the room, glaring at me. Her lips were set in a tight straight line as she showed me her true power as my Queen. My wife was angry, and fuck me, if I didn't love it.

"You are beautiful, Angel. I always knew that. But damn, when you're angry, you are even more beautiful. So fucking sexy. Your angry glare got me hard, kitten. All I want to do is throw you on the bed and give your pussy a thorough fuck."

"Alessio!" she snapped, her hands going to her hips. Ayla glared harder, and I smirked. Yeah, she was definitely getting nicely fucked tonight.

"Are you even listening to me?" she questioned, huffing in the most adorable way. She has exerted herself with yelling and giving me a long ass lecture. Her hands went to her rounded stomach, and she rubbed it gently before blowing a stray hair out of her face.

"Yeah, I'm listening to you," I replied absently.

She was standing a few feet away; maybe if I pull her into my arms, spread those legs, and give her pussy a long lick—

"Alessio!"

I snapped out of my thought at the same moment as a pillow kissed my face.

Thank fuck it wasn't a vase this time.

What happened to my sweet Ayla?

Oh yeah, pregnancy hormones happened.

Throwing the pillow on the bed, I faced my Angel again. She was no longer glaring or breathing fire. Nope, instead her eyes were filled in tears.

"Why didn't you wake me up, Alessio? I wanted to say good bye…you didn't let me say good bye," she whispered, her voice so soft I almost missed it. "I missed him."

Shaking my head, I opened my arms for her. Just like I knew, she didn't disappoint me. Her chin wobbled, and Ayla practically ran into my arms. I settled her on my lap, and she placed her head on my shoulders, her arms wrapping around my waist tightly.

Her round belly was pressed against my stomach, and I felt our baby kicking, letting us know of his—or her presence. I placed a palm over the bump, feeling it move with another kick.

"Viktor told me not to wake you up, Angel. You went to sleep late last night, and he left very early in the morning," I muttered in her hair, caressing her back.

"Did he see Maila before leaving?" she asked, burrowing deeper into my embrace. I fucking loved when she did that, like she couldn't get enough of me. Like she wanted to be closer.

I shook my head. "No. He didn't."

Ayla was silent for a few minutes. We just held each other—I held her and she held me, and I didn't want anything more. She was everything I wanted and needed.

"I'm scared," she whispered finally.

With furrowed eyebrows, I looked down at my Angel, forcing her to look up at me. "Why do you say that?"

Ayla blinked up at me, her eyes red with unshed tears. "I feel like everything is just...falling apart. Viktor is part of this family, yet it doesn't feel like that anymore, Alessio. He was gone for a year and now he's gone again. We don't even know when he will be back—or *if* he will be back."

Grabbing her shoulders, I gave her a small shake. "He will be back, Angel."

The mere thought of Viktor not making it out alive made me sick. It left a bitter taste in my mouth, and I rather chose not to think of it.

He was a motherfucking pain in the ass—one that I wanted to shoot multiple times in the ass, but he was still my *brother*. I have never doubted Viktor—it was my blind trust in him.

If there was someone I trusted enough to do this job, then it was Viktor. It was a gamble, a game—dangerous, but still a game to be played. Solonik needed to go down. Sooner rather than later.

As long as he was alive, my family and everyone else was in danger.

The only fucking problem was that he had too many connections. Behind our backs, he had build his empire, little by little—and now it was stronger. We knew only half of it.

It would have been easy to just kill him—put an end to this. But that would lead to a big fucking catastrophe. Everything was too connected. All our businesses. The whole corporation would go into chaos. He was too powerful to bring down without masking it and learning his plans.

"Princess doesn't even remember him. You should have seen his face when he held her, but she was so scared and started crying. He was devastated, Alessio."

Ayla's voice broke through my thoughts, and I looked down at her again. Her fingers feathered over my cheeks, softly caressing.

"I feel like *my* family isn't whole anymore, and I'm scared that it's only going to get worse," she continued.

Ayla gazed across the room, looking lost in her thoughts. Her face was drawn in, the look in her eyes making my heart clench. She looked so…desolated.

I knew how much family meant to Ayla. She has finally found her place—her family—and I knew she couldn't lose any of us. It would break her more than it would break me.

"You aren't going to lose us, Angel. I can promise you that. Nothing is going to happen to Viktor. After he's done with this shit, he will be back home where he belongs, with us," I said, kissing her forehead. "He's going to be okay."

My words held a hint of uncertainty, fuck, I didn't even know if whatever I just said was the truth. But I needed to soothe her worries.

"You think so?" Ayla questioned, her lips feathering over my neck. She laid gentle kisses there before looking me in the eyes again.

I stared into the green pools of her familiar eyes—eyes that I had fallen so in love with.

My reply was quick. "I know so."

She nodded silently. I knocked her forehead with mine. "Stop worrying, Angel. It's not good for you or the baby. Viktor is probably having fun with all the new pussies he's getting."

Ayla glared, but it didn't last long. When she stared at me through her doe eyes, her lips stretching into the most beautiful fucking smile, I couldn't help but smile too.

Her happiness always got my heart swelling and beating faster.

"I just worry," she mumbled under her breath. "I can't help it."

"Well, you shouldn't," I retorted, placing another kiss on her forehead, soothing the small frown lines.

Ayla laid her head on my shoulders again. While still holding on to her, I dragged both of us up the bed until we were laying on our sides. With our heads on the pillows, we faced each other.

My Angel cuddled closer to me, as close as the baby bump would let her. Her hand came up, resting over my cheek.

She let out a breathy sigh. "How is it that I love you more every day? I didn't think it would be possible, but every day I love you even more than the day before."

My hand tightened around her waist before

smiling down at her glowing face. She was beautiful—even more beautiful during her pregnancy.

Kissing the tip of her nose, I let my lips linger there before answering. "I don't know, Angel. I ask myself that question every day."

With a laugh, she kissed me on the lips—a quick peck that left me wanting more. I moved in for another kiss, but Ayla was already speaking again. "Do you remember the first time we met?"

I nodded silently, wanting another kiss, but she continued to speak. *Fuck, Ayla! I just want a damn kiss.*

Forcing back a frustrated growl, I listened to her. "You gave me three choices. What would you have done if I didn't choose to work for you? What if I chose something else? Maybe we wouldn't be here today."

I grabbed her by the hips, pulling her hard into my body. She stifled a laugh but quickly melted in my embrace.

"Angel, when I gave you three choices, it was just a show. In the end, I knew you wouldn't choose the others. You couldn't choose to go back on the street. All I knew was that you were running away from something dangerous and you needed somewhere safe. I was the only safety option you had. And you wouldn't choose option three. Why would you chose for me to kill you when you wanted to live? You hid in my car because you wanted freedom. You wanted a life…why choose death then?"

She was silent for a second, and I thought the

conversation was over. Finally! Bringing my head down, I went to kiss her. I was craving my wife's lips—I needed her kisses.

"But what if..."

For fuck's sake!

She ignored me even when I let out a loud breath, mixed with an annoyed growl. "What if I chose to go back on the street unsafe?"

I laughed because little did she know... "I would have dragged you back and tied you to my bed, Angel."

With our lips inches apart, almost touching, I stared into her green eyes. She stared back, her gaze never wavering.

Blue to green.

"It didn't matter what your choice was, I was keeping you."

My words were whispered, only for her ears. She shivered, her fingers now a tight hold on the collar of my suit.

"You just thought you had a choice...you didn't."

Ayla shook her head. "Are you saying it was love at first sight?" There was no mistaking the smile in her voice.

"Maybe."

I didn't know if it was love at first sight for us, but all I knew was that...the first time I had laid eyes on my Angel, she had me enraptured. I did fuck up multiple times before I finally took my head out of my ass and accepted my feeling for her. But I knew for a fact, the first time I saw Ayla, those green eyes of hers had charmed their way into my heart.

Ayla smiled fully now, her whole face lightening up in the process. She opened her mouth to speak again, but I gave her no chance.

Hell no. I need my kiss. Right fucking now.

I tilted her head up and crashed my lips to her, kissing her into silence. So deeply that she moaned into my kiss, her hands going around my neck.

Ayla dragged a leg over my hip, rubbing against me. I lost the battle. With my cock hardening in my pants, I pulled at her hair, angling her head to deepen our kiss.

When she pulled away, breathless, my lips never left her skin. Small kisses down her jaw and her neck, nipping gently at her soft skin.

"I want you," I muttered roughly against her neck.

Ayla brushed my hair back from my forehead before pulling me back to her lips. "You are always trying to get me in bed."

I kissed her lips again, taking her roughly before pulling away. Only to push Ayla on her back.

Her eyes held a needy lust as her legs spread open for me. I dragged her dress up and settled between her spread thighs, my face right over her soaking pussy.

"And this is exactly where you should always be. In bed. With me between your legs, my mouth on your pretty pussy," I said, my lips kissing her inner thighs, coming closer to where I knew she wanted me.

Ayla bucked against me, her fingers pulling at my hair, dragging me closer. I looked up to find her heated eyes already on me. She waited, her chest heaving with each anticipated breath.

"I'll have my breakfast now, Kitten."

Chapter 16

Viktor

I stood in front of the partially closed door. I shouldn't have been here—actually, I should have been far away from here.

But I couldn't help myself.

After catching a glimpse of Valerie walking down the hall, I followed and ended up here. Right outside her bedroom.

I was coming up the stairs and had paused at the sight of her standing in the middle of the corridor that led to her side of the house. She just stood there, staring into the distance as if wanting to take a step forward, but some invisible force was stopping her.

I saw her debating with herself, her fists clenching at her sides. Her heart wanting one thing but her mind stopping her.

It was that moment I knew she was never allowed outside of her bedroom. This must have been her first time. Did Igor let her out? Or maybe he wasn't present right now?

This was forbidden yet there she was—breaking the rules.

I was left wondering why, intrigued by the idea of her being forbidden and doing forbidden things. A feisty character buried deep inside the silent girl.

Then her eyes landed on mine. All thoughts went silent in my head. I could only stare at her, our gaze meeting and never wavering.

She paused, her lips parting, her eyes widening at the sight of me. Her hand went to her stomach, her fingers clenching the fabric of her dress.

Valerie took a step back; I took one forward.

She bit on her lips nervously before taking another step back. I took another forward, stalking her.

I was the hunter; she was the prey. And I couldn't wait to catch her.

And just like prey, she turned away and escaped, running away from me. That only made me want to catch her more. A wolf always enjoyed a good hunt.

Her quick footsteps faded away, and she disappeared into her bedroom. I stood there for a second, watching the empty hall until I took a step forward, following after her—wanting to be near her.

It was a strange, fucked-up feeling, but since I had woken this morning, she was the only one I could think of. Ayla's face had faded away in my dreams, replaced by the mute nun.

I had woken up in a sweat, confused at the sudden changed vision. And since then, she was all I could think of.

The blonde-haired nun, silent, with the most expressive beautiful eyes.

And now, here I stood, outside her door like a lost fucking puppy.

Alessio would be laughing his ass off. I would never hear the end of it from Phoenix.

Damn it!

But instead of turning away, I pushed the door open and walked inside. She was alone in the room, her bodyguard nowhere to be seen. Her room must have been left unlocked. I wasn't surprised, though. Looking at her now, I knew there was no chance she would escape. There was something trapping her here. Not Igor or these closed doors.

Valerie was sitting in the same chair, facing the windows—sitting in the same exact position as yesterday.

She didn't turn around at the sound of me. Closing the door behind me, I walked further into the room, anticipation licking its way through my body.

We were alone.

My lips tilted up in a smirk. There was nowhere for her to run now.

I spotted the notebook and pen on the bed. Walking toward it, I grabbed them and made my way to her. She still hadn't turned away, and my fists clenched at the idea of her purposely ignoring me.

Playing hard to get, baby?

I scoffed, shaking my head. I wasn't a man to play games with—she would be crushed in a matter of seconds.

THE MAFIA AND HIS OBSESSION PART 1

No games, silent myshka. You wouldn't like the consequences.

I was the only one allowed to play games. An interesting game was about to be played.

I wasn't going to take Valerie. No, she herself would ask me to—beg me to. It would be all her. As long as I played my cards right, her secrets would be mine, and Valerie would be asking me to fuck her in a few days.

Just a little bit of effort on my part—and then easy peasy.

My feet stopped in front of her, blocking her view of the window. She looked up at me, startled before masking her expression.

Placing the notepad and pen on her lap, I straightened up again. Valerie looked down at her lap and then up at me.

She stayed unmoving, silent, her gaze fixated on me.

I found that I couldn't tear my eyes off her, either.

After clearing my throat, I nodded toward the notepad. "How are you today?"

Are you fucking serious, Viktor? What are you—a fifteen-year-old virgin trying to get some pussy?

She took her eyes off mine and looked down at her lap. And then she took the pen in her hand, putting it on the paper.

I stared at her face; it was filled with concentration as she slowly wrote her words down.

I am fine. And you?

I read the words when she showed me the paper. Sending her a small smile, I shrugged. "I'm alive— biggest gift of the day."

Valerie frowned, her face changing from calm to worried.

Are you in danger?

After quickly writing, she showed me the paper again.

"Not really. Are you?" I questioned, taking the subject off me. She didn't need to know anything about it. The less she knew, the better.

The worry lines faded at my words, and then the silent *myskha* shook her head.

Not really.

I raised an eyebrow at her answer. "That's not an answer. Is it a yes or a no?"

Her lips settled in a straight line before she furiously started to write down on the notepad again.

You gave me the same answer.

I brought a fist to my mouth, trying to hide my laughter. Ah, there she was. The feisty nun peeking up at me again.

It left me wondering if I was the only one who saw that side of her. She appeared to be closed off, almost emotionless, but there was fire in her. And I wanted to explore that.

"It's the only answer you're getting," I replied, daring her to fight me.

She didn't. Instead her eyes met mine, and we were both lost yet again.

The sound of the door snapped my gaze away from her. I stared at Igor as he stood against the closed door, his eyes going from Valerie to me.

He frowned at the sight of me. Crossing his arms, he stood there but stayed silent. He knew better than to say anything back to me. Yesterday had served as a lesson to him.

I looked back at Valerie to see her staring at Igor now. Her face was filled with fear, her fingers clenching and then unclenching around the pen.

My lips curled back in anger. Fucking Igor.

He just ruined my moment with my *myshka*.

I ignored her bodyguard, acting as if he wasn't even there. He was irrelevant. I would deal with him later.

Placing a finger under Valerie's chin, I brought her attention back to me. Her eyes met mine, tears filling up in hers.

Instinctively, I brushed my thumbs over her cheeks and then under her eyes, caressing her face softly.

She hiccupped back a sob before tearing her eyes away from mine. Valerie looked down at her lap, and I was forced to move my hands away.

I watched her as she wrote down in her notepad. When she showed me the paper, I read the words slowly.

You shouldn't be here. If my husband finds out, you will be punished greatly.

Before I could answer, she took back the notepad and started writing again.

Nobody is allowed in here. You should leave.

I shook my head, and frustration glinted in her beautiful eyes.

Please.
He will hurt you.

I shook my head again, and she slammed her pen on the notepad, blinking away tears. She looked so devastated, scared—trembling with fear. *Hurt me...do you mean he will hurt you, my beautiful nun?*

Leaning forward until our faces were inches apart, I made sure her eyes were on me. "Valerie, this estate is as much mine as it is his. He can't hurt me. He wouldn't even dare. And your *husband* sure as hell can't kick me out of here. I can come and go as I please. Nobody will *dare* test my anger," I whispered to her.

Her lips parted, her mouth falling open at my words. Confusion clouded her gaze, and she only blinked up at me.

"Nobody will hurt me." *Nobody will hurt you.*

Valerie's confusion made me smile. She didn't even know who I was—what I meant to the Solonik family.

I was their only winning card—the master of this game. Her fucking *husband* was a nobody.

THE MAFIA AND HIS OBSESSION PART 1

"Sir, it is improper for you to be this close to Boss's wife."

I looked over Valerie's shoulder, raising an eyebrow at Igor. He swallowed nervously before averting his gaze.

My gaze went back to where it needed to be, and she seemed oblivious to Igor's words. There was no response from her. I had thought it would break our moment again, but her gaze was still fixated on mine.

Hmm...interesting.

She blinked up at me, and then her cheeks turned red. Smirking, I pulled away. What was the mute nun just thinking?

Did she imagine my lips on hers—kissing her? Or maybe more?

She blushed harder, looking down at her lap. Her fingers played the edge of the papers, and she licked her lips nervously.

I saw her peeking up at me shyly, her long eyelashes hiding her beautiful doe eyes. Taking my lighter from my pocket, I clicked it open.

Her gaze instantly went to the small fire, completely entranced by it. I took a cigarette out of the small box I kept in my pocket and placed it between my teeth. Her eyes went from the lighter to my lips, and she stared as I lit the end of the cigarette.

She gave me a strange look, like she was studying me, memorizing my face in that little head of hers.

I placed the lighter back into my pocket and inhaled before blowing the smoke out past my lips.

The smoke caressed her face, and she blinked her eyes once, still staring at me.

I stepped closer, inhaling at my cigarette again. Valerie's eyes were on my lips—watching before looking down at her lap.

Her attention was on her notepad as she started writing.

"I kinda hate it when your attention isn't on me, *myshka*," I muttered for her ears only.

There was no response. Not even a flinch. She didn't even look up at me to acknowledge my words. Cocking my head to the side, I stared at this beautiful woman.

There was so much about her that I still needed to learn. So much to explore. So much to see. She was filled with so many secrets that I didn't even know where to start.

Valerie kept writing and then showed me her paper.

You shouldn't smoke. It's bad for your health.

Reading the words, I busted out in laughter. Was that what she was worried about? My health?

I shook my head at her silly thoughts—*oh baby, that's the last thing you need to be worried about.*

I controlled my death, and I sure as fuck wasn't ready for it yet. Death could fuck itself in the ass with a splintered rod. I would call it when I was fucking ready for it to drag me to hell.

Smoking is bad.

THE MAFIA AND HIS OBSESSION PART 1

I hadn't noticed her writing until she showed me her notepad again.

"You are right. Smoking is bad." I shrugged. "And I like to do bad things."

She sucked in a harsh breath, her gaze quickly snapping to her lap. Moving closer into her space, I crowded in with my body. She was trapped with nowhere to go.

Leaning closer until my lips were next to her ears, I whispered. "I like to do…very bad things."

I expected her to push me away, any reaction to my words, but I only got a small shiver. Pulling away, I stared at her.

She swallowed hard, her chest heaving with each breath. I was tempted to tease her more—so tease her I did.

A single finger feathered over her cheek, slowly moving down while caressing her porcelain skin. So smooth, so soft. I wanted to bite it—turn her skin red with my marks.

The thought had my dick twitching in excitement. *Down, boy. Patience. I promise, your patience will be greatly rewarded by a warm pussy.*

My finger continued its downward path—her jaw, her neck. It lingered there for a second, tickling her skin near her ear before moving down again.

Her lips parted, her breathing louder and harsher. Valerie turned her head slightly to the side, inviting me for more. I knew she had done it unconsciously.

When my touch moved to her chest, her breath hitched with a silent gasp. I smirked at her reaction—fucking perfect.

My thumb soothed over her left tit before

circling her nipple. A soft touch through her dress, but she jumped like she had been shot with a bolt of lightning.

Valerie's lips moved, but no words came out—only silence. She was voiceless.

Her eyes fluttered, her breathing accelerating with each swipe of my thumb.

"Only my woman has the right tell me what to do or not do," I murmured, my thumb feathering over her nipple again. Her gaze quickly went to my lips and then my eyes again.

She shivered, her hands clenching her dress too tightly. "And you, *myshka*, you aren't my woman."

Yet.

The devil made its appearance again with one word before disappearing like it was nothing.

Fuck you, you nasty piece of shit.

Her hand came up, her fingers wrapping around my wrist, stalling my movement. I raised an eyebrow in surprise, staring down at her hold on me.

Her fingers tightened, and I looked back up again. Valerie stared at me with desperation—I couldn't read her. I knew she was attracted to me—she wanted more, but the fear was there. And rightfully so.

I was seducing her slowly, and she was falling in the trap laid out for her.

"You are so tempting, Valerie," I said. Her eyes were on my mouth, watching my words.

She blinked up at me, the sad look in her eyes making my heart clench tightly. Her gaze went back to my lips again. Letting her go, I took a small step back.

"It seems whenever I am with you, I forget what's right and wrong," I continued while watching her reaction.

Her shoulder dropped, her eyes leaving my face before falling to her lap. It hurt to see the defeated expression on her face.

But I had needed to know something, and my suspicion was just confirmed.

The way her eyes always went from my eyes to my lips whenever I was talking. She would only respond when she was looking at my face—other times it was as if I wasn't even speaking.

Shaking my head, I stared at her in complete astonishment. And a little bit in awe.

This beautiful nun, with alluring eyes, wasn't *just* mute.

She was fucking deaf.

Chapter 17

Valerie

His touch was electrifying. Every single swipe of his thumb, my skin burned with the sensation. I felt breathless, out of control.

Instead of moving into his touch, I should have pushed him away. I should have been disgusted by his touch. But I wanted it. I wanted more. I wanted everything he was doing to me. How my mind went blank and I seemed to forget everything except his touch and him.

He was all I could think of, and I never wanted it to end.

Every pain I felt before, it was forgotten as I stared into his brown eyes.

I used to hide, locked myself tight into my mind—numb to everyone and everything else, but with him, I felt alive. It was a strange feeling, one I wasn't familiar with. But even then, instead of hiding away like I always did, I let go and just—

THE MAFIA AND HIS OBSESSION PART 1

felt.

I let him show me how to feel.

My eyes fluttered close when he dragged his finger down my neck and then my chest, circling my nipple. It was wrong, so wrong. But it felt…right.

My fingers clenched around the fabric of my dress, wanting to hold onto something, anything to ground me to the present.

I shivered when he masterfully touched me again, and my eyes snapped open, our gaze meeting yet again. His eyes were heated, mixed with warmth and so much lust that I shuddered. I couldn't take my eyes off him.

Viktor was in control, the master of this situation while I was just a puppet caught in the strings of his play.

It was a dangerous game he and I were playing. There would be no ending, just a cliff-hanger that would pull us both into the depths of the crimson hellfire.

There was so much more about him than what he seemed. He was a breathing mystery, and I wanted to know more about him, his thoughts—his plans for me.

Why is he here?

The words twirled and twirled in my head, leaving me in a mistful daze. My fingers unclenched from my dress, and without thinking, I grabbed his wrist, stalling his movement.

I needed to think, and with him touching me, I couldn't even fabricate a coherent thought.

His gaze moved down to our hands. My eyes

followed the same path too, until they rested on our hands, my fingers around his wrist, holding him still.

His hand and mine were a stark contrast. His—tanned, strong, and rough, as if it never knew a gentle touch. Mine—pale, small, and soft, as if it never touched the sun.

This man belonged to the same world that destroyed me, yet I couldn't feel disgust. I looked up, and we just stared at each other.

I felt fear, desperation to know what he was thinking and what he wanted from me.

He is seducing me, but doesn't he know the results of this play?

Doesn't he know who I belong to?

If Valentin ever found out—Viktor would never make it out alive. And then I would have to bear the pain of both our mistakes.

The corner of his eyes wrinkled a little bit, and my gaze went to his lips to see him smirking. "You are so tempting, Valerie," he said.

I watched his lips closely, following each word before I blinked up at him again. My heart stuttered, and my chest clenched. What was he doing to me?

My gaze went back to his lips again, not wanting to miss any of his words. It was the only way I could listen to his words.

My ears were useless—the sound they heard were muted. All voices felt like a blanket, falling in a deep hollow pit.

There were no sound, just small whispers that I could barely make out. If I focused hard on the sound, maybe I would hear a word or two. But even

THE MAFIA AND HIS OBSESSION PART 1

then, it sounded weird, like I was submerged deep under water and someone was whispering from above.

My loss of hearing was my weapon, my strength. I didn't have to hear all the malice from my tormentors. The silence was a gift bestowed upon me in this chaotic darkness.

It was something everyone feared, a painful and regretful thing to others. But to me, I was blessed to have the silence. I praised it. I welcomed it with open arms.

But for the first time, I wanted to hear a voice— *his* voice. I wanted to listen to his words; maybe they would have been music to my ears.

For the first time, I felt the loss of my hearing cut me deep.

Viktor let me go, and I felt the cold wash over me in the most painful way. My hand fell to my lap, and my eyes moved to his hands. They were at his sides, his fists clenching tightly. The tattoos on the back of his hands looked more prominent with the angry lines of his veins.

Looking back up again, I stared at his face. He looked at me strangely, his head cocked to the side. Viktor studied my face for a second, his eyes moving from mine to my lips, and then up again.

"It seems whenever I am with you, I forget what's right and wrong," he said. I would have missed it if my gaze wasn't already on his lips.

It seems whenever I am with you, I forget what's right and wrong.

He couldn't have spoken any truer words than these. It was as if he picked them right out of my mind. My eyes flicked back to his, and I knew, whatever I was feeling—he was feeling the same.

A strange man I have never seen before. A complete stranger but he gave me more than my husband had ever given me.

He gave me a chance to use my words; his touch was gentle, his eyes soft—every look shooting straight into my heart. He was everything I had been secretly craving—dreaming of.

I looked at the notepad and pen on my lap. *Thank you, Viktor. I can't thank you enough, and you will never know how grateful I am to have those stolen forbidden moments.*

But whatever we had between us—we couldn't have it.

I had to shoot it, put a bullet through it, before it even bloomed to something else.

Without giving him another glance, I took the pen and started writing.

You shouldn't be here. Igor is watching us. He will tell Valentin, and my husband will hurt you. You say that he can't do anything to hurt you, but you are so wrong. He is a powerful man. He can do anything he wants...and if he wants to hurt you, he will find ways to wound you so deep. So please, you need to leave. Viktor, you shouldn't be here. Please, leave.

I showed him the notepad, and he read the words

slowly. When I saw no reaction from him, I started writing again. Feeling frustrated at his lack of understanding, I was close to begging now.

Why don't you understand? If I have to beg, I will. You really don't understand. Please.

With the notepad still on my lap, he was reading the words and then smirked. "Oh, I would love to hear you beg, silent *myshka*."

His face came closer, our noses almost touching. "Just not the type of begging you are thinking. Trust me, when you beg—you are going to do it for a whole different reason. And I'm going to love hearing you beg me."

My eyes widened in shock at his words. He couldn't mean…

His hand came up, and he thumbed my lips almost roughly, his fingers then moving to my cheek. They slowly inched their way to upward, his fingertips feathering just below my ear.

It tickled, but the warmth his fingers left in their path made me forget about everything.

"Were you always deaf?"

I blinked, and then my mouth fell open.

Wh-at?

How…? No! Nobody—

My thoughts screeched to a halt when he grasped my neck, pulling me closer. I trembled in shock and went limp, letting him control my body.

What's happening? I screamed in my head.

His fingers tightened around my neck. It wasn't

hurting—not like when Valentin would hold me. Viktor's hold held so much dominance in it, but it was…gentle.

I swallowed nervously, and his thumb rubbed the column of my neck softly, forcing my eyes on him again.

"Answer me, Valerie."

His face darkened and eyes glowed almost fiercely. Those brown irises were darker—almost black now. Viktor looked dangerous, angry. Like a killer, his mind set on his next victim. I saw him grinding his teeth together, his jaw locked.

Still staring at his face, I shook my head mutely.

If possible, Viktor looked even more furious.

"Did Valentin do this to you?"

The question left me shivering because, oh little did he know…

I shook my head again. Viktor raised an eyebrow at me, his hold tightening just a little. He pulled me closer, our lips now inches apart.

In this position, it was harder for me to see his lips. I couldn't see what he was saying. So I just closed my eyes. In closing my eyes, I let myself feel. His touch, his voice.

I felt his breath next to my ear, so close. Instinctively, I brought my hands up, my fingers latching on his arms.

Two different holds.

Dominance. And submissive.

Strong. And weak.

Powerful. And desperation.

I just held him, while he held me.

There were whispers, my ears trying so hard to

catch the words.

"...*Valerie.*"

My eyes snapped opened, and my heart froze for a half of a second before it started beating again, harder and louder.

My hands shook, and I held him tighter, tears blinding my vision.

Did I...?

My name...

He said my name...

I heard him...

He slowly moved his head in front of me, and I just stared at him.

Say it again, I begged. *Please. Say my name. I want to hear it.*

Viktor stared at me for a second before his lips moved again.

"Valerie."

I saw him speak...but my ears didn't catch his voice. His words fell into a pit of silence and darkness.

Closing my eyes, a tear fell down my cheek. I choked back a sob. *What a cruel fate.*

Before when I had heard his voice, it was almost silent. But I knew it was deep. I imagined that his voice was rough, deep and strong—just like him.

I want to hear you.

I felt his touch, this thumb brushing over my cheek. He swiped the tear away while his other hand released my neck. My eyes opened to look into his.

His brown ones were soft, focused intensely on me. As if I was the only one he could see.

Viktor brought his hand up, and his finger touched his lips. Instantly, my gaze went to his lips. He has found another way to communicate with me, letting me know that he was about to speak. He wanted me to catch every word he was saying.

"I don't know what you are hiding, Valerie. But I am going to figure it out. Whether you like it or not, I am going to figure *you* out. You can hide from Valentin, but not from me."

He brushed my hair out of my face. "All your secrets, Valerie. They will be mine. I want them. But I will wait for you to give them to me willingly."

His face was close to mine again, and he smiled, a beautiful, breathtaking smile. "Remember, I am not Valentin. I am Viktor. And you can't hide from me, silent *myshka.*"

With those as his final words, he stood straight. Viktor gave me a final glance, nodding, as if we now shared a secret. Maybe we did.

Our secret.

He left the room, and I was left staring at the wide windows, staring into the darkness of the night.

Minutes turned into hours. I lost track of time. When my back and shoulders started aching from sitting in the same position for too long, I finally stood up and moved from my chair.

I felt eyes on me, and I ignored them.

Igor was in the room—he was always present. I wondered how much he would tell Valentin.

Turning my head to the side, I looked at him. He was already looking at me, his eyes glaring holes into my body. Igor shook his head in warning, as if telling me to put an end to this game. Because it would lead to only chaos and pain.

I stared at him blankly, only because I didn't know how to end this—whatever it was between Viktor and me.

I didn't know how to end this beautiful secret.

Ignoring the eyes on me, I turned off the lights and crawled in my bed. I settled deeper into my pillows and mattress and closed my eyes.

Darkness welcomed me, and I fell into a deep sleep.

Where *he* was waiting for me.

In all his beautiful form, smirking teasingly, his brown eyes happy—his touch gentle and soft.

I felt a touch on my cheeks, almost featherlight, but it was enough to rouse me from my slumber. Blinking my sleepy eyes, I only saw darkness.

Huh?

I touched my cheek, it wasn't cold—it was warm and tingling, like it had just been touched.

Sitting up on my bed, I looked around the room. My lamp was the only light, but I saw nothing. The room was empty.

Shaking my head, I stared at the window, where Viktor had stood just hours ago. He was with me in my dreams, and now I could even feel this touch.

My body went limp, and I was about to turn to my side when something else caught my eyes.

On my nightstand, the pen and notepad sat there. Just where I had left them before I went to sleep.

Only difference, the notepad was opened, and on the paper, words were written in an unknown penmanship.

With trembling hands, I took the notepad and brought it closer to me.

I read the words slowly. I read them over and over again. Tracing each letter with my fingertips, I just stared at the words.

My chin wobbled, and then I smiled. A small, barely there smile, almost tearfully.

Okay, I replied in my head.

My fingers continued to trace the words.

Trust me, silent myshka.

Chapter 18

Valerie

I walked out of the shower and wrapped a towel around my body before staring at the mirror. It was glossed over with steam, but I quickly wiped it with my palms, just enough for me to see my face.

It had only been three days since I met Viktor. We had talked only twice. But both times, he was able to make my dead heart beat again. Just a little harder and a little faster. The drumming of the wings of a caged bird.

My heartbeat now drummed in my ears just at the thought of him.

The lips that had not known a smile for many years were now lifted up in the corners in the smallest smile. Just at the thought of *him*.

I stared at my reflection for the longest time, wondering if this was only temporary.

It is. This won't last, my mind argued with my hopeful heart. *You will only get hurt in the end. You are married to Valentin. Don't forget that.*

But just a little longer…I wanted to keep feeling this way just a little longer. Just a little bit of happiness, even if it was forbidden, I wanted to feel it. Even if it was just scraps, bits of light, I would take it.

I felt alive after so long, and that unknown feeling has quickly become addicting.

After drying my hair with a towel, I combed it. My gaze was still on the mirror, still lost in my thoughts. They all pointed in the same direction.

Viktor.

Maybe the reason why I was so infatuated with him was because the attention he gave me. I have been denied gentle touches and sweet words for many years. Valentin only gave me pain. I must have been stupid and naïve; maybe that was why I fell so easily for Viktor's attention.

Even now, I wondered what he was doing now. After last night, he disappeared, and I hadn't caught a glimpse of him again. When Igor had left my room for a quick minute this morning, I tried to walk out of my room again, just a step out. I had paused, my chest tightening almost painfully.

But when fear started to fuel inside of me, I took that step back and closed the door, hidden yet again from the outside world.

The rules were broken; the risk of losing everything now hung on my shoulders like dark clouds.

But still, I argued with my brain. I chose to follow my heart, like a child wanting a hug, a kiss…desperate for some quiet love.

When my long blonde hair hung loosely behind

my back, I pulled the white nightgown over my body. Now that I had felt a small taste of freedom, the high collar felt almost suffocating, the long sleeves itching.

A strange emotion filled my heart, and I quickly shook my head. *Don't think like that, Valerie.*

Giving my reflection a final glance, I took a step back. But instead of walking away, I paused.

Would he visit me again tonight?

Since the morning, I had tried not to think about it. It was almost as if I were craving his presence. He gave me something…and now I was left wanting more.

I looked at myself again, the mirror showing just a simple plain woman lost in her thoughts. It left me wondering how Viktor saw me?

Was I beautiful to him?

Just as the thought crossed my mind, my gaze went to the bathroom vanity. I walked closer and opened the drawers to find my makeup safely placed there.

I wasn't allowed to use them…except when ordered by Valentin.

When he would come to have his fun, he would ask me to *doll myself up* for him.

Don't disappoint me, Valeria. I want you ready for me, just like I asked. Be the nice little slut you are and wait for me on the bed.

I hated when he would order me to *prepare* myself. Lacy lingerie would be brought in. Pretty high heels. Makeup.

I was to make myself sexy, not as his wife, but as a whore. A courtesan for his pleasure.

My gaze drifted toward the makeup again. It was always used to humiliate me. But maybe, just maybe…I could use them differently.

I want to look beautiful for him.

My fingers feathered over the items, my hands shaking with nervousness. Before I could change my mind, I took the eyeliner in my hand.

Another rule broken.

Staring into the mirror, I applied the eyeliner. Just a little bit that made my brown eyes look bigger. The green speckles in my eyes appeared brighter.

Instead of wearing more makeup, I just applied some pink lip gloss, giving my lips a glossy look with a prettier shade.

When I was done, I closed the drawer quickly and with a bang, as if hiding a secret. My cheeks felt heated with embarrassment.

What am I doing?

You are a fool, Valerie.

I silently laughed at myself, shrugging away the idea that I was playing with fire.

Giving myself a final glance, I liked that it wasn't much. Maybe even Igor wouldn't notice. The corners of my mouth lifted up in a small smile, and I pressed a finger to my lips.

It will be our secret.

The smile was still present on my face when I walked out of the bathroom. But it slipped away when I saw Igor standing in the middle of the room.

His legs were spread in a defensive posture, his hands behind his back. He stared at me silently, his lips set in a straight line.

THE MAFIA AND HIS OBSESSION PART 1

"Your dinner is here," he said, nodding toward the nightstand.

I nodded silently, now wringing my hands nervously in front of me. When he didn't say anything else, I shifted my gaze away.

I walked toward my bed and settled down before bringing the food tray on my lap. The smell of pasta and garlic cheese bread made my mouth water.

I didn't pay attention to Igor as I dug into my food. Eating slowly, trying to make the time go by faster. My eyes went to the clock and then down again at my half-empty plate.

Eight-thirty p.m. Late but still early.

The first time Viktor had visited me, it was in the morning. Yesterday, he had visited me at night, but still earlier than now.

Maybe he isn't coming. Maybe I was being too hopeful.

I stared at my half-eaten food, my appetite long gone. When a pair of feet approached me, I snapped out of my thoughts and looked up at Igor.

He shook his head before speaking. "You are playing a dangerous game, Valerie."

I know that! I wanted to scream and cry. Cry because it was unfair. I was trapped here, and after so long, I finally felt something, but I couldn't have it.

I placed the tray on the nightstand again before looking at his lips, watching his words.

"Do you realize how bad this could get?" Igor continued. "Little girl, I am giving you the only warning I can. Whatever you're thinking about, don't. Whatever you are feeling, push it away. You will only get in trouble this way."

His words penetrated my mind, leaving tiny little wounds at the reminder. He was right. Whatever this was…there would be no happy ending.

I wanted something I couldn't have.

That alone could ruin everything.

When I didn't answer, Igor's shoulders dropped. It appeared as if he were sighing. His eyebrows furrowed sadly, a look I had never seen on his face before. He was always so…emotionless.

When he started speaking again, I could only stare, my breath caught in my throat. "I have to wait outside the door, knowing full well what Valentin is doing to you. If I could make a difference, Valerie, I would. But I can't. I know this won't change anything, but *I am sorry*."

My eyes widened at his words, my heart skipping a beat, and the sadness felt almost suffocating. All this time—I never knew he felt that way.

Igor wasn't a good man, he was far from it. He was an underdog, someone to do Valentin's dirty job.

To me, he was my captor. My jailor. When Valentin wasn't here to keep me trapped, Igor was.

But for the first time, he had let me see behind the cold armor.

"When he comes back, he will ask me. And I will have to tell him the truth. Whatever I had seen between you and Viktor, I will have to tell him. I have no choice. You made a mistake, and you will have to bear it. So take my warning and stop this fucking mess before it gets worse."

THE MAFIA AND HIS OBSESSION PART 1

My heart stuttered. The unshed tears stung my eyes, and they blinded my vision. My stomach twisted almost painfully, and I felt nauseous.

My chest tightened, and it hurt. It hurt so much. I pressed my hand over my chest and rubbed, hoping to alleviate the pain.

Igor took a step back, his eyes darker. He looked a little angry. "I can't put my family in danger to protect you. I am already risking their safety by bringing you those pills. If Valentin finds out..."

He left his words hanging, and I flinched. My fingers twisted around my dress, guilt consuming me. I knew the consequences, and it was frightening. Just the thought of it made me sick.

I nodded slowly, hoping he could see what I wanted to say. *I understand. We are all trapped. There is no escape. Valentin is the ringmaster. I don't blame you, Igor. You have a job as my guard. Your loyalty is toward Valentin. You have your family to protect, and I have mine to protect. It's a survival game.*

Igor stared at me for a few seconds before taking a deep breath. "Valentin is coming back in three days. He has asked for you to *prepare* yourself according to his *rules*. He will come for you first and then see to his other business."

As if cold water has been dumped over my head, I trembled, and my eyes closed. All I saw was my tortured body, Valentin taking his pleasure without asking. Just taking...forcing me.

A broken doll to do whatever he wanted with, his exact words.

My fingers dug deeper into my palms. The

stinging feeling of my nails pressing into my skin snapped me out of my thoughts. My gaze met Igor's face.

"Three days. That's all you have," he said before turning around and walking away.

I watched his retreating back. When he stopped, and then turned to face me again, I only stared at him.

"You don't know Viktor. He is not who you think he is."

I cocked my head to the side, curiosity now burning my inside. *What do you mean?*

"He is a very powerful man. And you…you are just a game. To men like him, someone forbidden like you, they see it as a conquest. Don't let yourself get swept away by his pretty words."

With that, he walked away and closed the door behind him.

I was left reeling, his words leaving a giant gaping hole in my chest. He…couldn't mean that. I stared at the closed door, my heart hurting more than before.

I wanted desperately to believe that Viktor was a good man. He spoke to me, he made me speak…he was sweet. He touched me gently. Viktor didn't hurt me like everyone else.

Trust me, silent myshka.

He had told me to trust him. His words had given me hope. I didn't know what to trust him about, but I wanted to *trust him*. I wanted to *believe* him.

He is a very powerful man. And you…you are just a game. To men like him, someone forbidden like you, they see it as a conquest. Don't let yourself get swept away by his pretty words.

The silent truth behind Igor's words spoke louder, though.

Did Viktor really care?

Or was I just a pawn to his boredom?

A single tear fell. I felt the drop on my cheek, tickling my skin. Swiping it away, I turned off the light and climbed under the covers.

Please don't hurt me, Viktor.

Chapter 19

Viktor

"Ayla?" My voice was loud in panic. I sounded frantic. I *was* frantic.

"Baby girl, why are you calling me? What's wrong? Did something happen?" I shot the questions before she could have a chance to answer.

"Huh? Oh no, everything is fine," she quickly replied.

I sagged against the wall, my heart thumping hard. She didn't sound scared, but even then, the panic didn't lessen.

"Then why are you calling, baby girl?" I asked quietly. Shit, didn't Alessio tell her not to call me?

"I wanted to check if you were okay. Are you okay?" her sweet voice replied.

Ah, for fuck's sake! This was bad. Very bad.

I wasn't supposed to have any communication with the Ivanshov like this. It would look too suspicious. Ayla just messed up big time.

THE MAFIA AND HIS OBSESSION PART 1

Taking a deep breath, I replied. "Don't worry about me, baby girl. I know you're worrying, but please don't. Remember, no stress during your pregnancy."

I could feel her nodding, and I almost smiled. "I know, but Alessio won't tell me anything. If you promise you are okay, then I won't worry anymore. I need to hear you say it instead of Alessio."

Instead of replying with what she wanted me to, I quickly spoke. "Ayla, you can't call me again. What you just did is very dangerous."

There was silence on the other side until I heard her whisper, her voice now masked with fear. "Did I just mess up?"

I shook my head. "No, baby girl. You didn't."

"But..."

"You just can't do that again. That's all. Hang up and go tell Alessio that you called me. He will handle it from there."

"Is he going to be angry at me?" she muttered. I could almost imagine her chewing on her bottom lip nervously.

Chuckling quietly, I shook my head. "No, Ayla. Alessio can never be mad at you. Now go."

"Okay."

Before she could hang up, I whispered the words for her to hear. "I am okay, baby girl."

And then I hung up.

Throwing the phone on the bed, I released a frustrated growl. Fucking shit! I couldn't even talk to her properly. Instead, the mere thought of Valentin catching me left me feeling cold and sick.

Only three days since I came back and I was

already suffocating.

A small ping from the second phone brought my attention back. Walking toward the bed, I picked it up to see a message.

I am here.

Ah. Everything was forgotten when I read the message. Instead, I could feel myself smirking.

How perfect.

It was true that I was suffocating here…but there was something—or someone—who could make me feel differently.

A few minutes with *her* was enough to make me forget *everything*. All the mess and how fucked up my life was, in her presence—everything was gone except *her*.

But I couldn't have her until something important was done.

I didn't reply to the text. Instead, I placed the phone in my pocket and walked out of my room. My steps faltered on the top of the stairs, my gaze drifting toward Valerie's wing of the estate.

Her room was at the end of the hall. Several steps and I could be with her.

But *business* came first.

Wait for me, myshka.

With a final look, I walked away. The car was already waiting for me. In the darkness of the night, the ride toward my destination was quick and silent.

When the car finally stopped, I stepped out and faced the dark alley. I walked forward, step after step, until I reached the mouth of the back alley.

THE MAFIA AND HIS OBSESSION PART 1

There was no one in the streets, and at this time, everyone was mostly sleeping. There was only darkness, me and *him*.

I walked forward and then stopped when I saw the figure standing against the wall.

"Hello, Igor."

He moved away quickly, his body defensive and ready for attack. I saw him reaching behind his back, probably for his gun.

Tsk tsk. Poor guy. Too bad, he already fell in my trap.

"Konstantin?" he asked quietly.

I walked forward under the single lamplight. His eyes widened at the sight of me.

"Surprised?" I asked instead.

"Wh—at? What are you doing here? I thought I was meeting…" he stuttered.

I chuckled and then shook my head. "Nope. You are meeting me."

"But…" He paused and then straightened. "What do you want, Konstantin?"

I sighed and leaned against the wall. I removed a small box from my pocket and placed a cigarette between my lips. Igor swallowed and watched as I lighted the end.

It was done slowly, dragging out the suspense. When he trembled slightly, I knew I had him right where I wanted.

"Do you really want to know?"

He didn't answer, so I just shrugged.

"Simple. I want you dead."

"You can't. Valentin…will know. And…"

"You don't need to worry about that," I said

before blowing out a puff of smoke.

I didn't give him a chance to answer. In a swift movement, I took the knife out and threw it at him. Bullseye.

It pierced his leg, and he yelped before falling to his knees. Igor groaned in pain, his chest heaving. He was an old guy, younger than Valentin, but still old.

Maybe I'll go gentle on him.

He was silent for a second. "Why are you doing this?"

Igor already knew the answer, yet he still asked. But considering what I was about to do, the poor guy deserved an answer.

"Here is something you need to know about me," I said, my voice quiet in the darkness of the night.

My words were only for his ears. He trembled, his eyes widening with fear when I took a menacing step closer.

"I always get what I want. It doesn't matter how or what I need to do to get it. In the end, it's mine if I want it," I continued. "I don't give a fuck about the consequences."

He shook his head, trying to beg for his life, but I ignored his desperate plea.

"And I want *her*."

I saw his throat working as he tried to speak, but he stopped when I crowded his space. Crouching down to his level, I smiled. I pulled the knife out, and he fell to his side, his face twisting in agony.

His eyes went to my knife as I twirled it around my fingers. The blade whispered over my skin but never cut through.

THE MAFIA AND HIS OBSESSION PART 1

I brought the knife closer to his face, dragging the tip of the blade down his face and then his neck, until I held him captive. One wrong movement…and his death would be signed.

I made a tsking sound at the back of my throat before speaking again. "Unfortunately for you, you are in my way. To get her, I will need to get rid of you. Sadly."

"When…Valentin finds out that you have taken an interest in Valerie…it will be war," Igor whispered through clenched teeth. "Don't do this. Remember, you and Valentin need to be one to bring down the Ivanshov. If you go against him…"

I laughed—because little did he know.

Leaning closer, I muttered in his ear. "Oh, I can't wait for this…*war*."

He opened his mouth, but no words came through as I dug my knife into his neck, breaking through his artery. Blood sprayed around us. It wasn't a clean kill—it was rather messy as he choked on his blood, the gurgling sound of his impending death music to my ears.

I dragged my knife out of his gouged throat and wiped it with my handkerchief. My suit was drenched with his dirty blood, but that was thing about black—it hid all the messiness of this beautifully fucked-up life.

Well, that was gentle enough.

Standing up, I gave him a final look and couldn't stop the smirk that pulled up across my lips.

With my gaze on the bloody gorgeous artwork, I watched the life drain out of him, his body convulsing and slowly going still.

I turned my back to him, but not before whispering words that he heard as his life left him completely.

"I will send my sincere condolences to your wife and kids."

Chapter 20

Viktor

The estate was dark and silent when I walked in. It was in the middle of the night, everyone locked in their room, sound asleep.

And here I was, walking down the corridor that led to Valerie's room.

Right after killing her bodyguard in cold blood. Removing the first obstacle in my path.

I would deal with the aftermath afterward, but now, I just needed to see *her*. Stopping in front of the closed door, I just stared and breathed. She was inside, sleeping. She would never hear me walking in.

She would never know I was in there, watching her. Touching her.

It would be my secret to keep.

I opened the door and walked inside. The door closed behind me, the lock clicking in place. Her room was dark, the night lamp casting a small glow around. From where I was standing, I saw her on the bed. She was still, sound asleep, her covers hiding her from my sight.

I stalked closer, stealthy—my gaze still on her.

My feet stopped next to her bed. My eyes drifted across and met her face. It glowed beautifully under the small light. Her blonde hair spilled over her pillows in soft waves, and my fingers itched with the need to touch them.

Her face was peaceful, her lush pink lips slightly parted as she breathed slowly in her sleep.

She was a vision I couldn't escape from—a beautiful goddess laid out to tempt me into doing something so wrong. Yet it felt…so right. This felt more right than anything in my life.

It wasn't my first time watching her sleep. Three nights in a row, I stood right in this spot and watched her sleep. Three nights and I still couldn't get enough. I wanted *more*.

Leaning closer, my fingers feathered over her cheeks, down her jaw and neck. Her eyes fluttered but didn't open. Valerie stayed still, but I saw her chest moving, her breathing accelerating just a little bit.

The comforter was up to her waist. My hand moved down her body, pushing it away. She trembled but still didn't wake up. *Good.*

Her body was covered with her white night dress. This way, with her dressed in pure white and sound asleep, she looked innocent.

Tempting.
Exquisite.
Ravishing.
Forbidden.

THE MAFIA AND HIS OBSESSION PART 1

It made me want her even more.

Tonight, nobody was here to stop me. Igor was dead. Valentin was gone, leaving his beautiful wife for the wolf to play with. He just didn't know that yet.

She moved slightly, turning on her back with her face toward me. So fucking beautiful, it almost hurt to look at her.

I climbed on the bed, curling toward her warm body. I forgot that my suit, my hands, and my face had dried blood on them. I forgot that I just killed a man to get *her*.

All that mattered was that I needed to be closer to her.

Wrapping an arm around her waist, I pulled her closer. She came willingly, her body soft and pliable to my touch.

I could feel her breathing against my neck, her lips slightly touching my skin. In her sleep, her hand glided up to my chest and rested there, right over my beating heart.

It thumped for *her*.

I was supposed to be seducing her, yet I was the one getting lost in *her*.

My fingers curled around her hand, holding it over my chest. She moved closer in her sleep, her legs rubbing against mine before she settled deeper into my embrace.

We laid there for what seemed like hours even though I knew it was only minutes.

I held her, she held me. We held each other.

For the first fucking time in so long, I felt *warm*. My chest tightened at the feeling; my heart drummed just a little faster.

I knew for a fact she would have never held on to her bastard of a husband like this.

The way she moved into my embrace so willingly, it was almost as if she knew it was *me*. As if she knew she was safe.

My eyes found her face again, which was now buried in the crook of my neck. I felt my lips turn up in a small smile. I couldn't help it. It was almost impossible to stop.

My fingers caressed her back, tracing some random patterns. She gave me a shiver in return, and my smile widened. Even in her sleep, she wasn't immune to my touch.

My hand drifted down and then toward her front. When my fingers brushed against her perky breasts, she shivered again, her breathing coming out in a small gasp.

Her nails dug into my chest. It only made me want to touch her more. My thumb feathered over her puckered nipple this time. She wasn't wearing a bra—just fucking perfect.

I continued touching her, so gently, so softly that I knew it must have been driving her insane. It was driving *me* insane.

I couldn't hear her moans, even though I wanted them desperately. Her silence only pushed me into wanting more.

Looking at her wasn't enough before. I had wanted to touch her.

Now, just holding her was no longer enough either.

She was *mine*.

THE MAFIA AND HIS OBSESSION PART 1

And I needed to lay my claim.

Pushing Valerie on her back, I stared at her sleeping face. I smirked in the darkness. She was still asleep, but I knew she was thinking of me. Even in her dreams, I was chasing her.

With my hand on her legs, I pushed her nightdress upward. My gaze never left her face, watching her reaction in her sleep.

Her lips parted again, and then her legs moved, falling open, giving me access.

Myshka, oh sweet myshka, you have no idea what you have just gotten yourself into.

Seduction always starts with words. Seduce her mind and her body will follow willingly without any fight.

Valerie had fallen in my trap since the very beginning. Her thoughts belonged to me the moment we saw each other. Little did she know, I was already seducing her mind for this moment.

My eyes shifted from her face and down her body, following a slow path. I watched her chest moving up and down with each breath. Through the fabric, I saw the puckered tips of her nipples. My mouth watered at the sight.

I didn't think...instead, I just leaned forward and tongued one of the tips through her dress.

Valerie trembled against the sudden assault, and I looked up to see her squeezing her eyes shut. Her fingers clenched at the bedsheets when I moved to her other nipple, doing the same thing.

But this time, I wrapped my lips around the tip and sucked, drawing her nipple between my teeth and biting softly.

Her back bowed, and I chuckled. *Hmm, more...I want more, myshka. This is not enough.*

I wanted her come on my lips. Only then would I be satisfied.

Sliding down the length of her body, I pushed her dress all the way up to her hips. I parted her legs further until I got a look where I wanted to be.

Black lace panties, hiding her pussy from me.

My fingers glided upward on her inner thighs. I saw the wet spot in the middle of the lace, but I wanted to feel it.

My thumb pressed against her core, and I sucked in a harsh breath. Wet. She was dripping for me.

I rubbed my thumb over the wet spot over her panties, and her legs shook as I continued my torturous touch. Crawling forward, my wide shoulders spread her legs wider, and I settled between them.

A forbidden fruit laid out for me—how could I not taste her?

With my face over her pussy, I smirked. *Got you right where I wanted, myshka.*

My lips met the skin on her inner thigh, and I placed small kisses as I went. Higher and higher, nipping softly but not leaving marks. *Yet.*

My tongue left wet trails until I was right where I wanted. I peeked up at Valerie to see her eyes still closed. They were squeezed shut, her breathing ragged, her body shaking—wanting more.

I kissed her covered pussy, my tongue outlining the wet spot before I sucked at her juices. Her body clenched, and her thighs tightened around my head.

I pushed her panties to the side and stared at the

THE MAFIA AND HIS OBSESSION PART 1

perfect sight in front of me. Trimmed blonde curls covered her pussy. I dragged a finger over her slit, parting her pink pussy lips for me.

I spread her wetness more and then pushed a finger inside her tight warmth. Just the first knuckle in, but her response inflated my ego way more than it should.

She creamed my finger, more wetness pooling between her thighs. Her pussy now glistened beautifully, looking perfect and ready to be devoured.

Having a big dick is impressive. But knowing how to lick and eat a pussy right—while making her feel desired, special and appreciated—is what makes you a real man.

You can fuck her sore, but the moment you master the art of eating her pussy and she is shaking like a leaf, her orgasm hitting her so hard that she creams your lips, mouth and chin—then you know you have possessed her mind and body.

And that was exactly what I was going to do to this little mute nun.

I was going to make her sin so bad…and so hard.

My mouth covered her pussy, and she shuddered as I lapped on her cream. Parting her pussy lips, my teeth grazed over her tiny nub before sucking on it. Her back bowed off the bed again, and I pressed a hand against her stomach, holding her down and captive to my mouth.

Her taste drove me delirious, and I was a starving animal, wanting more—wanting deeper.

Valerie tasted sweet, forbidden—she tasted sinful.

Her pussy was swollen as I continued to fuck her with my mouth. She was so fucking wet, her juices dripping down my chin as I dragged my tongue over her pussy lips and then poking against her heated core.

My heart pounded, and my cock ached in my pants. I was hard, desperate for release, but damn it to hell, I wasn't coming until I got her come covering my chin.

I groaned at the back of my throat when I pushed my tongue into her pussy, licking and sucking.

So fucking sweet and addictive.

I felt a touch on top of my head, and then she was holding me against her pussy, grinding into my face. Her body twisted underneath mine as I continued to worship her cunt. I rubbed my cock against the bed, needing some kind of friction.

Fuck. Fuck. Fuck.

I fucked her cunt with my tongue, in and out, and then swirling her wetness around her folds.

Valerie trembled, her body shaking so hard that I was worried for a second. But her pussy clenched, her thighs tightened around my head…and then she was coming. Hard.

I lapped all her juices, licking and sucking until she gave me everything. I could hear her breathing, loud and gasping.

When I was done, I placed a soft kiss on her pussy, and I saw her clenching again. Another kiss, just because.

Her thighs released their death grip, and her fingers unclenched from my hair. Her body went limp, tiny shivers still racking her lithe body.

THE MAFIA AND HIS OBSESSION PART 1

From my position, I looked up to see the most gorgeous eyes looking back at me. I could see the lust there. But it was mixed with confusion and sleep.

Valerie stared at me strangely, her eyes blinking once, twice, and a third time. She gazed into my face as if she were seeing a dream...an illusion.

Her lips were tilted up in a small, satisfied smile. Her face relaxed, but the beautiful confusion I saw there...it made me chuckle.

After kissing her inner thigh, I dragged my body up. With my elbows on either side of her face, I smiled. She smiled back. Valerie was in a state where her orgasm had left her thoughts foggy. She was floating right now, in a happy space.

Her thick eyelashes framed her hazel eyes, and she looked even more beautiful now. Her face was glowing—my beautiful nun was happy. And that made me want to beat my chest like a fucking caveman.

We stared at each other, our gazes never wavering.

In her eyes, I saw her questions.

Her lips parted, as if wanting to speak, but no words were spoken.

So I leaned down until our lips were touching. A feather light touch. So sweet, so soft, so gentle that my heart thumped hard and my chest ached.

I brushed my lips against hers in a small kiss before pulling away and staring into her eyes again. They were half closed, and I caressed her cheek with my thumb.

After minutes of silence, I finally spoke slowly.

"It's okay. It's a dream, *myshka*. Just a beautiful dream."

And she smiled, as if she knew it was…a dream.

Her eyes fluttered closed, the smile on her lips still there.

She was awake when I fucked her cunt with my tongue, but after her orgasm, in her dreamlike state, it was easy to manipulate her thoughts. Make her believe something else.

It's my secret, Valerie.

What just happened could get us killed…so for now, only I would know the truth.

Shifting away from her body, I dragged her dress back down and made sure she was covered properly. After pulling the comforter nicely around her body, I stood up and stared down.

I just stared at the exquisite sight in front of me.

After a long time, I finally forced myself to take a step back. And then another and another, until I was against the door.

Giving Valerie a final glance, I walked out and closed the door behind me. My cock was still hard and aching. I winced at the discomfort.

Looking down at myself, I shook my head and laughed.

I was covered in a dead person's dried blood yet I just ravaged the pussy of the woman I couldn't stop thinking about. I came at her like a starved mate, and fuck it if I didn't want to do it again.

I stared at the door, not wanting to walk away.

My hand came up, my fingers touching my lips. I could still smell her, her scent all over me, and I fucking loved it.

I licked my lips…I could still taste her. My cock throbbed painfully.

I wanted more.

One taste was never going to be enough.

One taste and there was no turning back.

One taste—that was all I needed to get me addicted.

Chapter 21

Valerie

I woke up feeling sated and completely confused. My mind was disoriented, and I laid on my back for several minutes, just trying to calm my breathing.

My eyes stayed closed. I refused to open them and face whatever was waiting for me early in the morning.

My shame.

Another secret.

I pressed my legs together and felt a lone tear run down my cheek. The spot between my thighs was sticky and drenched with pleasure I shouldn't have felt, yet here I laid, on my bed, filled with an all-consuming, forbidden feeling.

I squeezed my eyes at the reminder, my dream still replaying in my head over and over again. It felt so real. I had been so sure it was real.

His touch—his lips kissing me, his fingers caressing my skin, they all felt so real. As if he were right here touching me. Holding me. Making love to me.

It's okay. It's a dream, myshka. Just a beautiful dream.

I had confused my fantasy with reality. How can this be anything other than a dream?

Something so beautiful and as surreal as this couldn't be anything *but* a dream.

My eyes fluttered open, and I placed a palm over my racing heart, feeling each desperate, lonely thud. I have lived a cruel fate for a long time, so Viktor making love to me was something I could only dream of.

Rolling over to my side, I cuddled closer into my pillows. The sun was shining into my room, basking it with a beautiful morning glow. I stared at the landscape, wishing for so many things that didn't belong to me.

But no matter how much I wished upon a star, I continued living the life I was never meant to live.

I continued living as Valentin Solonik's wife. It was my identity now.

At the thought, my hand came up to swipe the wet trail that my tear left. In a matter of days, Viktor had made me weak in the most dangerous way.

He made my heart and body weak.

With only a word and a fleeting touch, Viktor had me under his thumb, controlling me every way he wanted, even when he wasn't here.

Not even Valentin had that type of power over me. The only reason my *husband* was able to control me was by using my family as my weakness.

Their safety was compromised, and in order to keep them safe and breathing, I sacrificed myself. I handed myself over on a silver platter to the devil and told him *it was okay to do whatever he wanted with me.*

As long as my family was safe.

I was the debt my family couldn't pay.

I was the unwilling collateral until I became willing.

Years ago, I promised myself that I wouldn't get weak. Ever. No matter what Valentin did to me, I would stand up on my two feet and repeat the day again.

But the moment my gaze met Viktor's, everything changed. Whatever resolve I had and the wall I had built around me, it came crumbling down until nothing was left but dust and the disaster in its wake.

One look was enough to make my heart beat just a little faster.

Viktor has weaved his way into my unwelcome heart, and no matter how hard I tried, I couldn't remove him.

He was just as deadly as the Devil, if not worse.

From the corner of my eyes, I saw movement in my room. I startled into a sitting position while holding a comforter to my heaving chest. In my fright, I saw a woman standing by my bed, holding a tray in her hand.

My eyes scanned the room, searching for Igor. He was the one who always brought me my food. Nobody else was allowed in the room, except on

THE MAFIA AND HIS OBSESSION PART 1

Valentin's command.

An unsettling feeling made its way in my heart, and my breathing became labored. A woman in my room, holding my food—this wasn't a usual occurrence.

What's happening? my mind screamed.

I panicked as my gaze met the woman's surprisingly kind eyes. She looked in her mid 40s, her black hair pinned over her head in a bun. Her chocolate skin appeared smooth. When she smiled, it made her look younger.

She walked closer and placed the tray on my night stand. I watched her lips, waiting for her to speak.

"Kons—" she started but then paused. My eyebrows furrowed as I waited again.

"I mean Mr. *Viktor* told me to bring your breakfast," she finally said. "My name is Sarah. From now on, I will be the one serving you. He said Igor is currently...*unavailable*."

That made no sense. Who was Viktor to command Igor? Only Valentin commanded his men.

Worry seeped into my pores. Was Igor okay? Was Viktor okay?

Viktor hadn't come to visit me last night. In my mind, I had created a fantasy where he would visit me and we would talk for hours. Just us. Just our moment. Our secret.

But now, I was left reeling at the sudden change in my everyday routine. What a laughable thought. I sounded almost like a dog—actually, dogs were treated better.

I stared at the tray and then nodded silently; after all, she would only get my silence.

Her feet shuffled near my bed as her weight moved from one leg to the other. I waited, and she waited too, or maybe she was speaking?

But I didn't lift my head to find out. After a few seconds, she moved away from the bed, and I tracked her feet as she walked out of my room. The door closed behind her, and I sagged against my pillows.

The food smelled good, teasing me to try it, but I couldn't get this unsettling feeling off my chest. My eyes closed, and I let my mind wander, overthinking and causing myself more stress. Even though I was shackled into this room, it had been both my hell and sanctuary. During the days Valentin didn't visit me, I found it peaceful here. I had learned to accept my fate.

But Viktor's appearance had changed everything. My normal routine. My thoughts. I was no longer filled with emptiness. It was strange and I still didn't know how to feel about it—this—him. *Us*.

My thoughts scrambled and then came to a screeching halt.

I shivered and then stilled. A gaze fell on my skin, caressing me slowly, silently. I could feel it. Someone was in my room.

I was almost scared to open my eyes, to face this intruder. Was it Valentin?

I forced myself not to move, but the seconds dragged, and I felt...*warmth*. The air felt more heavy, intense.

THE MAFIA AND HIS OBSESSION PART 1

Whenever Valentin was in my room, I knew the feeling—the sterile coldness that came with him. But this time, it was different.

The person who was watching me…it wasn't Valentin.

My eyes snapped open, and I met *his* gaze. Viktor's.

He sat in the couch, in the corner of my room, not too far from my bed. He leaned back comfortably, his left ankle crossed on top of his right knee. Viktor had ditched his black suit jacket. The sleeves of his white shirt were rolled up to his elbows. His tattoos—so very beautiful—adorned and curled around his arms. They were mesmerizing.

My gaze followed every inch of him. He was a big man, tall and muscular. Not overly, but he made my couch look dainty. The room was huge, yet his presence crowded me.

And the way Viktor was staring at me right now, he made me feel small.

When he finally caught my eyes again, he raised a questioning eyebrow. I sat forward in my bed, my legs hanging off at the edge.

He nodded toward the drawer where I kept *his*—and now *my*—pen and the notepad. Reaching inside the indicated drawer, I took them out and placed them on my lap. My pen whispered over the paper quickly as I wrote down my questions.

What are you doing here?

I showed him the paper, and then he shrugged

nonchalantly. Viktor didn't reply. Instead his eyes moved to the tray of food. He looked back at me expectantly. I knew that look.

It was a command without words.

I am not very hungry.

He refused to acknowledge the words written on the paper. Instead, his lips flattened in a straight line. Viktor gave me a hard look and uttered a single word. "Eat."

His arms were crossed over his chest as he waited for me to do as he demanded.

I sighed in response, knowing it was pointless to argue. I wouldn't win this fight. But strangely, instead of feeling weak and helpless, my heart fluttered in a weird way.

Did he care that I had enough to eat, that my belly was full and I was healthy?

Valentin usually didn't care if I had food or not. He never checked up on me. If I starved or not…

I picked up the freshly baked croissant. I ignored the scrambled eggs, bacon, and bowl of fruits while taking a small bite into my croissant. *Chocolate.* The flavor hit me hard, and I closed my eyes. I loved chocolate. It was melted into the croissant, sweet and savory.

I took another quick bite and chewed enthusiastically. This was my favorite.

But my chewing paused and my whole body stilled when the bed moved. That heavy presence of Viktor was now much closer, *really* close. His warmth spread over my skin, sinking into my pores

THE MAFIA AND HIS OBSESSION PART 1

and making me breathe harder. I tingled, and my stomach danced and fluttered.

I opened my eyes and turned to face him. He sat beside me, close but not touching. My lips were suddenly dry. I moistened them with my tongue and Viktor's eyes followed the movement.

He brought his hand up, and the urge to shrink away hit me hard. His dark gaze stopped me. The intensity had me trapped. His thumb brushed against the corner of my lips. "You had a little bit of chocolate there," he said in explanation before pulling his hand away.

I nodded silently.

"Eat," he pushed again.

I finished my croissant in a few bites. He never took his eyes off me, watching me eat, taking each bite, with rapt attention. I forced myself not to fidget, but it was so *hard*. My eyes fell on my lap as I finished my eggs too. I took a long breath, trying to settle my wild thumping heart. I exhaled, and I felt him inhale. We were a symphony, a dancing tune and a matching rhythm.

He watched me as I ate each bite slowly. Maybe I worried that he would leave after I finished eating. I dragged our moments, and we sat there in silence, drowning in each other.

I felt a tug on my head and noticed that Viktor had a lock of my blonde hair wrapped around his index finger. He gave it a slight tug again, bringing my attention back to him. *So demanding.*

Looking up, I focused on his face. He smiled, satisfied that my eyes were on him again.

My lips twitched, a small smile threatening to

make its appearance. He had that effect on me.

"You have beautiful hair," he finally said. Crimson heat rose up my neck and my face. The corner of his lips tilted up when he noticed my redness. "My fingers have been itching to touch, feel it. So silky and so smooth."

Bringing the lock of hair to his nose, he inhaled my scent. And then he smiled. "It reminds me of sunshine."

I was completely ensnared by Viktor.

Still holding my hair in his hand, he nodded toward my tray again. "Finish your breakfast."

I did as I was told. I didn't have the strength to argue, and honestly, I didn't want to say *no*.

Taking a few slow bites of my bacon, I watched Viktor from the corner of my eyes as he continued to play with my hair.

He tugged, and I brought my eyes to his lips again, knowing it was his indication that he wanted to speak.

"Did you sleep well last night?"

My breath froze, and my heart stuttered. Flashes of last night appeared in front of me. Viktor touching me…kissing me…caressing me between my legs.

Oh God.

I was even redder now, blushing, and just a complete shy mess.

He smirked as if he could read my thoughts, but I knew that was impossible.

It was an innocent question, yet…it was everything but innocent in my head. I licked my lips again and then gave him a sharp, quick nod.

His chest moved as he chuckled. "I didn't sleep that well. I was rather...*frustrated*," he offered.

I shrugged, not understanding his meaning. His smile widened, and I saw a teasing glint in his dark eyes.

I finished the rest of my breakfast in silence. When I pushed my empty tray away, Viktor released my hair. I felt the loss deep in my marrow.

I watched as he stood up in front of me, reaching inside the pocket of his black slacks. He took something out. Pushing his hand out to me, he opened his fist. In the middle of his palm was a small paper origami. It was white and orange. *Beautiful.*

Looking up at him in surprise, I waited for his explanation. "Take it. It's yours."

My lips parted with a silent gasp. He took my clenched fist in his other hand and forced my fingers open before placing the origami into my palm.

I held the fragile little thing. It was delicate and easily crushable. Scrambling for my paper and pen, I quickly wrote my words.

You made this? For me?

Viktor nodded. "Yes. I made it. For you."

A gift. Viktor gave me another gift. First his pen, and now *this*.

What is it?

It appeared to be a bird, but I wasn't sure.

"It's a swan."

A paper swan. Oh, how beautiful. I couldn't help but smile.

His words knocked my breath away before reviving me again. "It reminds me of you. Elegant and sweet. Beautiful. Graceful. An unspoken poetry."

Oh God. My eyes stung, but I blinked the tears away.

Do swans make dreams comes true?

He looked thoughtful for a moment before answering. Viktor never took his eyes off me. "Maybe they do."

What does this mean? You giving me this…?

He cocked his head to the side, as if he wasn't sure himself. "Maybe a symbol of friendship?"

I wondered if Viktor realized what he was doing to my heart…to *me*. Hope made its way in my chest, but then it shriveled just as fast as it bloomed.

We can't be friends.

He was so quick with his reply. "You're right. We can't."

His words hit me, the arrows sinking deep into my heart, wounding me. I almost missed his tiny smirk, but it was gone so quickly, I believed it was

THE MAFIA AND HIS OBSESSION PART 1

just my imagination.

Looking down at the origami still resting in the middle of my palm, I pushed it toward Viktor. I couldn't keep this.

Instead, he folded my fingers over the paper swan. His hand wrapped around mine, and he kept the delicate little thing safe in my fist.

"No. You can keep it. Who knows…maybe it will catch your nightmares and turn them into a beautiful dream."

I swallowed, feeling emotional and a little lost. My lips formed my silent words. *Thank you.*

Viktor let my hand go, and I held the paper swan closer to my chest. My gaze dropped from his, and I stared at my lap.

He stood there for a brief moment before he walked away. I tracked his movement as he left my room. Viktor had disappeared just as silently as he had come in. Now that he was gone, I wondered if this was a fantasy too, or did it really happen? Was Viktor really here…or was this another dream?

I opened my palm and saw the paper swan. No, this was real. He was here. He gave me a gift, a beautiful, thoughtful gift. My fingers feathered over the orange wing and then the little white head. It felt smooth under my exploring touch. Giving the swan a final look, I placed it in the drawer with my pen and notepad. Safe and treasured.

Minutes probably turned into hours, and I finally got off my bed. The stickiness between my thighs was partially dry now but still served as a reminder.

My dream. Viktor and I. Us. Together. His sweet exploring touch.

Even after years of unwanted touches from men, I have welcomed a stranger's—Viktor's—touch. I had craved it, and the dream left me wanting more.

I was almost ashamed to admit that I had liked it. I had enjoyed it without the effects of drugs that my husband pumped in my veins to make me feel the forced pleasure brought by him.

No drugs were needed for me to feel Viktor's exquisite—forbidden and sinful touch.

A shameful act in my dream—I have sinned, yet I couldn't seem to mind. When his lips met mine in a featherlight kiss, it was beautiful, and I wanted to bask in this beauty longer.

In the bathroom, I stood under the water spray—washing away any evidence of last night. My chest ached, and I closed my eyes, leaning against the shower wall.

I wanted to go back to sleep, so I could dream of *him* again. After our moment in my bedroom this morning, I wanted more. So much more.

After cleansing myself, I dressed myself in a similar black dress that I wore most of the time. Long sleeves, high collars, and the hem down to my ankles.

I looked like someone in the early 1900s. Those stay-at-home wives, good enough to only please their husbands and carry their husband's seeds in their wombs.

Valentin had made me into this person—someone who once had big dreams to someone with…nothing.

I stared at the mirror and imagined the old Valerie.

THE MAFIA AND HIS OBSESSION PART 1

The one who knew how to laugh. The one who adored and breathed dancing. Someone who belonged on the stage, dancing her heart away to the beautiful rhythmic music.

I had dreams, I had hopes…and then one night, I was stolen away.

I died in the arms of Valentin—and now I was just surviving.

With a final glance at the mirror, I walked away. My room was still empty, no sign of Igor. This time, I chose to shrug away the weird feeling in my chest.

I watched the outside world through my windows, in my room—in my cage. I spent the day knitting, and then I watched the beautiful sunset.

All the time, I was alone. Alone with my thoughts.

Alone with my fantasy—Viktor.

When night fell, leaving only darkness behind, I crawled under my covers and closed my eyes.

And in my dreams, he came for me again. We held each other, his lips pressed against my forehead.

In my dreams—in my fantasyland, he was my husband. And I was his wife.

The dream caused my fragile soul to wail in pain.

***

I opened my eyes, blinking once, twice, my eyelashes fluttering. My room was still dark, the night lamp the only source of light.

I knew it was still night…the dead dark silent night.

But the reason why my eyes had fluttered opened was because of the warmth beside me. A warmth that had seeped into my pores and made me feel warm inside and out.

My vision still clouded with sleep finally adjusted into the darkness to see…*him*.

Viktor, the man who haunted my dream beautifully, lay on his side. He was facing me, his eyes closed. He looked so peaceful, and his face was smooth with no worry lines.

Viktor was a beautiful, exotic man. Beautiful with a rough, hard look that he always wore. There was no mistaking that he was a bad man—not really a hero.

But I liked this villain, because in my dreams, he was my hero.

My eyes traveled down his body. He was under the covers with me, so close to me. He must have put the suit away because he was only wearing a crisp white shirt, which was left unbuttoned on top.

My gaze moved back to his face, and I couldn't stop staring. I couldn't stop looking.

And I couldn't help but touch him—feel him.

My hand came up, hovering over his face but not touching him yet. My heart thudded, and finally my fingers feathered over his cheek, feeling his rough stubble under my fingertips.

I smiled, still touching his face oh so gently.

Viktor didn't flinch. He stayed asleep. My fingers moved from his cheeks to his eyebrows, and then his nose, tracing a downward pattern to his

THE MAFIA AND HIS OBSESSION PART 1

lips. They were soft under my fingertips, and I wondered how they would feel on mine—if we kissed in real life.

Moving closer until our bodies were plastered together, I softly placed my lips on his. Just a brief touch, and then I moved away.

It's a dream. A beautiful dream that I never want to wake up from.

I laid my head on his chest and closed my eyes with a happy sigh.

At least I had this dream.

The next time my eyes opened, I was *really* awake. No longer in my fantasyland. The bed beside me was cold and empty, just like I knew it would be.

I touched the spot where I had dreamed of Viktor sleeping.

If it weren't for the words we had shared, it would have been as if he never existed.

As if he was a figment of my imagination.

But I knew it wasn't. I knew it was real.

Every day, every night, I traced the words he wrote for me.

Trust me, silent myshka.

I held these words close to my heart, and I waited for him to come to me again. The origami was also never far from my reach. I lost count how many times I held it, traced every edge of the paper swan he created with his hands.

It made me weak and naïve—but for a little while longer, I wanted to believe in this dream.

I got out of bed and followed my day. Sarah brought my food. I never saw Igor. After days of worry, I pushed him at the back of my mind. By the time night had fallen once again, I sat on my bed and faced the door.

I waited for Viktor—just like I did the other times.

My face held little makeup; my hair was brushed neatly. I even made two tiny braids on either side of my temple and tied it at the back. It made me look younger—prettier.

Bringing my knees to my chest, I crossed my arms on them and laid my head there.

I waited…and waited…and waited.

In the silence, I waited for my hero.

I smiled thinking about him.

And then the door opened.

My head snapped up, and my heart leaped. I stopped breathing for a second before my lungs kicked into action again, pumping blood into my veins almost furiously. My breathing accelerated, and my lips twitched with the smile.

After waiting for him, he finally came for me.

The joy I felt was too immense, and I wanted to sob. My heart beat just a little faster, thudding with each beat. I felt…warm.

My eyes stayed on the door, waiting for him to make his appearance.

He did.

He walked inside.

The only difference was…*he* wasn't the one I was waiting for.

My tiny smile fell, my heart faltered, and all the

warmth I felt drained from my body. I was left feeling cold again.

So cold and empty.

Lost and scared.

Broken.

The door closed behind him, and he locked it. He turned to face me, and my skin crawled. I fought the urge to throw up.

In front of me, instead of Viktor—instead of my dreams becoming a reality—my nightmares became real.

Valentin stood in front of the door, his heated eyes leering at me.

My husband had come back home.

Chapter 22

Viktor

I stared at the motherfucker's face. He stared back, his eyes dark with anger and the need to kill. He was raging.

Valentin Solonik was fucking pissed off.

And maybe I was enjoying it a little bit too much.

He came home to find his most trusted man killed. But what he didn't know was that the person sitting in front of him was the same one who slaughtered his man.

Too bad, so sad. But Valentin was a little late to the rescue.

Holding my fist against my lips, I cleared my throat and tried to look serious. And livid. After all, Igor was supposed to be my man too.

Igor's murder was a full circle. He was another piece on this chess game. I made a step, I moved the piece to create a path.

Not only to Valerie, but to my game—Alessio's

THE MAFIA AND HIS OBSESSION PART 1

game.

My King spoke. I listened, and then I made my move.

He made the plans; I made the kill.

"That doesn't even make any fucking sense," Valentin snarled, his lips curling back in fury. I saw his fingers tightening around the edge of the table, his knuckles almost white.

I shrugged. "Igor told me he was going to see Diego for an important meeting. He said Diego called with new information about the drug deal."

Valentin slammed his fist on the table before furiously pushing his chair away and standing up. "Diego wouldn't kill Igor. It makes no fucking sense. Diego works for Carlos. And Carlos would never attack one of my men."

"Just because we have dealings with the Mexican cartel, it doesn't mean we are best buddies with them, Valentin." My words brought his attention back to me. His eyes were furious, and his glare could kill anyone on the spot.

But I wasn't just *anyone*.

"If Alessio is the *Pakhan*, the King, then Carlos is no less. Carlos is the motherfucking Head. The Mexican cartel is his. Hell, he rules half of the world. The Ivanshovs deal with Carlos, but even Alessio doesn't want to mess with him. It's the unspoken treaty between them. But you must have royally pissed him off for him to kill Igor."

I planted the seed and watched it take root. Of course, Carlos didn't send Diego to kill Igor.

I killed Igor.

I also killed Diego.

Two birds with one stone. And now we just had to sit back and watch the drama begin.

"Our partnership runs deeper than you think, Konstantin."

I straightened in my chair at his words. *Our partnership runs deeper than you think, Konstantin.*

Ah, there we go.

The secrets—whatever Valentin was hiding. I fucking knew it had to do with the Mexican cartel. I just needed him to say the words.

Every piece we moved on the board, we moved diligently. We moved it with a purpose.

We moved it for a bigger picture.

And the bigger picture was right here. The reason why Valentin was so strong.

"What do you mean? Is there something I don't know?" I slowly asked.

His eyes widened for a second, and then he shook his head. "There are a lot of things you don't know and don't understand. Carlos and I go way back. We have been doing *business* together for decades."

I sat forward, placing my elbows on my knees and giving him a hard look. "And don't you think it's time I know?" I replied with a raised eyebrow.

Valentin lost his angry demeanor. Instead, a nervous look appeared on his face, and his eyes darted everywhere else except on me. He cleared his throat and rubbed the back of his neck.

"All in due time, Konstantin," he said instead, deflecting my point. "Why the hurry?"

I opened my mouth to rebuke, almost fucking desperate now to know his secrets. Fury curled

THE MAFIA AND HIS OBSESSION PART 1

inside of me, and impatience boiled underneath my skin. Taking this game slowly was hard. Maintaining my character as *Konstantin* was even harder. And it became worse with every passing day.

Taking a deep breath, I tried to calm myself before I went ape shit on him and lost whatever progress we had done. Valentin trusted me enough to speak about Igor's murder and for asking my thoughts. I couldn't lose that trust.

Valentin turned his back to me and faced the window, watching the darkness. "If Diego really killed Igor, do you know what that means?"

His words caused me to still, and then I smirked. "It means war."

He was silent, and then I heard him sigh. "No. We cannot go to war with Carlos. And I don't believe this. There must have been a misunderstanding."

I rubbed a hand over my face, infuriated with his reply.

Why was Valentin so sure it was a misunderstanding? Knowing Valentin, he was a man who would not think twice before declaring war.

His most trusted man was just killed—yet he was laying low.

It made no fucking sense.

Either he was a pussy or he and Carlos really did have a partnership deeper than the eyes could see.

"Igor was my man. But I have thousands like him. His death doesn't cost me anything," Valentin continued slowly.

I made a frustrated sound at the back of my throat before leaning back into my chair, acting nonchalant.

"But with Igor gone, Valeria—"

I paused at his words, my thoughts going blank and my heart stuttering.

Valerie.

Her name alone was enough to make me forget everything, whatever game I was supposed to be playing. I was no longer Konstantin; I was Viktor again.

Fuck. Get yourself together.

The Devil on my shoulder made his ugly appearance again, laughing his little ass off at my weakness.

I had spent days trying to get her off my mind. After the night I had touched her, worshipped her pussy until her come was covering my lips, I tried to forget.

I tried to get rid of that heavy feeling in my chest. I tried to forget how soft her eyes were when we had stared at each other.

I tried to forget how she melted into my arms when I gently kissed her lips for the first time.

But women were my weakness.

Valerie was my weakness.

I knew she was awake that night, awake and aware enough to know it was me touching her. Valerie had thought it was real, but then I fucked it up.

While I had her in my arms, knowing I had full control of her thoughts in that moment, I fucked her mind up.

THE MAFIA AND HIS OBSESSION PART 1

Broke her heart and told her it was a dream.

But I had to protect her. Even from herself.

That night, I found out the true meaning of being fucking *obsessed.*

Because after that night, no matter how hard I fought myself, I still went back to her.

I should have stayed away, but I went to her in the morning. She was surprised, but my presence was welcomed. She was the object of my obsession, to the point that I had sat there silently, like a fucking psycho, and watched her eat. It was just a simple act of eating, but I had been completely ensnared.

I remembered the look in her eyes. She had appeared emotional and so lost when I gave her that paper swan.

A gift for my silent *myshka.*

After I had walked away, I told myself I wouldn't come back. Not so soon. But fuck it, I hadn't been able to stay away.

In the darkness, every night, I joined her in bed. I watched her sleep. I held her in my arms, felt her breathing against my neck. She would pull me closer, she would hold me to her—and in return, I would hold her to me.

We just held each other.

She slept peacefully. I surrendered to her embrace and slept too but always left before she could wake up.

I didn't touch her intimately again. Only because I knew, next time fucking her pussy with my mouth wasn't going to be enough.

Next time, I had to have my cock inside her tight

pussy.

The need to take her was strong, but for some weird, fucked-up reasons, I waited. The thought made me smirk.

Waiting always made the forbidden fruit taste better—or, in this case, *feel* better.

"Forget it," Valentin said, pulling me away from my thoughts.

My eyebrows scrunched in confusion. "What were you saying about Valerie?"

He swiveled around and gave me a hard, deadly look. "How do you know about Valerie? Did you see her?" he growled low in his chest.

I shrugged, trying to act like she was nothing—as if she meant nothing.

"I stumbled upon her room. I was *exploring*," I replied slowly.

He nodded, losing the angry look again.

A deep and fruitful exploring. *Just not the type of exploring you're thinking of, you little piece of shit.*

Valentin walked over to his desk and sat down on the chair. With his elbows on the surface, he leaned forward, his expression serious—businesslike.

"With Igor gone, I will have to find someone trustworthy to keep an eye on her," he shared with me.

I internally smiled. *It appears I have won your trust when it comes to Valerie.*

"Why do you need someone to guard her?" I asked, acting curious for his sake.

He blinked and then looked at me like I was stupid. "To keep an eye on her."

THE MAFIA AND HIS OBSESSION PART 1

I laughed, mocking him in his face. "You look and sound weak, Valentin Solonik. Having a bodyguard twenty-four-seven, watching a helpless woman. It doesn't leave a good impression on you. If anyone ever finds out, they would think you're useless."

My words made him straighten his back, and he gave me an emotionless look. But I knew I had hit the target, so I continued.

"Even I thought you were weak. And the moment someone thinks you are...weak, then you're going down." With my hand, I made an act of an airplane crashing down. Just for the effect.

He swallowed hard and stayed silent. I could almost see the wheels turning in his head, my words taking root deep within.

"You don't need a guard for her. A woman like her doesn't need guarding. We can't waste manpower on her. Fuck, she looks as dumb as they come."

The words tasted bitter on my lips, and my fingers dug into my knees, hating myself for even saying those words.

And I hated myself more when I opened my mouth again.

"Please tell me she at least sucks dick good."

Valentin laughed at my words, like we were best buddies sharing a joke. I wanted to punch him in the face and then gouge his eyes out.

"Oh, she does. She's a fucking professional. Her pussy will suck your cock just as nicely." He winked before standing up.

My heart clenched, but I kept my eyes on

Valentin. I didn't let him see my weakness.

I didn't let him see that Valerie—my beautiful nun—was my weakness.

I played the cards right. I became Konstantin, and I gained his trust.

"The image is making me fucking hard, Valentin. Looks like I need to find some whores and a pussy to dip my cock in." I chuckled and stood up. "Or an ass. I don't mind breaking and fucking some tight assholes."

Valentin smiled sinisterly and clasped me on my back. "I'll send a virgin pussy and ass for you. Have fun tonight, son," he said.

I nodded, even though I was shaking with fury inside. "Best fucking idea you've had in a long time, old man."

He winked and then started to walk away. "It looks like I will be having my fun too. Time to see my wife."

Valentin walked out of the door, and I stood frozen—silent. My breath left me in a loud whoosh, and my knees weakened.

I closed my eyes and turned my head toward the ceiling, trying to get rid of this sick feeling inside of me.

My heart clenched, and I couldn't breathe. My stomach churned painfully, and I fought against the urge to retch at the thought of Valentin touching *my* sweet Valerie.

I am sorry, silent myshka.

Chapter 23

Valerie

All the hopes that I had shattered at the sight of my *husband* walking inside my room.

The dreams I had been holding on to—Viktor's touch, his kisses, his gentle hold, everything flashed in front of my eyes.

And then they came to a screeching halt, like I was suddenly submerged under cold water and drowning. In my mind, I was gasping for breath, struggling to stay afloat. Struggling to just breathe, but then I would be pushed under the water again. Drowning again.

Drowning in my own fear and sorrow. I was withering in the darkness.

Through blurred eyes, I watched my nightmare walk forward. He walked slowly, his gaze tracking his prey, his victim.

He smirked so sinisterly, and I shuddered, my whole body trembling in fear and agony. I hated his touch.

And now I hated it even more. Only because I knew how it felt to be touched differently.

Valentin stopped at the foot of the bed. He tugged at his tie, pulling it over his head, and then throwing it on the bed. His suit jacket came off next, and he rolled his sleeves up before starting to unbutton his shirt.

He raised a dark eyebrow, waiting. My heart stuttered painfully, and my training kicked in. My mouth parted in a silent cry as I knew I broke another rule.

Always kneel.

I was going to be punished.

Quickly getting off the bed, I knelt at the side. Sitting back on my heels, I pulled my dress up over my knees and spread my thighs a little. My head bowed in submission, and I waited.

I blinked the tears away and took a deep breath.

Strong. Be strong. You aren't weak, Valerie.

I repeated the words over and over again in my head. Closing my eyes, I willed myself to be strong.

Valentin would break me. He would hurt me. Humiliate me. Cause me indescribable pain.

But I was going to stand up again.

I was strong.

A lone tear fell down my cheek, and I didn't dare swipe it away. I didn't dare to move. My eyes opened, and I stared at the floor in front of me.

Valentin walked closer, and his shoes touched my knees, a silent command. I spread my thighs wider.

I could feel his gaze on my skin, scorching me with its uninvited lust. Disgust rolled underneath

THE MAFIA AND HIS OBSESSION PART 1

my skin, but still, I didn't move.

I waited. And waited.

He touched my hair, his fingers gentle at first. It was an illusion, because mere seconds later, his touch changed.

Valentin gripped my hair, twisting it around his wrist before snapping my head back. My neck ached at the sudden brutal touch, but I didn't wince or flinch. I didn't give him the satisfaction of seeing me hurt.

I breathed through my nose and tried to calm my wild, hurting heart. His smile made me nauseous, and his touch caused my skin to crawl, like thousands of tiny insects were moving under my skin, itching and bruising me.

I bled from inside, from my broken heart.

"Come do your wifely duties," he said.

His words were a slap to my face, reminding me who I really was, who I really belonged to.

Valerie Solonik.

His wife.

And it was time to pleasure my husband.

The fantasyland where I created my own story, where Viktor was my husband—it was just a dream and it would only ever be a dream.

The heartache caused by the realization was painful. I was robbed of my breath. How gullible and naïve I was.

I had let myself get swept away by Viktor and forgot my reality.

Valentin walked away, and I stood up, following after him as he went into the bathroom. My throat was tight, and my tongue felt heavy in my mouth.

He stood still as I started to undress him, removing his shirt first and then his pants. I even helped him take off his newly polished, expensive shoes.

Valentin stood naked in front of me, his leering eyes watching as I took off my dress and underwear.

He didn't touch me, yet I had to touch him. I was forced to touch him.

We got into the shower, the water cascading around us. He reached out and touched my cheek, his fingers going lower and then pinching my nipple.

I gasped silently at the pain, but it was quickly gone when he let go. I swallowed nervously, almost choking on my own distress. My breath caught in my chest as I started to wash him.

My movement was slow, making sure I was washing him properly. I remembered his furious face when I would hurry and mess even this simple task. My lessons were learned in the most painful way.

My punishments were carried out to be remembered and never forgotten.

The horror I would go through as I was made to feel—I felt them every time he touched me. Even if sometimes his touch was gentle, I would remember the times when he hurt me.

I remembered the times when blood would pool between my legs after the nights he would use me so relentlessly and unforgivingly.

My task was carried out perfectly, like a trained slave. I knelt at his feet, washing his legs. His length hardened, and I closed my eyes.

The water continued to cascade around us, washing away my tears.

I lost control, but I knew he wouldn't see my weakness. I breathed through my nose and then opened my eyes. My skin prickled, hating what was coming next.

My stomach rolled, yet I continued with my *wifely duties*. Taking his hardness in my hand, I pumped him once and then twice. Even though my ears were useless, I imagined him hissing in pleasure.

I looked up to see his eyes closed, his head thrown back and his smirk in place. My chest tightened, and my eyes burned with more tears as I moved closer.

My lips parted, and I took his cock in my mouth.

Heaviness settled in my stomach, and I fought against the urge to retch. His fingers wrapped around my hair, and he controlled my movement.

Valentin took my mouth hard, fucking it without a second thought. I gagged and struggled against the intrusion, yet he didn't seem to care.

He didn't give me a chance to catch my breath as he pumped his cock in my mouth. He kicked open my thighs, forcing them apart. I gasped when he pushed his foot hard against my core.

I tried to close my legs, but Valentin snapped my head forward, hard onto his length, and he hit the back of my throat.

Dizziness consumed me, the world swirling around me. My eyes blurred, black spots appearing in front of my sight. The warmth of the water was almost too much, my body heating, and I was floating.

Higher and higher, leaving the pain behind. Closing my eyes, I surrendered.

My body was limp in his hold as he continued to use my mouth. When his cum filled my mouth, I gagged and sputtered. He slipped out past my lips, the rest of his semen covering my body.

I wheezed for breath, my throat and chest hurting.

Through blurred eyes, I saw him speaking. "Wash yourself with it."

Swallowing hard, I pressed my lips together and did as I was told. My hands came up, pressing against my chest, and I rubbed his cum over my body.

His eyes flared with possessiveness—almost territorial. He nodded in satisfaction, letting me know he was pleased with me.

I stood up and let the water wash away his filth. After soaping up my body, I quickly rinsed myself. His gaze stayed on me, watching my every movement. When I was done, we stepped out of the shower.

Valentin stood still as I rubbed the towel over his body. Even at his age, he was a fit man. In his younger days, it was obvious he took great care of his body. His muscles still were defined, although he had gained a little more weight.

His hair was grey on both of his temples. The corners of his eyes wrinkled, and now he was keeping a beard. He was a handsome man, and I knew he was even handsomer when he was

THE MAFIA AND HIS OBSESSION PART 1

younger.

But sometimes beauty was only for the eyes. The outward appearance was pointless compared to the inner self of a person.

What was outside beauty when one held no inside beauty?

Valentin showed me the truth. He was a monster in disguise, and as long as I played the prey in this game, I had a chance at staying alive.

I snapped out of my thoughts when he gripped my cheeks and pulled me closer. His lips slammed on mine, kissing me hard, brutally. His teeth bit down on my plump lips, drawing blood.

He licked the droplets, his fingers digging into my skin. His grip on my jaw hardened to the point of pain, and I was almost scared he would shatter my bones.

The bruising grip didn't relent, and he was walking us backward, out of the bathroom and into the bedroom. He continued kissing me. I stayed lifeless in his arms, refusing to return his kiss.

When his lips released mine, his hand pushed down on my shoulders. I sank to my knees without a second thought.

I watched him walk away and retrieve something from the chair, something that wasn't there before. He must have placed it there when he walked in.

I had been too lost to notice.

With the box in his hands, he sat on the bed in front of me. Valentin opened it, showing me the inside. My breath left me in a loud whoosh.

My gaze snapped back up and he smiled. "It's beautiful, isn't it?" His voice dropped low, almost seductively.

It was beautiful. Truly.

But the meaning behind me left me shuddering. His depraved thoughts were written all over the beautiful jewel.

"It's made with diamonds and sapphire. The most expensive crystals just for you, Valeria. Something beautiful to match your beauty," he explained as he took it from the box.

He held the necklace for me to see.

It was thick, and I knew it would cover most of my neck. It was adorned with diamonds, both large and small. Around it, there were teardrop shapes made with sapphire. In the middle, there was a small crystalized loop.

It wasn't just a beautiful piece of jewelry.

It was a collar.

A reminder that I was nothing more but his doll, a pet. He fed me. He clothed me. He made me dance to his tunes. Without asking, Valentin leaned forward and held the collar to my neck, latching it from behind. He moved back and admired his handiwork, his eyes flashing dangerously.

Valentin looked like a man out of control, the beast inside of him ready to be unleashed. His new way of branding me had pleased him.

His finger went inside the loop, and he dragged me closer by it. His next words were used to break me. Completely and utterly broken.

I shattered at his demand, the few pieces left of my heart broke away—the shards lost in the empty darkness.

"Dance for me."

THE MAFIA AND HIS OBSESSION PART 1

I choked back a sob, my chest tightening and my throat working against the tears. My eyes burned, and I forced myself not to cry. How could someone be so cruel?

It was all for nothing. I had nothing left of me.

Dancing used to be my dream, my solace. My everything. It was my very breath.

When Valentin took me, I left dancing in its shielded box. He forbade me to dance, and I was thankful for it.

I thanked my lucky stars, because at least then…something so beautiful wouldn't be tainted by this cruel world.

Dancing was white and pure.

Valentin was dark and tainted.

The two would never merge, yet here he was—destroying another beauty.

Seven years and I hadn't danced—seven years, and I had protected myself. I had protected my dreams, the wings on my back that would help me fly when I would dance.

My head snapped to the side, my cheek aching at the sudden harsh slap. It brought me back to the present.

Dance for me.

A command, not a request.

So I stood up and did as I was commanded.

I danced.

I danced for the Devil.

I danced until my heart bled and I was left with nothing—just emptiness.

The collar felt heavy around my neck, suffocating me. I wore his jewels while dancing for him.

My body moved fluidly and with poise. Even without years of practice, the elegance of dancing didn't leave me.

Dancing used to be my art—an awe-inspiring art. A graceful and exquisite art. A beauty in the eye of the beholder. But as a dancer, I would feel its beauty too.

Every step I took, I felt it. I imagined it. I saw it.

But in this moment, my dancing wasn't an art.

I was dancing for seduction. I was dancing to seduce my husband. A temptress in the eyes of the man in front of me.

I was the seductress, and I played my part.

Valentin devoured me with his eyes, snickering, and I could almost imagine him growling as I moved my body for him.

I felt sickened, my naked body flushed with embarrassment and disgust.

The tears fell down my cheeks, my body growing weaker, my head becoming heavier. Humiliated and degraded to the core, I closed my eyes.

In my head, I imagined Viktor. I imagined being a soundless siren to only Viktor.

I danced.

But now, I was dancing for *him*.

I could see his beautiful smile and his dark brown eyes glowing with *adoration* as he stared at me dancing.

My body moved easily, and I twirled. I twirled and twirled and twirled.

I forgot the collar. I forgot Valentin.

THE MAFIA AND HIS OBSESSION PART 1

Instead, I floated away in my fantasyland to Viktor.

And I smiled.

Another tear dripped down my cheek, but I laughed silently, dancing and moving around the room with the same grace.

But now...for a small moment, I was happy. I could be happy with Viktor. My Viktor.

My hero in the world of villains.

I was breathless, high on an euphoric feeling—and then I crashed again.

Hitting the wall of a hard body, I stopped. My dream ended. My dance halted. And I was back in the present.

My eyes fluttered opened, and I silently gasped for breath. My cheeks felt heated and flushed—my whole body was warm.

But then I met the eyes of my husband. The coldness seeped into my body again.

"You dance so beautifully," he said. "A fucking seductress, making me so hard watching this naked body move around."

I trembled in his arms, but he held on tight. "Does it make your pussy wet to dance for me like this?"

NO! I mentally screamed and thrashed.

His hand moved down my body and pushed my legs open. His thigh moved in between, stopping me from closing them.

With his gaze still on mine, he thrust a finger inside me. Hard.

My lips parted, and I screamed. Silently.

My body shuddered and my stomach churned

when he pushed in another finger. I wasn't wet like he thought. The intrusion was painful, and it hurt so much. Too much for me to bear.

He thrust his fingers in and out, not caring that I wasn't responding to his touches.

It appeared like he was tsking at me. "Scream for me, Valeria."

No. I won't scream. I will never scream.

Silence. I continued to give him silence. And I would forever give him silence.

A third finger entered me. He tortured me ruthlessly.

"Scream for me!" he thundered. My ears picked up his words, faintly, only because his voice was louder than usual.

I pressed my lips together, refusing to give him the satisfaction.

My inside was being ruined, bruised, and injured. I didn't scream. I didn't cry out.

Briefly, I wondered why he wasn't giving me the drugs. Why not play with my senses and make me come using the drugs?

But then, that would have been too easy. He wanted to hurt me.

His fingers left me, and my eyes widened, feeling the relief for only a brief second. Valentin dragged me by the hair, and he pushed me on the bed.

With my front on the bed, my legs dangling down and my ass pushed toward him, he mounted me like an animal.

He slammed into me without warning.

My breath left me, and I pushed my face into the

mattress, my lips opening to silently scream and scream.

Valentin was rough, and I could feel blood dripping down between my legs. His fingers wrapped around my upper throat, and he squeezed.

I clawed at the mattress, begging for an escape. Begging for relief.

It hurt so much, my insides burning and being cut open, bleeding. My whole body was aching, hurting too much to move. He thrust painfully inside me.

With tears swimming in my eyes, I choked back a loud sob. My chin wobbled with the effort to keep myself from crying.

I didn't have the strength to fight him. But I never fought him. I let him do whatever he wanted. I always let him.

The tears fell, wetting the mattress until it was soaked where my face pressed against it.

With Valentin's breath on my neck, I imagined him laughing at my pain and demise.

With his cock hard in me, his fingers probed my ass. I felt him spit on my hole, and my eyes shut tight when he slowly pushed a finger in. And then two fingers.

He worked them slowly at the same time he continued to slam into my pussy. Within two seconds, the slow gentleness was gone and he was torturing my ass with hard, rough thrusts with his fingers.

My whole body was shaking and shuddering, the pain blinding me. It felt like I was being hit, thousands of lashes breaking my skin apart.

And then he was spilling inside of me, his semen coating my inside walls. He held himself still before he pulled out.

I sank to the floor, my legs too weak to hold me. My body was limp and battered.

My head thumped and I gagged, vomit now in my throat. I was shaking with agony and then I retched, throwing up on the floor where I lay lifelessly.

From the corner of my eyes, I saw Valentin getting dressed. When his clothes were covering his body, he walked forward. He knelt beside me, and in his hand, I saw the syringe.

He didn't say anything when the needle slipped into my flesh. I felt the drip…the flow in my veins.

Valentin looked at me, emotionless, and then left the room, the door closing behind him.

I was alone.

In pain.

Shattered.

And lost. So, so lost in this world.

Valentin took so much…until I had nothing.

I am nothing.

My heart clenched, and I closed my eyes, tired.

Finally, the drug started to play its effect. The pain dulled to a point where I didn't feel it anymore.

My ears rung with music, beautiful sound.

The world was colorful and bright. So bright and beautiful.

Perfect.

Just perfect.

I heard birds chirping and water rushing. I was in a magical land.

Floating far, far away.

And I swirled around, dancing to the beautiful music.

"It's beautiful," I laughed. My arms opened wide, and I swirled and twirled.

"You are beautiful."

That voice.

"You are the most beautiful, silent myshka."

I smiled.

"I am beautiful?"

He nodded. *"Your smiles are beautiful too."*

"Then I will smile. For you."

He wrapped his arms around me, anchoring me into his embrace. *"I will make you smile. Promise."*

"Promise?"

"Pinky promise, silent myshka."

I laid my head on his chest, and then we danced together. We held each other.

Oh, how beautiful it was.

Filled with peace, I drifted off—where my Viktor was.

Together, we smiled.

Chapter 24

Valerie

I must have laid there for hours, the drug coursing through my body. Making me feel things. Strange, beautiful things. And I wanted to continue basking in them.

I never wanted this to end—this beautiful dream. I never wanted to stop dancing and hearing the nature sounds and the enchanting music. And *his* voice. *His* laughter.

Viktor was there. Every step I took, he was there beside me, holding me. We were together, and there was nothing more beautiful than this moment.

But just like any drug, the effects eventually faded away.

I was thrust back into reality. The pain came back, my body aching everywhere. I struggled to a sitting position, my vision blurry and my head heavy.

Swiping a hand over my face, I took a deep breath. My muscles protested, but I took another deep breath. *Breathe in. Breathe out. Repeat.*

After some time, I finally got to my feet and limped to the bathroom. Standing under the curtain of water, I washed away all the evidence of Valentin.

I scrubbed my skin raw until I was red, itching, and sensitive. The collar was still around my neck. I didn't dare remove it. I also didn't dare to look at myself in the mirror.

The image in my head was enough to make my stomach churn painfully. I silently wished that Valentin would feed me those drugs every moment—every single minute and second.

They dulled my pain and sent me to a world where pain didn't even exist. There, I could be happy.

Here—I was a living corpse.

The dress I wore scratched at my sensitive skin. The material was smooth, made with the softest silk, yet it still itched.

Finally, I staggered toward my bed. Even climbing into it was painful. I struggled to breathe with the heavy feeling on my chest.

Valentin visited me and left. He took what he wanted and then left.

And now I was alone with my thoughts.

My eyes drifted toward my door, and I sleepily stared at it. A small smile kicked its way to my lips as I thought of my dream—my fantasyland.

Viktor.

My eyes started to drift closed at the thought, tiredness finally making its way into my body. Sleep overpowered me, and I slowly started to succumb to the peace it brought.

But then the door opened.

I blinked at the sudden change and sat up quickly in bed, holding the comforter close to my body. My heart raced, and I blinked again, trying to get rid of the sleepiness.

Was Valentin visiting me again?

I trembled—I couldn't take anymore right now.

But instead of my nightmare, my beautiful dream walked through the door. Just like it was meant to happen in the first place.

My breath was stolen from me, and I gasped this time. My heart accelerated and drummed harder than before, the wings of a bird—wanting to be let free.

The lights were still on, so I saw him clearly. Viktor closed the door behind him and locked it. In his hands, there was a tray of food.

My stomach rumbled at the sight; just now I realized that I was, in fact, hungry. My eyes met his unsmiling face—expressionless.

He was dressed in all black, but like last time, he'd left his suit jacket behind again. His sleeves were rolled up to his elbows, exposing the length of his tattoos. The first few buttons of his shirt were left undone.

With his harsh face, he looked deadly, but I wasn't scared of him.

Because he finally came for me. After waiting for so long, he was finally here. His eyes were trained on me as he walked closer.

I sat up straighter, our eyes never breaking from each other. The room felt less cold. His presence enveloped the room, creating a safe cocoon around me.

He made my heart warm, and the warmth continued to spread throughout my body. Whenever he was near, I seemed to forget everything. He was all I could see and think of.

Viktor really was a puppet master—and I was his willing victim.

He neared the bed and placed the tray on my nightstand. When he stood to his full height again, he towered over me, looking much bigger and more dangerous.

His lips were set in a straight line, and I watched his eyes glide over my body. His gaze paused at my neck, and then they continued in a downward path. His gaze left a trail of warmth until I knew I was blushing.

Finally, our eyes met again. Viktor stepped forward, and I breathed him in, locking this moment deep inside me.

His hand reached out and touched the top of my collar. My heart stuttered, finally realizing what he was seeing.

Viktor was seeing my husband's aftermath.

Embarrassed and filled with shame, I looked down at my lap. I refused to see the pity in his eyes. That was the last thing I wanted from him.

I didn't want Viktor to see me like this—weak and lost.

My nails dug into my palms as I stared straight ahead, wishing he would leave. But also secretly wishing he would stay—with me.

My feelings were a ball of confusion. But when

his fingers trailed up toward my chin and he turned my head toward him—our eyes meeting in silence—my feelings were clear as day.

I really did want him to stay—and hold me. I wanted my dreams to be real.

His other hand came up, and he touched his lips. My gaze immediately went there to see him speaking.

"Are you hungry?"

I shrugged, waiting for him to continue. "I brought you food. You should eat."

He didn't wait for my answer. Instead, he released me and then placed the tray on my lap. He nodded toward the food with a raised eyebrow, waiting while crossing his arms over his chest.

Viktor didn't seem like a man who waited for answers. He took and did whatever he wanted, expecting the others to listen and submit. He was demanding—his words a command, not a request.

Igor's words resonated through my ears. *He is a powerful man.*

I always knew that, but now I could see it more clearly.

Slowly, I ate what he brought for me. Viktor settled on the bed in front of me. Every once in a while, our eyes would meet, and every time, it became harder to look away.

The silence between us—it was beautiful.

Sometimes there aren't words. Sometimes silence is all you need.

Because even in the silence, I could hear his words—his voice. And in the deepest silence, that was when my heart danced so wildly for this beautiful, deadly man.

When Viktor reached forward to grab my hand, I paused and took in a shuddering breath. He smoothed his thumb over the inside of my wrist, slowly and so softly.

His thumb rubbed over my throbbing veins, and my breathing changed, racing with every swipe of his thumb.

His touch was electrifying, and it made me needy of him. Almost like an addiction.

That thought made me smile inwardly. Maybe I *was* addicted to Viktor. And this addiction was one I never wanted to escape from.

He pushed my long sleeves up above my elbows. The corner of his eyes tightened, and I saw his expression changing—becoming harsher and angrier.

I looked down to see the marks Valentin had left me.

When I tried to pull away, his hold tightened, and his eyes met mine again. Biting down on my lips at the look he was giving me, I stopped struggling.

Viktor pushed the tray away and scooted closer, until our knees were touching. I swallowed against the sudden lump in my throat.

He took something out of his pocket, a tiny round container. I blinked in confusion when he didn't explain.

But when Viktor opened it, I knew what it was. And it made my heart clench.

I looked up to see him intensely focused on his actions. Viktor applied the lavender-scented salve over my bruises. He made sure to cover all the red purplish marks, his touch gentle and soothing.

I have never had a man touch me so carefully before, as if he was scared to break me.

When he looked up at me, Viktor stared at me as if I was someone precious. Like he *truly* cared. And I believed it.

I believed the look in his eyes, and I held it close to my heart.

Viktor rolled up the sleeve on my other arm to check the damage too. This one had fewer bruises, but he still took care of them so sweetly. He didn't say a word—not that he needed to.

His hand trailed down toward my hips. His touch left me shivering, even though I felt hot.

Viktor looked at me questioningly, and I swallowed nervously. Pulling away, I rummaged through my drawer. Finally, I could use his pen and my notepad again.

Without another look at him, I quickly scribbled down.

Thank you. I will do the rest.

Viktor's hold grew tighter around my hips, but then he let go…only to touch the top of my collar. I knew it was bruising badly where Valentin had gripped my throat.

Viktor continued his gentle care. Dipping his finger into the salve, he brought his hand to my neck, slowly applying it to my itching, flaming skin.

His hand trailed across the collar, and his eyes grew darker. I wondered what was going on through

THE MAFIA AND HIS OBSESSION PART 1

his head.

In my dreams, he stole me away from here.

Would he do the same in reality?

Our eyes connected, and of my own accord, I moved closer. Like our bodies weren't our own anymore, we moved toward each other—so close, almost touching.

His lips were inches from mine, his fingers lingering over my neck, his touch featherlight. So different from Valentin's.

My eyes fluttered closed, but Viktor pulled away. He rubbed a hand over his face, looking frustrated for a second.

I missed his touch instantly, and I shook my head, trying to clear the web of thoughts. Thoughts of *him*—and us.

Viktor squeezed his hands into fists, his jaw and body locked tight. Hating the tortured expression on his face, I took the notepad in my hand again.

His eyes drifted toward it, and he waited for me to write.

Why are you here?

It appeared like he was clearing his throat, and then he was speaking. I watched his lips, listening to his words through the silence.

"Valentin came back, and I knew—" He paused and then sighed. "I wanted to see if you were okay."

I wasn't okay before, but I think I am now.

With a heavy heart, I stared at my lap, staring at the pen pressed against the paper. I had replied without thinking. The truth has spilled out, and when I looked up, Viktor's eyes meeting my own—I saw him truly looking at me.

I knew he wasn't just seeing a face.

He was seeing my soul, because I chose to bare it to him.

Viktor opened his mouth, and then he closed it again, as if he was lost for words. Wanting him to continue speaking, I scribbled down on the paper.

Where is Valentin?

He took my free hand in his and then spoke. "He is drunk and passed out."

Is that why you are here? Because he is passed out?

Viktor nodded without saying a word. I didn't know what to say either. We both knew it was wrong—this was wrong. So wrong, yet we continued to play this game.

His fingers entwined with mine. "Valerie, I am sorry—"

I lurched forward, dropping the notepad and pen on the bed as I covered his mouth with my free hand, stopping his tirade of words.

I was on my knees beside him on the bed. In this position, I towered over him a little. Viktor had to look up into my eyes, and I hope he saw all my unsaid words.

THE MAFIA AND HIS OBSESSION PART 1

His fingers tightened around mine, and he pulled me closer, our chests touching, our breathing harsher. My heart pounded as I stared into his dark brown eyes. My chest heaved with each labored breath.

I wanted to succumb to his embrace and forget everything. My palm stayed on his lips, our eyes looking, searching—doing the talking for us.

Finally, he moved. The mattress bent under his weight as his body came even closer. Until the other side of my hand was pressed against my lips.

My body locked tight, my eyes widening. Viktor watched my reaction—his focus only on me.

I gasped, my lips parting and touching my own hand. I felt his lips move against my palm, placing the smallest kiss there.

For a brief moment, I wondered what if his lips were on mine—what it would feel like.

But just as sudden as the thought was, I quickly pushed it away.

I knew Viktor saw the indecisiveness in me. His hold on my hand grew tighter, and he pulled me forward until I was tumbling into his lap.

My head twirled—he was everywhere and everything. He was everything I could feel. And he was making me want it—want him.

Closing my eyes, I took a deep breath and then let go. I released him and pulled away. Viktor let go too, his arms falling to the bed—empty and no longer holding me.

I took the notepad and furiously started writing. The tears blurred my vision, but I spoke only the truth—my truth.

The truth that could end us.

This is wrong. I am married.

Chapter 25

Viktor

The truth stared right at me, glaring. I fought against the urge to scrunch the paper up and throw it away. And then I wanted to shake some sense into Valerie.

This is wrong. I am married.

I mentally laughed. Married? Fuck no. She was married by name, but it fucking meant nothing.

Valentin only wanted to corrupt her innocence—mold her into something she wasn't.

I had been way past raging when I walked into Valerie's room. In her presence, little by little—I felt myself warming up again.

But now, I remembered everything Valentin said.

He had stumbled into the library, holding a bottle of rum in his hand. It was probably his second or third bottle, because he was drunk enough to fall flat on his ugly face.

His drunken words—it snapped something in

me. For a moment, I had almost forgotten that I was supposed to be Konstantin.

Tightest pussy ever.
You gotta try it sometime.
Best lay I ever had.
Made her bleed. Sweetest fucking thing.
Maybe I'll fuck her ass tomorrow.
Collared the little bitch. Made her my whore.

He told me in detail how he broke her and how he intended to break her more.

I sat there—listening, raging, and wishing I could give him the worst death.

If he thought hell would be his final destination, his final death—then he needed to rethink, because by the time I was done with him, hell would be his heaven.

He was going to beg me to send him there—but I wouldn't.

The marks he left on Valerie, he needed to feel those marks ten times worse.

I knew my *silent myshka* would be hurting—my heart clenching and my chest hurting at the mere thought.

When Valentin fell into his drunken slumber, I couldn't wait anymore.

And now—I just wanted to hold her.

I glanced at her written words again and up at her face. Her hazel eyes, they were filled with so much sadness. As if saying the words had broken something in her.

It might have been the truth—but we could turn this wrong into something right.

Only if she was willing.

THE MAFIA AND HIS OBSESSION PART 1

"Do you want me to leave?" I asked, hoping and wishing she would say *no*.

Valerie looked down at the paper again, and I saw her tear fall. A single drop, wetting the paper, right over the word *"wrong."*

She looked up, another tear trailing down her cheek. Her tears were my undoing. They had the power to break me.

Valerie didn't answer. She bit on her lips and looked down again, her fists clenching around her notepad.

I knew she didn't want me to go—but I needed her to make a choice.

Standing up, I gave her a final glance and turned around—walking away.

I was crossing the middle of the room when I heard rustling and then feet padding quickly across the room. I swiveled around, just in time to catch Valerie in my arms.

She wrapped her arms around my waist, holding on tight. I blinked in shock, my body frozen in place. I could only hold her in my embrace.

It was almost in slow motion as she went on her tip-toes, moving closer until our lips were inches apart.

And then she closed the little distance between our lips.

She kissed me. Slowly and softly. So gently. A chaste kiss, just our lips touching, meeting, and making slow, sweet love.

It wasn't a kiss I was accustomed to. I had never had someone kiss me like this.

My lips didn't move against hers, too shocked to

respond. Valerie shyly pulled back, her cheeks red, beautifully blushing. She stared up at me through her thick eyelashes, biting on her pink full lips.

Her chest heaved, her lips parting as she took in deep, harsh breaths. Her arms grew tight around my waist, and then she was letting go.

I let her.

Valerie took a step back, her hand coming up to her lips. She appeared surprised too at her action.

She took another step back. When the distance grew between us, my arm lashed forward, gripping her wrist and stopping her retreat.

Our arms were outstretched. My hand trailed down from her wrist until our fingers were laced together.

I didn't think she would, but her fingers gripped mine back, accepting my hold. We stayed like for what felt like hours—but I knew it was seconds. This was us—our moment.

"Pull me closer," I said, my voice low and rough to my own ears, filled with unsaid emotions. "Tell me not to leave."

Her fingers tightened around mine, and she blinked, her lips parting and her breathing accelerating. "But I am going to give you a warning." I looked into her eyes. "If you pull me closer, I am going to kiss you. I am going to *really* kiss you, Valerie."

I waited.

She stopped breathing.

Maybe I did too.

And when Valerie stepped toward me, we breathed.

THE MAFIA AND HIS OBSESSION PART 1

She pulled me closer.

Another step and my heart thumped harder.

Finally, we stood inches apart. So close, our chests touching—our bodies molding into each other's embrace.

I brought my free hand up, holding the back of her neck and pulling her toward me. She gasped silently and then I kissed her.

I *really* kissed her.

I kissed her the way I'd always wanted to.

And I kissed her the way she deserved to be kissed.

Her lips parted, and I took the chance to explore her. There was nothing soft and gentle about the kiss.

It was a kiss that wasn't meant to be forgotten. Our tongues danced together, swirling, teasing, and making us crave more.

The kiss—it told her was she *mine*.

I deepened the kiss, and she returned it with the same fervor.

This moment, it was intense, passionate, wild, dangerous. And it felt so fucking right. More right than ever.

I fisted her hair, keeping her face angled just right. With one of our hands laced together, her other hand came up to my face. She touched me—oh so gently. Her fingers feathered over my rough stubble, holding me into our kiss.

We anchored each other.

Valerie deepened the kiss, and I captured her bottom lip, biting softly before plunging my tongue into her mouth again.

We were both gasping for breath when we finally pulled away. Valerie sagged into my arms, burying her face into my chest. Our clasped hands stayed locked together, between us, right over my wildly treacherous beating heart.

I didn't believe in fate and destiny. That shit didn't work for us, made men. We controlled our own lives. *I* controlled my own fucking life. It was in my hands, and I decided what happened to it.

But right this moment, against my own beliefs, I just knew this was it.

The moment we laid eyes on each other—this was meant to happen.

Our fates were sealed. Together.

My fingers feathered over her skin, right over her fucking collar. Gripping the back of her neck gently, I made her look up at me.

I dropped my forehead to hers, and we breathed together, lost in this forbidden moment. When I knew her eyes were on my lips, I finally spoke.

"There is no turning back, silent *myshka*."

Chapter 26

Viktor

"The shipment will arrive in a matter of days, Mr. Solonik. I can assure you that. It won't be late this time." The man standing in front of me rambled nervously. His nervousness made me choke back a laugh. Shaking my head, I sat back against my chair before crossing my left ankle over my right knee.

Abram was a few years older than me. His tall figure, dark skin, deadly smile, and scars across his face and neck made everyone cower. He was the *Undertaker*. Yet he was scared of *me*.

"Valentin gave you a chance last time. This time, I am the one overlooking all the incoming shipments. You won't get another lucky chance," I replied offhandedly.

He was Valentin's trusted man. The one who took care of all the incoming and outgoing cargos.

Abram nodded before looking over his shoulders. "*Sluzhitel'*, bring me one the white packets. It's labeled *ZA*."

A young boy, a *Sluzhitel'*, a servant boy, probably around the age of fifteen, came around the corner, a white packet in his hands. His head was cast down, his skinny frame looking too fragile to be living in this fucked-up world.

He handed me the packet and backed away, his head still cast down and still facing me until he was out of sight.

Abram gave me a small smile and nodded toward the item I was holding. "Our most prized drug. Specifically made for our associates. The black-market shakes under its price and dealings."

Already knowing this information, I only brought the white packet closer to my nose. "And who are your associates?" I questioned lightly, digging deeper.

"Many. We have many. The Mexican cartel—Carlos is one of our most important clients. We trade our drugs. This one for the one he produces. Fair trade."

I ripped open the packet carefully, dipping my finger into the white power. It was silky against my fingertips, and I brought my coated fingers to my nose.

Holy fuck.

"What is this? This is the strongest shit I have ever snorted," I growled, taking another long sniff of whatever this shit was.

Abram gave me disgusting smile, a pleased look on his face. "We make the best. Little amount, but the effect lasts longer and better. More money this way. Our clients fucking love it."

How did Alessio not know about this?

THE MAFIA AND HIS OBSESSION PART 1

No wonder Solonik was cashing so hard. The sneaky little shit.

"You said Carlos trades with us. What type of drug does he trade?" I asked. I kept hearing his fucking name. Valentin practically worshipped his dick and now Abram...

Abram raised a questioning eyebrow, looking surprised at my question. "You don't know?"

I stayed silent, neither confirming nor denying. When the silence stretched and the tension increased, Abram finally swallowed and gave me a tight smile. "Aphrodisiac drugs. A drug specially for sex. It is still being tested on—it's a new drug, and Carlos is still working on it."

"The sensation is usually too much to bear. The effect will slowly disappear only after multiple orgasms," he explained when I stayed silent.

I nodded. This fact was known around the black market. Especially the underworld—our own fucking people.

Aphrodisiac drugs. They were used everywhere and on anyone.

But I had a feeling the drugs Carlos was making weren't the same. There was something else—something only Valentin and Carlos knew about and were silently trafficking.

Feeling frustrated at myself, I pushed the white packet away and placed it on the table beside me. I wiped my fingers with a handkerchief and stood up.

More than a whole fucking year—and I was still lost. Alessio trusted me on this job. I was sent here to gain information yet I hadn't even taken a step in the right direction.

"I'll leave the rest to you, Abram. Don't disappoint me," I muttered.

He straightened and nodded. "I won't."

Without wasting another second, I speared him with a final hard glare and walked away. Yegor followed closely behind me. He was always in the background, present and vigil.

"Where to?" he asked when we got to the car.

Closing my eyes, I leaned against the seats. "The estate."

The drugs were strong, just like Abram said. I barely snorted that shit, and the effect was still lasting in my body. I could feel the way my muscles were losing all their tension. My body prickled with awareness, and then I felt light, almost like I was floating.

It was silent and soothing.

Until chaos erupted.

"There's someone tailgating us. Two cars. Black-tinted windows. I can't see the people driving."

My eyes snapped open at Yegor's voice. "For how long?"

"Since we left Abram's warehouse."

I looked behind me, and just like Yegor said, we were being followed. Fuck this shit. Why did my life have to be so fucking dramatic all the time?

"Go north, away from the estate. Lead them to the abandoned highway," I quickly ordered.

My gun was already in my hand, and I waited—the race driving a crazy adrenaline rush through me. Minutes later, the fun began.

The sounds rung through my ears, loud and

clear.

Pop! Pop! Pop!

Tires screeched, and the gunshots were loud through the night. Cars were stopped, but the bullets didn't.

When I heard the doors slam behind me, I knew the men were out and coming for us. Yegor nodded at me through the rearview mirror, and then he was out of the car.

I followed, our guns blasting bullets at whoever those fuckers were. A tall figure crumpled into the dirt as my bullet pierced through his chest.

Yegor shot someone else down. I crouched behind the car and waited. There were shouts, and then another man was down. Another grunt of agony as I shot the fucker closer to me.

I heard someone bellow out in pain—a voice I recognized very well.

"Yegor!" I roared, coming out from behind the car. My bullet was tearing through the head of the bastard who shot my man.

Fuck! How many men were there?

My blood coursed furiously through my body. I was aiming at the next man when someone grabbed my ankle and yanked me down.

I aimed my gun behind me, but the punch that landed on the side of my head blinded me for a second.

Another shot rang through the air. I saw Yegor struggling to sit up and knew he just saved my life.

With a snarl, I twisted around and grabbed the man by his neck. I pulled his body under mine before landing a punch in his face. Yegor's bullet had pierced his stomach, but he was still alive.

"Seriously?" I snapped, looking down at my now blood-covered clothes. "Are you kidding me?"

The man shuddered when I turned my glare on him. "And here I was thinking of not taking a shower tonight."

Landing another punch on his already broken nose, more blood squirted. "But I have no choice with your dirty fucking blood on me now."

Another punch in his pathetic ugly face. "Do you know how fucking hard it is to get in the shower after a long ass day, when you could be doing something better instead? Maybe in bed sleeping."

This time I landed a punch on his ribs. "Or better yet, eating an appetizer, breakfast, lunch and dinner. Also known as pussy."

"Seriously?" Yegor wheezed from behind me. "At this time?"

"Italian pussy. Blonde pussy. Red pussy. Black pussy. Russian pussy. Hell, give me any pussy and I will be a happy man," I growled.

"Are you going through pussy withdrawal?" My man laughed.

"Also known as pussy starvation," I mumbled back before breaking my captor's face again.

I had never gone this long without sex. For the past few weeks, my dick has only known my hand. Poor guy was about to call it quits on me and probably shrink a few inches as my punishment.

At the thought of pussy, Valerie's face flashed before my eyes.

I shook my head to clear my throat. Now was not the time to think of my beautiful nun.

THE MAFIA AND HIS OBSESSION PART 1

I turned my attention to the bloodied man—the only one left in this attack. "Who sent you?"

He gurgled something and then spat blood out with two broken teeth. Tsk tsk. Poor baby.

"...Carlos..."

I barely heard the name through his vicious coughing, but then he said it again. And this time, my body went cold.

Well, shit.

"Why?" I snarled into his face.

He smiled—and then brought his hand up. The moment was quick and I couldn't stop him. He placed the pill between his lips and bit down.

I reacted before he could take his last breath. Taking my gun, I shot him. Right between his eyes.

"I own your fucking death."

I stood over the dead body and gave Yegor a look. "Valentin doesn't need to know about this."

He nodded silently and limped away to inspect the mess.

Carlos knew. He fucking knew the truth.

I rolled my neck from left to right and took a deep breath. This was the moment where I wished I had taken those drugs from Abram. I needed the strongest shit to get over this.

Taking my phone out of my pocket, I went to make a call—someone to clean this up. Instead my attention was diverted to something else—or someone else.

A paper fell out from my pocket. I picked it up and stared at the beautiful penmanship.

I couldn't help it. A small smile curved up my lips as I read the words.

You don't scare me.

Valerie's words.

She wrote it down when we were speaking. After she fell asleep, I stole the paper.

Valerie was everywhere—consuming me. Every fucking waking hour. In my thoughts. In my dreams. She was deep under my skin.

It has been three weeks since our kiss in her bedroom. Three weeks since we both fell into this trap and didn't do anything to escape from it.

We kept falling deeper—until there was no fucking escape.

Taking a deep breath, I straightened up and placed the paper back into my pocket. Safe—like always.

I walked away from the dead bodies and smiled at the realization. I didn't need any of those fucked up drugs.

Valerie was my drug.

"Time to see my girl."

Chapter 27

Valerie

I walked out of the bathroom, braiding my hair at the same time. My feet stalled when I found Viktor in my room.

His back was to me while he faced the wide windows. His hands were clasped behind his back, his figure looking very intimidating.

His presence took over my room, a deadly, strong presence that made me shiver in both apprehension and anticipation. Viktor could be frightening. But he didn't scare me like Valentin did.

Only because Viktor had proved he didn't want to hurt me.

After our first kiss three weeks ago, Viktor and I have grown closer—closer than I could ever imagine. What I used to think and could only dream of…it slowly became my reality. He visited me almost every night.

When Valentin would come for me, those nights

were filled with horror.

But the moment Viktor walked through the doors, my pain would vanish and he would cocoon me in his warmth.

His embrace kept me strong. His gentle kisses made me feel treasured. His soft looks made me feel beautiful—at the end of each night, he made my soul sing.

I thought in my dreams we were beautiful.

But I realized, in reality, together we were even more beautiful.

Viktor turned around to face me, his back now to the dark night. The lights were off too, only the nightlamp casting a glow around the room. His face was visible in the small soft light.

He appeared darker and meaner. More vicious. Dangerous. His face was expressionless, barely a smile there.

His eyes bored into mine, fixing me onto the stop. I couldn't move. Viktor walked toward me, stealthily. Almost like he was tracking his prey in the dark.

I licked my lips before biting down nervously. He stopped in front of me; we were less than an inch apart. Our bodies were so close together.

Closing my eyes, I leaned into him. His warmth enveloped me, shielding me from any coldness from this messy world.

Viktor's arm wrapped around my waist, and he pulled me into his body. I felt his fingers on my neck, drifting up, and then he was pulling my lips from between my teeth.

He thumbed my lips roughly, and then his lips

THE MAFIA AND HIS OBSESSION PART 1

descended on mine. Viktor kissed me so softly and oh so sweetly.

It was hard to believe. A man like him, unbreakable—to kiss as if he was scared to break me.

As he pulled away slightly, I opened my eyes and we stared into each other.

Viktor and I—together we glowed. Just like the moonlight shone in the dark sky, our light illuminated this dark world.

Even though our ending was not a guaranteed happy ending, we still chased it.

Viktor gave me a half smile, the corner of his lips turning up in a small smirk. His other hand wrapped around my waist, and he lifted me up high.

I laughed silently, holding on to his shoulders as he carried us to the bed. He laid me in the middle and climbed beside me. When he placed the notepad and pen between us, my smile widened.

This was our moment. We would talk about nothing and everything. We shared the little things in our lives. Small happy moments. He would find ways to make me smile—and that was all that mattered.

"How are you today?" he asked.

I am better, now that you are here.

Valentin didn't visit me today. I was thankful for that, only because I didn't want him to taint whatever Viktor and I had.

When he would visit me, I wasn't my own afterward. I knew Viktor hated it—he loathed it. If he could, he would have killed Valentin.

I knew that—but I also knew he was helpless.

I didn't know Viktor's reasons, he wouldn't tell me, but whatever they were—I understood.

I understood because I was just as helpless.

Viktor dragged a finger through my hair, and I moved closer, laying my head on his chest. He held me while I bathed in his smell.

Except something was different.

Pulling away, I found my notepad and pen again.

You smell like blood.

Viktor froze, and his arm tightened around my hips, his fingers digging into my flesh. I winced, and he quickly let go. He breathed out, and his lips twisted ruefully.

"Yes. You are right. I smell like blood," he replied.

I swallowed nervously, blinking up at him through the darkness.

Did you hurt someone?

He read my words and then stared at me unblinkingly before opening his mouth to speak again. "I didn't just *hurt* someone. I killed someone. Not one. Four men."

The news stole my breath away. I knew the type of man Viktor was. He wasn't exactly a Prince Charming, although I liked to think of him as one.

He was a killer—as dangerous as a crime lord.

But I didn't expect him to say those words as if he didn't care, almost heartlessly.

"Valerie, I do things you will hate. I kill men for a living. You knew that before, then why that expression on your face? Why did you just lose this beautiful smile I love so much?"

His thumb caressed my cheek softly, his eyes never leaving mine. Viktor touched the corner of my lips. "Smile for me, silent *myshka*."

I imagined his voice soft and smooth as he said those words. Like I always knew, he was the puppet master. And he manipulated my fragile heart with his words.

"Your smiles are beautiful too."
"Then I will smile. For you."
"I will make you smile. Promise."
"Promise?"
"Pinky promise, silent myshka."

I remembered those words—his voice ringing through my ears. The dream I had after Valentin had drugged me.

Taking the pen in my hand again, I quickly scribbled down.

You said that my smiles are beautiful. In my dream.

He looked down at the paper and then smiled. "They are, Valerie."

Swallowing nervously, I wrote down my next words.

Then I will smile. For you.

I stared at his face, watching his eyes move over the words. I watched his reaction, waiting and waiting.

Finally, our gazes met again. His appeared darker, unreadable. He stared at me for a moment, his expression so serious. My heart thumped hard, and my veins throbbed in my neck.

Maybe this was a mistake. Maybe my words were a mistake.

But his fingers threaded through my hair, fisting the strands around his hand. I sucked in a harsh breath. He pulled me closer and claimed my lips hard.

A hard kiss—a promise.

Viktor pulled away, his lips so close to my ear. I felt him talk, although his words were soundless.

"*...make you smile...*"

My eyes widened, and I quickly pulled away. It wasn't the first time this happened. The first day his voice—barely, but it was there.

This time again, his voice sounded underwater, the words hidden under blankets, but I heard them. Very slightly. Softly spoken.

My gaze went to his lips again. "I will make you smile, Valerie."

My vision blurred with unshed tears, and I sniffled quietly. "I'll be the reason for your smiles, silent *myshka*. Promise."

Through a tearful gaze, I wrote on the notepad.

Promise?

"Promise," he swore.

Just like in my dream. Except this wasn't a dream. It was reality—our reality. Our truth.

Viktor. You make me smile. Always. You make me happy. With you, I feel safe. I feel protected. And treasured...and loved. I feel different when I am with you. Like I am invincible. You make it easy to live in this dark world. I don't hurt when I am with you.

Viktor read the words slowly, as if he were memorizing them in his mind. He touched the paper, and then our gaze met again.

For the first time, I saw all his unsaid emotions. I saw the *real* Viktor.

Not the killer. Not the Prince Charming I liked to dream of. Not the façade he built around himself, the shield he always had up.

I saw the man behind the angry looks. The man with a hidden gentle soul.

Viktor was dangerous. Our lives entwined together in a dangerous path. A wild beginning. We knew what it meant to be together, yet we continued to sneak through the darkness to find each other.

The heart did what it wanted. Words could be silenced. But the heart could not.

Chapter 28

Viktor

I faced the window, trying to keep the anger at bay. It became harder every time I was in Valentin's presence. If the fury living inside of me wasn't for Valerie, then it was for my family.

Alessio.
Ayla.
Princess.

The people I vowed to protect with my dying breath.

Valerie wasn't part of the plan—I wasn't meant to see her—to meet her, to touch her, to kiss her. Nothing was meant to be, but it still happened.

Fate is a cruel thing. It likes to fuck us all up with a huge fucking cucumber in the ass.

And now the game has changed.

Shaking my head, I let out a deep sigh. Valentin was still talking—about the new *business* deal with Carlos. And I was still back to square one.

Every time I asked a question, Valentin changed

THE MAFIA AND HIS OBSESSION PART 1

the topic. Every time I had a lead—it was a dead end. They covered up their tracks perfectly.

I should have known. If Alessio was powerful, then Carlos was just as powerful.

Two Kings against each other. Fighting one battle.

With Valentin not on our side, we were fucked sideways until I could crack him and his *dealings*.

I turned away from the darkness and faced Valentin. He was looking down at a paper on his table, but at my question, he snapped his head up.

"Abram told me Carlos trades aphrodisiac drugs with us. What exactly are they for?"

Valentin swallowed but remained quiet. Stalking forward, I gripped him by the neck, pulling his face close before snarling. "I am done with your bullshit. You want me to fight for you—you want to win this fucking war, but you forget that to win this war, you need *me*. You also seem to forget that this war is *mine*."

He glared at me before his sputtering started. I blocked his airway passage, and Valentin fought for each useless breath. It was tempting—so fucking tempting to end his life right here and now.

Valerie's face flashed in front of my eyes. Her tears. Her pain. Her silent cries—silently begging me—silently beckoning me to be her dark warrior.

I squeezed his throat tighter, bloodlust coursing through my veins. His face turned red, but he didn't lose the motherfucking glare.

Just keep playing, Viktor. A game never stops until there's a winner.

At the end of it, only one person will be standing

and left breathing. And there are only two choices. Me or Solonik.

I heard Alessio's voice in my head, and my fingers loosened around Valentin's neck. I let him go—because a game still had to be played.

He coughed, sputtered, and finally started breathing again. It took him some time, but he swore and cursed at me.

I shrugged it off. "I have given you the reins for too long. Now what the fuck is going on? I am a *Solonik*—and I have every fucking right to know what *my* family and what *my* business is dealing with."

Valentin struggled for another moment before he turned his furious face to mine. "I thought you weren't ready for this yet, but it appears I have underestimated you, Konstantin."

And then he smiled. "You are my *heir*, after all. I was waiting for you to snap and demand answers."

His smile turned sadistic, and I had a bad fucking feeling about it. Actually, about his whole ugly old face.

Valentin got off his chair and walked toward me. He clasped me on the back and then laughed. "Aphrodisiac drug, you ask?"

His laughter died down but not the evil glint in his eyes. "We use them for a lot of things. But the best use…" He paused and then smirked. "Women. They work best on those whores. It makes their pussy so fucking wet. Best fucking sight, let me tell you."

I knew that. I fucking knew that. But that wasn't all. There was more.

THE MAFIA AND HIS OBSESSION PART 1

I stayed silent, waiting. And waiting. Finally, he shook his head.

"How do you think I built my empire, Konstantin? How do you think I am still this strong? If I had followed Alessio like a lost puppy—the *Solonik* wouldn't have been this powerful. You are lucky, my son. Very lucky that I am giving you all that I have earned through years of work."

The blood in my veins froze, and my heart stuttered. My heart twirled because I knew where this was going. I didn't want to see it, believe it, but it was there, right in my face. I should have known.

"Buy and sell."

His words broke through the fog around my head. I clenched my fists and took a deep breath. *Calm down, Viktor. Calm. The. Fuck. Down.*

"You mean human trafficking?" I elaborated slowly.

He nodded, his smirk still in place. "You can make millions in one night."

"I thought we weren't doing this. Alessio was against this," I continued, trying to understand where this was coming from.

"*We* are doing this. *They* aren't. Alessio didn't know, and he doesn't need to know. For a Boss, he's pretty pathetic," Valentin mocked.

Nodding, I breathed through my nose and played my part. "You are right. Their loss. Our gain."

Valentin clasped me on the back again, a proud look on his face—like he was a proud father and I, his son. And when he spoke, the pride was there in his voice too. "I always knew you were the right man for this. To officially welcoming you and announce you as my *heir*, a grand party is being held in a week. All our closest associates will be there."

I was silent, lost in my thoughts—lost in this sudden reveal. What the fuck was I supposed to do now? Play along? Fuck those innocent souls—just so I could convince Valentin? Buy them, use them—sell them?

The thought made me sick, and my stomach twisted. I clenched and then unclenched my fists again, desperate to hold on to the rest on my fucked-up sanity.

"I invited Alessio too."

At Alessio's name, I snapped out of my thoughts and gave Valentin a dirty look. "Why?"

He laughed. "Boy. Do you hate him that much?"

If only you knew…

"A few weeks ago, my man traced a call. Ayla called you," he stated slowly.

My heart stuttered to a stop, and it felt like I stopped breathing air. I coughed and then hid it with a laugh and a shrug. "Just like I said—she fell for it. So fucking easy. No wonder Alessio fell for her. Her pussy must have been an easy access for him." I paused and took a deep breath. "Or maybe it was loose. After all that time Alberto fucked that used pussy."

"I underestimated you yet again." He laughed and nodded in response. Valentin looked pleased with himself, like he had finally won the best thing in the whole world.

My full loyalty—what he always wanted.

THE MAFIA AND HIS OBSESSION PART 1

"I have heard news...that Italian *blyad* is pregnant again. You didn't say anything when you came back," he muttered, rubbing his chin thoughtfully.

I swallowed hard, nervously. Fuck me. We were treading on a bad line.

"I had other more important things," I replied slowly, watching his reaction.

He tsked at me, shaking his head in disappointment. "You don't understand what this means, right? We were lucky it was a *girl* the first time."

Gun shot...right through my heart.

"What if it's a *son* this time? A boy—to take the Ivanshov name forward, to continue their legacy? We lose all our chances, Konstantin."

I stayed silent, my tongue feeling heavy in my mouth. I couldn't speak; no words could be made from me.

Valentin continued, pacing around the room like a caged animal. He told me of his plans.

"Convince Ayla to come to the party," he announced, smirking wickedly. "This *your* war, after all...you can do the honors."

My body was cold, my hands ice as I listened to his words. The baby, an innocent child—Alessio and Ayla's baby wasn't even born yet—but his death was already being planned.

I did the only thing I could.

I nodded.

I fucking nodded...to kill my brother's baby.

My head swirled with too much. Valentin thought he underestimated me...but it was *me* who underestimated *him*.

For the first time, Alessio underestimated his opponent—by a long damn shot.

Valentin looked amused and winked. "You look nervous, son."

Shaking my head, I cleared my thoughts and then chuckled low. It sounded vicious and cold to my own ears.

"No, old man. I am not nervous. I'm just thinking of different ways to spill blood."

"You will find one very fitting. You always do. Make it painful for her—and him. Reserve the best for *family,* right?"

I stared at him, right through the eyes. "Right. You are so fucking right. Leave the best for last."

He nodded. "Good. I am proud of you, son. I know you will not disgrace my name, our name."

Valentin turned around and faced the full-length mirror on the wall. He fixed his tie and ran his fingers through his grey hair. "Now that this is out of the way, I would like to visit my wife. I am sure she has missed me."

His words sent me through a dark spiral mess. My heart clenched, and I found it hard to breathe. It fucking…hurt.

My beautiful silent *myshka*. The one trapped in her tower…waiting for *me*.

I had to fight against the urge to rub at my aching chest. Clearing my throat, I looked around the room, trying to appear disinterested.

"Will she be attending the party?"

Valentin shook his head. "She never does. She isn't allowed to leave her room."

THE MAFIA AND HIS OBSESSION PART 1

"Well, that's boring. I thought it would be fun. Parading your property around, letting everyone see—but no one can touch and have her. If I was you, I would have proudly presented her around and made all those horny bastards jealous. Let them know she is *mine*."

A small possessive growl escaped past his lips at my words. I waited—watching his reaction. Finally, he smirked.

"Well, fuck, Konstantin. You always have the best ideas," he replied, his laughter booming across the walls.

I lifted my chin in acknowledgement. "This will be…fun."

Valentin didn't reply. Instead, he started to walk away toward his destination—*my* destination.

And I couldn't let him.

Not today. I just…couldn't.

I couldn't let him hurt her.

Just not fucking today. Not after everything I had just learned.

Tonight, my Valerie would not feel pain.

"Wait," I called out, stopping Valentin in his tracks. "How about we have a toast tonight? Celebrating our win a little early? I'm sure her pussy can wait just a little longer."

He turned around, looking thoughtful for a second.

I waited…and waited…

I stopped breathing, hoping…fucking praying.

He nodded.

I was hit with a rush of relief and almost fell on my ass.

My sweet Valerie.

"I'll bring the drink! A toast. To our win." He winked and walked away.

I stumbled back and sank down on the couch. Burrowing my face in my hands, I sagged against the seat.

Valentin had dropped several bombs, and I was still reeling.

Our war.

Those innocent women.

Alessio.

Ayla.

The baby.

And…Valerie.

What the fuck was I supposed to do now?

Chapter 29

Valerie

Fifty-one…fifty-two…fifty-three…fifty-four…fifty-five…fifty-six.

I recounted the tally marks again.

Fifty-six.

A round fifty-six.

Fifty-six days.

Sixty days since our gazes first met.

Fifty-six days since I met Viktor and shared our first words.

Twenty-four days since I kissed Viktor for the first time.

I recounted the tally marks again, memorizing those dates.

Memorizing our moments again…and again. They were ingrained in my memories, never to be forgotten.

First look. First touch. First kiss. Every touch after that. And every kiss after that.

Every soft look…heated look after the first.

The burning desire built in the pit of my stomach and traveled all the way to my heart, clenching and hooking there—forever to stay.

I was still looking at the paper when I felt a hand on the back of my neck.

The softest touch—but I could feel the possessiveness in the way he gripped me. I relaxed and closed my eyes, already knowing who it was.

His touch—I had it memorized. My body knew it, and I welcomed him.

Leaning back into his warm body, I let out a soft sigh. This was my favorite moment. When he would sneakily enter my room, and spend all the little time we had…together.

We stayed like this, him holding me, and I leaning into him. My anchor.

Finally, I opened my eyes and turned around. He stared down at me through unsmiling eyes. But I knew, those dark cold eyes, they could be so gentle.

His fingers trailed up my neck, and he thumbed my lips. I shivered against his touch and leaned into him for more. Viktor's forehead dropped to mine, and we breathed.

He closed his eyes tightly, as if he was fighting some kind of demon…like he was in pain.

I wrapped my arms around him, holding him to me. I laid down on my back and pulled him on top of me. The bed cushioned our weight. He buried his face between my breasts and just stayed there—silent and holding me so tight.

We held each other.

Another moment to memorize.

Finally, he looked up at me, his eyes filled with

so many indescribable emotions. Bringing a hand up, I caressed his face gently. He burrowed his cheek into my palm and placed a kiss there.

Viktor then kissed my lips sweetly. I savored the kiss because I didn't know for how long I had it.

He pulled away slightly and gave me a small smile. "You once said you wished to see outside this room. Just for a moment you wanted to step out and explore a little."

I nodded, waiting for him to continue.

"I have found a way, Valerie."

His words made my heart stutter, and my eyes widened. *How?*

He saw the question in my eyes and replied, without needing me to voice it out. "There is a party. I convinced Valentin to let you attend."

My heart exploded, and my stomach filled with wild butterflies. Tears stung my eyes, but I blinked them away.

With Viktor, tears were not needed. With him, I was strong.

"I know it's not what you had in mind. But *for now*, this is all what I can give you, baby."

I palmed his cheeks, wanting him to see my words. He watched my lips as I mumbled silently.

This is enough.

His forehead touched mine again. I loved when he would do that. There was something so soothing in it—like we were connected in some ways. Maybe he felt the same way, because his eyes always softened when our foreheads would touch.

"One day…one day, *I promise*. One day, I will get you out of here. I will steal you away. Forever."

...and I will wait for that day. I will wait...for you.

I smiled and leaned up. Our lips met, and we kissed. We just…kissed.

***

The day was here.
The day of the party.
My dress was placed on the bed.
A different dress from usual.

I didn't know who chose it or who brought it for me. I had walked out of my bathroom to find it on my bed.

It was long and white, made with beautiful lace patterns. The dress was also covered with a few pearls, making it slightly heavy. My sleeves were long but with a cut in the middle. It came together at my wrist. It wasn't high neck. Actually, the cut was pretty low. It was the most skin I had ever shown while being dressed in a very long time. My blonde hair was up in a twisted bun, with a few strands of hair falling on either side of my temple.

I didn't look at myself in the mirror. I couldn't bring myself to. Closing my eyes, I brought my hand up and touched the collar that was always present.

I let out a loud breath and opened my eyes again.
Don't think of it, Valerie.
Think of Viktor.
He is waiting for you.

I walked out of the room, repeating those words. I descended the stairs slowly and felt everyone's eyes on me.

My palms grew sweaty, and I trembled, my legs shaking.

You can do this, Valerie.

A few more stairs…

I caught *his* eyes.

I was breathless. Breathless for *him*. Only for *him*. Always for *him*. My heart danced. Oh, how it danced so wildly and beautifully for *him*.

His brown eyes never left mine.

He stared…and stared…and never looked away.

I didn't look away either as I stepped down the rest of the stairs.

I realized that I didn't have to look in the mirror.

Viktor's eyes were the mirror to my soul. And in his eyes—I was beautiful.

I smiled.

Love was crazy. It was a beautiful madness. An euphoric chaos I never wanted to escape from.

Chapter 30

Valerie

I stepped off the last staircase, and Viktor took a step forward. Almost like he was unconsciously drawn to me. When we were in the same room—it was just us. Nobody else mattered.

But our moment was ruined, like the ashes after a fire, scattered throughout the air.

Valentin stepped in front of Viktor, blocking our path to each other. I stilled, my feet refusing to move as Valentin walked closer, a smirk on his face.

He was dressed up in an expensive three-piece suit, his hair styled nicely and a champagne flute in his hand. My eyes roamed around the room, taking everyone in. They looked like rich businessmen—billionaires. No one would have guessed their reality. The most depraved men to ever live on this earth.

The things they had done—the things they do on a daily basis. Hurting innocent people. Ruining

THE MAFIA AND HIS OBSESSION PART 1

lives. It was all hidden behind a careful, sophisticated mask.

My husband stopped in front of me, his body close to mine. He leaned down and placed a quick, hard kiss on my lips. His arm went around my waist, a band of steel—my body his prisoner.

When his lips released mine, I fought against the urge to wipe at my lips. I stayed still in his arms as he turned to face everyone. My gaze lifted to his lips, watching him speak.

"I would like to present to everyone—my beautiful wife," he said, a huge smile plastered on his face.

My eyes went to the room again. Some people clapped. Others raised their glass as a toast. There were snickers and smirks. Laughter that I didn't hear and I was thankful for that.

I didn't want to hear their degrading laughs and words. Seeing it all was enough for a lifetime.

My gaze finally met Viktor's again. My heart stumbled just like always, whenever our eyes would meet.

He was there, in the shadows, leaning against the wall, a glass in his hand too. Viktor was dressed very similarly to everyone else.

But for some reason, out of everyone—he looked the most dangerous.

He was dark and brooding. A vicious glare and his lips in a firm straight line. An animal ready to strike. A killer on the loose.

And his eyes were on mine. His whole attention was trained on me.

I saw his gaze moving below, and it stilled on

Valentin's arm around my waist. Even with this distance between us, I saw the way his hand tightened around the fragile glass—something that could easily break under his force.

My attention was snapped away from him when Valentin steered me away. We walked to one of the chairs in the corner, and he pushed me in it.

Fear slithered its way into my body at his glare. "Stay."

I nodded and folded my hands over my lap, my feet planted firmly on the floor. It was hard not to shake or bounce my legs with nervousness.

Valentin stood beside the chair, a hand on my shoulder as he greeted and chatted with people. The world around me moved and tilted—everyone enjoyed their night as I stayed sitting, trapped yet again.

Around me, men and women danced—waltzing around the room. I watched everything in a daze, my body feeling heavy and my mind numb.

The man who was standing in front me moved away, and I saw Viktor. He was still standing there—where he was before.

Our eyes met again, and he stepped out of the shadows, moving forward stealthily. With each step toward me, I grew nervous.

What was he doing?

He stopped in front of Valentin and me. His gaze never left mine. A waiter passed by him, and Viktor placed his glass on the tray without breaking our eye contact.

Chewing on my lips nervously, I tried to look down, but his intense stare stopped me. It trapped

THE MAFIA AND HIS OBSESSION PART 1

me in place.

It was ironic. I hated being trapped, like how I was in this chair, yet I didn't mind being trapped by Viktor.

It was something I welcomed with open arms. He could trap me however he wanted, with his eyes, his words, his body—and I would welcome it.

He could be the puppet master, and I his marionette, and still I wouldn't fight those taut strings.

Viktor smirked, and I trembled in anticipation. This shouldn't be happening. Not in front of Valentin. If he knew whatever Viktor and I had, we would lose it all.

From everything to nothing.

Just empty broken hearts.

I couldn't bear the thought of that. My stomach twisted, and I felt sick just imagining being without my Viktor.

My thought was interrupted when I saw Viktor speaking, his unwavering gaze never leaving mine. My eyes widened, and I sucked in a deep silent breath.

"You have a lovely wife there, Valentin."

My fingers clenched at the soft fabric of my dress. *What is he doing?*

Valentin's hand tightened on my shoulder, his fingers digging in my skin almost painfully. I winced, and Viktor's eyes grew darker, murderous.

But he continued speaking, refusing to act on his anger. A part of me was thankful for that, but another part of me—an irrational part of me—wanted him to fight for me.

"If Ayla was here, I would have asked her for a dance, considering she is my Queen. It would have been an honor," Viktor said, nodding toward my left. "But since she isn't…"

Ayla? That Ivanshov woman? The one Valentin always swore at?

But…

Confused, I looked to my left. My breath left me, and I froze.

I hadn't seen him before, but he had clearly seen me. His hard blue eyes were on me, looking just as dangerous as Viktor's. His black hair was smoothed back nicely, but a few stubborn dark strands fell over his forehead.

He was big and very tall, his shoulders easily twice mine, and he was probably a foot taller. If I thought Viktor was a big man and dwarfed me, then I was clearly mistaken.

Viktor had a dark aura around him, all the time—and when he was angry, he was vicious. But this man—I could tell he was someone everyone bowed to. This man was deadly.

And without even asking for his name, I already knew who he was.

This was the infamous, the one and only, Alessio Ivanshov.

And he was staring at me, like I was someone under a magnifying glass and he was trying to figure me out.

He was staring right into my soul, and I shivered, shrinking away and pushing myself deeper into the chair, away from him. My heart did several flips in fear, panic now coursing through my body.

THE MAFIA AND HIS OBSESSION PART 1

I always imagined Alessio as a dangerous man, but with him glaring at me like that, I just wanted to run away.

Quickly averting my gaze, I looked at Viktor instead. My anchor. He would protect me.

He was still staring at me. All thoughts of the dangerous man standing beside me was gone. This time, Viktor extended his hand toward me.

"It is only fair that I ask you for a dance. So, may I have this dance…Mrs. Solonik?"

I flinched, but the burning sensation in the pit of my stomach was only for a moment, because behind his words, I saw what he really wanted to say. I saw it in his eyes.

May I have this dance, my silent myshka?

My lips twitched in a small smile before I quickly hid it. I would give him my smiles later. Right now, we had a little game to play.

My head turned to my right, and I waited for Valentin. For him to give me his permission.

Valentin stared at me through cold eyes, his lips thinned in a straight line. He dragged the silence—the suspense—until he finally nodded. My breath left me a relieved sigh, and I looked back at Viktor. He smirked and raised an eyebrow, waiting.

Slowly, I released my dress from my tight hold and brought my hand up. My fingers had barely touched his palm when Viktor grasped my hand firmly in his. His grip was soft but unyielding.

He pulled me up, and I stumbled into his chest. His other arm went around my waist.

Protective and possessive.

His eyes told me, *"Mine."*

My eyes told him, *"Yours."*

My heart said, *"His."*

Viktor walked us backward, toward the middle of the room. A few people moved out of our path. We finally stopped, and I waited, my heart in my throat and my stomach twisting nervously.

Butterflies.

I had butterflies.

My lips stretched into a smile, and I wanted to laugh freely.

Even in a moment like this, while I could feel my husband's glare on my back—scorching my skin, I wanted to laugh.

Because I was…happy.

Even for a little moment…I was happy.

With a hand in his, my other on his shoulder and his arm around my waist, Viktor started moving.

My ears were useless—but I didn't have to hear the music to dance.

I followed Viktor. Every step he took, I followed and matched him.

We were one.

Everything and everyone disappeared, until it was just Viktor and me. Almost like the whole world had darkened and the light was only shining on us.

We moved around the room, lost in each other.

And oh, how beautiful it was.

Tears pricked my eyes, and I quickly blinked them away. Viktor smiled, his arm tightening around my waist before he pulled me closer.

"Don't cry, Valerie. Your tears are my undoing. They decimate me."

THE MAFIA AND HIS OBSESSION PART 1

My smile widened at his words.

I never wanted this to end.

But eventually, just like any happy moment—this ended too.

Our feet stopped, and I tried to catch my breath. Viktor lost his smile, and he gave me a small nod.

I swallowed hard because I knew what this meant.

It was time to go back to my husband.

Viktor gripped my hand and walked me back to where Valentin was waiting. I sat on the chair, refusing to meet his gaze.

Viktor's grip tightened, and then he let go. My eyes widened, and I pressed my fist against my thighs, my heart racing wildly in my chest.

Viktor walked away, and I released a shuddering breath. Valentin pressed a hand on my shoulder. I felt his hot breath near my ear, and I knew he was speaking to me—but it was useless. I didn't hear any word.

He released me too and walked away, joining a group of men, talking and laughing.

I stayed still, waiting—confused and lost. Not knowing exactly what to do.

Finally, when I knew everyone's attention was off me, I opened my palm.

There laid a small, crunched-up paper. The one Viktor had slipped into my palm before letting me go.

I opened the paper, and I was no longer lost anymore.

Because I knew where my place was.

Meet me in the back garden—10 minutes.

My gaze quickly flitted to the corridor that led to the back garden. It was empty. Everyone was in the middle or scattered around the room, chatting or dancing.

My heart thumped, and I waited.

I saw everyone's attention moving to one spot. My gaze followed, and I winced at the sight.

A maid was bent over a table. Her tray was on the floor, glass broken and scattered everywhere. Her dress was pulled up to her waist, and a man I didn't recognize mounted her from behind.

Oh God. No.

I wanted to lurch forward and scream.

I wanted to scream and stop him.

I wanted to save her.

Everyone watched.

Nobody did anything.

Tears fell down my cheeks as I stayed seated…I didn't do anything, either.

I watched as my *husband* walked around the girl, unbuttoning his pants before gripping the girl's jaw and bringing her mouth to his waiting cock.

I could taste the bile in my mouth, and I fought against the urge to gag and throw up. Snapping my gaze away, I looked toward the corridor—toward my Viktor.

He was waiting for me.

With everyone's attention away from me, I quickly got up and walked away. My steps were quick, my dress swishing around my ankles as I tried to meet Viktor before anyone could catch me.

It felt exhilarating. Forbidden...and my heart thumped again.

I walked outside, just a few steps out the door. The cool air caressed my skin, and I breathed it in. After so long—this was...beautiful.

It was the only word I could use.

Beautiful.

This was what freedom felt like.

And then I saw the reason for my freedom.

Viktor walked toward me, and unconsciously, I took a step toward him.

We met in the middle, crashing into each other's arms.

His lips met mine, softly and then hungrily. As if he was craving me. I kissed him back with the same fervor.

In this moment, I forgot about the depravity that was happening behind us.

I focused on Viktor—on this moment.

We kissed under the moonlight while it cast its glow on us.

Our lips separated, and Viktor smiled. *Beautiful.*

I laid my head on his chest and just breathed him in. I didn't know how long we stayed like this, but in the end, he moved away and we had to let go.

We had to go back inside—back to reality.

A final glance and I walked away—back to my husband.

I walked inside to find the girl quickly picking up her tray and the glass shards. They were done with her. My heart ached for her, yet I couldn't do anything.

I was helpless, just like she was.

Quickly moving to my seat, I sat down and looked at my lap, closing my eyes and wishing I was anywhere but here.

The night went on. Dinner came and went, although I could barely stomach anything.

By the end of the night, I just wanted to go back to my room.

I'd rather be trapped there with Viktor—than here.

Chapter 31

Viktor

I watched Valentin's drunken ass as he sprawled on the bed, snoring like a fucking pig.

He was passed out cold—and I was thankful for that. Maybe drugging his drinks after all had been the best idea. He wouldn't know. Valentin would think he just happened to drink too much and he passed out because of it. It wouldn't be the first time anyway.

He had plans to visit Valerie tonight, but too sad for him, now he couldn't.

I would be the one visiting my silent *myshka*.

Smiling at the thought, I turned away and walked out of the room, closing the door behind me.

Time to see my girl.

After dinner, Valerie was escorted upstairs, back to her room. The party went on, and finally, when everyone started to leave, I could breathe again. Alessio nodded at me and left too. Thank fuck, I told him about the crazy, fucked-up plans. We would deal with that shit later.

For now, Ayla was at home, safe and sound. Just like it was meant to be.

Valentin was stumbling over his own feet, making his way to his room. He drank some more, celebrating our so-called early win.

I walked into Valerie's room to find her on the bed. She was sitting with her knees brought up to her chest, her head lying over her arms.

She looked so innocent like this—so fragile. So pure. She appeared untouched by corruption.

But seeing her like this—I wanted to corrupt her.

Valerie's head snapped up, and our gazes met. She smiled sleepily before opening her arms for me.

Oh, the innocence. She was inviting the wolf with open arms, and she didn't even know it yet.

I walked toward her, tugging my tie as I went and pulling it over my head. I threw it aimlessly around the room. My jacket followed, and finally I crawled into bed with her.

Valerie's arms were still wide open, waiting for me. And like a fucking puppy and an animal wanting his mate's touch, I savored her touch and crawled into her waiting arms.

She giggled silently as I pushed her on her back and laid on top of her. Her thighs opened and cradled my hips between them as I laid my head on her breast, nuzzling between the heavy weights.

I breathed in her sweet scent and let out a sigh, all tension being released from my body. Fuck, this was exactly what I needed after a long-ass day.

We stayed like this for some time, me cradled in her arms while she gently played with my hair. I knew I was heavy on her, but she didn't make a move to push me away.

Eventually, I lifted my head up to see her serene smile, her face soft and filled with so much adoration. I couldn't look away.

So I did the only thing I could.

I kissed her. She gasped against my lips, and I kissed her harder, forcing my tongue into her mouth. Taking what she was giving.

It started with the sweetest kiss until there was nothing sweet with the way we were kissing. Our tongues battled fiercely, dancing, and it was…everything and more.

The kiss went straight to my cock, and fuck me, I loved it. I loved being hard for this woman—I fucking loved wanting her.

Because I knew she wanted me just as much.

The kiss deepened, and the heat between us could probably scorch our skin. She clung to me, whimpering and kissing me harder, as if she wanted to bury herself into me—into my soul.

Valerie's fingers curled around my hair, tugging and begging silently. We were lost—so lost in each other. We were drowning, and I'd rather drown than take my next breath.

And I wanted more.

I dragged my lips away from hers and made my way down, kissing her jaw and neck until I came in contact with her fucking collar.

We both stilled at the same time, our breathing harsh and heavy.

Our gazes locked, and I saw the heated look in her eyes—and through the heated look, I saw her pain and sadness.

Fuck me. She was going to kill me one day.

One look was enough to break my cold motherfucking heart.

Pulling Valerie to a sitting position, I moved closer until our bodies were molded together. She looked down at her collar, losing her soft smile in the process.

I lifted her chin up, our gaze meeting again. With a shake of my head, I touched our foreheads together.

"Don't think about him, Valerie. It's us. Just us. Me and you," I mumbled, making sure she was seeing my words.

Valerie gave me a small nod, but I wasn't satisfied with it. My hand went behind her neck, and I did something I had never done before.

Her eyes widened, and her mouth opened in shock.

My fingers met the lock behind her collar, and I unlatched it, removing the stupid collar from her neck.

Valerie froze, her breath leaving her. My heart was in my throat too, and I could barely breathe.

Her hand came up, touching her neck—her bare skin. Tears spilled down her cheeks, breaking my heart further.

"Shhh...don't cry, *myshka*. Don't cry," I whispered, my voice coarse, kissing her tears away.

Her arms went around my neck, and she held on tight as I kissed her lips again. We kissed as I slowly removed her dress, our lips only leaving each other to pull her dress over her head before we were kissing again.

Her fingers unbuttoned my shirt, and I let her. She slowly peeled it off my body, her hand touching my bare chest. I sucked in a harsh breath and kissed her harder, nipping at her lips before groaning into the kiss.

My pants came off next while I laid her on her back again. Valerie never stopped touching me, her hands roaming my shoulders, my back—her nails digging into my skin—marking me as *hers*.

I wanted to tattoo those marks into my body, for them to never fade away. I wanted to wear those proudly and shout on top of the roof that my woman fucking gave them to me.

"Valerie…" I whispered against her lips.

She arched her back, and I slowly made my way down. I kissed a path down her neck until I reached those beautiful round globes. I took her bra off, and my eyes worshipped her tits.

So. Fucking. Perfect.

Small but big enough to fill my hands. Her nipples were a dark rosy color. My favourite kind. I wanted to feast on them for the rest of my life.

I kissed my way down, toward the valley of her breasts. My tongue peeked out, and I tasted a fully erected nipple. Hmmm.

I worshipped her tits with my mouth, teasing her nipples into fiery points. I licked the hardened buds and then sucked until she was arching her back and practically ripping my hair out.

My lips continued their downward path, tasting the skin of her stomach and leaving a wet trail. Her legs opened for me, and I smirked.

I wanted nothing between us, but right now, her panties were in the way. I shrugged and then ripped it away.

Well, there we go. Nothing in my way now. She was bare for me—completely at my mercy.

And I was the beast who was going to devour her sweet nectar.

She quivered in anticipation, her nails dragging almost painfully into my shoulders. I imagined how it would sound to have her begging for me.

I couldn't hear her moans, but fuck, the way she was touching me, pulling my body closer to hers—I knew this was what she wanted.

I looked up to see her already looking at me. When I spoke, my voice was rough and husky to my own ears. Full of desire for this beautiful woman laid out for me.

"You've got me, *myshka*. You've got all of me, beautiful Valerie. Just wait a little longer. I need to make sure you're ready for my cock, baby. I need to make sure your cunt is wet enough to take me deep inside you."

Her lips parted in a silent moan, and her head fell back to her pillows, her eyes closing tightly. My gaze went back to my destination.

Her sweet pussy.

I pushed her legs wide to accommodate my shoulders, and I settled between her spread thighs, my head right over where I wanted to be.

My cock ached painfully, and I rubbed it against the mattress, hoping some kind of friction would help, but bad fucking idea. My length hardened more, and all it wanted was to be buried deep inside her cunt—fucking her into oblivion.

I kissed her quivering pussy. She writhed underneath me when I slowly dragged my tongue over her pussy lips, parting them so I could probe her entrance.

Her hips left the bed, her thighs tightening around my head. I chuckled against her wet pussy when she creamed my lips with more wetness.

She was so fucking wet that she was dripping on the bed, drenching the bedsheets with her desire. I inhaled her sweet scent and almost came right there while licking her cunt.

Holy. Fuck.

I didn't know pussy could be this addicting. But apparently, it could be.

I lapped at her juices and then penetrated her entrance just with the tip. I sucked at her clit, biting softly at the tiny bud. When I pushed a finger inside her, she flinched and grabbed my head, pulling me closer into her pussy.

Plunging two fingers inside her, I sucked on her tender swollen clit—sending her into a frenzied orgasm. A growl escaped past my throat as I enjoyed the sweet nectar she was giving me.

She writhed against me as the climatic wave overtook her. Wetness pooled between her legs, creaming my fingers and lips until she was drenched and ready to take my cock.

I pulled up and smirked down at her face. Her eyes were still closed, her chest heaving with each breath. Her lips were pink and swollen from being freshly kissed. Her face was flushed and red—she was breathless.

And so fucking beautiful. And just like the paper swan I gave her, Valerie was delicate and fragile.

I quickly pulled down my boxers and settled between her thighs again. Her lips parted as she breathed, her eyes opening. They were unfocused on my face, and a lazy smile spread across her lips.

"You are so beautiful, Valerie. Do you know that? I want to look at you forever. You make my heart ache in a dangerous way," I whispered before kissing her lips softly. "I can't seem to get enough of you, my sweet *myshka*."

I pulled away slightly, looking down at those gorgeous eyes of hers. "I am going to make love to you, baby."

Valerie closed her eyes, her fingers biting into my shoulders again. I kissed her again, and a tear slipped down her cheeks.

Gripping my cock, I rubbed the tip against her wetness before finding her heated core and slowly thrusting inside, pressing into her body.

My eyes closed at the sensation, completely lost in this moment.

My heart cracked and then molded together again. What was once cold turned into warmth.

I grunted as I sunk into her snug pussy. Valerie shuddered under me, her arms tight around my shoulders.

My lips blindly found her again when I was fully seated inside her warmth. I stayed there, our bodies locked together.

I never thought a moment like this could be beautiful.

I never thought sex could be breathtaking.

THE MAFIA AND HIS OBSESSION PART 1

But with Valerie…it was everything and so much fucking more.

She trembled under my body, and then I heard quiet sobbing. What the—

My eyes snapped opened to find hers tightly shut. Her body was taut, tears spilling down her cheeks.

My eyes widened, and my heart stumbled, fear skyrocketing through me.

What have I done?

Panic coursed through my body, and I suddenly felt sick. I thought she wanted this, but did I misread the situation? I thought…the fiery need in her eyes told me she wanted me as much as I wanted her. But…

What have I done?

My self-control had snapped, and I had used her.

Just like Valentin had.

Fuck, I was worse.

She trusted me.

"No. No. No. Oh, my sweet Valerie. What have I done?" I choked while stroking her hair.

My cock was still buried deep inside her. Ashamed and sick to the stomach, I tried to pull away. Valerie's eyes snapped open, and her lips parted in a silent cry, panic in her gaze.

I stilled as she shook her head, her throat working as she swallowed hard and cried at the same time.

More tears spilled down her cheeks, and Valerie—she clung to me as if in desperation.

Like I was her savior…her anchor…her everything.

"I am sorry," I tried to say, but the words were like a rumble from my aching chest. I closed my eyes and rested my forehead against hers.

I couldn't look at her—in her eyes—I couldn't look at what I had broken when I had promised to fix her.

I tried to pull out of her heated core again but fuck—I couldn't.

"...*No*..."

My heart stilled and then erupted with chaos.

This wasn't possible...it couldn't be. It couldn't fucking be.

I stopped breathing only because I couldn't.

I struggled with my next breath, and my eyes snapped open.

Valerie palmed my cheek, her other arm around my shoulder and pulling me closer. She wrapped her legs around me, her ankles locking around my thighs.

She moved her hips, thrusting my cock inside her again.

My gaze went to her lips

Valerie swallowed hard and shook her head again. Valerie took a deep breath through her tears and her lips parted again—as if to speak.

My gut spasmed and my body trembled, my ears throbbing and praying to listen to her. Wishing this was real.

Her eyes were filled with so much pain—but I saw something else there.

She was staring at me like I was her everything. Like I was her whole world—the moon, the sun, the light, the darkness—everything.

THE MAFIA AND HIS OBSESSION PART 1

When my ears picked up the next word, this time I was sure it wasn't a dream. It wasn't a fragment of my imagination.

It was real.

It was *her*.

Valerie decimated me.

She left me bleeding, the inside of my soul scratched and cut open.

Valerie annihilated me.

Her arms tightened around me, and she curled into my embrace, forcing herself into my soul.

Valerie destroyed me.

Her sweet faint voice, unused and barely out of her throat…destroyed me.

"Please…Viktor."

Chapter 32

Valerie

I was drunk, high on Viktor, his touches driving me to the point of insanity. There was no other way to describe what I was feeling.

What started out as a kiss, just a simple kiss—turned into something so much more. I was naked underneath him, my neck bare of the collar that kept me trapped—my soul open to his. Our hearts dancing to the same wild, beautiful symphony.

Viktor has given me pleasure that I had never known before. What used to be my dreams was now my reality. The way he touched me, his hands, his lips filled with certainty, as if he knew how to play me, a master at playing the notes of my body.

A moan and then a groan. A whimper and then a shudder. My body craving what he was giving me—becoming an addict to his sinful touches.

I should have been cowering away from him, but my arms were opened wide. His beautiful heart was tainted—and I wanted him to tarnish mine. With each kiss, I fell deeper into his soulless eyes.

With each nibble on my skin, my body grew soft and pliant underneath his. My legs spread to accommodate his body. The heating core between my thighs pulsed, almost aching with need.

I could feel my dripping wetness, my body working itself—ready to take him inside of me, very much how a female's body prepares itself, for breeding—to take her mate between her legs and inside her clenching core, and for her womb to nourish his seeds.

The pressure deep at the bottom of my stomach built, flooding my mind and body like molten lava. Sweat slid down across my skin, my body warm—too warm. The feel of him against me, rubbing against my sensitive skin, the sensation driving an igniting pleasure between my thighs. My body was hyperaware of every inch of my Viktor.

In this moment, the world could have gone into a dark chaos, casting us all into a never-ending oblivion and still, I wouldn't have noticed. I wouldn't have cared. All that mattered was Viktor and for him to keep touching me.

I caught his fevered eyes when he crawled back over my body. His lips glistened with my sin, the sweetness that had dripped for him and he'd tasted on his lips.

My fingers tangled in his black hair, my eyes staring into the pools of his aroused dark eyes. I could smell liquor from his breath. I inhaled his scent, a masculine, earthy smell, and his unique cologne teased my nostrils. I breathed him in again, the scent that only belong to Viktor.

I filled my senses with him while my hands never stopped exploring every inch of his chest and back. I memorized every indent, every curve, every bone, and every muscle twitch.

His skin was covered with tattoos—my fingers tracing them, but when his head tilted to the sides and he claimed my lips again, I decided that I would explore another time.

His lips were firm on mine, the kiss hard, like him. Male, Viktor, *mine*. My heart had claimed him before, and now my body was ready for him.

Sparks tingled across my skin, and I was breathless as the kiss felt like it was never ending. I could taste my own tang on his lips, and I savored it as he plunged his soft tongue between my lips, kissing me deeper. My eyes closed, kissing him back with just the same passion.

I felt his hard length between my thighs as he pressed against my weeping slit, so wet and sticky. Viktor rubbed his tip against me, coating himself with my cream. His hardness teased my clit, making my empty core clench desperately for him to fill me.

My toes curled, and my thighs spread wider when he touched my entrance, pushing the slightest bit against my slits. My back bowed and I panted, waiting on edge.

Instead of thrusting inside of me hard, like I had expected him to, he slowly pushed himself inside me. Viktor took his time, taking me slow, letting me accommodate to this size. He held himself over my body, his kisses turning sweet and gentle.

My breath hiccupped as I gasped. He thrust his

cock in easily, until he was fully seated inside my warmth. My whole body clenched tight at his sheer size, and I hiccupped back a sob.

Tears spilled down my cheeks as he continued to kiss me—claiming me softly. Just like he said. *He was making love to me.*

My heart shattered, the pieces flying apart.

Viktor obliterated me.

How could a man like him, a man born in the darkness—surviving in the darkness—hold so much gentleness in him?

Viktor thought he was the savage in the dark—what he didn't realize was that he was the savage who brought me light in my own pile of darkness.

Viktor ruined me.

He tainted my soul with his own, placing an invisible bond there that marked me as *his*. He *ruined* me. For any other man. He made me *his*. Irrevocably his. Only his. Mind. Body. Soul.

For the first time, I gave someone my everything.

Viktor wrecked me.

The next time, my husband would touch me, his touch would be erased by the memories of Viktor's. He *wrecked* me. And I wanted more of the damnation he had placed on my heart.

I felt him starting to pull out, and panic pressured over my chest. My eyes snapped open, and my lips parted with a silent cry.

"...No..."

My eyes widened, and I sobbed louder. My throat worked, painful. I didn't hear it, but I knew Viktor heard it.

He heard *me*. No longer the mute broken soul.

No longer *his* silent *myshka*.

How this happened—how did I break years of silence—I couldn't tell. But I knew the reason was right in front of me, his dark eyes penetrating mine.

Through blurred eyes, I could see him apologizing. He thought he hurt me, but little did he know…

He *did* hurt me. My soul was bleeding for him, only because I was scared our ending wouldn't be happy. I was scared that this would be our last moment.

I lifted my hand up and caressed his cheeks, my tears leaving wet trails down my own. He was still buried deep inside me. Viktor tried to pull out again, but I clenched around his cock.

He gritted his teeth, and I imagined him hissing as I clenched again. My ankles locked around his thighs, and I thrust my hips upward. I gasped at the sensation.

"Please…Viktor."

Viktor has given me something so precious and so fragile that it could be broken so easily. And I was *scared*. Scared of losing *him*. Scared of losing *us*.

Please. Please. Please.

His eyes were wide, his chest heaving with each labored breath. His gaze went to my lips, staying there for a moment before moving to my eyes again.

"Valerie…" he started and then shook his head, like he couldn't believe *this* was happening.

I opened my mouth again, ready to speak. My throat was hurting, practically on fire. After years of not using it, the inside felt like it was being scratched raw and bleeding.

"…Viktor," I muttered.

"Ah fuck!" he swore, his forehead dropping to mine, his eyes closing tight as if he were in pain.

I didn't realize this would hurt him just as much. I didn't realize that I had the power to destroy *him*.

But in the moment, Viktor looked like I had just left his heart bleeding on the floor.

We *obliterated* each other.

We were drowning in each other.

Breathless and fighting. For each other.

My lips brushed against his, kissing him softly. He kissed me back, hungrily, and I tasted the saltiness of my tears. Or was it *his*?

Closing my eyes, I drowned in our wounded kiss. My soul was feeling something that it had never known.

I was falling…falling…falling…

Viktor was falling…falling…falling…

My heart wanted to wrap around him and never let go, whispers of wings growing around the beat of my heart to carry our love.

Viktor tore our lips apart, and I opened my eyes to stare into his dark irises. They were heated again, but I saw all the unsaid emotions there.

"You are going to be the death of me one day, Valerie."

I gave him a quick peck on the lips, my heart squeezing at his words. *But I want to be the reason for you to live.*

His lips feathered over mine. "*Myshka*. One day soon, I will steal you away. But right now, I *need* to make love to you."

I nodded, my arms around his neck. Holding him to me, I smiled through my tears. "Yes…make…love…to…me, Viktor."

His thumb brushed against my plump lips. "Your voice. Fuck. Your voice is the sweetest thing I have ever heard. A fucking melody to my ears, baby."

My whole body hummed with energy as he ground against me. Viktor slowly pulled away, and I moaned at the loss of him. His chuckle vibrated through his chest when he thrust inside me again.

Once he was fully seated inside me again—his tip touching the entrance of my womb—those broken shards of my heart molded together again. Creating a perfect piece. A beating heart for Viktor.

My breathing accelerated, and desire pooled between my thighs, drenching the spot between us where we were connected. My wet core made it easier for him to thrust in and out of my waiting pussy.

He was *big,* and I almost whimpered at how full and stretched I was. The slight sting of pain brought me pleasure I never knew was possible.

My heart fluttered and my pussy gripped him tight every time he pulled out, almost like it hated the loss of him. And every time he pushed inside of me, the flames built, aching and burning me.

Viktor kissed down my throat, nibbling the skin and sucking. He continued a downward path and took a lonely erect nipple into his mouth. He suckled on it, worshipping it with his tongue.

His teeth grazed my skin, and the feel of his rough stubble against my sensitive flesh was driving

THE MAFIA AND HIS OBSESSION PART 1

me insane.

His thrust quickened, and I held on to him, my nails digging painfully into his shoulders. He grunted against my skin, forcing his cock inside my pussy over and over again. Forcing out a pleasure hidden deep within me.

Skin slapping together, our bodies sliding against each other, sweat covering us, our arms around each other, our bodies connected in the most intimate way—this moment was forbidden yet so *beautiful*.

His fingers drifted between our connected bodies, where his hard, thick cock continued to pummel inside me, his thumb brushing against my tiny nub before giving me the smallest pinch. I arched off the bed, and I bit on my lips, holding back my scream.

I was trembling and gasping for air. He licked between the valley of my breasts before moving up. My eyes went to his lips, watching him speak through my hazy, lustful eyes.

"Come for me, Valerie. Let that pretty tight pussy come all over my cock. Give it to me, baby."

Oh God.

He kissed me, hard, almost brutal and so dominant. With a hand over my hips, his fingers dug into my skin. I bit on his lips, and he hissed before he savagely took my lips again.

Viktor pulled almost all the way out before thrusting hard into me. I gasped, and then I was spiraling down and down. The intense crackling wave hit me hard, the ache between my thighs intensifying before slowly turning into a dull feeling.

Our eyes met and we stared...never breaking contact.

Viktor's hips bucked against mine before he thrust inside me one last time. His whole cock was buried into my warmth as I continued to clench and milk him. I felt the warmth of his seeds as he filled me.

He was deeply ingrained inside me.

I was a limp mess, gasping and panting. His chest heaved with each breath, and we were both silent.

Silence. Our sanctuary. In the silence, we found power—we found *us*.

Viktor rolled us on our sides, facing each other, but he stayed buried inside me. He pushed my hair away from my sweaty forehead and placed a kiss there before speaking.

"That was..." He broke off and shook his head. "I don't even know how to..."

My fingers feathered over his cheeks. "We...can't...describe it."

His eyes widened again, and he sucked in a deep breath. "That's going to take some time getting used to, Valerie. Do you realize that you practically just cut my chest open and ripped my heart out?"

"Is...that bad?" I asked. Now that I was speaking, I started wondering how I sounded to Viktor. He said my voice was *sweet*, but...

He gently nudged my chin up. "Louder. I can't hear you."

Oh. "Is...that bad?" I tried again.

He winced and quickly looked toward the door before meeting my eyes again. "Too loud, baby."

THE MAFIA AND HIS OBSESSION PART 1

"Sorry," I mumbled.

Viktor smiled. "That was perfect."

He kissed me, a quick stolen kiss before speaking again. "*You* are perfect. You can speak. You can actually fucking speak. And right now, I am drawing blanks. *Why?*"

One simple word...a question that weighed so heavily.

Unconsciously, my hand came up to touch my bare neck. Viktor noticed, because he noticed *everything*.

"Why did you stop speaking? Because of Valentin? Are you really deaf too...or...?" He left the sentence hanging, waiting for my answer.

"No...I can't hear. But I can...speak."

Viktor stayed silent, waiting for me to continue. Taking a deep breath, I explained the unsaid history. "I wasn't deaf before. But a few years ago, I lost my hearing."

I broke off with a cough, my throat burning more with each word. Viktor quickly pulled away, slipping out of my tight heat. I hissed at the loss of him, and he closed his eyes at the same time.

"Holy fuck. I could live inside you for the rest of my life," he said, opening his eyes again. Turning away from me, he leaned over and took the glass of water from the nightstand.

I sat up as he handed the glass to me. "Drink," he ordered, no place for argument.

The glass was empty within seconds as I drank all the water, like a starved animal. The freshness soothed my inflamed throat, and I took a deep breath.

"Better?" Viktor asked, taking the glass from my hand.

I nodded. "Yes. Thank you."

Viktor smiled, and his fingers touched my lips. "A little louder. You are speaking too soft for me to hear."

I cleared my throat and tried again. "I said, *thank you*."

He bent down and stole a quick kiss before pulling away again. "You are welcome, Valerie."

We laid on our sides again. Viktor wrapped an arm around my hips and brought me close to his body. Between my thighs, I could feel my wetness dripping and his seeds leaving my warmth. I clenched my thighs together, not wanting any trace of him to spill away.

"Valerie, talk to me," he urged, nudging the tip of my nose with his.

"It's in my genes. My mother is deaf, since she was born. At the age of eleven, I was told that I would eventually go deaf too. My sister was six then, but she was diagnosed too. They gave me an estimated of five years before I would start losing my hearing, and maybe two years after that, I would be completely deaf," I explained slowly.

While I was speaking, Viktor never stopped touching me. Whether it was his fingers drawing random patterns or his lips feathering over my skin, he was always touching me.

"That's how I can read lips. My mother reads lips too. It's hard, but I have been training my brain since I was eleven. Back then, I wasn't deaf, so it was easier to learn. I listened and watched the lips at the same time, until I got used to it and the voice would just blend in the background and I would listen by just reading the lips. I know sign language too," I continued.

"When did you go deaf?" Viktor asked, his fingertips grazing my ear softly.

I thought for a moment, trying to remember the dates. "Maybe three years ago. I think."

"The doctor was wrong," he said, a small smile on his lips.

I nodded. "My hearing lasted longer than they thought. I was very slowly going deaf; it was just six months when I had realized it. But then…"

The words caught in my throat, and I swallowed hard as the memories assaulted me.

"What happened?"

I buried my head in his chest, a whimper caught in my throat. "*Valentin*…I can't remember much. It was a bad night. He hit me, and by accident, my head bumped against the bed post hard. I had lost consciousness and woke up two days later…I didn't hear anything when I woke up. No matter how loud I screamed, I couldn't hear anything. No words. No sound. It was just silence. I went from hearing to complete silence in a matter of days."

Viktor's arm tightened around me, trapping me into his embrace. "I know I was supposed to go deaf, eventually. It was meant to happen. But it still feels like he robbed me of my hearing. Maybe if I hadn't hit that bed post, my hearing would have lasted longer…a few more months even."

He pulled away and made me look up into his face. "Does it hurt? Being deaf…do you hate it?"

My hand came up to touch his cheek, rubbing his days of rough stubble. My throat had started hurting again from talking too much, but I continued speaking. For Viktor.

"No. I learned to accept it and be happy with it. I am deaf…not broken. It's part of me. And in some ways, I have found strength in it. Because then, I didn't have to hear his cruel words. Surprisingly, the silence is beautiful."

Viktor waited…because he knew, he just knew a *"but"* was coming.

"*But* right now, I wish I could hear *you*. It *hurts* not being able to hear you." *Or the sound of your heartbeat.*

Viktor's eyes darkened, and our foreheads touched in a soothing way. "If I had the power to give you that wish, I would grant you it. Fuck, I would even cut my own arm off to give you this wish. I would leave a bloodbath behind me—just to give you this wish, *myshka*."

Shaking my head, I couldn't help but smile at his words. "I don't need you to cause a bloodbath for me."

At my words, Viktor smirked…a dark sinister smirk. It was quick, and then it was gone, like it was never there. Almost like it was my imagination.

"Why did you stop speaking?" I closed my eyes at his next question.

"He loved it when I screamed my pain. It was his drug. My screams were his power over me. And after I lost my hearing, my speech pattern changed too. I couldn't control how loud or soft I spoke, like now. He said my voice was ugly…that I sounded weird. Eventually, I realized that my power lay in my voice. If I took it away, he wouldn't win. He couldn't control me. Every time he begged me to scream and I wouldn't—I won."

Viktor pulled me closer into his body, until we were plastered against each other. "That's a long time to stay voiceless, even when you aren't. You are so strong, Valerie. Do you know that?"

I shrugged at his choice of words.

"You are, *myshka*," he forced out.

We fell into silence, both of us basking in this moment. My mind was reeling. So much has happened. Viktor and I—and then finding my voice again.

Viktor eventually pulled away and went to the bathroom. A few minutes later, he came back with a glass filled with water. I drank it without any question.

"Your throat is hurting," he stated. Not a question, just a simple fact.

I nodded, placing the glass on my nightstand. Viktor got in bed again and pulled the covers over us. Without hesitation, I curled into his embrace, and we held on to each other.

Our gaze never wavered and slowly sleep started to seep into my languid body. Viktor placed a kiss on my nose before speaking.

"Why did you speak for me?" he asked. I imagined him whispering the words—our secret.

I opened my mouth to answer, but my throat burned, and I coughed when the words wouldn't come out. Quickly fishing out my notepad and pen from my drawer, I started writing down.

A smile touched my lips as I held his pen while my fingers feathered over the paper. The memories—our moments flashed in front of my eyes.

This was how everything started. This was how we became *us*. When our hearts decided to dance for each other.

Because you deserve my voice. You earned it, Viktor.

Viktor read my words and he entwined our fingers together. "Was *it* everything you dreamed of?"

My smile widened at his question. "It…was…much more."

The words were barely past my lips when Viktor started kissing me. We kissed until we were breathless. And then we just held each other.

Our eyes closed…and I was filled with peace.

It was much more.

I spoke the truth.

Because it truly was much more.

This was my dream. My *first*.

My first time wasn't when Valentin stole my virginity and pushed his cock inside me, breaking through my barrier. My first time wasn't when I cried in agony and begged him to stop.

My first time wasn't with my husband.

This was my first.

I believe…tonight was my first time.

Viktor was my first.

And my last.

Chapter 33

Viktor

Valerie was a beautiful woman. But she was even more beautiful when she was sleeping. All the worries and the pain—they all disappeared from her face, leaving just a soft, peaceful look.

Her hair was spread over my pillow, where her cheek rested, her body as close to mine as possible. With my arm around her hips, I kept her anchored to my body.

It was morning already, yet I couldn't bring myself to leave.

Valerie made a little sleepy noise, and her eyes fluttered open. Her lips quirked up on the side, a small smile appearing on her lips.

She fluttered her eyes shyly, almost innocently, and then she buried her face in my chest. Not before I caught sight of her cheeks blushing with a rosy color—such a beautiful fucking sight to see first thing in the morning.

Pulling her face away so she could see me

speaking, I winked at her. "It's a little too late to be shy now, baby."

She pouted and then shrugged, never once losing her smile along the way. After taking her one more time in the middle of the night, Valerie fell right asleep—with my cock still buried in her tight pussy.

I stayed awake, just holding her and savoring her warmth around my cock before eventually pulling out. She had mewled, a disappointed sound in her sleep before cuddling closer into me.

I barely slept last night, not wanting to miss a single moment. The way her eyebrows would rise, her forehead crunching up during her dreams. Her sleepy sighs. When her lips would part when she breathed. The small muscle twitches. Or the random little sleepy smiles that would appear on her lips. I found out she also had a habit of tapping her fingers on the pillow while sleeping.

I memorized everything until they were deeply ingrained in my memories.

In her presence, I forgot what I was supposed to do—what I was meant to do. I forgot why Alessio sent me here.

And *Ayla*...Ayla would disappear from my mind, like she had never been there.

Valerie was the forbidden fruit everyone warned me about...but I still took a bite. I didn't realize the taste would be this addicting.

She once was someone untouchable...until she became *my obsession.*

And fuck me, I needed her like I needed my next breath.

I wasn't a poet—hell, I was far from being a man

with words to give her. But for Valerie, I would become the man with action behind the words I could give her—words I never gave anyone before. Because they were only meant for her.

Valerie caressed my cheeks, taking me away from my thoughts. Her lips parted as if to speak, but then she broke off with a cough. She rubbed her throat and tried again.

"What...are...you thinking...about?" she asked slowly and almost too quietly. But I didn't miss it. I couldn't miss her voice, her fucking sweet voice and the small slur in her speech that made her even more perfect.

I was still reeling from the fact that she could speak. Relieved that she could and pride that I was the one she chose to speak for.

She definitely mind-fucked me last night, and damn it, if my dick didn't like the sound of her voice. And her fucking whimpers. And those dangerous sexy moans.

"...Viktor?"

Ah, fuck there we go again. My heart doing that fluttering shit and squeezing until it was hard to breathe.

Every time I heard her voice—every fucking time—she stole my breath away.

Swallowing past the lump in my throat, I looked at her face. Her eyes were serious, but she hadn't lost her smile. I knew she could tell I had a lot on my mind—all the mess I had to figure out. All the games I still had to play.

Her fingers smoothed over my lips gently. Unconsciously, I kissed her fingertips and her smile widened.

"Show me…your soul, and I will…show you mine," she whispered.

A small chuckle vibrated through my chest. "Valerie, my soul has some really dark places. You won't be able to see them…you'll run away at first sight. You should never visit them because my soul is no place for you to live in, baby."

Her smile turned into a frown, but she stayed silent. Our stares never wavered, and I could tell she wanted to say something; it was right at the tip of her tongue.

The moment was broken when my phone vibrated on my nightstand, our eyes breaking away and our bodies pulling apart.

"I should be going," I muttered, quickly getting off the bed. "It's morning already. If someone sees me coming out of your room…"

I left the sentence hanging, but Valerie understood and nodded. Her eyes clouded over, her eyebrows pinching together as if she were in pain. She sat up and pulled the sheets up to her neck, covering her nakedness.

Grabbing my clothes from the floor, I made my way to the bathroom, but not without casting her one last glance to see her gaze moving to her lap, looking almost sorrowful.

After freshening up and fully clothed, I walked out to see Valerie in the same position. I saw her fidgeting with the bedsheet as I walked closer. With a knee on the bed, I leaned down and placed a kiss on her forehead.

She leaned more into me, her hands now

gripping my shirt. But I couldn't bear that lost look in her eyes.

So I kissed her.

I kissed her deep and hard until she gasped for breath. When we pulled apart, her eyes were hazy, her lips swollen and pink—and there it was, that smile I was looking for. A tiny shy smile graced her eyes, accenting her glorious beauty even more.

"I have to go, Valerie. But I promise, I'll come for you tonight."

"Okay," she murmured with a slight slur. I found it endearing, the way she spoke. Fuck, I found myself fascinated with every piece of her.

Shaking my head, I continued. "But before I go, I need to tell you something about me."

Valerie cocked her head to the side, waiting. Curiosity was about to kill the cat.

"I saw the way you looked at Alessio," I started. She opened her mouth as if to speak, but then quickly snapped it shut with a slight shiver of fear.

Ah, little innocent *myshka*.

"He isn't the bad guy, baby." I paused, and then shook my head with a laugh. "Well, he is. But not *really*."

Valerie looked confused, but she waited patiently for me to continue. "My name isn't Konstantin Solonik, like everyone seems to call me. You know that I am Valentin's nephew. But baby, I belong to the Ivanshov family. My real name is Viktor Konstantin Ivanshov."

Her eyebrows furrowed together, and she cleared her throat before speaking. "You mean…you aren't…the heir…"

"No. I am Valentin's heir. But I am also one of Alessio's men. His second in command. Valentin hates the Ivanhovs, but I don't. They are my *family*, Valerie. Alessio is my fucking *brother*."

The crinkling between her forehead deepened, and she looked at me like I had grown two heads and was doing the Macarena.

"But…how…I don't…understand," she spoke quietly.

Nudging the tip of her nose with mine, I gave her a small smile. "It's okay. You will understand more later…when shit will go down. All you need to know is that Alessio is on our side, *myshka*. All I need to do is…make sure Valentin is ten feet under the ground. Soon."

Her mouth hung open in shock, and she stared at me with wide eyes. Leaning forward, I captured her lips with a raw kiss. She gasped into my lips before kissing me back, hesitant but then confident with each passing second.

I released her lips, and Valerie blinked several times. Pulling away, I winked at her.

That was how I left Valerie…with her mind reeling. *Get a taste of what you do to me, my beautiful myshka.*

Closing her door softly behind me, I made my way to my quarters. The smile on my fucking face couldn't be wiped off.

Until…I saw Valentin waiting for me in front of my door.

My back straightened, and I lost my smile at the expression on his face.

He looked happy. Too happy. His stupid old face

was glowing, and the dark smile on his face made my stomach roll.

Fuck. My heart clenched, because I knew...I just *fucking* knew.

I could practically feel my heart dropping into the vast pit of my stomach.

"Alessio just left," he started, chuckling with a shake of his head. "He got a call."

I took a deep breath and waited...I waited for the words I already knew was going to be said.

"Ayla had a little accident."

My heart squeezed, my chest feeling heavy. My breath left me with a loud whoosh. Struggling with my next breath, I gave out a small cough and cleared my throat.

The walls I had built around my heart formed again, creating a cage. The fake façade I had created—Konstantin Solonik—was back in place. A perfect illusion to convince my foes. A tainted mirror. They saw what I wanted them to see.

First rule for a made man to remember.

Everything was a lie. Everyone was a lie. Every fucking day was a game to play.

Believe nothing. Whatever you see or hear is a lie.

Apparently Solonik didn't follow the same rules, for he fell into my trap so fucking easily. Easy for him. A fucking nightmare for me.

My back straightened, and I could feel my lips stretching in a smirk. His smile grew at the expression on my face.

"I got news from Abram. He was there to witness it. Saw Ayla fall," he continued, pushing off the wall. With his hands behind his back, he paced the hall.

I leaned against the door and crossed my ankles, my arms crossed over my chest.

Breathe. Don't fucking break. Ayla has to be okay. Ayla is okay. She has to be.

I tried to repeat the words in my head, hoping to believe them. But fuck it, I didn't even know if she was okay.

It was a wild game—the chase never ending. The darkness never ceasing. I was the Master. And Ayla was my unwilling victim.

"The baby didn't make it."

His words chilled me to the bone.

The words I was waiting for.

I just didn't realize they would hurt this much.

But then again…I was Viktor. *Viktor Ivanshov never lets anyone get in his way. Viktor Ivanshov never fails on a mission. Viktor Ivanshov never loses a game.*

Taking a deep breath, I fished out my lighter from my pants and the cigarette box. Valentin watched me with closed eyes, judging my *lack* of reaction. The only thing he got from me was a smirk…a playful one, filled with victory.

Placing a cigarette between my teeth, I lit the end and inhaled. The puff of smoke drifted when I exhaled. The lighter was lit, my thumb moving over the small flame. Just never touching. Another illusion to play with the mind.

Playing with fire.

Inhaling another breath of my cigarette, I released a chuckle. It sounded dark to my own ears.

THE MAFIA AND HIS OBSESSION PART 1

"Just because she didn't come to the party, it doesn't mean my plans can't be put in motion, Valentin," I drawled, clicking the lighter on and off. The *tick tick* it made sounded harsh in the empty, silent halls.

"So it was your plan?" Valentin asked, his eyes widening a fraction of an inch. "But how? I don't—"

"I have my ways," I cut him off with a raised eyebrow. "I told you, Valentin. I do things my own way. I don't play to lose."

"I can see that now," he replied, nodding with satisfaction.

Pushing away from the wall, I walked past him. "If I had a chance, the bitch would be dead too—but then again, why kill them off so easily? Alessio needs to feel the pain. One down. The baby had to go. Sooner rather than later. I'd like to say we're winning."

Valentin let out a booming laugh. When he spoke, his words caused my teeth to grit with fury.

"I like the way you think. I didn't think you could do it—but clearly, I keep underestimating you. Good job, son. For the first time, you have made me proud. Your father is a fool. He didn't see your potential. They made you second in command under a fucking Boss. But you—you deserve to be the fucking *Pakhan*. And one day, you will be."

I didn't reply. My eyes met his in a hard, unflinching gaze. He stilled, and I looked away, effectively shutting him up.

Without sparing him another glance, I walked into my room and closed the door behind me. His footsteps eventually faded away and then silence.

The silence sickened me, and I fought the urge to throw up.

My insides tightened, and once again my emotions derailed. I breathed through my nose, trying to calm my nerves and the never-ending cramps in my stomach. Sweat dripped down the back of my neck. My hands started shaking, and I clenched them into tight fists. The lump in my throat grew until it was hard to swallow, my tongue feeling heavy—speechless. Motionless.

I felt…crippled.

What have I just done?

***

A week later

Half of Valerie's body laid on top of mine, covering me with her warmth. She cuddled closer, burying her face in my chest. Her fingers drew random patterns, her touch feathering over the art on my skin.

She loved them and couldn't seem to stop touching the intricate designs, always exploring with her touch. Skin to skin. Sometimes, she would lay kisses along the path of my tattoos.

Over the week, I had successfully been able to keep Valentin away from Valerie. Using various tactics, I was the one who ended up in her bedroom every night. Not the fuck face who was supposedly her husband.

"…Viktor."

THE MAFIA AND HIS OBSESSION PART 1

Snapping out of my thoughts, I looked down at Valerie to see her eyes already on me.

Something indescribable would always ignite me when she'd breathed my name.

Her voice was so sweet…still unused with years of silence. Sometimes her voice was too soft to hear, or too loud. Her tone was low at the beginning of a sentence and then rose until I would tell her it was too loud. Valerie's voice was a little scratchy but beautiful nonetheless.

I think maybe I found it more beautiful because it was…different. It was her. It was perfect.

"You are always…lost in your…thoughts."

Valerie sat up, leaning over my face. Her bare tits were right over my mouth, and I was tempted to take a bite…maybe even a lick. My dick hardened at the lush sight, and I swore under my breath.

She palmed my face—while I was wishing she would palm my hard cock—and her forehead came down to touch mine.

"Why won't you talk to…me? I know…something is troubling…you," she whispered.

Ah. There it was. The unspoken words between us. The one thing I didn't want to talk about.

"You have changed. You are more silent…and…brooding," Valerie continued, her lips touching my cheek in a small kiss now.

"It's nothing," I mumbled. Her eyes fixated on my lips, and I saw the disbelief there. Her lips pursed in a small, frustrated pout.

"You are a bad liar, Viktor."

"Valerie…" I started, but she shushed me. My

little nun *actually* shushed me.

With a finger on my lips, she said, "Don't lie to me. You ask me to trust you and I do, yet...you don't trust me. You won't...tell me what is...hurting you. And I *know* you *are* hurting. Something worries you."

I stared into her warm brown eyes, filled with so much understanding. I wondered if she would still be so understanding if she knew my truth.

Quickly rolling us over so she was under me, I hovered over her naked body. "You are right. I *am* hurting. I *am* worrying. And I have done terrible things, Valerie."

Valerie's finger tangled in my hair, and she brought my face closer, our lips mere inches apart. "What have you done, Viktor?"

"I hurt someone who is very close to me. I *hurt* her, and she means everything...but I think I have hurt her, and I don't know if she's okay or not," I finally confessed, my voice rough with unsaid emotions and my words catching in my throat.

Valerie stayed silent, her gaze never leaving mine. So I continued. "The mere thought of something happening to Ayla cripples me, Valerie. But knowing I am the reason behind it...Alessio would never forgive me."

Her warm eyes turned confused. "Maybe you shouldn't...be so hard on yourself. I don't know what to say. She seems important to you. If you think you have hurt...her, then you...should apologize."

"I don't think apologies will ever be enough," I admitted.

THE MAFIA AND HIS OBSESSION PART 1

Valerie shook her head, her eyebrows bunching sadly, as if she were feeling *my* pain. She leaned up and stole a kiss. I kissed her back. What was meant to be a quick peck turned into a long kiss, one that left us breathless.

For a brief moment, I forgot my worries. I forgot about Ayla and Alessio. I forgot about the *baby*.

I savored Valerie's kiss and continued sinking into the sea of *love* she was giving me, the depth never ending.

"Tomorrow is a new day. Everything…will…be fine, Viktor," she muttered against my lips.

Settling beside Valerie, I pulled her into my embrace. "Let's not think about tomorrow. I want to live in the *now*. And right now, I just want to hold you."

Valerie smiled, and my heart stuttered—like it always did whenever she would look my way.

We stayed like this for what felt like hours. In our own bubble where nobody could hurt us.

She eventually got up to take her shower. I watched her go, my eyes on the slick warmth that dripped between her legs. Shaking my head, I held back my laugh. She would just get dirty again.

While listening to the shower run, I went through her drawer. Valerie had spoken enough for the day. I had noticed her slurring her speeches more in the end. The wince every now and then couldn't be mistaken either.

But instead of finding her pen and paper…I found a box.

Confused, I took it out of the drawer. Valerie's room only had the bare necessities. Her closet with filled with some clothes, but that was it.

There was nothing for herself in her room. No personal touches that made the room truly hers.

It was just a cage. Hiding her. Trapping her like a prisoner.

Sitting against the headboard, I opened the box.

What the—

Inside, I found something I never expected.

Holding the shoes in my hands, I inspected them. They were flat, very light, and made with what seemed like expensive beige satin. There were white pearls scattered on the surface, with long ribbons that would probably tie at the ankles. A very feminine touch. It was actually *pretty*.

The soles were almost worn out. But these weren't just normal shoes.

They were fucking ballet shoes.

Chapter 34

Valerie

My hands drifted between my legs, washing off the remains of Viktor. His seeds coated my inner thighs, where our mixed scent had dripped from my sex.

I ached between my legs, where he had taken me both ruthlessly and slowly. Clenching at the thought of him inside me, I could still feel him. His rough thrust. His lips against my skin. His groan vibrating off his chest.

Walking out of the shower, I toweled myself off with a smile. What was the use? Viktor would just get me dirty again. Maybe I cleaned just for him to get me dirty. It was apparently his mission.

My gaze caught my naked body in the mirror. I smiled at the sight of my bare neck. When I was with Viktor, I didn't wear my collar. With him, I was free. It was just us, hiding from the rest of the world.

My room, what used to be my cage, my hell on

earth, was now my—*our*—sanctuary. This was where we met, first touched, where our lips first kissed, and where he first made love to my soul.

After putting on my dress, I opened the drawer and took out the small white bottle. The one hidden at the back, behind my accessories. Emptying the bottle in my hand, I counted the small capsules.

Only twenty-three left. I would need more. But since Igor wasn't here to bring me any, I was going to have to ask Viktor. He knew about the pills, but I had told him there was more left. I didn't realize so many days had passed already.

I placed all the pills back into the bottle and hid it in the drawer again, away from all eyes. This was my secret. A secret I had kept for many years. Igor wasn't perfect. He was my captor along with Valentin, but he was good enough to give me something nobody else would.

Walking out of the bathroom, I saw the bed was empty. My eyes tracked for Viktor and found him next to the window. He was staring outside, while leaning against the wall with only his boxers on.

He must have heard my approach because he turned around. Viktor's eyes met mine, and I felt myself smiling under his intense penetrating gaze. My body tingled and my stomach flipped at the way he watched me.

My eyes traveled down, tracing every part of his wide, muscled chest. The intricate design covering his exposed skin fascinated me. They were beautiful, and it took me hours tracing every line. I wanted to memorize every part of Viktor.

But my gaze froze at his hands, finally seeing

THE MAFIA AND HIS OBSESSION PART 1

what he was holding.

My world stilled.

It felt like everything had darkened and disappeared around me. The light only shone on Viktor. All I could see was him and what was in his hands.

I stopped in the middle of the room, my feet refusing to take another step forward. My vision blurred, and my blood roared through me. I could feel my throbbing veins in my neck, and I desperately tried to breathe.

How?

Viktor being Viktor, he read my unspoken question. I stayed in the same spot, my body shaking slightly with shock as he walked toward me. He met me in the middle of the room in three long steps until our bodies were so close together.

His breath feathered over my cheek as he leaned down. His lips kissed mine softly. He held the back of my neck firmly in his hold, keeping me anchored to him as he devoured my lips.

Viktor purposely made me *forget*.

With his kiss, all the worry and pain seeped out of my body, leaving me breathless and limp in his arms.

When we pulled away, he laid his forehead against mine. He appeared just as breathless. I watched his lips as he spoke, not wanting to miss anything. "They were in the nightstand. I found them in your drawer."

My eyes squeezed shut at his words. Viktor had brought out something from my past—something I wanted to forget. A part of me that was stolen and ripped into shreds right in front of my eyes.

"Valerie! Valerie!"

My head snapped up at my name being called. Turning around, I saw the director coming my way. I waved, letting him know I heard him.

He came to stand in front of me, breathless, but his eyes were shining with admiration and happiness. "I thought you were gonna leave and I wouldn't be able to give you the news."

I smiled back at the show of his enthusiasm. "What news?"

"You are going to want to sit down for this," he said, pointing at the bench behind me.

Mathew Easton was a middle-aged man, married with two kids and another one on the way. His father owned this theater before him, and now it was his.

To him, we weren't his investments or just his dancers. We were more. He built us, made us who we were today. A perfect unit. The perfect dancers that everyone admired. Funnily, he liked to call us his little petals. His children. Together, we were a family built on the same ground—the same passion that lived in us.

Ballet.

"Sit down," he ordered again. I did as I was told. Sitting down, I bent forward and started to unlace my ballet flats.

My feet were sore, but I smiled at the pain. Hours and hours of dancing, doing the one thing I loved the most in the world, had brought me beautiful pain.

THE MAFIA AND HIS OBSESSION PART 1

"Now will you tell me what has gotten you so excited?" I questioned with a raised eyebrow.

"This is big, Valerie. I am almost sad that I will lose you after this. But Goddamn it, I am so happy for you," he mumbled before taking a deep breath.

Confused, I only stared at him mutely. Mr. Easton sighed and handed me the portfolio he was holding. Taking it from his hands, I opened it and read the first paper.

I saw my name in bold letters, and my heart stuttered as I continued reading. No way! Impossible. I read the paper again. And again. Maybe three times.

"You are the best dancer I have, Valerie. At such a young age, you have come so far. Only eighteen—not a lot of dancers can do this," he continued when I stayed silent.

"This…" I started but then broke off. Tears blinded my vision. *"How…I don't…"*

I was in shock—my heart in tatters as I read the words again. My body trembled with the force of my happiness.

"Remember the last dance? That was our best performance. A few people from The Royal Opera House were our guests. They saw you, Valerie. They approached me after the performance. Their director wanted you as one of his dancers. Not just one of his—he wants you to play his female lead." Matthew paused when I still hadn't said a word.

I was…speechless. This was my dream. But it felt so surreal.

Mr. Easton sighed and placed a hand on my shoulders. I looked up at him through tearful eyes.

He gave me a small gentle smile, his own happiness evident in his eyes. "He said he will send an official invitation. I didn't believe him at first. I thought he was just being nice, and I didn't tell you because I didn't want to get your hopes up. But then this arrived in the mail today. The real invitation. Your name in golden bold letters, Valerie."

"He wants me to dance for The Royal Opera House in London? One of the most famous ballet theatres? As the female lead?" I finally choked out.

He nodded and touched the paper on my lap. "Yes. He is only asking for one performance. For now. But like the invitations says—if you want and like his theatre, he would like to hire you as his female lead. He's asking for one dance for now—and I am sure if this is a success, which I know it will be, he might just rope you in as an official female lead dance. You might be able continue with The Royal Opera House."

I closed the portfolio and jumped up. Mr. Easton staggered back when I wrapped my arms around his waist, hugging him tight.

He laughed and patted me on my back. "I guess that's a yes?"

Instead of answering, the tears continued to fall down my cheeks. I sobbed into his chest, feeling too overwhelmed to do anything else.

"Are those happy tears, Val? You know very well that I jump right out of the window when a girl cries," he joked lightly.

I pulled away, smiling, laughing while crying. "This is my dream, Mr. Easton! I...I don't...oh my...God..." I broke off again, not being able to

THE MAFIA AND HIS OBSESSION PART 1

finish a sentence, let alone hold a conversation.

"I...am...going to dance for The. Royal. Opera. House!" I exclaimed.

Mr. Easton stepped away and looked over my shoulder. "That's not all. There is another surprise. Turn the next page." He pushed me back toward the bench.

Swiping my tears away, I opened the portfolio again and turned to the page he indicated.

My stomach flipped again, butterflies dancing merrily, and my heart burst for the second time.

"Congratulations," he said from behind me.

"This is impossible," I whispered, staring into the paper.

"Nothing is impossible when you believe in it."

I closed the portfolio and shook my head. "I don't think I deserve this, Mathew."

He grasped my shoulders and turned me around to face him. His eyes hardened as he spoke, his tone filled with seriousness. "You deserve this and so much more, Val. Full scholarship to the Royal Ballet School of Dance, in London. An almost three-year program. Plus, a job as the female lead dancer at The Royal Opera House. This is the perfect opportunity. Both in the same place. You're getting everything that you deserve. You worked your ass off for this, Val."

My body pulled away from his hold as I slid to the ground. Sitting on my butt, I stared into space. Holy. Shit. Wake me up from this dream right now!

Wait, no—never wake me up. This was too beautiful to wake up from.

"I don't think I can move. My body feels a little

weak," I muttered to Mr. Easton.

He laughed and then sat down beside me. "So what are you going to do?"

I swallowed against the lump in my throat. "If I say yes, then that means I leave you behind. This theater is a part of my life, Mathew. Everyone here, my friends, my family—I can't imagine leaving you all behind."

Mr. Easton smiled. "You are like a daughter to me, Val. You know that, right?"

When I nodded in response, he continued. "I am proud of you. Every day, when you complained why I would push you so hard...make you work harder than everyone else—this is the reason. I saw a potential in you, Valerie. My theater is small, and you deserve bigger than this. I knew one day you would leave all of us behind to chase this dream, and I purposely pushed you for it. You may not be my biological daughter, but I am a proud father today."

I sniffled away my tears, but it was so hard when Mr. Easton was saying such things. It was true, out of all the dancers, I was the closest to him. For him to say he was proud of me, it was everything.

Today, I made my mentor proud.

Tomorrow, I would make him fly—for believing in me. The next time I danced on the stage of The Royal Opera House, I wanted him to be able to puff his chest out and proudly say, "This girl was one of my dancers."

"Thank you, Mathew," I whispered, returning his smile with one of my own.

"So?" he asked, raising an eyebrow in

THE MAFIA AND HIS OBSESSION PART 1

challenge.

I stared down at the portfolio before bringing it to my chest, hugging it tightly. "I will do it. My answer is yes. To all of it."

"Good girl," Mr. Easton said, standing on his feet again. "Time to give your parents the good news."

I stood up, and my smile widened. "I can't wait to tell them!"

"Hurry on home then, Val."

We hugged again. He patted me on the head and nodded proudly before leaving. I quickly changed out of my dress and packed everything in my bag.

As I was leaving, I saw Mr. Easton waiting for me in front of the entrance. He was holding a box in his hand.

"This is for you. New ballet shoes. This is my gift to you," he said, his voice a little rough with emotion.

Taking it from his hand, I held it to my chest. "Thank you, Mr. Easton. For everything."

I waved at him as I walked out. "Goodbye!"

"Make me proud, Val!"

"I will!"

Promise, I thought to myself.

My mind was reeling as I walked to the bus stop. A mixture of nervousness, anticipation, and giddiness. I couldn't wait until I could give my parents the news.

They knew how much ballet meant to me. I remembered how at first, they didn't approve, but this—this would make them proud of me.

Looking down at my watch, I saw that it would

be another thirty minutes until the next bus. I had missed my usual one while speaking to Mr. Easton.

My feet kicked under me as I started running. No point in waiting for the bus. Running would take me home faster. My legs burned, but I didn't care.

Thunderstorms wrecked through the sky, and a few minutes later, it started to pour. I wasn't surprised with the change in weather. This was New York City, anyway. Expect the unexpected.

I continued running through the rain, laughing. I could already imagine my parents' faces when I told them the good news. Best day ever!

By the time I reached home, I was soaked through my bones. Opening the door, I walked inside and called out, "Mom? Dad? I am home!"

The house was silent. Confused, I left my wet shoes at the front door and walked further inside, leaving water puddles behind me.

I froze when I saw what greeted me. We had guests, and everyone turned to stare at me. I almost felt like hitting my head into the wall.

I recognized two older men. I had seen them before, a few years ago. The elder one, probably in his late fifties, stared at my chest. He was the same one who had leered at me the first time we met.

Feeling self-conscious and uncomfortable, I took a step back. My skin crawled, and I shivered. I didn't like the way he was looking at me.

My mother stood up, blocking my view of the man. Her expression was drawn in, and I saw tears in her eyes.

"Mom..."

She shook her head. "Go to your room, Val. And

change your clothes."

I nodded without saying anything. The air around us felt stale and dark. All the happiness I felt before dissolved because I knew something was terribly wrong.

I quickly went upstairs and straight in my bathroom. My lips parted in a silent gasp at the sight of me. My beige shirt and light pink skirt were so wet and stuck to my body. It almost looked inappropriate. I winced as I remembered that everyone downstairs had seen me like this.

After toweling myself off, I quickly dressed again, this time choosing black jeans and matching blouse.

I made sure I was presentable before walking downstairs again. Except my steps faltered on the top of the stairs.

"I told you I would come for her on her eighteenth birthday. You are lucky, I have come a week later."

"Please," *I heard my father beg. He sounded so broken, so lost.*

"Jacob, this is not the time to beg. You had years to repay the debt you took. You still can't pay me back. I told you—my money or your daughter."

My eyes widened, and I plastered myself against the wall, hiding myself from view. Oh God. No.

No. No. No.

This couldn't be happening.

I covered my mouth with a hand, trying to hold in my shocked cry. My chest tightened, and it felt like I would suffocate.

"I need more time. Please," *my father said*

again. "I'll find a way to pay you back. I promise. Just not my daughter."

I heard my mother sobbing. "She is still so young. Please give us some more time."

"You were supposed to pay me my debt three years ago!" the voice thundered, and I flinched. My stomach rolled, and I fought against the urge to throw up.

Three years ago—I was fifteen. That was when I met that man for the first time.

"I already gave you more years, you pathetic bastard. She was supposed to be mine three years ago. You asked for some time. You asked until she was eighteen. Guess what? She is eighteen now, and I am taking her with me, whether you like it or not. I don't give a fuck if she screams her head off—I am going to drag her out of here."

I choked back a cry, and bile rose in my throat. I gagged and closed my eyes tightly, listening to his words. The more he spoke, the most my heart cracked into pieces.

He laughed maniacally. "Don't worry. I won't take her in front of you. But I will warn you now. First and last warning. If you resist, maybe I'll just fuck her right here, on your floor—take that little precious virginity she kept for so long. Would you like that, Jacob? Huh?"

I didn't hear my father's reply. Sinking to the floor, I gripped my head. Pushing my palms against my ears, I desperately tried to forget the words I just heard.

What is happening? Everything was perfect just moments ago.

THE MAFIA AND HIS OBSESSION PART 1

My head swirled and my body shook with each silent sob.

"Do you want all her virgin blood on your floor?"

Stop!

I scratched at my ears and slapped a hand against my temple repeatedly.

Wake up, Valerie. This is a dream. Wake up. Wake up!

My throat closed up and my chest felt on fire as I fought for each breath.

And then I heard the words—the words that changed me—changed everything.

"A choice. I give you a choice. Valerie or Malory."

My eyes snapped open, and I lurched forward on my knees.

No!

I almost cried out but quickly clamped a hand over my mouth. My teeth bit down on my lips viciously, and I tasted blood.

"But I won't wait for Malory to turn eighteen. I will take her now. So, Jacob, the choice is yours."

How could someone be so cruel and heartless?

Malory. My sweet little sister. My precious little doll. My little princess.

Her smile flashed in front of my eyes. I could almost hear her laughter when I would spin her around.

She was only thirteen.

And he would take her now...

My mind screamed, and I covered my face with my hands, silently wailing.

I tuned out everyone, refusing to accept this reality. When I tried to stand up again, my knees weakened and sank down on the floor again. With whatever strength was left inside of me, I crawled to my sister's bedroom.

Opening the door, I found her sleeping peacefully on her bed. She looked so innocent and vulnerable.

The tears fell down my cheeks, and I hiccupped back another sob as I kissed her forehead. My lips lingered there, and I breathed in her sweet flowery smell.

"I love you, doll. Remember that. Always." Goodbye, Malory.

My gaze stayed on my sister for one last time before I walked away and closed the door. Stepping into my room, I closed my door too. I swiped away my tears with the sleeves of my shirt.

A decision needed to be made. My father wouldn't make it. I would.

The box that Mr. Easton gave me was still on my bed. The black portfolio was there too. My vision blurred with tears again.

There would be no new beginning.

The dreams I had—everything was lost.

Pacing the length of my room, I tried to breathe. Minutes probably turned into hours. Finally, I heard my door open.

I didn't turn around. Instead, I faced my bed, still staring at the white box and the portfolio.

"Valerie..." my mother started.

I could hear her crying. I heard my father sniffling too—as if he were trying to keep his tears at bay.

Covering my face with my palms, I took a deep breath. My tears had dried, and I made sure to swipe away any wetness that was still there.

I turned around to see my parents standing in front of the door. They looked completely ruined. Now, I remembered. They had the same exact expression three years ago—when that man had visited us.

But they were given more time.

And now—we had run out of time.

"Valerie…your sister…" my mother cried. "You have…to save your sister. He will…hurt…"

My father opened his mouth to say something—maybe to explain his situation, his faults. But I shook my head.

"She is…so…young…" My mother continued to sob for my sister's life.

My lips wobbled, and my nose tingled with the effort to not cry. My stomach twisted again, and my fingers curled into fists.

Instead of responding, I walked to my closet and took out a grey, glittery box. Inside, I found the pair of ballet flats that I wore during my last performance. The same performance where The Royal Opera House had decided to make me their female lead.

My favorite pair of ballet flats. My lucky charm.

My voice came out as a whisper when I finally spoke. "I heard…you talking."

There was silence. A tear fell down my cheek, and I let it roll, sliding down my neck, leaving a wet, lonely trail.

"Can I take this box with me? That's all I want."

"Val," my father started, but I cut him off.

"Will he let me take this box?"

"I think..."

Closing the box again, I held it to my chest as if it would give me protection. I turned around to see my father holding my mother, who looked pale and almost sick from crying.

I saw the shame in my father's eyes before he looked down. "I am sorry," he whispered. "I am so fucking sorry, Valerie. This is my fault...this is all my fault......my sweet girl..."

My throat felt tight, almost suffocating me. I opened my mouth to say something—anything—but no words came out.

"It's okay."

My mind screamed. Liar! It's not okay!

I walked past my parents and out of my bedroom, still holding the box like it was my saving grace.

"Promise me you will never let anything happen to Malory," I said, stopping at the stairs.

"I promise," my father replied.

My body trembled in pain, and another tear fell down my cheek. This time, I lifted my chin up. And then I took a step forward—toward the man who sought to own me—to destroy me.

"Myshka."

I silently gasped as pain assaulted my body. Viktor's voice. So soft—and far, far away, almost like it was deep underwater. I could barely even hear it. Maybe I didn't hear it. Maybe it was my dream.

THE MAFIA AND HIS OBSESSION PART 1

Viktor's hand tightened at the back of my neck. Not hard enough to hurt me, but there was a commanding pressure in his hold. My eyes snapped open, my gaze on his lips.

"Look at me, Valerie." I stared up into his deep chocolate brown eyes.

My lips parted, and I took a deep breath before whispering. "I used to…dance. Until it was…stolen from me."

Chapter 35

Valerie

I didn't realize that my words had the power to hurt this much. *I used to dance. Until it was stolen from me.* The truth tasted bitter on my tongue, and I hated that they were my reality. I hated that once I had everything—and then in a matter of minutes, I lost it all.

And I *hated* Viktor for reminding me of what I had lost.

My ballet flats were kept hidden. They were a reminder of what I could have had. A different beginning, a different present, and a different future.

I wanted to keep it locked away, but how long was I supposed to keep my past buried? One day soon, the truth would have had to come out. But I wasn't ready for it *now*.

Viktor's hand went from the back of my neck to my cheek, lifting my face up so he could look into my eyes. He was searching for something, his gaze never leaving mine. Then he sighed, his forehead dropping to mine again.

My heart thumped, just like always when he would touch me. So gently and so sweetly. He handled me as if I was someone precious to him. Looking into his eyes, riddled with so many unsaid emotions, I believed that. I believed in *him*.

Viktor cupped my cheek before speaking. "Talk to me. I want to know, Valerie. I want to know everything about you."

"There is so much to say, Viktor. I don't...know...where to start," I replied. Instinctively, my hands gripped his waist, my body folding into his.

He walked us backward until the back of my legs hit the bed. I sat down, my hands on my lap, playing with the fabric of my dress nervously.

Instead of sitting beside me, Viktor knelt to his knees.

He lifted my long dress up until it was bunched on my thighs. Without waiting for my response, his body settled between my legs. In this position, we were closer. Him on his knees for me, our faces the same level, our eyes meeting and never wavering.

Viktor took my hands in his and gave me a small squeeze. His lips moved, and my eyes quickly went there to catch his words. "Start from the beginning, baby."

So I did.

I told him how much I loved dancing.

I told him how I used to breathe ballet, morning till night. Until my feet were sore and my toes were bleeding. Until I was breathless and my legs couldn't walk anymore.

To me, ballet and I—we weren't two separate things. Without one, the other didn't exist. We were *one*. My body would move to the music without thought, lost in its rhythm. I would feel its beat in my heart. Each step was deeply ingrained in my brain.

And then I told him about the *good news*. The same ones I never got a chance to tell my parents.

The room was filled with my choked cries. A tear slid down my cheek before I could stop myself. But instead of making a lonely wet trail, like before, in my room—this time, there was someone to swipe it away.

Viktor's fingers touched my cheeks gently, and he thumbed away my tears. Another drop fell, and he caught it, this time with his lips.

His lips feathered over my skin so gently. And now, I was crying for a whole different reason. Why did he have to be so…sweet?

A man like him—who held so much darkness, yet could hold so much gentleness. He was both light and dark. He was both the angel of heaven and the devil of hell. He had the power to crush bones yet mend a broken heart, piece by piece.

"You are so brave; do you know that?" he muttered. My gaze went to our entwined fingers.

"I don't feel so brave now. I feel weak. But as long as it's me…not my sister. I would have never been able to live with myself if I had sacrificed Malory for my own happiness," I replied, my eyes never leaving our hands. I found myself fascinated with his thumbs rubbing soothing circles over my knuckles.

THE MAFIA AND HIS OBSESSION PART 1

Viktor nudged the tip of my nose with his gently, and I looked up at him. "I am going to get you out of here, Valerie. Just give me some more time. I need you to be strong for a little bit more."

I shook my head at his words. There was no point. I was living in a fantasy before—with him, where I had let him sweep me off my feet and away from this cruel world.

But Viktor...couldn't save me. I was beyond saving.

Only because saving me meant pulling my sister into this darkness.

"You can't. I am the debt my parents owe. If Valentin doesn't have me, then he will go for my sister."

"When I take you out of here, I will make sure that Valentin can never hurt another innocent soul," he said to me. Anger danced in those fiery eyes of his. Viktor evoked a brutal sense of danger.

I stayed silent, refusing to say *yes* or *no*. I trusted and believed in Viktor—but if it meant living in this hellhole to protect Malory, then I would gladly leave Viktor behind.

Viktor took my ballet flats from the floor and placed them on my lap. He folded my fingers over them, forcing me to hold my worn-out flats.

"You will dance again," Viktor said.

They weren't just *meaningless words*, from a *boy* who held no power.

It was a *promise* made by a *man* hell bent on saving my soul—with his tainted one.

My fingers caressed the ribbons, speechless. We were both silent for a moment before Viktor broke my dreamlike daze. He took the ballet flats from me and placed them back into the box before hiding it in the drawer again, sealing it away from eyes that wanted to hurt it.

I crawled into my bed, laying on my side with my knees curled to my chest. Viktor climbed in from behind me, molding his body into mine—a perfect puzzle.

His lips were on my neck, and he placed the sweetest kiss there. My eyes closed, and I released a deep breath.

Even though my heart was hurting and I felt strangely empty—Viktor was slowly filling that black void in me. He made my aching heart peaceful.

***

1 week later

A slight touch in my shoulder roused me from my sleep. I rubbed my eyes and blinked them open to see Viktor staring down at me with a small smile on his face.

We just made love...I must have slept for only thirty minutes.

Groaning, I closed my eyes again. His fingers slowly drifted from my shoulders to my sides before tickling me.

My eyes snapped open, and I quickly tried to move away from his torturous hands. "Viktor, stop!" I giggled and quickly smothered it by pushing my face into the pillow.

THE MAFIA AND HIS OBSESSION PART 1

He stopped and pulled me into a sitting position before nudging me to sit on the edge of the bed. Confused, I did as silently commanded. With my legs hanging over the edge, I anxiously waited.

Viktor appeared slightly nervous—his small smile told me so. And the way his eyes would meet mine before quickly looking down, it was strange yet endearing. For someone else, I would have said they looked *shy*.

But for Viktor—the word *shy* could never be associated with him.

Even through his nervousness, there was still that commanding presence around him. He was all rugged and alpha male. Strikingly confident with every step.

He knelt at my feet, and my eyes widened when I finally noticed what he was holding. In his hands, there was a white box. Viktor slowly opened the lid, showing me what was inside.

My heart stuttered at the sight of what was inside the box. Almost, like it was a siren call and I was completely mesmerized, waiting for it to pull me into its dark, never-ending depth.

With a finger under my chin, he lifted my face up. Our eyes met, and the world stilled. My stomach clenched, and I was suddenly breathless at the look he was giving me. Heated with a mix of sweetness.

"I want you to dance for me," he spoke. I could almost imagine his voice against my ears, like soft velvet.

His thumb brushed my cheek gently. His caress was intimate, reserved for me—our moment. "Will you dance for me, sweet Valerie?"

My throat closed with unspoken emotions. The lump grew, and I gasped for my next breath. My hands shook, my blood pumping and roaring through my veins furiously at his words.

Taking the ballet flats from the box, he placed them on my lap. "They are new. I had them made for you."

Finally, I tore my gaze away from his and looked down at my lap. The most beautiful pair of ballet flats sat in front of me. They were a soft pink, made with silk. Golden vine designs laid on top with pearls scattered all over the surface. The long ribbons were pink and almost see through.

My fingers caressed the ballet flats, and tears blurred my vision. I looked up into Viktor's face, and he was regarding me with understanding eyes—my own guardian angel in this crimson hell fire.

"New ones. For a new beginning," he said.

For a new beginning.

What was once lost had been returned to me.

Another broken piece of my soul glued to the cracked puzzle. Slowly, Viktor was putting all the scattered pieces together. Until it was revived into its old mold—not perfectly, but enough to truly *live*.

But...

"I can't," I whispered back.

Viktor stared at me, unblinking and clearly not surprised by my words. "Yes, you can."

I shook my head. I wanted to—almost desperately, but I *couldn't*. "I haven't danced for eight years. It's been so long, Viktor."

His hands gripped mine tightly. His eyes turned hard, those black orbs turning darker as he spoke.

THE MAFIA AND HIS OBSESSION PART 1

Viktor looked beautifully vicious. "It doesn't matter. You still have it in you. I want to see you in your element. I want to see you let go and be free."

"I can't..." I broke off, touching my ears. "I can't...I can't hear. How will I dance if I can't hear the music?"

Something else was stolen from me. Another preciousness that many took for granted.

Viktor stood up, and his lips stretched with a knowing smile. He took his phone out of his pocket and quickly tapped something and then placed it on the bed beside me.

My heart did a pitter patter dance because I just *knew*. "What song is that?"

"*Ave Maria*," he replied, our gazes never leaving each other. "I remember. You told me you loved dancing to this song. It is your favorite."

Something so small, yet he remembered it. A choked sob escaped past my lips, and the tears streamed down my cheeks. "Please...don't make me do this. I can't..."

Viktor cupped my cheeks and swiped the tears away, like he has done so many times. His words made my chest clench tightly. "You don't have to hear the song. You know it by heart."

His hand came up to my chest, and he laid his palm right over my beating heart—that was racing for *him*. "So you just have to feel it from here. Feel the music and dance."

He didn't wait for my reply. Taking the ballet flats, he bent down and made me wear them. He tied the long ribbons around my ankle and up my calves.

The ballet flats looked even more beautiful on my feet—made just for *me*. A perfect fit. A perfect match. A perfect beginning.

Viktor pulled up and walked us in the middle of the room. We stood there, silently, just holding each other.

"Dance for me, my sweet Valerie."

With those words, he left my embrace and went back to the bed. Settling on the edge, he placed his elbows over his knees and his chin over his interlocked fingers. He watched me, his fevered eyes solely on me.

His lips moved, and I watched him speak. "Let me see *you*. Show me your beautiful soul."

My heart was beating in my throat when I saw him take his phone in his hand. "I restarted the song, Valerie," he said, as if that was my cue.

My eyes closed, and I breathed in a deep breath. The muscles corded with tension slowly relaxed. My body felt like it was floating, the air light around me.

In my head, I remembered the song. The tune and the beat. Every step I took flashed behind my closed lids, like it was just yesterday. Extending a leg in front of me and with my arms in position, as I remembered, I twirled.

My body moved effortlessly as I danced for him. I danced to the rhythm of my own heartbeat—I danced to awaken my dormant soul that was now singing loudly for *him*.

I opened my eyes, and our gazes met. The world stilled even while I was twirling and dancing for *him*. His gaze never moved from me.

THE MAFIA AND HIS OBSESSION PART 1

Like Viktor said, I didn't need the music to dance. I didn't need to hear it—I just had to feel it. And I felt it—the music, the steps...the dance.

With each beat of my heart, I felt *Viktor*.

I wasn't a siren to lure him or a seductress to tempt him. I was just a broken woman who was dancing for the broken man she felt deep inside her veins.

Viktor stood up and walked to me. His arms captured my hips, and he brought me close into his body. His embrace was warm and firm—everything I wanted and needed.

His darkened eyes were fevered for me, and when his lips descended to mine, so softly and sweetly, he kissed me. Viktor wasn't just kissing me, he was tasting my soul. Stealing it and locking it away, for it belonged to him now.

Driving his tongue past my lips, he forced me to take his kiss. I took it willingly and gave him more in return. His hands gripped my hips, keeping me anchored against his. I felt his hard bulge pushing into my lower stomach, and he captured my moan into the kiss.

We pulled away when we were breathless. His hungry eyes caused my thighs to clench in anticipation. My heart was racing, adrenaline rushing through me without any consideration.

My chest grew tight at his words. "I know you think this is what you are meant to do, to protect your family. But *trust me*. Let me be your strength, Valerie. Let me carry your burden, your sadness, your pain—your anger. Give them to me, baby."

Unshed tears blinded my vision, and I blinked

them away with quiet sniffles. "Viktor…"

He cupped my cheeks before continuing. "I know you're strong. I know you can *survive* in this fucked-up world. But I don't want you to *just* survive. I want you to *live*."

I want to live too, I cried silently.

I couldn't speak, but Viktor continued. His words enough for both of us. "I will make sure that you are standing on that stage, dancing your heart like you always wanted. What was once stolen from you, I will give it to you. They will clap for you. The audience will cheer for you. I will make your dreams come true, Valerie."

"I won't hear them…" I finally managed to say, my heart breaking further. Viktor painted such a beautiful canvas for me to see, yet…God, it couldn't be this easy.

"You don't have to hear them," he replied. His hand touched my chest again, over my heart. "You will feel it, right here. Your heart will beat to the rhythm of their cheers."

The image of me dancing flashed in front of my eyes. Under the lights, on the stage, the dark audience—me lost to the flow of my steps.

A beautiful moment that I missed with my every breath. Something lost in the shadows yet this man promised to return it to me.

"Let me steal you away from here, Valerie." There he was, mending my broken heart. "Let me give you what you deserve," he said before claiming my lips again.

When we pulled apart this time, I didn't want to let go. Ever. So, in his palms, I gave him what I had

locked deep inside of me. I gave him my heart.
 The softest whisper, "Steal me away, Viktor."

Chapter 36

Viktor

"Steal me away, Viktor."

That was all I needed. Her words. Her permission. In this moment, she truly gave herself to me. Body, mind, heart, and soul. I was a greedy son of a bitch, taking everything she was giving and still wanting more.

A few more days, Valerie—and then we would be far, far away from here. Back to where we belonged. Together. With my family.

Gripping her waist, I lifted her off the ground and carried her to bed. She moved back and fell on the pillows. Her blonde hair was spread over our pillows, and she opened her arms for me, inviting me into her embrace.

The shadow and pain in her eyes were now lightened, and Valerie smiled up at me. "You are beautiful like this. When you're smiling. I hate when you're hurt, Valerie. It makes me want to rage and kill anyone who has a hand in causing you pain," I muttered, covering her body with my own.

My lips feathered over her ears, and I knew she wouldn't hear the words. I didn't want her to hear *this* promise. No matter how much darkness Valerie has experienced in this world, she was not ready for this one.

A soft whisper—a promise to her, "There will be bloodshed. I will start a war for you."

My lips found hers again, and she kissed me back with starving passion. Clothes were taken off quickly and thrown on the ground. Her ballet flats followed shortly until our naked skins were pressed against each other.

I *needed* to feel her. And I knew she needed me just as much.

Her legs spread open to accommodate me, her nails biting into my shoulders, pushing me forward for more. I sucked on her lower lip before biting gently on it. Pulling away, I saw it was plump and ripe, a dark pink.

Valerie released a throaty moan when I rubbed the tip of my cock against her wet slit. Her back bowed, and she rubbed against me desperately. With my eyes searing into hers, I teased her until she was breathless and begging for more.

Her moans made my cock jolt in excitement, wanting to be sheathed in her tight heat. Her eyes were flaming with hunger and a desire she had kept in for so long. Valerie whimpered as my cock slid up between her pussy lips, pushing but never entering her clenching core.

Her hand came between us, and she took hold of

my length, trying to put me inside her. Slapping her hand away with a growl, I pinned her arms above her head.

"Don't fucking touch me, baby," I growled, cupping her between her legs. "This pussy is mine, and I decide when to give it my cock." She creamed between her thighs, and my dick was coated with her sweet juices.

The thought of her sucking and taking my cock deep inside her throat flashed in front of my eyes. With a smirk, I pulled away and stood by the bed. Valerie sat up with a start, surprised as she stared up at me.

I beckoned her forward with a finger, and she crawled to the edge of the bed. "Do you want it?" I asked. My voice sounded rough to my own ears, filled with lust for this beautiful woman on her knees for me.

Her gaze flitted below my stomach where I was gripping my hardened length. She bit on her lips before nodding. I waited until her eyes were on my face again before speaking. "Use your words. Tell me what you want exactly."

"I want you," she whispered. I saw her cheeks blushing beautifully.

"What do you want, baby? Do you want to suck my cock? Say it," I urged her when she stayed quiet. If possible, her cheeks turned redder. Her breathing accelerated, her gorgeous tits bouncing slightly with each breath she took.

"I want you…" she started slowly. Her eyes went to where I was gripping myself again. "I want to suck your cock."

THE MAFIA AND HIS OBSESSION PART 1

If possible, I swelled bigger in my hand. Fuck, those words between her sweet lips. With innocent looking eyes, heated with hunger for me, she was the most beautiful in this moment. A fucking seductress she was.

Her whole body was blushing, and her breathlessness urged me on. "Take me then, Valerie. Take what you want. Own it, baby." *Own me. I am fucking yours.*

Valerie brought her hand up, and she cupped my hardened cock in a soft palm. She lifted her head and caught my eyes just as she squeezed me, ever so slightly. I let out a hiss, and her lips quirked up in a small, confident smile.

The little Vixen licked her lips teasingly. "Fuck," I swore when her head descended toward my waiting hardness.

In the next moment, my cock was wrapped between her fuckable lips. Her sweet hot mouth was on me, sucking and teasing. She was slow and deliberate.

My sweet ballerina took her sweet time tasting me.

I couldn't stop the grunt of pleasure from escaping past my lips. Valerie moaned in response and took me deeper into her mouth. I willed myself—trying to be strong—and thrust myself up in all her tight warmth.

But fuck—it was hard. So fucking hard when she was being such a little tease.

She tongued the tip, tasting my pre-cum before taking me deep again. Her lips tightened around the length before she sucked. Her teeth slightly grazed the underside of my cock, and I let out another hiss. Fuck!

I let her play…putting myself at her mercy, to do as she pleased.

Until I grew impatient.

Grasping her hair, I wrapped it around my wrist and pulled her hard over my cock. I felt the tip brushing the back of the throat, and my eyes rolled back in pleasure, another deep groan vibrating from my chest.

I heard her gagging around my cock, her throat working overtime to please me. "I don't play nice, baby," I muttered.

Valerie readjusted her jaw, trying to get accustomed to my size. Holding the back of her head, I kept my ruthless pace, pumping into her mouth—in and out, forcing her to take me deep and rough.

She hummed around my cock, her saliva dribbling down her chin as she pleased me—oh, how she fucking pleased me.

Her doe brown eyes stared up at me submissively, her mouth opened for me to take and fuck. A beautiful perfect sight.

My legs shook, and I could feel my muscles bunching. When I was close, I pulled out of her sweet mouth. "As much as I want my cum coating those pretty lips of yours, I am coming in your pussy, Valerie."

Her breath hitched, and Valerie blinked up innocently at me. Grasping her shoulders, I turned her around. She let out a startled gasp at the sudden move.

THE MAFIA AND HIS OBSESSION PART 1

Her knees were planted over the edge of the bed, and she was on all fours for me. Her ass was in the air, and I could see her sweet honey dripping between her parted legs. Her pussy lips were pink and puffy, a tempting sight. She looked deliciously ready to be thoroughly fucked.

I gripped her hips and pulled her back into me. My tip teased her opening, and she moaned out loud before pushing her head into the mattress, masking her sounds made for me.

My hand wrapped around her hair once again. Pulling her head up, my lips touched the back of her neck. Valerie turned her head to the side, looking at me. Her gaze went to my lips as I spoke.

"I don't want gentle and sweet love-making. I want to leave you quivering with my marks all over your body," I muttered. "I want to own you. And I will. I'm going to pound that sweet tight pussy."

She gulped hard. Instead of fear, her eyes lit up with need. She *trusted* me. Valentin took her without her permission.

I would *own* Valerie but only with her consent. She would be *mine*—only if she said *yes*. I would make her say *yes*.

"I am going to fuck you, *myshka*."

"Please," she begged quietly. "I need you."

Smirking, my lips feathered over her ear, out of her sight. She wouldn't hear me. But I almost wished she could.

"Like this?" I asked, thrusting inside her hard. Valerie bit on her lips to keep from screaming.

Her pussy clenched around me desperately. She moaned again, a sound mixed with pain and pleasure. I wanted to hear her screams...I wanted to pull them from her, forcing her to take my cock and hearing her screams as she would.

But fuck...as much as I wanted to hear her screams, I couldn't...we couldn't.

Not only did we have to keep us a secret—I was also possessive of her voice. I didn't want anyone else to hear her sweet melodious voice, her moans, or her fucking needy screams.

Pulling out, I thrust back into her willing body. Her heat enveloped me once more, and I never wanted to leave her pussy. Being inside her was the best fucking feeling and a blessing. She was tight and responsive, perfect, and *mine*.

I groaned as her pussy clenched around me. I pulled out and push back in. I suckled at the tender flesh behind her ear and on her neck. My body molded the back of hers as I continued to pound her.

Our fucking was almost animalistic. Rough and deep. I didn't care. I just needed my cock deep inside her cunt so she could feel me for days.

I wanted her to feel me tomorrow morning and have her pussy wet with her honey just at the thought of us fucking.

Her body quivered, and I knew she was close. My cock swelled inside her tight warmth. My hand gripped the front of her neck, and I pulled her head back. With my lips touching her forehead, I pulled out and thrust back in one last time.

Valerie shuddered with her orgasm. She bit on her lips to keep from screaming, and I closed my eyes at the sensation, the feel of her milking my

THE MAFIA AND HIS OBSESSION PART 1

cock as I pumped my cum inside her.

Only our breathing could be heard. Our skin was drenched with our sweat, our cum leaking from between us. Valerie sagged into the mattress, her body limp.

My fingers went between her legs, where we were still joined. Her inner thighs were coated with her juices and my cum. Rubbing two fingers over her skin, I gathered our mixed essence.

Valerie opened her eyes when I brought my fingers to her lips. She stared at me with a small, tired smile. "Suck," I ordered. Her lips parted, and she lazily sucked at my fingers, tasting *us*. She hummed in response, and her eyes closed again.

I pulled out and we both groaned at the loss. Quickly going to the bathroom, I cleaned up and came back with some paper towels. After making sure Valerie was comfortable in bed again, I cleaned between her legs.

I got into bed too, and Valerie curled into my side. A happy sigh escaped past her lips. With an arm over my stomach, she laid her head on my shoulder and made herself comfortable, as if my embrace was her home.

We stayed like this for a long time, silent and just basking in the afterglow. I thought she had fallen asleep until I felt her move. She slid down a little and rolled over, half of her body covering mine. Crossing her arms over my chest, she settled her chin on them and stared up at me.

I was transfixed, ensnared in her soft gaze. Valerie's lips were quirked up to the side in a small smile as she stared at me in complete adoration.

My fingers traced a path up her cheek and pushed her hair behind her ear. Her smile widened at the simple action.

"You are so sweet to me, Viktor."

Her whispered confession had my heart clenching and racing. "For the longest time, I didn't know how to be *sweet*. Someone taught me that. She made me realize what it means to *feel*. But still, I had kept it locked inside. It was not *my* place to feel. But when I am with you, you bring out the side that I didn't know I had. With you, I can let go and feel whatever I want."

Because you are mine.

Valerie cocked her head to the side curiously, but she didn't ask for more. She took what I was giving her—little bits of me. But what she didn't realize…slowly, I was giving her everything of me.

We were quiet for some time again. Staring at each other and lost in each other. I wrapped an arm around her waist, holding her to me. "Tell me about your sister."

Valerie sighed, and a faraway look appeared in her gaze. "Malory was always more cheerful. Loud. A happy kid. She was very kind. I remember once we found a bird in our yard. Its wings were severely broken, and it appeared dead. I told her maybe we should bury it, but she insisted on taking care of it and nursing it back to health. I was very sure it would die in a few hours, but Malory didn't give up. She nursed it back…and a few days later, we had a happy bird. It couldn't fly again, but they became best friends quickly."

Valerie continued to tell me stories about her

little sister. How much she loved animals. Malory loved singing and had a beautiful voice but hated dancing, while Valerie was the opposite. She was bubbly, while Val was quiet and reserved. The sisters were almost the opposite in everything, yet they were inseparable.

"We have the same nose and eyebrows, but other than that, we don't look very much alike. She has bright blue eyes, and her blonde hair is very light, almost platinum, while mine is a darker shade of blonde. She has fuller lips. Malory is my beautiful doll," Valerie said. "She is so precious."

Everything was perfect for them…until hearts were broken and lives were shattered.

"They loved me…"

My arm tightened around Valerie at her words. "Not enough. Your parents didn't love you enough."

Valerie's fierce gaze met mine. "You can't say that. They did love me. I know that."

I released a long sigh. She was right but… "Valerie, if they loved you…they would have never sacrificed you. Yes, they did love you, but not enough. Not the way you deserved to be loved. No parents should have sacrificed their own daughter for the other. Whether Malory was younger or not, you were still a child too. You were still innocent. Yet you became the unwilling collateral."

Tears filled her eyes, and her voice was a mere whisper when she spoke. "My father was powerless against him. He was one of Valentin's business associates, but he was powerless. He was Solonik's dog. It wasn't his fault. It was *my* choice to go with

Valentin."

Her voice cracked as if it hurt to say the words. My sweet innocent Valerie. Valentin took the heart of a blossoming girl and broke it. He made her grow up faster, forced her to survive through darkness, while she was meant to live through the light.

It was my choice to go with Valentin.

I shook my head and sputtered a heartless laugh. What a fucking joke.

"No, it *wasn't* your choice. Don't fucking say that. It was *never* your choice. You think you made a choice, Valerie, but whether you had said yes or no, Valentin was going to take you away. Your parents were going to sell you away. They came to beg you to go with Valentin—to save your sister's life. They didn't choose you just like it wasn't your choice."

Valerie choked back a sob and buried her face in my chest. "I don't want to hate them, Viktor. They are my parents, and they have hurt me...but I don't want to hate them."

I held her to me as she cried her little heart out. The broken girl inside her crying for what was stolen from her. "I...always...wanted them to save me...but they never came...back for me. I waited...and waited...they never came back for...me. They...left me...with...*him*. They...didn't come for me. They forgot...me."

I closed my eyes, feeling sick in my stomach. My chest grew tight, and my heart squeezed. Valerie poured out all her hidden emotions. All the unsaid words, she finally said them.

"I am sorry, *myshka*."

THE MAFIA AND HIS OBSESSION PART 1

The world was a cruel place. I lived in it. I thrived in it. The darkness became me...I moved into the shadows until wherever I went, the darkness followed. I had wreaked havoc over innocent lives. Left bloodshed behind.

Yet...in the middle of this cruel world, hidden innocence lived. Valerie lived. If only I had found her sooner...only if...I would have stolen her away.

Because my darkness needed her light. And Valerie needed the chaos I brought with me.

I continued to hold her until eventually her tears dried. We both fell silent. Her sniffles filled the room until they slowly disappeared too.

When she spoke again, her voice was hollow and sad. She sounded so lost. "I was always so alone. Always locked in this room. If it wasn't Igor watching me, then it was Valentin visiting me. Sometimes, I would be completely alone. Just with the memories of who I used to be. I lost myself, Viktor. I became a puppet...I didn't know to feel anymore."

Lifting her chin up, I made sure she was looking at me. Her eyes were swollen and glassy with unshed tears. "Nobody else was allowed in this room?" I asked.

She shook her head once and then looked thoughtful. "Well, no one really. But there was a girl. She was the only one allowed in my room. To bring me food and clean my room. Every morning, she would help me dress up."

I stared into her gaze, waiting for her to continue. Valerie's shoulders slumped down. "We became very close. Every day she would come and we would talk. Not a lot. The silence between us was comforting. At least we weren't alone. At least we had each other."

"Was she your friend?" I asked curiously.

Valerie nodded, and she gave me a tiny smile. "My only friend here. We were together for years. She was the sweetest, Viktor. Someone with a very kind heart. I saw it rarely, but she had the most beautiful smile. We bonded until I couldn't imagine being separated from her. She became my *sister*," Valerie whispered her last word.

Past tense. Valerie was using past tense...*Fuck*. She had a friend, yet this one was probably stolen away too. "Who is she? Where is she now?"

Her gaze shadowed over. "She is slave 2107."

My heart clenched, and it felt like I had been punch in the fucking throat. "What?" I whispered.

"She has been hurt so much, Viktor," Valerie answered tearfully. "I thought my life was hard...until I met her. At least I had the title of being Valentin's *wife*. Powerless, yet I had a position. But she was a *slave*. Valentin's slave. The other woman he would release all his depravity on. I got the better end of the rope—she got the never-ending nightmare of it."

I stayed silent, only because I didn't know what to say.

A *slave*. A motherfucking slave. Another innocent soul. Fuck!

"When Valentin started to notice how close we were, he took her away. He ripped her away by the hair and dragged her out..." Valerie stopped with a choked sob. Pressing a hand over her lips, she tried to keep it in as she continued to speak. "I don't know…if she is okay. I don't know…if she is alive. She didn't deserve this, Viktor. She didn't deserve to be used. By anyone. She deserved to be free. Happy and loved."

I held Valerie tighter and pinched my eyes closed.

She didn't deserve this, Viktor. She deserved so much love and happiness. She didn't deserve to be used. By anyone.

How many more lives would be destroyed? How fucking unfair would this world continue to be?

"Wherever she is now, I hope she's okay. Valentin used to do all kind of things to her. Sometimes he would spend more time with her, and I was left alone for days—sometimes *weeks*. But after he took her away, he started to visit me more. At first, I was worried and thought she was dead. But I hope…I hope she is okay."

Valerie's words snapped me out of my thoughts. I stared down at her, and she looked so sad…so lost…so fucking broken. I *hated* it.

Our eyes met, and she sighed. "Valentin hasn't come for me in weeks. I wonder who he's hurting now…who is bearing all his painful, depraved marks. I just hope it's not her. I hope she is far, far away from him. From this cruel world."

I cupped her cheeks and swiped away her tears. "I hope so too, baby."

Just like I am going to take you far, far away from him.

"You would have liked her," Valerie said. She finally gave me the smallest smile. Something so precious—I wanted to memorize it.

"What's her name?" I asked, still lost in Valerie.

"Irina."

Irina.

Irina.

Irina.

Why did that name sound so familiar?

I had heard it somewhere, yet I couldn't...

Irina.

That name...

When realization finally dawned, my stomach rolled, and I fought the urge the throw up. My lungs squeezed until I was breathless.

I heard Valerie's voice. "Viktor, are you all right? What's wrong?"

It sounded far away. I felt heavy; all of me was sinking. Everything was drowned by the tidal waves of nothingness. Except the Devil's laughter. That I heard, clear and loud. He had been gone for so long. I thought I had finally escaped his taunting, but there he was again. His reappearance made me clench my eyes closed.

The devil on my shoulder mocked me. He reveled in my suffering.

His tongue slithered out, and he hissed in my ears. *You fucked up yet again, Viktor. I knew you would. And now...now you have to face the consequences.*

Fuck.

Irina's words echoed in my head.

I also hope you find a good woman. One who will not make you so heartless anymore. A woman who will actually teach you to be good and how to

THE MAFIA AND HIS OBSESSION PART 1

show compassion.

Valerie called out to me again. I couldn't respond. The devil continued to laugh. I wished he would choke, but instead, he stayed perched on my shoulders, crossing his legs, watching the drama unfold. My life was his favorite fucking soap opera.

The name whispered through my head again.

Irina.

Fuck my life.

THE END

Acknowledgements

I think first and foremost, I want to thank Viktor and Valerie. This story wouldn't have been possible without their forever presence in my little head. They spoke, and I wrote. Viktor is the type of character that you can't say *no* to. He will scream loud until I give in and write his story the way *he* wants.

I want to thank Vivvi. My girl. My best friend. You are everything. Thank you for being there for me. Thank you for always pushing me up when I am falling down. Thank you for loving my characters, my babies, just as much as I do, if not more. Actually, saying thank you is not enough. I am so glad to have you in my life.

My parents, thank you for your never-ending support and love.

To Jessica and Chelsea, my girls. What would I do without you? Seriously, I would be drowning if it wasn't for you two keeping me afloat. Thank you for being there and supporting me through all this craziness. It has been a wild ride, and you have stuck with me till now—thank you will never be enough. Cheers, to so much more now.

To my beta readers and author friends– Dani Rene, Skyla Madi, Brianna Hale, Tania Varela, Julia Lis, Giana Darling, Rebecca Scarlett – thank you for reading this book, thank you for being gentle with my babies and thank you for loving them. You guys have been so amazing and supportive. I have no words to explain my gratitude. Love you all!

The biggest thank you goes to my Publisher. Thank you for giving *The Mafia and His Obsession* a chance.

To my editor, Toni—what would I do without you? Seriously. You are a life saver, and I am so glad you didn't hunt me down, tie me to a chair, and make me write this book faster without procrastinating so much. Your patience has been so amazing. *Thank you.* I am so glad we worked together on this book. You truly did wonders.

Thank you to everyone else who had a hand in making this book—my proofreader, formatter…you guys are stars.

To Deranged Doctor Design—This cover is GORGEOUS. You always paint my vision beautifully. Thank you.

To the bloggers and everyone who took their time to promote *The Mafia and His Obsession*, you are awesome! My big thanks to you.

To my beautiful readers, a huge thank you to every single one of you. My lovelies. Your never-ending support and love has taken us on this path. From the first word to the last, you have been here with me. I am proud we took this journey together. I am so thankful for that. Thank you for standing with me, even through my craziness. To all the fan accounts and groups out there, thank you! All the beautiful edits and posters you have made, they are my inspiration and motivation. Cheers. To many more!

About the Author

Lylah James uses all her spare time to write. If she is not studying, sleeping, writing or working—she can be found with her nose buried in a good romance book, preferably with a hot alpha male.

Writing is her passion. The voices in her head won't stop, and she believes they deserve to be heard and read. Lylah James writes about drool worthy and total alpha males, with strong and sweet heroines. She makes her readers cry—sob their eyes out, swoon, curse, rage, and fall in love. Mostly known as the Queen of cliffhanger and the #evilauthorwithablacksoul, she likes to break her readers' hearts and then mend them again.

FOLLOW LYLAH AT:

Facebook page:
https://www.facebook.com/AuthorLy.James/

Twitter page:
https://twitter.com/AuthorLy_James

Instagram page:
https://www.instagram.com/authorlylahjames/

Goodreads:
https://www.goodreads.com/author/show/16045951.Lylah_James

Wattpad account:
https://www.wattpad.com/user/HumB01

Or you can drop me an email at:
AuthorLylah.James@Hotmail.com

Or check out my website:
http://authorlylahjames.com/

You can also join my newsletter list for updates, teasers, major giveaways and so much more!
http://eepurl.com/c2EJ4z

Printed in Great Britain
by Amazon